TRADE
SECRETS

TRADE
SECRETS

MAYNARD F. THOMSON

POCKET BOOKS

New York   London   Toronto   Sydney   Tokyo   Singapore

This book is a work of fiction. Names, characters, places and inci-
dents are either products of the author's imagination or are used
fictitiously. Any resemblance to actual events or locales or per-
sons, living or dead, is entirely coincidental.

POCKET BOOKS, a division of Simon & Schuster Inc.
1230 Avenue of the Americas, New York, NY 10020

ISBN: 0-671-74899-8

First Pocket Books hardcover printing January 1993

10 9 8 7 6 5 4 3 2 1

To Laura, Alec, and Hannah,
with love and gratitude

ACKNOWLEDGMENTS

I thank my friend and secretary,
Deborah Kelbach, for her tireless assistance
in preparing the manuscript.

TRADE
SECRETS

CHAPTER

I jerked the receiver off the wall: "Speak."

There was a lull, then a harsh, vaguely human sound: "Ah, Mr. Nichols. How nice to find you home, at last. Gretchen Lukacs-Skizenta, Mr. Nichols. Remember me? I've been trying to reach you for three days; didn't you get the messages I left on that machine?"

"I had a spot of work down on the Cape . . ."

A lie born dead: "Really? How wonderful you're working again. That means you won't have any difficulty coming up with the three thousand six hundred dollars you owe Brenda. The alimony, Mr. Nichols; you do remember the alimony?"

"I remember. I certainly do."

"When can I expect the money, Mr. Nichols?"

Money. Money for Brenda. She had taken my love, my self-respect, my confidence, almost all my worldly possessions, and the cat. I hated the cat, but I missed the other things. How much money would I have to have before I would willingly give some to Brenda? More than I had. Much more than the one thousand seventy-six dollars and thirty-three cents the

Commonwealth National Bank computer reported as my net worth.

"The old man can't hang on forever. Heart, you know? If we could just wait for my ship to come in, I'm sure we could manage something. Perhaps this century?"

"I want that money, now!" She throttled back a decibel: "If I have the check by Friday I won't have to have you thrown in jail for nonsupport. Do you have any doubt that Judge Tyrone will do that, Mr. Nichols?"

I conjured an image of the good judge declaring that I had forced Brenda "to live in conflict with her need for selfhood" to satisfy my "macho chauvinism" just before awarding her everything but my macho parts. No, I didn't doubt she'd be glad to see me again.

"Now, listen . . ."

"No, *you* listen. Brenda and I have had enough of your games. She called me in tears today. Tears! The university's told her she's out if she doesn't pay the tuition next week. Her therapist needs to be paid—the therapist you drove her to. She had to send her away for self-awareness counseling; that costs money, too. I'm warning you: I want that check by Friday or no more nice guy . . . uh, no more nice . . . Never mind. I'm calling on Friday and you better have that check ready for me."

I remembered the preserves I'd been stirring and grabbed the spoon I'd left in the pot. It was white-hot. The last thing I heard before I slammed down the receiver and dashed for the tap was "You can yell all you like—you've no one to blame. . . ."

My right hand was in a bucket of ice water when the phone rang again. I ripped the receiver off its hook: "Listen, you bloodsucking stoat—you tell Brenda I'm the one who should be getting therapy for being crazy enough to have married her!

2

Now get off my back or I'll rip out your tongue and beat you to death with the bloody stump!"

A long pause, and then a voice I didn't recognize: "Could I . . . *possibly* have the office of Mr. Nason Nichols?"

Business? I did my best to control my panting. "Why, yes. Yes, this is Mr. Nichols's office."

"Mr. Nichols?" The voice nervous, hesitant.

I dropped my voice a register. "Just a second, I'll see if he's in. Who's calling?"

"This is Mr. Holtree's secretary. At Proctor, Needham and Choate. Mr. Holtree would like . . ."

"I'll get Mr. Nichols," I mumbled. "I hear him now." I didn't know anyone named Holtree, but Proctor, Needham & Choate was one of Boston's largest and oldest law firms—well out of Brenda's league. I slammed the kitchen door, stomped my feet, clattered the receiver on the counter for a few seconds, then picked it up again.

"Nichols here."

"Mr. Nichols? Uh, excuse me. The strangest man . . ."

"Who? Oh, yes—one of our clients. Severely stressed, I'm afraid. Ex-wife's been calling him at all hours, says she'll have her biker paramour dismember him. Apologize for his unseemly behavior."

"Oh," she said. "My goodness. I see. Yes, I see." She drew herself together: "Well, in any case, Mr. Holtree asked me to call and see if you'd be able to see him about some work he has. As soon as possible."

"Well, I'm rather tied up right now."

"Oh, dear. Mr. Holtree so hoped . . ."

"However, my secretary tells me that my afternoon appointment canceled. About three?"

There was a mirror on the wall and I stopped to check the effect. Half an hour with the shower running had taken the worst wrinkles out of the jacket, and the rep tie matched, sort of. The khakis had a decent crease, and if the cordovans wouldn't take the place of the mirror, they didn't look like I'd got them at Morgan Memorial, either. I'd missed a spot shaving but I knew I could pass for thirty-eight, thirty-nine tops. I pushed the hair into place, assured myself the slight salting of gray added the right tone of gravity, and stepped into Proctor, Needham.

The reception room was a different world. On the outside, 147 State Street was just another of the thirty-story glass-and-steel monoliths that were turning downtown Boston into a mini-Manhattan; inside the heavy oak door on the nineteenth floor, a decorator with several million dollars to work with had done a reasonable job of repealing the twentieth century. All it needed was Bartleby the Scrivener sitting at a counting-desk to complete the picture. Most of the lawyers I work for have their offices in a phone booth in the basement of the courthouse; I recalculated my daily rate.

I had barely gotten to *The Wall Street Journal* in the reception room when Holtree's secretary appeared. She led me through a couple of miles of dark corridors to a large corner office.

Holtree rose and stuck out his hand. He withdrew it when he saw the bandage on mine. "Been in a scrape?"

"Got into a bit of a jam, you might say. Prefer not to use my fists, but sometimes you can't avoid it." The look in Holtree's eyes made the pain worth it.

The lawyer was a thin, pinched fellow with close-cropped gray hair and the kind of glasses Old Doc Smithers wore before he went mod. He was wearing the vest and trousers of a Jay Press herringbone a shade or two lighter than the hair. I picked a Windsor chair with a Harvard seal on the back, and sat.

4

"Thank you for coming at such short notice, Mr. Nichols. I appreciate that. It concerns a matter of some urgency." Holtree had mastered the trick of talking as though he had a mouthful of marbles. It was very Back Bay, and slightly irritating. "I trust you are . . . ah . . . shall we say, discreet?"

"Priest and penitent."

"Beg pardon?" His eyebrows twisted into a question mark, then straightened again. "Ah, yes. 'Priest and penitent.' Just so. Very good. Anyway, it could be dicey, very dicey indeed, if this were to become public. It's a most delicate matter."

"I understand. What's up?"

Holtree picked a pipe off his desk and lit it with an old Zippo. Soon his head was wreathed in smoke. "We represent a company called Zoltec Industries. You've heard of Zoltec?"

I nodded. "Zoltec makes integrated circuits—computer chips. They're unquestionably the world's leading producer of high-speed, high-capacity chips." Holtree glanced down at some notes on a yellow legal pad. "These chips are the heart of the computer. No chips, no computers. No computers, well . . ." He shrugged.

I pursed my lips and nodded again. Satisfied, Holtree continued: "Zoltec enjoys a commanding lead in the manufacture of state-of-the-art chips because of certain proprietary manufacturing techniques it has developed over the years. Those techniques, which the law recognizes as trade secrets, have enabled Zoltec to derive what we might call, um, supra-competitive returns, for many years." He spoke like an annual report.

"You mean Zoltec knows how to do things the other guys don't, so it makes lots more money than they do?"

He winced; lawyers are not programmed for concision. "You could put it like that."

"Let me guess—now somebody, probably an ex-employee, has run off with the know-how and is about to set up shop himself?" It seemed a safe bet.

It was. "Very good, Mr. Nichols. I take it you've handled matters of this type before?"

"Sure. In my experience, your only chance of getting the stuff back is to move fast. When did Zoltec discover the loss?"

"Friday. One of their senior engineers resigned a couple of weeks ago, a fellow named Platt. Said he was going to start a cellular-phone business. Friday was his last day. He left early. His secretary found this"—he gestured at a sheet of paper— "when she was cleaning out his desk. She had the good sense to take it to Platt's supervisor, Dr. Bingham. That brought us in." Holtree pushed the sheet across his desk.

It was a piece of graph paper containing notes in block print. THE PLATT GROUP—BRUCE C. PLATT, PRESIDENT AND CHAIRMAN was printed at the top. Under that, someone—presumably Platt —had written: "Consultant in integrated-circuit technology. Zoltec process." "Zoltec process" was circled in red. There were some calculations and scribbling about start-up costs. I tossed the paper back on the desk.

"So this Platt doesn't know you know what his real plans are?"

"We assume that as far as he knows, Zoltec still thinks he's going into the phone business."

"Well, that's some help. No reason for him to hurry, at least. May give you some time. Is the 'Zoltec process' something he could carry away in his head?"

"I'm told not. If he's planning to sell Zoltec's technology, presumably it means he's gone off with blueprints, documents, that sort of thing. Dr. Bingham's trying to figure out what he might have taken right now."

"Why not call the cops?"

"Too much chance of a leak. If news of this gets out, Zoltec's bankers will have a fit. The stock would collapse. Any clumsiness in the investigation and any documents would be on the next plane out of the country."

"Makes sense. So I'm the alternative?"

"Exactly. We want you to find out if he's got anything belonging to Zoltec so we can get a court order and go in and get it before it disappears."

"Okay, I get the idea. I get one thousand a day, plus expenses." It was twice my normal rate.

He pursed his lips, then nodded. He was still well ahead of me. "I don't think that will be any problem. Zoltec has millions of dollars a year riding on this. Can you meet with Dr. Bingham tomorrow? He can give you the technical details. One o'clock? That should give Zoltec time to complete its investigation."

"I think I can squeeze that in."

"Splendid. I look forward to working with you."

"Likewise, I'm sure." We exchanged the facial tics that pass for smiles in old Boston circles. Holtree was thumbing through a Brooks Brothers catalogue when I left.

CHAPTER 2

When I got back on the street it was late afternoon on one of those Indian summer days New England does better than anyplace else on earth, a day for a stroll along the Charles with a Wellesley girl. Those days were behind me, so I called Bucky Hanrahan to see if he could join me for a drink at the Ritz. I left word at his office and ambled down Washington Street toward the Common.

I love Washington Street, love the seamy raunch of it, the pure, uncompromising squalor. Girlie bars, strip joints, filthy movies, and the pungent odor of man elemental—flypaper to the scum of the earth: I love it all.

Every old city sported a Washington Street until the urban development crew came along, squealed, "Ohh, city life is so *stimulating*, but . . . maybe just a little—tacky?" and set about suburbanizing everything remotely urban. They made Scolly Square into a shopping center, Disneyfied the South End, and now they're sandblasting their way down Washington Street like an army of dental hygienists warring on plaque. Any day the Pussycat Cinex will mount a major Bergman retrospective,

8

the only dance will be aerobic, and the Combat Zone will be a memory, its former inhabitants as remote as Hogarth's.

It was too early for the hookers, pimps, dealers, and slimeballs to be out in force, but the joyless music was pouring out of the bars, and the usual assortment of pockmarked, whey-faced deviates was slithering in and out of the porn shops. A couple of burly shore patrolmen were starting their evening round, strolling with that swagger that comes when you know you can break any head on the block and don't have long to wait.

Tony was propped up outside a hotdog stand at the corner of Washington and Boylston, trying to sell the windup penguins grazing around him. A swaying drunk watched transfixed, but I was glad penguins weren't Tony's main line; the only toys that do well on Washington Street are the ones you blow up and date when even the hookers won't touch you.

"Hey Nase—fuckya been? Too long, man." He raised his hand. I had to bend to slap it, since Tony's south half lay somewhere in the Mekong Delta and the wagon he rested on was only a few inches above the sidewalk.

"Been around, been around. When'd you start pushing these little guys?" One of the penguins came to rest against my shoe, its wheels racing as it pecked at my toe.

"Oh, man—can you believe this shit?" He swiped at a penguin, careening it into the street. The drunk lurched after it, lost his balance, and fell into the gutter. "That mofo Reilly, came on the beat wha', six, seven months ago? You know the dude. How long I been selling stink books on this corner, huh? Whataya guess, five years, Chrissake? Huh? Am I right, man, huh—five fuggin' years?"

"Hey, at least, Tone. Maybe six."

Tony thought for a few seconds, then shook his head. "Fucksa difference. Long enough. You know, I got like, squatter's rights, huh?"

"Right on, bro." Tony loved it when I slipped into patois.

"Sure. So anyhow the man, he come along, say 'Okay, Stubs,' call me Stubs like it's real funny, get yer balls blown off fightin' for yo' country, crawl around on a fuggin' wagon all yer life, 'ya can't keep selling that filth, gotta get another scam.' Just like that. Five years I been here selling T & A books, make a few bucks, fuggin' street's maybe the stinkbook capital of the universe or sumpin, and this asshole say 'Ya gotta get another scam.' So I say, 'Fuckya talkin' about, fine Jesus or sumpin,' and Reilly say 'Naw, that ain't it, pad he's on don't cover me for no skin books, only cover me for numbers.' Fucksa world comin' to?"

"Amen."

"So I gotta bunch a this shit, from some guinea wha' Doreen, tricks for Sugar Man, know, boosted 'em someplace." He shook his head, cleared his throat, and hockered on the drunk's leg. "Fuggin' sweet boys only ones buy 'em. Sailor, maybe, got a load on, for his ol' lady or sumpin, but mosely it's some dicklicker." Tony hated homosexuals; he also hated whites, blacks, Italians, the Irish, Jews, Muslims, priests, cops, and every other known subgroup. He seemed to like me and the whores who worked the street; maybe he just needed to be looked at from time to time. A lot of people find it hard to look at two-thirds of a black man in a dirty overcoat with a medal pinned on his chest.

"That's a bitch, Tone. Tell you what—here's two dollars. Number one thirty-seven. I got a hunch."

He took the money, wrote out the slip and handed it to me. "Ya wanna bird?"

"Hey, come on, Tone—think I've gone gay?" He mumbled "fuck" and was winding penguins when I left. Patrolman Reilly arrived and started to pull the drunk out of the gutter. Washington Street's a grand thoroughfare, and I had a spring in my step as I hastened across the Common to see Bucky.

10

I met him during my sabbatical in Southeast Asia. Bucky had dropped out of Boston College about the same time that Harvard suggested I take a few years off to "find myself." Vietnam was where a young man found himself in 1968 if he lost his student deferment.

Bucky was the only other person in my military police unit who cared about anything besides killing, getting killed, getting laid, and blowing dope. We got out at about the same time, but with different compulsions: I'd had enough of authority, military or academic, and became a glorified process-server; Bucky had had enough of poverty, so he completed BC, got a master's degree in computer science from MIT, then bullied his way into a job with one of Boston's major brokerage houses, where he followed the high-tech industries that made Route 128, outside Boston, the East's answer to Silicon Valley. He also followed the Red Sox, which was one of the reasons we remained friends. He could give me a quick course on Zoltec.

I got to the Ritz and went into the bar, a dark, quiet place where good taste reigns. I asked Henry for a pair of specials, up, and found a corner table. Bucky ambled in a few minutes later.

"I'm pleased to see you in surroundings worthy of your station, Nase. I take it you've found a client?" Bucky knew the Ritz was my expense-account haunt; necessity made me a beer-and-shot man on my own tab.

"Let's just say I'd be interested in whatever you can tell me about Zoltec Industries. I buy the marts."

"Zoltec, hum?" Bucky smiled. "You're in the tall cotton, Boyo."

"Tell."

"Great outfit. One of the best-run companies in the country. Started by a guy named Armand Zoller. He came over from Europe after the war and taught at MIT. Physics. If he'd stayed

11

he'd probably have a Nobel by now, but he hated that ivory-tower academic bullshit and the departmental politics, so he started Zoltec thirty years ago. He still dominates the place, and Hitler would have envied the way he runs it. There's a trust fund, Putnam, old Yankee money, held maybe a quarter of the stock for years. Gotta few guys on the board, put some financial type named Truscott in to mind the store a few years ago, but basically passive. Zoller's the man. Gotta be in his late sixties, early seventies, but very much top dog."

"Makes a lot of money?"

"Zoltec or Zoller?"

"Either. Both."

"Zoltec, definitely. Terrific returns, year in and year out. Zoller?" Bucky shook his head. "Negative. Decent salary, of course, but gave up all his equity to the money people to raise the capital to get started. Probably doesn't give a shit, anyway —above all the grubby stuff that obsesses crass scum like us." He glanced at my tattered tweed jacket. "Well, like me, anyway."

I let this pass. "They make computer chips, I gather?"

"Well, that's sort of like saying Ferrari makes cars. Dozens of companies make chips. Every Apple on every kid's desk runs on chips. Zoltec makes the chips that run the computers that matter—the ones that control an entire factory, or that tell the missiles how to land right on the hanky on Saddam's head." He pushed a peanut around the tabletop with a drink stirrer. "At that level, nobody cares what they cost, so Zoltec makes *lots* of money."

"Who's the competition?"

"For high-capacity chips?"

"Um."

"In the U.S., nobody. The Japanese try, but they're always a step behind. Ditto the krauts. It's all in the speed and amount

12

of data that can be processed. When Zoltec was turning out chips that could move two gigabytes, everybody else was at one. They catch up, Zoltec moved up to four. Now they've got chips that'll tell you what the temperature will be in Dedham, an elephant farts in Uganda. That's why the U.S. dominates the mainframe computer business."

"Anything else you know about them?" I signaled Henry for another round.

"Not a hell of a lot. Rumor has it they're working on a megachip, the granddaddy of them all, but I don't know. I do know I'd give my right one to know anything that might affect their stock." He glared at me over his glass.

"Sorry, Buckeroo—I don't know anything myself, and if I did I couldn't tell you, at least not yet."

He let out a long sigh. "Sure, sure. Just remember, Nase, you owe me one."

"Lean over." I beckoned so that our heads almost met in the middle of the table. "Little down payment. DeJames Packer's been doing so much coke his nose looks like a snow cone." DeJames was a young, ninety-seven-mile-an-hour left-handed reliever the Sox were counting on to carry them to the playoffs, or better. "Yesterday he crashed like a a 747 they forgot to fuel. They sneaked him off to the funny farm late last night. Call your book and get something down on New York. This isn't our boys' year—for a change."

Bucky reared back like I had kicked him in the groin. "Jesus, Nase, are you sure? We had a lock."

"Shhhh!" The bar looked like one of those stockbroker ads, every head turned to catch the word. I barely mouthed the words: "Gospel, Buck; they'll announce it tomorrow, next day latest. He's bouncing off walls. Give him a rosin bag, he'd suck it dry. Might as well make some money on the downside."

"Your source reliable?"

"The best." My informant, a sometime client, had been supplying DeJames with a thousand dollars' worth a week of his favorite decongestant. I tossed off my martini, left Bucky muttering about the perversity of the Irish God, and caught the MTA back to Cambridge.

CHAPTER 3

I used the next morning to finish canning the preserves, and the sun was already honey on dry leaves when I left for Zoltec. I stopped on the steps to drink it in. Across the street a gaggle of Radcliffe girls were tossing a Frisbee, their squeals puncturing the crisp air. They were keeping it away from a tiny white West Highland terrier that dashed back and forth in frantic pursuit. I was trying to remember when I had last done anything for the sheer joy of it when I overheard Mrs. Serafina and McGinty in the litter-strewn side lot exchanging pleasantries, Cambridge fashion: "He never; Magellan's a good boy!" A small ball of gray Brillo quivered at her side, adding his part to the discussion.

"You fulla shit. You keep that dog outa my yard or you outa here." McGinty's prune face, flushed by his morning pint of rock & rye, darkened toward purple.

"Is not your yard. Is everybody what lives here yard. I gotta right use it, same as you. Magellan's gotta use it, got no place else." Mrs. Serafina's prodigious bosom heaved.

"Why, you old . . ." McGinty took a step forward. Mrs. Sera-

15

fina could take care of herself, but I thought I'd save her the trouble.

Magellan beat me to it, darting in and growling as ferociously as a fifteen-pound dog can. McGinty kicked at him but missed, exposing a fishbelly ankle. The little dog dodged, then whirled and struck.

"God damn it!" McGinty's foot jerked loose, then shot out and caught the dog in the side hard enough to somersault him sideways. "Get outa here, you goddamned cur." Magellan scrambled to his feet with a yelp, then retreated to the safe place between Mrs. Serafina's legs, whimpering and cringing.

"Don' you touch him! What kinda man, kick a little dog?" Mrs. Serafina looked ready to do some stomping herself.

"Okay, McGinty, cool off." I stepped between them. Across the street the girls and the little white Westie had stopped to watch the action.

"Wassit to you? Get outta my way. I'm gonna kill that dog." McGinty put his hand on my chest and pushed.

I slapped his hand away. "It's this to me, McGinty; I don't like you. Now, why don't you crawl back into your hole? Or maybe you'd like me to kick you back there like you kicked the dog?"

McGinty held my stare for a few seconds but he hadn't taken on enough courage yet to feel like swinging at me, considering I was twenty-five years younger and looked like Charles Atlas next to him. "Nahh!" With a derisory gesture he turned and shuffled back into the basement door, where he turned and yelled, "Remember what I said—you keep that damn mutt outta my way or I'll kill it."

Mrs. Serafina saluted McGinty with a sharp upward thrust of a thumb protruding between her first two fingers, then bent over and picked up the dog, who peered over her shoulder at the Westie yapping across the street. "Is you okay, Magellan, huh? That man hurt you?" She rubbed a wrinkled cheek

16

against his and got a lick in return. She put the dog on the pile of laundry she had been carrying in a plastic basket and strained to lift it.

"Let me."

"Wha', I'm an ol' lady, can' take care of hersel'?"

"Oosh!" The basket weighed a ton. "No way. I want to hear about my friend McGinty. What's the trouble?" We walked back inside, Magellan's face bobbing inches from mine, his little pink tongue shooting out to give me the first kisses I had had in some time.

"That *filho da puta*. He mad 'cause he step in Magellan's business. I tole him sorry, I clean up his shoe. Wern' drunk alla time, he see it anyhow."

"That's it? Stepped in a little dog doo? I would have thought he'd have felt right at home."

"Hey, thas' good. Yeah, he right at home in kaka. You right." She stopped on a step, breathing hard.

"One of these days McGinty'll fix the elevator." The rest gave me a chance to contemplate the peeling green walls. It was probably a good thing that there was almost no light.

"Sure, he will—an I'll be Mis' Portugal."

We finally made it to the top. "Jussa minute." Mrs. Serafina fumbled in a string bag until she found her keys, then opened three locks.

Magellan sprang down and bolted into the apartment. I stepped forward and he rushed back and gummed my ankle.

"Hey, Magellan, what you do Nase leg, huh? He you friend. Leave him lone. Come on in, Nase, havva cup coffee, little flan." She beckoned with a heavy forearm.

I flicked Magellan off. "I can't stay, Mrs. Serafina, but thanks. Another time?"

"You gotta eat more, Nase—you too skinny." She snatched a wad of skin just above my belt and squeezed. "Looka that; ain' got enough for a woman to hang onto. How you gonna

17

make a woman happy, huh, she no able to hang on? Woman, she wanna hang onna man." She flashed a golden smile.

"Ouch. Afraid this is one man women don't want to hang onto, Mrs. Serafina, and somehow I don't think gaining three hundred pounds is going to help much."

"Fsst!" Mrs. Serafina let go and made a smacking sound with her fingers against her lips. "Don' be thinking bout that woman, that Brenda. She don' know how to make a man happy, 'cause she never happy herself. Alla time complaining, never anything right for her. 'Men do this, men do that, system do this, system do that.' Alla time, blame her troubles on this an' that. You forget about her. There lotsa other women roun, real women, know there ain' no troubles 'cept with people. Not men, not women, no system, jus' people. You fine one." The golden teeth reappeared. "You a coupla years older, go after you myself. Ain' that right, Magellan?"

"Arf!" Magellan pounded his tail on the floor.

Take off forty years, a hundred pounds, and the mustache, I might have been interested. "You're too much woman for me, Mrs. Serafina. I couldn't keep up."

She brayed. "Hey, you probably right!" She smacked me on the shoulder with a hamlike fist. "My Fer'nan', he say the same thing, God res' his soul. An' he right. Ten years ago, Nase, ten years ago this January, my Fer'nan' leave this life. Couldn' keep up with me, jus' got wore out."

She looked down at the dog with a smile, then thrust arthritic fingers out for a lick. "Magellan, he the firs' man been able to keep up with me. He start hangin' 'roun last year, I know right away—Magellan, he the man for me. We gonna grow old together, ain' we, Magellan? Anyway, you fin' somebody soon, I know; I gotta vision."

I cast a glance at the yellowing wedding picture of the Serafinas on the table by the couch. He had certainly had plenty for a woman to hang onto. "If she's half the woman you are, Mrs.

Serafina, I'll be a lucky man, but I better go now." I turned for the door.

"Hey, you come up soon, havva glass wine, some flan, you unnerstan'? Put some weight on you."

"It's a deal." I started down the steps.

"Magellan, you say good-bye Nase, thassa good boy."

"Arf."

I headed out Route 2 to pick up 128. Most of the traffic was heading in but as usual the road was torn up and the congestion was savage. A cab started to cut me off at a traffic circle, and the cabbie gave me the finger when I didn't give way. The Boston Irish have poetry in their wrists.

Things lightened up once I got on 128. I put the car on autopilot and reflected on Mrs. Serafina's observation about Brenda. I hadn't realized that she'd made such an impact in so short a time. She'd moved out in less than a year, and now she was a stranger, searching for self-awareness at some East Coast Esalen. Pity she hadn't asked for mine as part of the property settlement—I would have happily surrendered all I had. Yet as much as I'd come to wonder what I had ever seen in her, I couldn't bring myself to hope she'd find what she thought she wanted; even Brenda didn't deserve a truly heavy dose of insight. She didn't really want it, anyway. It was the quest, not the capture, that obsessed middle-class intellectualoids in Boston. They were like dogs chasing cars, cars named "self-fulfillment" or "the real me." I was glad I'd never joined that race— I lacked the energy.

I only got lost once looking for Zoltec, so it was just after one when I pulled up to the entrance. A huge security guard slid open a glass window in the gate house and took my name.

"Yessir, been expecting you. Why don't you pull in over

there"—he gestured toward a parking space—"and come on in. Got to sign you in."

Inside the guardhouse an overhead battery of television monitors displayed shifting scenes from remote cameras. One wall was almost covered with rows of green lights. Under each one was a black plastic label indicating a location.

A similar label over the guard's breast pocket told me his name. "You guys aren't fooling around with the security, are you, Gene?"

"No, sir." He pushed a notebook across a counter and handed me a pen. "They're pretty strict about that. Everybody in, everybody out, one of us marks it down. Sign here, please." A thick finger thumped the space where he'd noted my license number and the time.

I signed and he pulled out a visitor's badge, recorded the number next to my name, then handed it to me. "Why don't you pin that on and have a seat? I'll let Mr. Truscott know you're here."

"Mr. Truscott?"

"Yessir—left word he wanted to see you first thing."

In a couple of minutes another guard pulled up in a golf cart and zipped me a quarter mile to a low brick building marked "Zoltec Industries—Administrative Offices." Inside, a secretary escorted me to an office labeled "Z. Truscott–V.P. Finance." She knocked softly, then waved me in and disappeared.

A tall thin man looked up from behind a desk. A computer displaying a spreadsheet hummed quietly on a table next to him. Next to it was a picture of a pretty woman in a wedding dress, and a smaller picture of the same woman in an Austin-Healey. A squash racquet leaned against the wall in the corner.

The man rose with a smile. "Zachariah Truscott, Mr. Nichols. Appreciate your coming in."

He was a few years younger than I, three inches taller, and a couple pounds lighter, wiry and fit.

Truscott cut a fine figure: blond hair combed straight back, even features, a healthy tan, and gray eyes that sparkled through fatigue. His suit coat hung over the back of his chair so that the red flannel suspenders stood out against the blue shirt, white collar, and gold collar pin, setting off the yellow silk tie. I glanced down at his feet: black tassel loafers—a full B-School.

"Won't you have a seat?" Truscott waggled a long finger at a chair behind me, then lowered himself into his. He tossed one arm over the back and crossed his legs. "I don't know how much you've been told about our problem, Mr. Nichols, but Dr. Zoller and I thought I should have a chat with you before you got together with the others." He ran his hand back through his hair, then shook his head.

"Well, Mr. Truscott, I gathered from Mr. Holtree . . ."

"Zach, please. I'm afraid yesterday Holtree didn't know the half of it. I won't waste your time with the details, since Dr. Bingham will be going over those, but there are some things he and his people don't know that maybe you should know, just so you'll understand our"—he looked up at the ceiling, searching for the word—"panic, if you will, about what's happened." He gave me a rueful smile, as though anything as human as panic could get him drummed out of the Business School Alumni Association.

"From what I understand, I don't blame you for being upset."

He responded hurriedly, "You see, this couldn't have come at a worse time. I mean, there's no good time for this sort of thing, I guess, but . . ." he broke off. "Oh, hell, I'm not making any sense. Let me start from the beginning. Sorry. Anyway, I'm the chief financial officer out here. I'm the guy who watches the money. The place is filled with scientific geniuses, Dr. Zoller first and foremost, but someone's got to remember the shareholders, see to it a few dollars go their way every now and then. That's me."

"I gather quite a few dollars go their way."

This drew another smile. It wiped away the drained look. "I guess we've done all right." The pride faded from his voice as quickly as it had come. "I've also got to deal with the lenders —you know, banks, pension funds, keep them happy."

I nodded. I had to keep my bank happy, too.

"We were about to announce a new development. It would have been a major breakthrough, a really important competitive advantage. Something we'd been working on for a long time, that only proved feasible a short while ago. The market would have been"—again, the skyward look for the right word —"wildly enthusiastic. That was going to be our opportunity to issue some new stock and use the proceeds to pay off debt. Now all that's on hold, because it appears that it's the technology for this new process that this Platt fellow stole."

"I see." I did, a little.

"It's simple, really; the lawyers tell us we can't announce our new development unless we also announce that it's been stolen." He snorted, then shook his head. "Violation of the securities laws otherwise, because we'd be implying we had a competitive advantage that won't be an advantage at all if this fellow Platt sells our secrets to somebody else."

He took another sip of coffee. "Of course, if it gets out our secrets were stolen, the market's going the other way, and I'm going to have shareholders ringing my phone off the hook. To say nothing of bankers calling loans. And issuing new shares would be out of the question. *Is* out of the question, unless we get our secrets back. All of which means"—he took off his glasses, leaned forward and gave me a suppliant look—"Dr. Zoller and I will be wishing you well, to put it mildly. Any questions?" He smiled.

"Just one. Why me? You want the best chance of finding the

stuff, you should get a big agency, put a round-the-clock watch on. There's only one of me. Pretty thin."

"We thought about getting in a major agency, or the authorities, but decided against it. The lawyers persuaded us the police would do more harm than good, and too many people would know about our problem if we brought in a big agency. The market, the lenders—too much chance they'd get word." He shook his head. "This just can't get out, at least until there's no more hope of recovering our data. Dr. Zoller had gotten your name somewhere. You're an unavoidable trade-off."

"Unavoidable trade-off" beat "hopeless jack-off," which was what my father used to call me. I shrugged. "I'll do my best."

"I know you will. We have every confidence in you." He sounded like he meant it.

Truscott untangled himself and walked around the desk. As he did, the smaller picture fell on its face and he stopped to prop it up.

"I used to have one of those."

Truscott looked up. "An Austin-Healey?"

"Well, a wife, too, but I meant the Healey. Had a used one in college. Great cars. A classic."

He chuckled and cast a fond look at the picture. "Bitsy says I'm the only man she's ever heard of whose mistress is older than his wife."

"Probably be easier to keep a real mistress running, if your Healey's anything like mine was."

Truscott laughed. "Easier, and cheaper. I think I'm putting my mechanic's kids through college. Now I better get you over to Bingham's group so you can get to work." He took me by the arm and led me to the door. He paused before opening it. "Maybe it would be best if you don't say anything about our talk to the others. The scientists would just assume I was thinking up a new way to cut their budgets. We operate pretty much on a need-to-know basis around here anyway, and the fewer people who know about this crimp in our financial plans, the better."

"No problem."

"Great. Just keep me posted. Call me anytime. In fact, let me know as soon as you even think you know where this guy's gone with our stuff. That'll give me some lead time in the market. That's critical." He handed me a business card. "I've put down my home phone. Call anytime, day or night." He patted my shoulder. "And Nase? Thanks. And good luck."

The next meeting was in the Research and Development Building. Holtree, thumbing through some legal papers in the anteroom, greeted me like an old chum. Maybe he had looked me up and found out that I, too, was a son of Harvard, sort of.

A secretary led us through a pair of doors marked "Authorized Personnel Only" into a windowless conference room. It held a long table and the kinds of chairs you find in hospital cafeterias. There was a blackboard at one end.

Two men arrived just behind us. The first introduced himself as Dr. Bingham, a solidly built, distinguished-looking man in his late fifties. The other man, a Dr. Quarles, was perhaps forty-five, pudgy and short. He was wearing a white lab coat and looked more like a chef than a scientist.

Bingham shut the door. "Well, Mr. Nichols, I gather you've been informed of our problem?"

"I've got the broad outline, Doctor," I said, "but maybe you can give me a better idea of what I'm going to be looking for. It would also help if you could tell me as much as you can about the man who did this, so I'll have an idea where to start looking."

He reached into the pocket of his lab coat and pulled out a cellophane envelope, then dumped the contents onto the table. Out fell a small black rectangle. "This is a microprocessor—a chip." He pushed it over. There were half a dozen tiny wires coming out of each side. It looked like a squashed spider.

"That's a four-megabyte chip—it can hold four *million* bits of data at one time. It can process more information, faster, than any other chip ever made. It will be the heart of the most powerful computers on earth."

Quarles chimed in, "It's a quantum leap in computer technology."

"Just so," said Bingham. "Anyway, that's what this is all about. Let's move on." He scooped the chip back into the envelope. "Winston"—Bingham nodded at Quarles—"worked through the night, and we know what Platt took." His voice trailed off. "It's a disaster."

Quarles glanced at a sheet of notes he had pulled out of a side pocket of his coat. A fine sheen of perspiration glistened on his face. "We keep all our blueprints and process specifications in a vault here at headquarters. In order to check out materials, to work on them in your office, for example, you must first log them with the vault custodian. That way, we have a record of everything anyone has had access to." Quarles had a soft, schoolmasterish voice with a slight nervous halt every several words.

"I gather from what Dr. Bingham said, Doctor, that you think Platt may have checked out materials for his own purposes?"

Quarles looked at Bingham. I waited for an answer. It was Bingham who finally spoke: "Dr. Quarles has determined that Dr. Platt has stolen the specifications for the new chip." He whispered the last words.

"The materials are gone?"

"No. He must have taken copies."

"How do you know he stole them? Maybe he just took them out to do his job."

"That's the point—he didn't have anything to do with the new chip. He had no business with those materials, but he

25

logged them out overnight. Plenty of time to copy them." The pencil Bingham had been holding in his fist snapped. "It took us five years to develop that process. Five years of trial and error, and that son of a bitch will sell it for a song." Bingham's couth was slipping, and I approved; clients that hate well are less likely to flyspeck the bill.

"Who will he take it to?" I asked.

"There are only a few possibilities," Bingham answered. "You saw his notes—he plans to be a 'chip technology consultant'—selling our technology! My guess . . ."

A random thought made me interrupt. "Yeah—I did see the notes. That was thoughtful of him—leaving them, I mean."

The lawyer looked up. "Thoughtful? I'm not sure that's quite the right word. We're just lucky . . ." Irony puzzled Holtree.

"No, I guess you're right. That was awfully careless, though." I swiveled to look at Bingham. "Was he careless? No disrespect, but my experience with engineers is that they're usually pretty neat. Careful."

Quarles seemed about to say something, but Bingham answered first. "As Elton says"—he nodded at the lawyer— "we're lucky he was careless this time. I really wouldn't care to speculate on what's typical of engineers."

Out of the corner of my eye I saw Quarles deflate like a soufflé in a draft. I gave it up. "Right. I guess it doesn't matter. You were saying where you thought Platt might try to sell your technology?"

"As I was saying, there are half a dozen companies that would understand the value of our technology, but the Japanese are where I'd go first. We've always managed to stay a few years ahead of them, and their computer manufacturers hate having to buy chips from us; it humiliates them to depend on foreigners for anything. With the materials Platt took, any one of the Japanese companies could be making the new chip in a year or so."

"Can't they just buy one of your chips, take it apart and see how you make it?"

Bingham snorted. "Never. You can take it apart, but that won't tell you how we managed to quadruple the capacity while reducing the cost. It's all in the manufacturing process, and we only got that right last month. They could look at one of the new chips forever. They'd never figure out how to make it."

"What can you all tell me about Platt himself? You know—address, habits, that sort of thing." I pulled a little spiral notebook and a pen out of my pocket. That always impressed clients.

Bingham answered, "One of my staff members, Dr. Ornstein, knew Platt better than anybody. She's also a first-rate physicist who knows the new process from the bottom up; she developed the voltage stabilization curves herself—a brilliant piece of work. I'd like her to join us now. In addition to filling you in on Platt, she'll be available to work with you until we have this situation under control."

Holtree must have seen my reaction to the news I was going to have an assistant. "You'll need someone who can recognize Zoltec's materials and swear out an affidavit; that wouldn't be you."

"I suppose, but . . ."

Bingham cut in: "Rachel is a fine scientist; she worked closely with Dr. Zoller and me on many aspects of this project. Understandably, she feels proprietary about it. We all do, but perhaps Dr. Ornstein more than most." He paused, looking at Holtree and me. "In addition, I think Dr. Ornstein may have personal reasons for resenting what Platt has done. I'm sure she'll give you every assistance."

"Gotcha." I wondered what that meant. Bingham was a joyless sack of spleen; I didn't envy anyone working under him.

Bingham's call brought Dr. Ornstein in short order. She was

carrying an armload of black binders enveloped in an oversize sheaf of blueprints. She plopped them on the table and turned to meet us. Bingham handled introductions. "You met Elton Holtree, I believe, Rachel. I'd like you to meet Nason Nichols. He's the investigator who's going to try and recover our materials. He's interested in knowing about Dr. Platt."

Dr. Ornstein forced a smile that failed halfway through. "I'm not sure I can help much, but I'll tell you what I can. Rachel Ornstein, Mr. Nichols." We shook hands. Her voice was low, with just a hint of hoarseness. She was a head shorter than my six feet, and a few years younger than I, but old enough to have some lines in her face, and some character, too.

Bingham and Quarles rose to leave. "Well, Mr. Nichols, I think Winston and I have probably told you as much as we can at this time. I'm sure you appreciate that it is impossible to overstate the importance to Zoltec of getting our materials back. Dr. Zoller views their loss as the most serious threat the company has ever known. I do hope you're able to accomplish something."

Bingham turned to Dr. Ornstein. "Rachel has agreed that this will have her highest priority; she's available to help you in any way. Now if you'll excuse us." He left, Quarles scurrying after.

"Well, that seems to take care of that, em?" Holtree pulled a thin gold pocket watch out of his vest pocket. "I'm not sure I have anything more to contribute at this time. As you can tell, Mr. Nichols, finding those materials quickly is of the utmost importance. How you do it is your business, and, frankly, I'd just as soon not know." He gave me the raised eyebrows.

"Signal received. Dr. Ornstein and I will figure out a plan of attack. I'll let you know as soon as I have anything."

Holtree stuffed his legal pad back into an ancient briefcase, nodded vaguely in our direction, and left.

I turned to my new partner. "Well, Doctor, what can you tell me about the oh-so-naughty Dr. Platt?"

She had just taken off her glasses and was rubbing her temples in a circular motion, and at first I thought she hadn't heard me. Then she spoke, but her voice was low and I had to strain to hear. "I don't know. I don't know if I can tell you anything that will help. I thought I knew Bruce, but I must have been wrong." Her voice trailed off, then rose slightly as she pushed a file across to me: "Here. I got his file from Personnel; I thought it might help." She went back to rubbing her temples.

"Good thinking. Rough time around here, huh?"

She nodded without opening her eyes.

"Suppose you first give me a quick tour of what we assume are the stolen documents. I'd like to know what we're looking for. These are the originals?" I pointed to the pile she had brought in.

She nodded again. "This is a complete set, blueprints and process sheets, for what we call the laser lithography process." She pulled a black binder over and opened it. I don't know what I had been expecting, but not what I saw: page after page of computer printouts, as meaningful to me as the Rosetta stone.

"What's it mean? But the short course, please."

That drew a quick half-smile. "Basically, the power of a computer—its speed and capacity—depends on getting as many circuits as possible into as small a space as possible. The circuitry is microscopic, and under traditional manufacturing methods you run up against absolute limits on your ability to compress them. We developed a new way of doing it, using lasers, that gets around those limits. It isn't easy; there are dozens of different steps, and hundreds of variables have to be controlled at each step—temperature, voltages, that sort of thing; a tiny deviation in one of them and nothing happens, or at least nothing good. These sheets show what the ranges have to be, and how to achieve them." She rubbed the palm of her hand over an open page and smiled at it. It was a lover's caress. The fatigue seemed to lift for a second, her features softened; she was pretty.

I turned away and picked up the personnel file. "Look: there's no reason for you to hang around here while I review this. Why don't I go through it, take a few notes, then give you a call?"

She nodded gratefully, told me what extension to call, and left. I settled in, stoked the nicotine beast for the first time that day, and opened the file.

I've looked at a fair number of employment files, and they have a depressing sameness: the initial application, filled with eagerness and hype—"looking for a more challenging opportunity with a dynamic, growing company"; the offer, written with personnel-manager palsiness—"we know, Bill, you'll be an exciting addition to the Acme team, and Wally, Frank, and all the folks in Marketing can't wait to work with you"; the annual evaluations, with their humiliating and usually absurd critiques—"and you've agreed, Bill, that you need to improve your people skills in 1991"; and then the predictable tawdry conclusion, or I wouldn't be the reader—"discharged for alcoholism," or "wages garnished," or "terminated for personal reasons."

Platt's was about par, except they hadn't gotten around to sticking in the closing entry. Ph.D. in electrical engineering from Purdue, a few years of teaching at a state college, then a succession of jobs in industry. The last one before coming to Zoltec had been with a cellular telephone company: "Responsible for budgeting and contracting a $25,000,000 satellite communications facility," the application said. That meant he'd probably helped install an office phone system. Under "Career Objective" the interviewer had entered "applicant seeks major supervisory responsibility on an executive path." No doubt they had told him that was what he was getting, too. Ah, well, Brenda and I had also made promises to each other. Except when she walked out I didn't have any secrets left to steal.

The last page in the file was a copy of a payroll department change-of-address form, dated the past February. Platt had gone from an area of Newton popular with faculty types to an address on Boston Harbor, probably a condo in one of the restored nineteenth-century warehouses. Chichi. Also expensive. I wondered how he swung it on the sixty thousand he was making when he left. I flipped back to the employment application, which said he was single and about my age. I added his address to my notes, and a bank reference. There wasn't much else, so I called Dr. Ornstein. She answered on the first ring.

"I've gone through the file, and it's pretty lean. Could we get together now? I'm hoping you can tell me a little more."

"Of course. I'll be right in."

I wasn't thrilled at the prospect of any more time within four pea-green walls. "Tell you what, Doctor, I'm about tapped out here; suppose we adjourn and continue this over dinner?"

I could hear her brain calculating. Duty won out. "Sure. Sure, that's a good idea. I've had it, too. Just give me a minute. I'll meet you in the reception area."

The thought was probably criminal in certain Boston circles, where the existence of two sexes is grimly acknowledged but viewed as a vestigial defect in the species, but as I waited for Dr. Ornstein I realized I was looking forward to an evening with a woman. It had been a long time.

C H A P T E R 4

We got past "Doctor" and "Mr." halfway through the first glass of wine. I had followed her back to her apartment, the top floor of a townhouse on Beacon Hill, then drove to Rita's, in the North End. I wanted someplace quiet, where the waiter wouldn't want to be my friend. Rita's is dark and warm, the food aggressively pre-nouvelle.

I waited until we ordered, then broached business by asking how Platt might try to move the stuff.

She looked startled. "Why, I don't know. Couldn't he just call people he thinks might be interested, then have them come and look at it?"

"He could, but that wouldn't show much instinct for self-preservation."

"I'm not sure I follow you."

"I assume this guy plans to stay around to enjoy the fruits of his labor once he manages to sell the stuff. That means he won't want to leave tracks in case someone starts raising questions about how all of a sudden the competition has caught up. In other words, he isn't going to be running any ads in the *Globe*.

At the same time, he's got to feel the market out pretty carefully. He just walks up to somebody, the wrong somebody, says, 'How'd you like a great deal in computer chips?' and he could find himself housed at state expense the next few years. Ruins the résumé."

The image rattled her. "Prison?"

"Ho. Dr. Platt's running around with, what—a million dollars' worth of stolen property? You tell me. What's more, the person who buys is risking a lot, too, if he knows what he's getting's stolen, which he will. I don't think companies with the bucks and morals to be interested are going to be stupid enough to hang around on his doorstep. They'll want to be able to say 'Who's he?' if things get tight. Dr. Platt's moved into a lonely world."

"Oh, God," she said. "What a fool. What a goddamned fool." She reached out and took a cigarette from the pack I had lying on the table. She blew out a long stream of smoke, then gave one of those snorts and shoulder shrugs that say "Ask me what's so funny?" so I asked her what was so funny.

She shook her head, then shrugged again. "Oh, hell, I guess it's no secret. Dr. Bingham probably already told you." She pulled on the cigarette, then continued. "Bruce—Dr. Platt—and I were very close for a while. There was a time I even thought we might get married." She looked off in the distance for a moment, then went on, "Then I decided he was totally egocentric, full of big talk and self-delusion." She leaned over the table until I felt I had to, too, so that our noses were no more than a foot apart. "I just got so I couldn't stand hearing him talk about himself and his big plans anymore." She chuckled, but there was no humor in it. "And now it turns out I was wrong; he's not a talker—he's a doer all right—a big-time thief. Funny, huh?"

She drained the last of her wine and I signaled for another round.

"You don't mean he talked about walking off with . . ."

"Oh, no; nothing like that. Nothing illegal." She leaned back. I liked nose-to-nose better. "It was just that he wasn't content being just an employee, even a successful one, which we are— I mean, people like Bruce and me. He called us 'technocrats' and said we 'gave away our intellectual capital for a pittance.' Bruce talked about 'embodying the Nietzschean synthesis,' or some garbage like that; being a major scientific thinker who's able to translate his thoughts into a great enterprise through sheer force of will. Someone like Land at Polaroid, or Dr. Zoller, for that matter."

"I'm not sure there's anything wrong with wanting to be something more than you are, although it can be frustrating." Her voice had taken on an intensity, a note of bitter disdain. I didn't understand it. I wanted to, although I couldn't have said why.

"This town is knee-deep in smart people who've never gotten over the fact that there are lots of even smarter people around. Everything came easy to them when they were kids in Detroit or wherever, and they got by on sheer brainpower. Then they got to Boston and they discover brainpower's no big deal —the place is full of smart kids—and they fall apart because they're going to have to work really hard to stay even."

"I bet you were one of those smart kids; how've you managed?" The waiter delivered the clams and a split of Lacryma Christi.

She thought about this for a minute. "I *was* one of those smart kids. I'm a pretty smart adult, too. But I never had a chance to sit around thinking great thoughts all day, because I had a father who took care of that. A sweet, gentle man who wanted nothing more in life than to read the Talmud and argue fine points of Jewish law with a bunch of old windbags."

Her face twisted. "He thought great thoughts, and talked—

Jesus, did he talk—and my mother and I worked. She worked two, sometimes three, jobs so that I could have a book, take a trip, go to a better school, but there was never enough. Do you have any idea what it's like to get your clothes from a second-hand shop because your father's so busy translating Maimonides he can't be bothered with a job?"

I shook my head, but she wasn't really looking for an answer —she had retreated to a world of old remembered hurt, where visitors never get past the waiting room. "No matter how tired she was, or how worried about money, how we were going to pay the rent, get my braces, all of that, my mother always had time to listen to my father, nod while he went on about some meaningless point he had scored at shul. Then she'd tell him how wonderful he was. She died of a heart attack my last year in college. My father still lives in Evanston, and I visit him every now and then because my mother would want me to, but I've had enough of talkers and dreamers. When I realized Bruce was just some Freudian phase I had wandered into, I got out. People like that are useless." She tossed it off with as much feeling as I had used to order the clams.

"Maybe she loved him." I was making white sound, just to hear her talk. "Was she happy?"

"Love." She said it slowly, as though uncertain of the meaning. "Oh, she loved him all right, and it killed her. Love can cost too much."

She sucked the meat out of a clamshell, then continued: "I hated him for what he did to my mother, for what he did to me. I struggled to get through college, then to get my doctorate. You know how I paid for my graduate work? With the money I got from a small insurance policy my mother had taken out. She never told me she had it."

I poured more wine. Rachel took a deep drink. I watched her neck relax as she leaned back, then broke into a smile.

"Phew. I really got wound up. Sorry. You must be a good detective."

"Wine makes a great interrogator—beats a rubber hose every time."

Whatever our subject had done to Rachel's mood, it hadn't put her off her feed. She ate with a lusty appetite, and I was pressed to keep up. We chased the clams with osso buco and a bottle of barbaresco. We made small talk until Rachel came back to business: "What's the next step?"

"Tomorrow morning we go hunting. Start at Platt's apartment, see if we can find him. He doesn't know we're on to him, so it shouldn't be hard. Maybe he's opened an office, someplace he can do business. He'll probably have to if he wants a cover. Then, once we find him, we follow him, see who he meets, see if he brings things with him to meetings that might show where he's keeping the stuff. You got any ideas?"

"No, except I think you're right about the office; Bruce will have to have an office—it's part of the thing about being a big operator. That's where he'd keep the documents, wouldn't he?"

"Good guess, but we'll need more than a guess. Luck won't hurt." I remembered something I had seen in Platt's personnel file. "I saw that Platt moved a while ago. What—eight, nine months ago, maybe? Into the high-rent district. Know anything about that?"

She started to speak, hesitated, then shook her head. "Not really. That was about when we broke up. I really wasn't concentrating on anything except the project. I think he got a lot of . . . new things around then. A Porsche, too. He's the kind of man who needs a Porsche, if you know what I mean."

"There's another kind?"

She laughed. "He's got a little vacation cottage up in New Hampshire; I suppose he could have the materials there?"

"That's a shot, too. So's his Great Aunt Tilly's. He's the key —he'll lead us to the materials, if he's got them."

I dropped Rachel at her apartment. We shook hands, very businesslike. It felt good.

CHAPTER 5

I woke knowing the last glass of wine had been a mistake. A shower, two cups of coffee, and the *Globe* helped, but my fighting edge was still dulled when I called Platt's apartment. After a dozen rings I called information and asked for any new listings under Platt. The electro-adenoidal tones of a computer told me that I had a hit—The Platt Group had a phone. From the exchange, it was out toward Milton—a tasteful, understated place to have an office. If Bruce was making a statement, as Rachel had said, it was an oblique way to start. Maybe he figured stealing Zoltec's lifeblood was statement enough.

Five rings and I gave up. Either too early for anyone to be in or Platt was on the road. I hoped he hadn't already packed his sample bag, set off making sales calls; that could make things difficult.

I'd arranged to pick Rachel up at nine. Careful maneuvering to avoid the insanity of Harvard Square enabled me to pull up in front of her apartment a few minutes before. She was standing just inside the glass doors, waiting. I liked that.

Vogue must have run a recent spread on "Smart New Designs

For Fall Sleuthing," or else Rachel was just one of those people with innate chic. She wore a pants suit in a muted autumnal rust, with a black silk blouse. The effect was stunning, with the look of an accident.

We cut over to Quincy Market after only twenty minutes of curb-climbing, fender-bending car hockey. I wedged the Scout into a No Parking zone on a side street and we headed for Platt's condo.

The weather had turned, and the air, laden with sea mist, had a bite to it; I hoped we weren't going to have to do too much outside work. We found Platt's address after a few minutes' stroll, and I had called it right: it was one of the old stone warehouses renovated a few years before, at the same time the nearby market area had been dolled up to have all the kitschy charm of a theme park. It made for top-drawer conspicuous consumption. As I stared up at the massive gray building, three stories tall and half a block long, one of my most human qualities surfaced: envy. This was going to be an easy man to dislike.

There were two BMWs out front, and a few Volvos and Saabs for the underachievers, but no Porsches. Either Platt had left early or he was staying somewhere else. We opened the front door into a small anteroom. A row of mailboxes was recessed in the wall. The second one from the left had a business card in the slot: "Bruce Platt, Ph.D."

"If he buzzes us in, we depart fast." I pushed the button above the box a half dozen times, then waited a couple of minutes. "Let me know if you see anyone coming."

I got out my pocketknife and wedged a blade under the mailbox door. It popped open easily, because it was jammed with an accumulation of mail, most of which slid out onto the floor. I quickly pawed through the pile. Platt hadn't picked up his mail since he'd left Zoltec. I crammed everything back into the box and slammed the door shut.

"What do you think that means?" Rachel handed me a Star Market flyer I'd missed.

I jammed it back through the slot. "Not sure, except that Platt probably hasn't been home for a while. You said he has a place in New Hampshire?"

"Near North Conway. Maybe he's staying there?"

"Maybe." We walked over to Quincy Market for a cup of coffee. I left Rachel at a table while I made a couple of phone calls. The first was to an Area D police captain named Hairston who owed me a favor; he'd been going with Brenda until I met her. He was in my debt forever.

"Hey, Buddy—how you been?"

"Nase, Nase—good to hear your voice. Whatcha gonna bribe me for today?" Hal's a cute guy, likes to have his little joke; I say he does me a favor, he says I bribe him.

"Hal, you ever worry Internal Affairs going to wire your phone, put you away about a hundred twenty years?"

"IA? You gotta be kidding! I got signed receipts from half the guys in IA. Only thing they care about is if you give them their cut. Good guys to do business with."

"I'll sleep better, Hal, knowing that. Hey—I need a little favor. Not a big favor, a little favor."

For ten dollars on my tab he got me Platt's license number. He was still driving the Porsche. I hoped things never came to a high-speed chase—the Scout labored a bit over forty-five, which was about where Platt'd be shifting into second.

The second call was to the number I had gotten for The Platt Group. A woman answered on the third ring.

"Is Dr. Platt in, please?"

"I'll check. Who's calling, please?"

"This is Burford Werkins, from VSI."

"Well, Mr., uh, Berkin, I believe Dr. Platt is tied up right now."

"Splendid. Keep him that way. I have a presentation he'll be most interested in. Be by momentarily. Where did you say you're located?"

"Waverly Office Park, in Milton. Third building in, on your right. Uh, who did you say . . . ?"

"Bye now."

The Waverly Office Park was one of those developments that look more like a technical college than a center of commerce. The directory at the entrance listed several acronymic company names on a blue background. At the end of the list someone had inserted "The Platt Group" on a hand-lettered sign. I swung the Scout into a parking lot opposite Platt's headquarters and hoped no one would notice us and call the cops. The Scout wasn't the most inconspicuous place for a stakeout, and there was no way to know what kind of wait we were in for.

"That's Platt's car?" I asked, pointing at the silver Porsche across the road.

"Um, looks like it." Rachel nodded. "Now what?"

"Now we wait."

"For what?"

"I dunno. Guys with shopping bags, I guess. See if Platt leaves, where he goes. That sort of thing."

Rachel gave me a troubled look. "Do you have any idea what we're doing, Nase?"

"Sure. There are two of us trying to do a job that requires three shifts of three men each to do properly. I know exactly what we're doing; we're shooting in the dark." I lit a cigarette.

"I'm sorry. I didn't mean to sound critical." She leaned back against the seat. "Wake me when the customers arrive." In a few minutes she was breathing regularly, asleep. Her face softened and she curled her arm and cradled her head against it. She murmured softly and I wished I had a blanket to put over her, even though it wasn't cold. It would have felt right. Instead I hoped she was comfortable.

After an hour the waiting game got stale. For all I knew, Platt was doing the *Times* crossword. I opened the door as quietly as I could. Rachel stirred, then settled back and didn't wake. She looked very young. I walked across to Platt's office.

The receptionist sat hunched over a gray metal desk in a tiny front room. "Yes, sir?" She arched eyebrows that were more pencil than brow.

"Hi. Is Dr. Platt in?"

"May I say who you are?"

"Of course. Burford Werkins, of VSI. I called."

It took a few beats. "Oh, yes. Sure."

I followed her eye to the phone on the desk. The light in one of the buttons was lit. "Dr. Platt is engaged."

"Hey, that's great—just when a man needs insurance the most."

"Huh?"

"Little joke. Mind if I wait?"

"Dr. Platt's very busy. I don't know if he can see you. He just returned from vacation."

"New Hampshire, I bet?"

"Why, yes. How . . . ?"

"Uncanny, isn't it? Little woman says I must have second sight. Maybe I'll wait just a little while."

"Do as you like, but I warned you." She picked up the *Cosmopolitan* she'd been reading when I came in, and I asked her the way to the bathroom.

I walked down a short hallway until I saw a partially open door. I stopped just outside and listened to a man's deep voice.

". . . any time. The sooner the better, as far as I'm concerned." A pause, then, "You bet it's theirs." Another pause, then, "Of course I can show it to you, but it'll take a few days. Why don't I call you . . . ?"

I poked my head around the door. Platt looked up from his desk with a startled expression, and a large hand engulfed the mouthpiece of a phone. "What's going on? What do you want?" He was a big man with what I suppose are called earnest good looks. He didn't look happy to see me.

I stepped into the room. "Hi. Werkins here. Burford Werkins. Just call me Bud. Wondered if you'd have a few minutes to talk about your insurance portfolio? Got a great new product, just take a second." I thrust out my hand and advanced on him, insurance agent's loopy grin plastered across my face.

"No! Excuse me." He put the receiver to his mouth: "Just a second, somebody came in. Hold on, Harry." He covered the mouthpiece again. "Now, see here!"

I held my hand in his face until he grabbed it. "Nice to meet you, Bruce. You don't mind if I call you Bruce, do you? Say, that's great. You're going to love this program, builds equity while affording complete protection. Lotsa . . ."

Platt ripped his hand out of mine. His strength was impressive. "Look here, Mr., uh . . ."

"Please, Bruce, let's not stand on formalities. Everyone calls me Bud. 'Cept the better half—she calls me often. Hah! Just kidding, of course. Seriously, if anything should happen to you, God forbid . . ."

"God damn it, I don't care what your name is, just get the hell out of here!" Platt jerked at the receiver and the phone fell off his desk onto the floor with a crash. "Shit." He yelled into the mouthpiece, "Hello. Hello! Harry? God damn it." He started snapping the button on the top of the phone, then yelled. "Sandy. Sandy! Get me that number again." He slammed the handset down and shot me a look of pure malice. "Will you get out of here or . . . ?" He started to rise.

"Whoa, Bruce. Gotta watch that fuse, guy. Terrible for the old pump, know what I mean? Catch you later." I started out the door, then stopped and turned back. "Say, Bruce—have you thought about convertible term?" I left quickly.

Back in the waiting room Sandy was muttering into the phone, "Go ahead, Dr. Platt. You're through." She hung up and looked at me. "I told you . . ."

"Absolutely right, hon. Shoulda listened. Boss tells me I'm too aggressive for my own good. Say, Bruce wondered if you'd bring him a glassa water, couple aspirin?"

As she walked down the hall I copied the number on the slip of paper she'd read from when she dialed. As I left it occurred to me that I didn't envy insurance salesmen; they're in a risky business.

CHAPTER 6

Rachel woke when I climbed back in the car. "Where did you go?" She blinked and rubbed her eyes, then covered a yawn.

"Little scouting expedition. Wanted to see the good doctor in operation, maybe get something going." I handed Rachel the number I had copied. It had a Manhattan area code. "This mean anything to you?"

She yawned again, then shook her head. "Never saw it before. Why? What's going on?"

"Platt was on the phone with a guy called Harry when I came in. This is Harry's phone number, and I think he's a potential customer. The proverbial hot prospect."

I sketched what had gone on. When I finished, Rachel looked at me out of the corners of her eyes. "Do you always work like this?"

"Textbook stuff. Fully approved by the Massachusetts Board of Detective Standards." We settled back to wait.

By two o'clock I was hungry enough to gnaw the gearshift knob. I was wondering whether Rachel could hear the noises my stomach was making, when Platt came out of his headquarters. "Look." Platt was striding toward the Porsche, keys dangling from one hand, an overnight bag from the other.

"Head down!" I cranked over the Scout. By the time I looked up, the Porsche was moving toward the exit. I pulled out after it, keeping a good distance back. I said a silent prayer that Dr. Platt had more respect for the Commonwealth's traffic laws than he did for its notions about theft.

"Okay, I'll bite—would you mind telling me where we're going?" Excitement melded with curiosity in Rachel's low voice.

"I think he's going to get a sample. Want to bet on New Hampshire?"

"You know, you're pretty good at this."

"Yes'm. I'm probably the best there is."

C H A P T E R 1

We picked up 95 North and followed it to Route 16, the road into New Hampshire and the White Mountains. I'd won my bet. The traffic had thinned and I took pains to keep a car or two between us and Platt. The late afternoon light and crisp air combined to give the countryside the focused colors of a Maxfield Parrish painting. We smoked and murmured a few comments but for the most part settled into the rhythm of the ride, so that our bodies tossed like rag dolls and our brains went with them.

I was certain we were heading for Platt's camp. Rachel had made this trip before, when the quarry had been her lover, and I could feel the poignancy of the change. For my part, I was eager to see if our luck would hold. If it did, we'd have Platt nailed in a day or two. I looked over at her, lost in thought. I hoped we'd be lucky, but not too soon—I liked being with her.

The light was fading fast and I almost missed it when Platt turned off. A signpost pointed the way to Liberty. As soon as we turned off the main road we were in the heart of rural New Hampshire, passing ramshackle houses in need of paint, scattered trailers, and northern New England's last crop, rusted-out cars abandoned in fields. In a few minutes we pulled into Liberty.

There wasn't much to it, just a scattering of white frame houses, a general store, and a church. One of Norman Rockwell's *Saturday Evening Post* covers, a little contrived now, but on balance a pretty bit of Americana.

"His cottage is on the other side of the village, on a dirt road that runs down to the lake."

"Roger." I followed the Porsche through town. This was rusty Scout country, so I wasn't so concerned about Platt spotting us, but when he pulled off onto a dirt track just past the last house in the village I kept going a hundred yards before swinging off the road and burying the Scout in a clearing. "How far to his camp?"

"I don't know—a half mile, maybe."

"Let's walk."

"What're we doing? Walk where?"

"I don't know; let's go peeping. We're here, aren't we? There's got to be a reason."

We were a hundred miles north of Boston and had some altitude, and it was a lot colder than it had been in the city. I grabbed a sweater and tossed Rachel an old Harvard sweatshirt that had been in the back of the car for the last ten years. She grimaced but pulled it on. We started down the dirt road into a pine forest.

The air smelled wonderful after the stink of the city. Wood smoke blended with the resinous bite of cut trees. A dog was barking across the lake ahead, the noise carrying as though the beast were walking beside us. Our shoes made scrunching noises on the dirt. Overhead, though there was still a little daylight, Venus winked. It was a lovely place to be alive. I murmured as much to Rachel, and she patted my arm and nodded. I thought of the word "camaraderie." It was not something I had known with a woman before.

The scraggly pines let enough light through to mark our way. We walked in silence until the road dipped, and then there was a clearing and a white frame cabin. The Porsche was parked next to it. Platt must have just gone in because a light went on as we watched.

We wouldn't pass as the Welcome Wagon if he glanced out. I skipped off the road into a clump of scrub, tugging Rachel's arm so she'd follow.

"Now what?" Rachel leaned over to whisper into my ear, her breath making vapor trails. I whispered back, "We wait here for a little while." I looked at my watch. "It's five o'clock. If he's going to grab a sample and turn around tonight, he'll probably do it pretty soon. Let's just wait and see."

Rachel nodded. I slipped down to the ground and she followed. We sat in silence.

After half an hour of increasing discomfort and boredom, the door to the cabin opened. Platt stood framed in light, his large body filling the doorway, until he stepped out into the clearing. I couldn't see anything in his hands, so I assumed he wasn't ready to take off.

He walked in our direction, and for a minute I thought he must have seen us, until he turned toward a woodpile off to our left. He filled his arms with a load and turned back into the house. In a few minutes smoke came out of the chimney.

I tapped Rachel on the shoulder and mouthed, "Let's go." We stopped at the top of the rise and looked back. I imagined Platt poring over his secrets, dreaming of the wealth to come. I didn't know what Rachel was thinking as she stared at the cabin. A loon made the most desolate sound on earth. We trudged back to the car.

. . .

We waited until almost midnight in case he planned an evening departure; when it reached the point that only yawns would come out, I took a solo stroll back to the cabin. The road was dark as the pit and I thought about bears and wolves and inbred bumpkins with axes. By the time I reached the clearing I was delighted to see that Platt had turned off the lights.

We headed north until we found a motel just outside North Conway. Rachel pumped change into a candy machine while I pounded on the office door. It took a few minutes to rouse the proprietor of the Wee Resting, but it was the off-season and we were the Wee; in fifteen minutes I was in my own tiny house, pushing dinner out of my back teeth. I could hear Rachel on the other side of the thin partition, soft clicks and rustles, water running. I was turning down the thin blanket when she tapped on the wall. "Nase?"

"Yes?"

"Good-night. Sleep well."

"You too. Sleep well." Then the sound of a bed creaking. I let my thoughts roam, warm and protective. Before I was ready, I was asleep, dreaming of pizza.

We woke at first light, stopping for coffee and doughnuts and taking some spares. The mist was still lifting when we arrived back at duty station.

We spent the morning chatting and getting out of the car for an occasional stretch. Around noon we cracked the doughnuts and cold coffee.

By one o'clock the conversational lapses were showing real staying power. Finally Rachel broke one that was acquiring a life of its own: "Nase?"

"Um?"

"What if . . . ?"

"Don't say it." It was the question I'd been ducking since Boston.

"But seriously. What if he's not here to get our data? What if he's planning to spend the winter here, for God's sake?"

"O ye of little faith; trust me, trust me. He's here to pick up a sample, my instincts tell me so. As soon as we can swear to an affidavit saying we *know* the stuff is here, we're gone. You have to have patience in this business; that's half the game. Why, last year I . . ."

"Your *instincts*?"

"Okay, okay—you've got a point. I'll go back to the cabin, see if there's any indication what he's up to."

When I reached the clearing I stepped back into the brush we'd hidden in the night before. I sank down on the ground, chanced a cigarette, and waited. Weak sunlight caressed the slate-and-silver lake, unruffled by the slightest breeze.

Every few minutes Platt's silhouette appeared behind a shade. At least he wasn't hunkering down over his stamp collection. I basked in the sense of voyeurism, of seeing and not being seen.

After half an hour the shadow play lost its fascination. I had just lumbered to my feet and stepped back into the clearing when Platt's silhouette crossed the shade nearest me, heading toward the door.

I hit the cover seconds before the door swung open. He shut the cabin door with a bang and crossed to the Porsche without looking around, swinging a manila envelope by a corner. As he fumbled the keys in the lock, the little inner voice with the know-it-all tone demanded attention: "Nichols, you are a world-class moron." Dr. Platt was going to be ancient history before I got back to the Scout. I looked around but there was no way I could head out until he left; he'd see me if I moved any sooner.

The car broke into life with a growl that violated the stillness. Wheels kicking up a hail of gravel and dust, Platt fishtailed up the rise and down the road.

51

I bolted after it, choking on the beige cloud that hung like a pall. The road was twice as long as it had been earlier, and by the time I was halfway back to the Scout I knew I had screwed up hopelessly. I just hoped we could catch up and follow him.

I pulled around the corner where I'd left Rachel. No Rachel. No car. I stood and stared. I cursed the day man was born of woman and flopped down under a tree.

An hour went by. I alternated between frigid contempt and slobbering rage. Each felt right in its own way, but I never got to pick, because when the Scout lurched to a shuddering stop and Rachel called to jump in quick, I was too startled to do anything but obey. We were underway before I had the door closed, halfway through the village before Rachel responded to my stare.

"Bruce could have been pulling in any minute—he probably wouldn't have been too happy to see his insurance agent lying under a tree." She smiled, downshifted, missed the shift, stuck the tip of her tongue between her lips, ground some gears, tried again, cursed, made it, smiled again, drifted wide around a corner and left Liberty behind us.

"May I ask where you went while I was visiting Platt?"

"You certainly may." Another smile.

"Very well. Where did you . . . holy shit!" We swerved to miss a cow that had wandered out in the road. Rachel gave it a puzzled look, downshifted, and shot back into our lane seconds before we would have demolished a haywagon going the other way.

"Yes?" Still the cat-with-canary smile.

I wrestled myself into the seat belt. "Damn it, where did you go? What happened and where are we going? Will you please fill me in?"

"Now, now—don't get so excited. Do you have a cigarette?" She lit the one I handed her, looked at the tip, exhaled. "I went after Bruce. Wasn't that the idea? He came tearing down the road and was out of sight and you still hadn't shown up. Brr, it's cold." She pulled the no-draft shut. "So I followed him."

"You followed him."

"Well, exactly. That's what I said. It's a good thing he has a conspicuous car. I just followed the road until I came to the shopping center outside Ossipee and saw it. So I pulled in. He was parked outside the supermarket."

"So? What was he doing in the supermarket? He went to buy groceries?"

"Of course not. We know what he was doing up here; don't tell me you've forgotten your 'instincts'?"

"Okay—no more fooling around; I'm tuning in Paul Harvey, full volume. In five minutes you'll be a hopeless imbecile." I reached for the radio.

That did it. "All right, all right—anything but that."

"Bruce was in the drugstore next to the grocery. I saw him through the window. And do you know what he was doing?" She didn't make me answer. "He was making a copy of something on their copier." She held on to the wheel with one hand while she fished a piece of paper out of her pocket with the other. She thrust it at me. "Ta ta!"

I unfolded it. It had been crumpled and the maze of tiny creases made it hard to read. Two thirds was black and couldn't be read at all, but I could make out columns of numbers like those I had seen at Zoltec. I looked up: "Jesus, Rachel —where'd you . . . ?"

She cradled the wheel in both arms: "I watched him through the window. The first copy came out—well, you can see—and he balled it up and ran another. I couldn't believe it when he tossed it away." Her voice dropped. "The look on his face was so intense; he was like a . . . a madman, I guess. I think I could have walked in and stood next to him and he wouldn't have noticed. Oh, God, Nase . . ." She shook her head, then continued in her normal tone. "As soon as he drove off I ran in and grabbed that. I about wet my pants when I saw what it was. My only worry then was that he'd get back and find you running around, but I passed him a minute later, getting gas."

I was awestruck, blown away, and told her so.

" 'I'm probably the best there is,' I believe the expression goes." And then she whooped and I yelled and she did the one-handed driving thing that scared the hell out of me but I didn't care because she was using her other arm to pull me over while she pressed a wet, sloppy kiss on my cheek, and we went down the road that way, red-eyed and dirty and a little crazy.

CHAPTER 8

We stopped at a gas station just above the Massachusetts line and squeezed into a phone booth, still giggling and grabbing and filled with the joy of success and maybe something more. I dialed the number I'd copied in Platt's office, then tilted the receiver so Rachel could hear.

"Fesco North America—Good afternoon."

"I'd like to speak to Harry, please."

"Who?"

"Harry. Just . . . Harry."

"Don't you have a last name, sir?"

"No. You see, I met this gentleman the other day. At a meeting. And he said to call him at work. At Vesco."

Rachel whispered, "Fesco, not Vesco," then bit her lip but giggled anyway.

"Fesco. And he gave me his number. But I forgot his last name."

"I see. Well, there's nobody here named Harry. I'm sorry."

"Oh."

"Unless . . ."

"Yes?"

"Well, there is one man who's sometimes called Harry. Is the man you met Japanese?"

"Why, ah . . ."

"Because I've heard Mr. Matsami tell Americans to call him Harry."

"Of course—Matsami; that was his name! Harry Matsami."

"Well, actually it's Haroki, but I guess Harry's easier for Americans. Just a minute, puleeze, I'll connect you. May I tell him who's calling?"

"Sorry, wrong number." I hung up.

I dropped Rachel at her place. Driving to Cambridge I felt bereft, a lonely, irrelevant man again, and almost regretted the success that would soon separate us.

The apartment was dark and depressing until I turned on the lights, when it became just depressing: yellow cracked walls, stained ceilings, fixtures from which all detail had been obliterated by countless coats of cheap paint, decor by Goodwill. It was hard to believe that Brenda and I had been ecstatic to find it, had for those first few months before it all went to hell lain awake talking about color schemes and curtains. Yet I was lucky I had leased it before the latest real estate bubble had swept Cambridge, or I'd be living in a walkup next to a rendering plant in some grimy industrial backwater like Somerville or Watertown. At least in Cambridge most of the people you met had all their fingers. Some of them were successful, too, and on good days I could pretend I was one of them. This was one of those days.

Truscott had wanted to know as soon as we knew anything. Now we did. I called his office. He was in a meeting, but his secretary passed along a question: Could I meet him for dinner after his squash match? The Union Boat Club at eight. Bucky was right; I *had* moved into the tall cotton.

I brewed a pot of coffee and ran a tub. While I waited I played back my answering machine: a nameless nag from American Express, reminding me that payment was due in full the end of each month; then, "Hi, Nase, it's the Old Buckeroo, calling to thank you for the tidbit on our ex-pitcher—Sal must of shit when the news broke after I got ten large down on New York. 'Bout time I got some back. Let's get together soon. Gimme a call." Finally, after an ominous pause through the electronic ether, the hiss of succubus: "Mr. Nichols, this is Gretchen Lukacs-Skizenta. Today is Thursday. Remember: if I don't have three thousand six hundred dollars by close of business tomorrow, you're going to jail—I swear you are." Click and hum.

The phone rang as I was toweling off. I let the machine run until I heard "Hello, Nase, this is . . . ," then grabbed the receiver.

"Hi, Rachel."

"How high-tech."

"Security measure. Can't be too careful. What's up?"

"Well, I know this isn't much notice, but I called Dr. Zoller to report and he wondered if by any chance you'd be able to meet with him tonight. With us, actually. He wants me to be there, too."

All of a sudden no party was complete without me. "Sure, I can do that. Where we meeting?"

"Zoltec at five-thirty—the boardroom."

Not the Ritz, but I'd get to meet the Great Man himself. "See you there."

CHAPTER 9

I'd been expecting to find Holtree, and maybe Bingham or Truscott, waiting behind the huge doors the receptionist opened, but the room seemed empty. It was a far cry from the windowless cell I'd been in the first time I visited Zoltec.

The boardroom was smaller than a football field, but not a lot. The fading sun transfused raw silk curtains running the length of the room. A third of the opposite wall was covered by a collage of geometric objects. Stepping closer, I saw that it was a printed circuit board on which computer chips had been arranged to form patterns.

A teak directors' table occupied the center of the room, flanked by a couple dozen Barcelona chairs. The tabletop was bare except for a stack of architectural drawings, illuminated by a cone of light from an overhead spot.

I stepped over and glanced at the drawings, renderings of a post-modernist complex half a city block long. "ZOLLER FOUNDATION RESEARCH PARK, LINCOLN, MASSACHUSETTS" appeared in block letters in the lower right corner.

Rachel stepped out of the shadows in the far corner and came to me. She had changed into a tailored charcoal pants suit, white blouse, and high heels. A woven rope of turquoise and silver circled her neck. *Playboy*'s idea of Madame Curie. "Hello again." She extended her hands and I took them in mine. Her eyes roamed over my face. "Dr. Zoller will be joining us in a minute. I got here early and he was showing me those." She spoke softly, almost in a whisper. She gestured toward the drawings. "It's his dream. Isn't it . . . incredible?" Her voice had a breathy quality, as though she had caught cold in the car, but there was an intensity that matched the life shining in her eyes. "He'll be right back. Oh, Nase—he's so pleased. I told him how you'd got on to Bruce so quickly, and he was speechless, almost stunned. I think he must have prepared himself for for the worst. He can't wait to meet you; he's got something he wants to discuss with you. He's very excited about it." She squeezed my hands hard enough to hurt, then dropped them as though she had forgotten they were there.

"What is it?"

"I don't know. He's acting terribly mysterious. I do know he wants to see you alone for a minute."

"Huh?"

"Relax, Nase—he doesn't bite. He probably just wants to thank you for what you did."

Greed perked up its ears, whining for attention: "Bonus time, bonus time." I gave it a kick and it slunk off into the corner where it lives. "I hope you told him what you did," I muttered. It seemed indecent to speak in a normal voice in the sepulchral light. "You deserve the credit."

"We both do. We're a team, aren't we?" She put her arm through mine, then turned to face me. "And do you know something, Nase? I haven't had as much fun in years as I've had with you the last couple of days. I hope we'll . . ."

I didn't get to hear what Rachel hoped because she was cut off by a door opening at the far end of the room.

I had fantasized a cadaverous figure with electric hair and googly eyes—Dr. Zorba on speed, perhaps. I hadn't anticipated the short, powerful, barrel-chested figure that advanced toward me.

Zoller may have been in his seventies, but nothing betrayed his age except the white hair that crowned his large head. Even that was thick and carefully groomed, framing a prominent, unlined forehead. His step was slow but deliberate; measured, not tentative. With his erect carriage and dark blue pinstripe suit, he could have been the foreign minister of Switzerland receiving our ambassador at Geneva airport.

He walked toward us without a word until he stood within the territory my mind tells me is my own, so that I took an involuntary step backward. "Mr. Nichols." He extended his hand and I took it. There was none of the sticklike quality that makes you fear you'll crush an old person's hand. "Armand Zoller. You do me a great honor by coming. Dr. Ornstein has told me of your efforts."

His voice was deep and firm, with just a trace of central Europe.

"I'm delighted to be here, Doctor, and pleased that things have worked out so well. Frankly, luck had a lot to do with it. That, and Rachel's—Dr. Ornstein's—quick thinking."

Zoller looked from me to Rachel, and back again. He nodded slowly. "I don't doubt luck played a part, Mr. Nichols, but I don't understand why men speak of luck as though its assistance depreciates their own efforts. Luck is as likely to be bad as good, no? It neither discredits our successes nor excuses our failures. Over time, only will and intellect matter." He broke off. "Here, here—what am I going on about? It is evening already. You both must be thirsty. Come—something to drink? Rachel?" He gestured at a bar cart at the end of the room.

"I'd love one, Armand, but I have some things to catch up with in my office. In a few minutes, perhaps?"

"Of course. We will wait, then. Please hurry back." Zoller gave a half-bow, the image of the European diplomat. Rachel disappeared in the dim light even before the door clicked shut behind her.

Zoller led the way to some armchairs around a coffee table in a corner. "Please be seated, Mr. Nichols—you must be tired. I hope you will accept my gratitude for your efforts; it is always a pleasure to deal with a man who knows how to do his work efficiently."

"Thank you, Doctor. I hope the rest of it goes as well." I glanced around the room. "Is Elton Holtree expected? We could put together the affidavit for the seizure order tonight."

"We can get to those details in a minute." Zoller waved his right hand dismissively. "First, I would like to give you some idea why I am so grateful to you."

Zoller cut off my protest: "Please, indulge me. I have a proposal to make, but first there are certain things you must understand." At my nod, he continued: "The technology that . . . that person stole is invaluable. I mean not only that it represents the potential for a great deal of money for Zoltec. No, I mean that it is not in this country's interests for that technology to be available to others. That is far more serious than the money."

Zoller's deep, quiet voice had a hypnotic quality to it, and I found myself swaying imperceptibly with the rhythm of his words.

"This is my adopted country. Like many converts, I suppose, I love it with a passion that those of you born to it cannot know. I came here after the war because I belonged to a class my Russian liberators scheduled for extermination: the class of people who think for themselves. My mother, a sister, various others—all gone. The Germans were more efficient, but the Russians made up in zeal what they lacked in efficiency."

"I'm sorry" seemed a bit flaccid so I said nothing, but lit a cigarette. Zoller didn't seem to notice.

"Here I found a climate in which a man could think for himself. With energy, with will, and"—he nodded at me—"with luck, a man can succeed. As I have."

I wondered if Zoller were using a captive audience to indulge in an old man's maundering, although that wasn't the way I had sized him up. He went on: "There are no other countries like this one, you know—countries to which a penniless immigrant can flee, then control his own destiny. You can become an American—you cannot become a Frenchman, or an Englishman, or a Japanese. We are unique, and we must remain rich enough and powerful enough to continue drawing and sheltering the world's exiles. The countries that are challenging us most certainly won't, will they?"

"I'm not sure I . . ."

"I have made Zoltec the world's leading producer of computer chips. Brilliant scientists like Dr. Ornstein have kept it that way, and that is why companies like IBM and Kray produce the computers the rest of the world clamors for. It is a constant effort. Other companies, other countries would like to catch up, pass us. It is important they not do so. In the future, even more than today, our economic well-being will depend on our superior computer technology. Our factories, our military capability—everything. It is the battleground of the world economy. If we are to remain the world's dominant economic and cultural force in the twenty-first century, we must remain the leader in computer technology. And Zoltec's chips are the key."

Zoller leaned toward me, his arms resting lightly on the chair arms. "I don't think other societies should move ahead of us—societies that do not share our values. Do you, Mr. Nichols?"

Rhetorical questions have always struck me as slow sport. "No," I muttered. "That probably isn't a very good idea."

Zoller laughed, a quick, harsh bark. "Not a very good idea! You have the Yankee gift for understatement, Mr. Nichols. Indeed, 'not a very good idea.' Which is why I was particularly horrified to learn that this Platt"—he said the name as though it left a rancid taste—"is proposing to sell my property, the greatest advance in computer technology in a generation, to the Japanese. 'Not a very good idea.' " He snorted, whether with rage or amusement I couldn't tell. Probably both.

"It's definitely the Japanese, then?"

"Of course. Fesco North America, the company you called? It's the American subsidiary of Fujima Electronics. The leading Japanese chip producer—our principle competitor."

"Don't you see"—he leaned over and put a hand on my knee, something I've never liked very much—"once our data passes to the Japanese, it is gone forever. It happens all the time, believe me. I've watched it for years. It's why we stopped patenting our technology—all patents did was tell them how to copy us. There is no effective response. Their government protects them, denies everything, while our childish leaders wring their hands and speak of 'free trade.' The Japanese smile, and nod, and lecture us about working harder, while their products flood the world, built on our technology. And another American industry dies. Only this one mustn't die, or in a few years Japan will be the most powerful nation on earth. Real power, Mr. Nichols, not guns and bombs no one dares use, but control of knowledge, and the wealth that goes with it. Don't you agree?" He leaned back, taking his hand with him.

"Of course I agree. Shouldn't we be getting that seizure order?" I squinted at Zoller; only shadows and ivory glints remained of his face.

"No, Mr. Nichols, I don't think so. Tell me honestly—can you guarantee me that we'll succeed in getting the materials back if we become involved with lawyers and courts? How long does it take to get a stack of paper out of the country? Do you think an American court order means anything in Japan? They laugh at our legal procedures. They think nothing of stealing from us, lying to us. And one day soon they mean to own us. I don't want that."

"Then what . . . ?"

"Please, Mr. Nichols—hear me out. That is all I ask."

I reached for another cigarette and settled back. "I'm all ears, Doctor."

"Thank you. I propose we let Dr. Platt sell our technology to this 'Harry.' To the Japanese."

I took a few beats to recover. "Okay. Fine. It's yours. I'm sure the Japanese will be very grateful. I'm also sure there's a catch here somewhere?"

Zoller laughed, a dry, mirthless sound. "The catch, as you call it, is this: Fujima is always just behind us in chip technology. Always breathing down our necks; two years, three, five at most. If we have the new process, and they do not, they will be farther behind, but they will catch up, and we will have to repeat the whole cycle—if we can. If we have the new process, and they do not, but *think they do*, and commit everything to it"—Zoller thrust his head forward—"they will be even farther behind by the time they realize they have been going nowhere. We would gain years. Now do you see?"

"There's something wrong with the stuff Platt stole? It doesn't work?" I shook my head. "But Rachel said . . ."

"No, no, Mr. Nichols—it works, it works. It did not, it is true, a year ago, even six months ago, but Dr. Ornstein—she found the way." His voice softened momentarily when he mentioned Rachel's name, then resumed the hard, staccato pulse it had held before.

"What Dr. Ornstein told you is quite correct, Mr. Nichols; Platt has our technology, and the process works—of this I have no doubt. I had doubts, but I was wrong. She proved me wrong."

"Then how . . . ?"

"I propose we alter the documents. Subtly, so that nobody would guess, but in such a way as to send those thieves off in a totally wrong direction. A few changes to the frequencies and temperatures, restating the laser impulse rates—Dr. Ornstein could do it easily. Getting things wrong will be no problem, I assure you. God knows it took us long enough to get them right." Zoller's harsh laugh crackled through the dark room like the first static of winter.

"Alter the documents?"

"Exactly."

"I see."

"Excellent. Then . . . ."

"There's just one tiny detail I'm afraid I must have missed. Forgive me if I seem obtuse, but how are you going to arrange the transformation of the technology Platt has, which works, into the technology you would like him to have, which wouldn't?"

"I hope, Mr. Nichols, that you will help me in that regard."

"Help you?"

"Certainly."

"Exactly what do you see me doing?"

Zoller flicked his hand in that European way. "I think it would not be too difficult a thing for a man of your talents to recover the documents temporarily, without Platt knowing of it. Just long enough to permit Dr. Ornstein to make these changes. Then you would return the altered documents, restore the real ones to Zoltec, and the rest takes care of itself, I think. It is really very simple."

I ran it back a few times, then shook my head. "What does Rachel—Dr. Ornstein—think about all this?"

"We haven't discussed it. I wanted to get your agreement first. I'm sure she will be eager to help."

I took a long drag on my cigarette, holding the smoke deep

until I had to exhale. "I think we're mincing words. I believe you're suggesting I burglarize Platt's cabin. That's a major felony. Matter of fact," I ruminated, "I think technically I'd be burglarizing it twice—once when I took the documents, and once when I returned them. They'd probably be willing to drop one, though, in return for a plea on the other. Doubt I'd wind up doing more than a year or two." I looked up at Zoller. "Have I missed anything?"

"Don't you see, Mr. Nichols—Platt is the only person who could complain if anything went wrong, and he can't; what could he say? Someone broke into his house to steal something he had stolen?"

"It's still burglary, and it's still risky."

"How can it be burglary to remove our own property? Besides which, there is no reason for you to be caught. Of course, you would be well paid. Would twenty-five thousand dollars be appropriate?"

"Dr. Zoller, I . . . ."

"I don't want to haggle, Mr. Nichols—what do you think would be fair?"

If I had an answer I didn't have time to form it before the door opened at the far end of the room and Rachel peered around it. "I was wondering if that drink is still available?" She spoke to Zoller, but smiled at me, and I felt it the length of the room.

"Mr. Nichols?" It was just a whisper. Rachel stood in the door, expectantly. I couldn't tear my eyes away.

"What is your answer, Mr. Nichols?"

I turned back to him, but it wasn't Zoller I saw. "My answer is it's crazy."

"Perhaps we should get Rachel's view?"

"I don't think . . ."

Zoller rose. "Come in, my dear, come in. Do join us. Mr.

Nichols has something to tell you. Come sit here, while I fix your drinks."

"Oh, Nase! What a wonderful idea." She looked at Zoller as though he had just cured cancer.

"You understand the risks? I mean, this isn't Capture the Flag."

"Yes, but I think Dr. Zoller's right, don't you?"

"Maybe."

"I assure you, Mr. Nichols, if I had the slightest doubt, I would never let Dr. Ornstein be involved. Or you, of course."

"What will you tell the others?"

"The others? What others?"

"Holtree. Bingham. Truscott. Quarles. Anyone else who knows we've been looking for your missing technology."

"No one else knows. Holtree will be told that we've changed our plans, that I have decided not to pursue the matter because of the risk of adverse publicity. Why doesn't matter. He is a lawyer; they do not question the one who pays. You have not talked to him since your return?"

"No."

"Good. He will be no problem. I will call him."

"What about Zach Truscott?"

"What about him?"

"I was told to report to him. We're having dinner tonight so I can fill him in. What do I tell him now?"

"You must not tell him what we are doing. He is so eager to tell his banker friends about the new process. It means nothing but money to him." He waved contemptuously. "He'd whine about the effect on the financial markets"—he pronounced it *vynanshull*—"and threaten to go to the Board." He glanced over at the long table as though Truscott were already standing at one end, ratting to the assembled directors.

"Tell him you haven't had any luck. It is very simple; you have made no progress."

"I don't like to lie."

"It is only for a few days. After you have accomplished the task, I will tell him what we have done. Then he can make his announcements, and rejoice as his stock goes up. It will not hurt him to wait a little. He will make his money soon enough, and be quiet."

"Still, I . . ." I glanced at Rachel. The look she returned was much like the one she had given Zoller earlier.

"That should work nicely. The others will simply be told that you were unsuccessful."

We held the look, Rachel with her hand raised. No, she hadn't looked at Zoller the way she looked at me. She jerked her eyes down, away from mine.

I took a deep breath, then another, as though preparing for a long swim under water. "We'll have to move quickly." I stared at Rachel until she looked up again. "He'll be meeting with that man to show him the sample; we'll have to get in before he gets back. He won't waste any time. We'll go tomorrow."

Zoller looked at me and nodded slowly. "Good. Very good. I'm delighted Truscott suggested you; you are the right man." He nodded again. "Yes, it is good. Truscott picked well." He raised his glass in my direction.

CHAPTER 10

"Pres Thacker, Nason Nichols."

"Howjado."

Naked men pawed themselves with threadbare towels, discussing this or that shot that had proved old Rumford's undoing.

The Union Boat Club is cold roast Haut Yankee, a redoubt of perverse spartanism nestled between Beacon Hill and the Charles, where scions of merchant-banking families that financed the revolution go to row, play squash, and escape their women. Decrepit squash courts, the gym where Teddy Roosevelt swung Indian clubs, varnished wooden walls hung with fading pictures of bearded eights of yore, and a locker room that would get an army base a Congressional investigation. I couldn't imagine why they didn't have an old housemaster from St. Grottlesex administering canings.

"Nason's working with me on a project we've got going." Truscott turned to me. "Pres is with Putnam."

"What's your area, Mase?"

"Consulting, Fess—what's yours?"

"Oh, I push a little money around. Who you with, Ace?"

"Free lance, Les. Used to be with Farquhar, in London."

"Really?"

"A true fact." Nothing wrong with rudeness in these circles; it was friendliness that was non-U: "*Such a nice little man, but, um, just a tiny bit . . . um . . . familiar, don't you think?*"

"Pleasure meeting you, Blace."

"Have to do lunch, Wes."

We tromped across the Common to Locke-Ober. "Farquhar. I love it. Thacker'll be trying to look up Farquhar first thing Monday morning, wondering what your interest is in Zoltec. He'll go crazy." He slapped his thigh.

"Think so?"

"Oh, God, yes. Putnam holds a pretty big position in our stock. Thacker follows Zoltec like a hawk. Not a bad fellow, really. Known him since B-school. Hell of a securities man, actually."

We swung off into Winter Place and the Edwardian excess of Locke-Ober. The maitre d' greeted Truscott as though he were Anastasia at the White Russian Ball, and led us to a corner table in the Men's Grill.

Truscott leaned forward conspiratorily. "Well, any luck?"

I sipped my wine and thought of money, lots of it. Peace-of-mind money. "Not really."

His face fell. "You haven't found him?"

I shook my head. "Not yet."

"Any leads, any ideas?"

The head shake was good because I didn't trust my voice not to give me away, so I worked it again.

He slumped back. "Damn. I was hoping you'd have something by now. I guess I assumed, when you called . . ."

"I'm sorry. I just thought you might want a progress report. Even though there wasn't any to report."

Truscott was contrite. "Oh, I'm delighted you called. Really.

It's just what I asked you to do. And I'm certainly not blaming you. I'm sure it's very hard. What will you do next?"

"Just keep doing the same thing, I guess. Wait around, try to find out where he is, see if we can spot your stuff." Mom had been right; lying really did get to be a habit. "I still say a big agency . . ."

"No, I don't think so. The risk of a leak is just too great. We'll stick with you." He reached across the table and gave my arm a quick tap. "Don't worry; you'll get on to him."

"Thanks for the vote of confidence, Zach. I hope you're right."

He laughed, a pleasant sound. "I do too. And frankly, not just for the company's sake."

"How's that?"

He leaned toward me. "Well, it's a matter of public record that as an officer of the company I've got stock options that won't be worth anything until the stock goes up quite a bit. If we get our materials back and announce the new process I should be able to exercise my options. I've waited a while. We have, I mean—Bitsy and I"—he got a far-off look—"Bitsy's the light of my life, but she sure can spend money."

"Lucky you."

"I'm lucky my wife likes to spend money?"

"You're lucky your life's got a light."

He thought about it, the idea dancing across his face. "You're so right. I'm the luckiest man alive." His smile was a boy's, and it took an effort for him to switch subjects. "You think you may make some headway soon?"

I shrugged. Lying to the man was getting less pleasant by the minute. "I sure hope so." I threw him a bone: "I think so."

He nodded, then leaned across the table. "I know this is a tough one, but next week I've got to decide whether to roll over some lines of credit. It would make a big difference to know which way the stock's going in the near future. You'll let me know the second you think you've got any leads, won't you? I mean, right away?"

The waiter deposited oysters Rockefeller in front us, and I took another glass of wine. Alcohol's always been a liar's friend. "Of course, Zach—you'll be the first to know."

"Thanks, Nase. Believe me, we appreciate all your help." He called the waiter over and ordered a '78 Montrachet. Just the thing with Lobster Savannah.

CHAPTER 11

After the wine and a few Armagnacs I floated into bed, my last thought a vow I'd finish the thing fast, then apologize to Truscott for keeping him in the dark. Bended-knee stuff. Then I promised my conscience a good, long rest.

It was doing just fine, too, until I was wrenched awake by a pounding on my door that could have been the Gestapo, if they'd started recruiting old Portuguese women.

"Nase, Nase, lemme in, you gotta help me. Please, Nase, lemme in, he kilt him." The pounding resumed.

"I'm coming, I'm coming." The clock said 7 A.M. Not good. As I fumbled at the dead bolts, locks, and burglar chains that are basic survival gear in Boston, Mrs. Serafina's cries tapered off into shuddering sobs. She threw herself on me as soon as the door opened.

"Hey, calm down, calm down." Her stocky old body shook rhythmically as I led her in and sat her on the couch. I squatted by her side. "Now, what's wrong? Who killed him? Who's him, for that matter?"

"*Ele mató Magalhaes!*"

"Whoa. Hold on, Mrs. Serafina, please. I don't understand. Someone hurt Magellan?"

She started to answer, but only gasps came out at first. I took her hands and she gradually gained some control. "Tha', tha' man, tha' McGinty. He, he kill Magellan." She let out a wail as though her heart were being cut out.

"No! He wouldn't do that." I settled onto the couch beside Mrs. Serafina and put my arm around her. "Why don't you tell me why you think that?"

She wiped her forearm across her eyes and nodded, then sniffed. "I, I took him down for his morning walk. You know, ever' morning I gotta take him out." More sniffles, until I assured her I knew and she went on: "I leave him in the yard for jussa momen', while I walk down to the corner to getta paper. When I got back, he gone—Magellan gone!" She finished on a trailing upnote; if I'd been a car I would've pulled over.

"Well, maybe he just wandered off. He's probably down there now."

I used my comfort-the-afflicted voice, and it seemed to calm her because she stopped wailing and took on a resigned, hopeless tone. "Thas wha' I thought, only he never does, but I was hopin', you know, an' callin' for him, like 'Here, boy, here Magellan,' an' then McGinty, he come outta the basemen', an' he jus' stan' there, he stan' there smiling, an' finally he say 'Wassa matter?' real slow like. An' I say, I say, I can' fine Magellan, an' has he seen him. An' he say, yeah, he seen him, he seen him in his yard, an' he kill him an' throw away his body! An' then he laugh an' go back in the basemen'." She buried her face in her hands and threw herself against my shoulder.

"Jesus Christ, that's the sickest . . ." I hugged her to me as she started to keen again. "Look, I can't believe that. Even McGinty isn't that sick. I'll go talk to him. He's got to be lying. Magellan's probably waiting downstairs now."

"Oh, Nase—you think so?" She pulled away and stared

through red, watery eyes. Her old head shook. "No, he's mean enough, he'd do that. Kill a little dog. I don' wanna live!"

"Shit!" I leaped to my feet. "I'm going to go talk to that mother. I'm sure there's some misunderstanding. Now you go up to your place and I'll come see you as soon as I know anything." I started out the door, stopped, then grabbed an old roll of film out of a drawer, shoved it in my pocket, and left to confront a man, or what passed for one.

I took a quick walk around the building but didn't see any sign of Magellan. In spite of what I'd told Mrs. Serafina I'd seen enough pure viciousness, and of McGinty, to figure it was possible, maybe likely, he'd done what he'd said. As I walked into his lair I wondered if I would kill him if I decided he had. I hoped so, but had no great faith; I was civilized.

"McGinty!" He had his back turned and was shoveling out the incinerator when I found him. He brought the shovel up across his chest as he lurched around, then stood, trembling, with the shovel raised. He had the look of an astigmatic rabbit cornered by the hounds, and I knew I wouldn't kill him, no matter what.

"Whataya want? Get outta here." He hiked the shovel and stepped back.

"I want to know about the dog, McGinty. I don't think you killed it. Where is it?" I stepped toward him.

He pulled the shovel back as though to launch it at me. "Get outta here, God damn it! I killed the little bastard, just like I told the old woman. And I'll kill you, too."

He lurched forward and launched the shovel at my head, moving with more speed than I would have thought possible from a blown rummy. I hadn't been expecting it and only missed catching the blade between my eyes by getting my hand up in time. There was a sudden, cold jolt somewhere alongside my head and then I had the handle of the shovel buried across

McGinty's wattles and he was backed up against the wall and I really was going to kill him.

"You're probably the sorriest excuse for a human I've ever seen, McGinty. I'd be doing the world a favor if I strangled you on the spot." I could feel blood dripping down the side of my face onto my shirt. It was everything I could do to keep from throwing all my weight against the shovel and crushing his throat.

"Stop! You're choking me." It came out as a croak. Gobs of spit bubbled on purple lips. His breath was foul.

"The dog, McGinty! Mrs. Serafina's dog. What'd you do with it?"

I could almost feel the calculations whirling through Mc-Ginty's sodden brain. I leaned a little harder on the handle, then backed off fractionally.

"I didn' do nothin'. I swear!" His eyes danced and his legs buckled, so that for a second he was hanging by his chin from the handle.

"Where is it, then?"

"How should . . . ow, Jesus Christ!" I shoved his head back. "I don't know, I swear I don't. I was only fooling the old woman. I didn't mean anything by it."

McGinty's face was almost blue. Slowly I withdrew the handle but kept it raised to his chin level. His hand shot to his neck and rubbed.

"You coulda killed me." It was a sob, all bluster gone.

"Should have, McGinty, should have. And I probably will, if I find out you're lying."

"I'm not lying. I don't know anything about the damn dog. I was just joking."

"You're a funny guy, McGinty. You should go on television." I tossed the shovel into a corner, then reached into my pocket and pulled out the roll of film. The blood was still dripping, but I wasn't going to give McGinty the satisfaction of seeing me wipe it. "As a matter of fact, McGinty, I've already given you a screen test." I held the roll up so he could see it.

He stared at it uncomprehendingly. "Huh?"

"I'm a detective, McGinty; you know that."

He nodded slowly, not sure what he was committing to.

"You think I've missed you loading stuff from the building into your car? It's my business to see things like that, Mc-Ginty."

"Hey, I dunno . . ."

"Save it, asshole—I got it right here on film: the cleaning stuff, the fixtures, the stuff you were supposed to impound when old man Edwards skipped, even the lawn mower, for Chrissake. You tell Wenal it was stolen?"

"It's not . . ."

"Shut up. You're on film, McGinty, and I bet Wenal would just love some cameos of his custodian at work. You'll be sleeping in the Harbor Light Mission the night after he gets these." I tossed the roll into the air and caught it.

"Whataya want?" Everything about him sagged like a twenty-year-old girdle. I could barely make out his words.

"You're going to behave, McGinty. It's not going to be easy for you, but you're going to behave like a human being. Just as though you'd been born one. Do you get what I mean?"

He just stared at me. "You're going to leave Mrs. Serafina alone. When I find her dog—and I better find her dog—you're going to leave it alone. And you're going to stay out of my sight. Got it?"

He finally gave me a sullen, whipped nod and I left him slumped against the wall next to the coal bin. I stumbled toward the stairwell with a drowning man's need to breathe, and stood at the top, my chest heaving, drawing in the damp morning air.

The girls from Radcliffe were out early, tossing the Frisbee again; their raucous, certain voices rolled over me, bidding the neighborhood rise and be young. I watched them hungrily, drinking in their energy, indifferent to their sex; it was age, not sex, that distinguished us.

I reached in my pocket, pulled out the roll of film, and tried to imagine why I'd held on to pictures of my wedding. I flipped the roll into a storm drain and went back upstairs to report.

"So he isn' dead? You think maybe he alive?" She dabbed at my ear with a warm washcloth.

"Ouch! I think so, Mrs. Serafina. I'll go look for him in a minute."

"Oh, would you? I pay you to fine him."

"Of course you won't pay me. I wouldn't take your money."

She pulled a small, worn leather purse out of a drawer and fumbled it open. "Wha's a matter, my money not good enough? You a detective, ain' you? I wan' you be my detective. Fine Magellan. Here." She thrust a battered ten-dollar bill into my hand.

I unfolded it slowly. "Mrs. Serafina, I can't . . ." I looked up into her eyes staring at me, pride and a small dog all she had left, and maybe just the pride. "Okay. I'm your detective. Thanks." I pushed the bill into my pocket and got to my feet. "You know, I can't promise anything. He may be gone."

She sniffled. "I know. But I gotta know. Unnerstan'? I can' stand it, not knowing. You fine out an tell me. Either way, you tell me. Okay?"

"Okay." And now I had two clients.

By ten o'clock I'd combed the building and every side street in a ten-block radius. I'd questioned a dozen people and commissioned a small army of neighborhood kids to be on the lookout for a small gray dog. Rewards were offered, business cards distributed. I reported to my client, then returned to my apartment. I was almost on time when I left to pick up Rachel.

CHAPTER 12

We were an hour north of Boston when it occured to me that it wasn't a New Hampshire burglary that was going to put me in jail, but Massachusetts nonsupport. It was Friday—Ms. Lukacs-Skizenta's deadline. I thought of stopping to call and beg for mercy, then shrugged; I planned on paying Brenda when hell froze over. She'd have to catch me first, and at the rate I'd been moving that could take some doing, even for a rabid mongoose like her lawyer.

"Psst! Hey, Nichols!" Rachel broke into my musings. "I gather you have some reservations about this." She dived into her purse, came back with a cigarette, then looked at me quizzically over the flame of her lighter.

"Yes, you might say that."

"Then why are you doing it?"

I looked over at her. "I need the money."

"You don't strike me as a man who's done a lot of things for money."

"That's why I need the money. Look—just leave it, okay? I'm here of my own free will. Why doesn't matter."

She seemed not to have noticed. "Because I wouldn't want you to do it because . . . Oh, hell—I feel like an idiot." She turned and stared out the window.

"Because why?"

She turned back, and her face was flushed. "Well, maybe this is presumptuous, but I think we . . . get along. I feel comfortable with you."

She swayed back and forth with the pitching of the Scout. "This thing with Bruce and the Japanese and the trade secrets and all that—that's my fight, mine and Dr. Zoller's. We both have our reasons for wanting to do this. I don't think you do. I just wouldn't want you to feel that you had to do this."

"Had to? Of course I don't have to. Why would I feel I had to do this?"

"You know—for me." Her voice trailed off into an embarrassed silence while she stabbed out her cigarette.

I found the whole thing intensely uncomfortable. "Rachel, how many times . . . ?"

"I know, I know—'You need the money.' You're a nice man, Nase. A very nice man. Even if you are a liar. But thank you."

"You're welcome. I don't know what for, but you're welcome anyway. Now can we please talk about something else?"

Rachel laughed. "Of course. What would you like to talk about?"

"Tell me about Platt; how'd you ever get hooked up with a guy like that?"

The laugh died. "It was just a fling; it was no big deal."

She turned and stared out the window, an empty expression on her face, until I couldn't take it anymore. "Look, forget it. I was out of line."

For a minute she didn't answer. I watched the reflection of her face in the window glass. She was a long way away. Finally, she turned back to face me.

"No, you weren't. I'm the one who's been out of line. I've

been kidding you, kidding myself. You should know the truth." Her voice was raspy, the words starting with a rush, as though to get them over quickly: "I told you I broke things off with Bruce. That isn't true. I told you that because it's less . . . humiliating than the truth. He tossed me out. All of a sudden. Just like that." She snapped her fingers.

She choked, fumbled in her purse, pulled out a handkerchief, and wiped her eyes. "He got rid of his old car, his apartment, and me. Just . . . like . . . that." She snapped her fingers together again, but this time they didn't make any noise. She looked at them for a second, then continued: "I was in love with him. Growing up, I hadn't had much time for boys. I was just a plain girl with glasses and braces who had to work all the time. When Bruce came along, with his energy, his self-assurance, his sense of who he was and what he wanted, and he wanted me, I fell hard."

"Hey, look, I . . ."

She fluttered her hand at me. "It's all right. Let me get this out. I had always prided myself on my independence, my ability to get along without depending on a man, and then Bruce came along and I was jelly. It was true, what I said about his talk, his posing. I knew all that, but I made allowances, excuses. I didn't care. And then, after he had had his fun with me, he threw me away. He just stopped calling. When it became obvious something was wrong I confronted him and he told me. 'The chemistry isn't right.' An aunt had left him some money and he was going to start living. I was too serious, didn't know how to loosen up. I 'lacked sparkle,' was his phrase."

She was looking down at her hands, working the fingers as though they hurt, speaking in a low, insistent voice. "That was in January. I threw myself into work, which has always been my refuge. At first it was hell seeing him at work every day, so I just worked harder, longer. It was stuck, going nowhere. Even Dr. Zoller hadn't been able to make it work. They were ready to abandon it, give up. I'd never seen people at Zoltec so discouraged. It was as though the company had lost its energy."

Rachel gasped as I negotiated with a flatbed that wanted to play chicken. After I let it win she went on: "Dr. Zoller was wonderful. He's a very special man; I'll always be grateful to him for what he did for me. Very, very grateful. More than I can say."

"How do you mean?"

"I think he realized I had a personal problem, although he never said anything. He was attentive, gentle, encouraging. He put me on the project full time. I put in sixteen hours a day, seven days a week. It was his form of therapy for me, I think, and it worked; I forgot about Bruce, got over the hurt. Dr. Zoller and I were together constantly, but he never pressed for results, never set deadlines. It was as though he didn't really care. Finally, though, I figured out how to do it—make it work, I mean."

Rachel went far away again, but only for a second. "Dr. Zoller's reaction when I got it—I'll never forget. He was dumbstruck. He just couldn't believe it, until I showed him, again and again. And then he was so gracious, so generous in his praise. He made me feel like the most special person on earth, because of this thing that we could do, that no one else could do."

She got a dreamy look as she remembered that sweet triumph, then returned to the present, hard. "And then Bruce took that, too." It came out a choking rasp.

She brushed away a tear. "A stupid story. The woman scorned." Self-contempt oozed. "But there's more to it than that. It's Dr. Zoller. He gave me the way to get my self-respect back. I owe him more than I can ever repay, and this is something he wants. I think he'd like to kill Bruce if he could, but he can do this. I think his reasons are good, but even if they weren't, I'd do this for him. That's why I'm here, Nase. A woman of few words, huh?" She gave me a wry lopsided grin. Her eyes were red, and she sniffed a few times and blew her nose. I'd never seen a lovelier face.

We pulled into Liberty about four. I drove through without stopping until we came to the place we'd pulled off the road before. Rachel waited in the car while I trotted down the road.

The tall grasses and sprawling junipers gave up their smells to the thin, cool air. My Reeboks scrunched on the dirt road. I thought of Rachel's story and was glad we were doing what we were doing. I felt better than I had in a long time.

The bright road dipped and turned into the pine-shadowed clearing, the cabin before me. I stepped into the woods before anyone inside could have seen me, and waited.

There was no car, no smoke from the chimney, although most of the houses in town had been cranking it out against the evening chill. I could see the kitchen and dining area, and they were dark. No shadows moved behind the windows. Short of going up and knocking on the door, I didn't know what else I could do. We'd go set up someplace, then come back at first light and do it. I walked back, whistling an old camp song.

I told Rachel my conclusion: Nobody home at Platt Lodge.

"Well, then, why are we driving away? Why not do it now?" A hint of impatience; Rachel had the blood lust on her.

"Distaste for prison life. Said to be terribly confining. Food's bad, too."

"But you said . . ."

"That he's probably gone. But I could be wrong. I know you find that hard to believe, and I admit it's almost unheard of, but it could happen. He may just have gone around the corner to buy cigarettes, in which case he would be very surprised to find his ex-girlfriend and Bud Werkins waiting to greet him."

"Bruce doesn't smoke. And I wasn't his 'girlfriend.' That's a horrible expression."

"Whatever. Anyway, we aren't set up, and night's coming fast. If he's still around, he'll be in tonight and we'll know it tomorrow, because he'll leave tracks. And if he's gone, nothing will have changed tomorrow, and we won't have to 'enter a dwelling house in the night season,' as the statute books put it, which automatically adds five years if you're caught. Which, if we're seen poking around at night in a car with Massachusetts plates, we're more likely to be. Does all of that make sense? Does any of it?" I couldn't see any holes in Zoller's argument that Platt would be in no position to press charges if we were caught, but I preferred not to trust my future to the mad notion that the world was rational.

After a few seconds Rachel's jut-jawed look softened. "Of course you're right. I wasn't thinking. My emotions got in the way of my judgment. We'll do it your way."

"Don't misunderstand me—I'm in this all the way or I wouldn't be here at all. We'll get it done."

She patted my hand and nodded, and the warmth of her fingertips stayed with me all the way to North Conway, under the gray bulk of Mount Washington, where we found a motel set back from the Vegas strip that scarred the valley.

Rachel popped the doors while I did a staggering drunk routine, muscling the copier into the closest room. My heart was putting in for overtime when I lowered the copier onto the cheap credenza.

Rachel plugged in the copier and waited for it to warm. "Look—we used to do this at school." She bent over it, holding her hair back with one hand. She pressed her face against the copying surface and fumbled for the start button. There was a sudden flash of green light and for a second her face looked Martian, or at least the way Martians ought to look. The counter that kept track of the copies flipped over with a click.

Rachel snatched up the copy. Her face, distorted by the glass, looked enough like her to make the death-mask quality of it unsettling. "Come on, Nase—your turn."

"I've no intention of doing that; it'll probably make your hair fall out."

"Come on—don't be an old poop."

"It'll look ridiculous. You'll laugh."

"I won't laugh—I promise. Come on, try it."

So I did.

Rachel squealed. "God, Nase, that's the ugliest face I ever saw!"

"I think, if you're all done playing, I'll go to my room and clean up."

We were sitting in a restaurant called Sam 'n Ella's, which was tucked between Adam's Ribs and Mother Clucker's Chickin' Lickin'.

We each poked at our food. Rachel's mood had shifted. The playful girl was gone, replaced by a pensive woman. During the ride in she had stared out the window, silent. I guessed she was back with the Platt thing.

I made a few attempts to get things back where they had been but gave up when all I could draw were listless mumbles. I worked on a pair of martinis instead, and mused about the life that had brought me, in a round forty years, to half a college degree, a failed marriage, a negative net worth, and a budding criminal career. A cognac helped manage that. Then I thought about Platt, and how annoyed the Japanese were going to be when they finally figured out they'd been taken. I hoped, for Platt's sake, they had a sense of humor.

We drove back in silence. I parked behind the motel and asked her what the trouble was. She told me she didn't know what I meant, there was no trouble. I asked her why she hadn't said ten words during dinner and she told me it was because she hadn't felt like talking. I asked her if something was bothering her and she told me to mind my own business.

I jumped out, eager for my own company. Rachel mumbled something and went to her room, closing the door behind her.

Behind the motel the valley swam in the light of a harvest moon and the pinpricks of stars Boston never saw. I lit a cigarette and wondered about a woman I hardly knew. I told myself I was a fool, that I had a job to do, that it was absurd to have thought of anything developing between us; objectively, I wasn't in Rachel's league. Then I replayed the exchanges, the laughter and tears, the kiss in the car, the touch of her hand on my arm. Subjectively, it had worked, fit, felt right. And now it was gone. Rachel had gotten what she wanted, and now it was going to be all business. I drew one last time on the cigarette and threw it to the ground.

When I turned to walk back Rachel stepped out of the shadows and into the moonlight, ten feet away. The night breeze lifted her hair and set the leaves to whispering. "Nase? I'm sorry. It isn't you. Please forgive me." She spoke so softly I could have been hearing the wind.

"What is it, Rachel—what's wrong? I'll help you if you'll let me."

She hugged herself and bowed her head. "I'm afraid, Nase. Keep me from being afraid—please? Please?"

I walked to her and took her into my arms. "Oh, God, Nase, hold me—I'm so scared. I've never been so scared before."

I cradled her head on my shoulder. After a moment she lifted it and put her arms around me. She locked her mouth on mine and we stood like that, swaying softly.

Later, while we were still in each other's arms, she whispered of the fear that had rolled over her earlier, that wanted to consume her: fear of what we were about to do, of being caught; fear of failure; fear of being middle-aged and alone; fear of the hurt that Platt had left her; fear of wanting, expecting, hoping for anything else.

Her tears made tracks on my arm as I stroked her back and whispered of my fears, because they were the same as hers. And then, our lips brushing, I whispered the fear she hadn't mentioned, the fear that would heal itself and all the others if only she shared it—the fear that she didn't need me as I needed her. Her answer came as we sank to the ground, came in rustling clothes and sweet endearments, in warm skin and feathery touches, in murmured promises and cradling arms, in shadows and contours, in ivory beauty and gentle demands. In a long, low sigh.

Later, she opened her eyes and looked up at me, a shy smile lighting her face. "Nase, there's one more thing I'm afraid of."

"What?"

"I'm afraid we're lying in poison ivy."

CHAPTER 13

We drifted off in Rachel's room. When I kissed her awake it was barely seven. We dressed quickly. It was still dark when we pulled out onto the highway. We didn't talk about what had happened.

I found our parking spot and pulled in, then rummaged in the junkyard I carry in the back until I found the cardboard box I was looking for. "Here." I handed Rachel a walkie-talkie and pulled on an old pair of gloves.

"What's this for?"

"You push this little button to talk, see. I'll have the other one; anyone comes, let me know."

Rachel was battle-ready. "No way, Nase. I want to come."

"Rachel, honey—we're not raiding Mom's cookie jar. I get caught in there, I'm looking at serious time. You be the lookout; all burglars use a lookout."

"But I know how his cabin's arranged. . . ." She saw something in my face and trailed off. "You're right. Show me how to work this thing."

We did a few "testing, one, two's" until I was sure she had the hang of it, and it was time to go.

She hugged me, hard. "Good luck—and be careful," she whispered. A quick kiss and she stepped back into the bushes as I turned and started down the road again. After I had gone a few hundred feet I looked back; I was alone again.

It was my fifth time on Platt's access road, I knew the route better than his garbage man, and I was pretty sure he was gone, but my heart was beating and my ears were ringing as though it were my first time on patrol in Vietnam. A couple of minutes brought me to the edge of Platt's clearing, which looked as it had when I left the night before. One glance at the ground told me no one had been back; there was no reason to wait.

Once around the cabin to check for alarms. Platt didn't have a warning sign, which is 90 percent of any home burglar alarm, but I checked for window contacts on the off chance. Nothing.

I went around again, this time going slowly and trying to figure out how I was going to get in. It would have been a piece of cake if I just wanted to rip off the appliances, but Platt might think something was up if he came back and found his windows kicked out or the door ripped off its hinges.

I tried the door, then each downstairs window, then the door again, but Platt hadn't been as accommodating as he might have been. I applied some pressure to the door with my shoulder, but it held fast.

I vented my five favorite oaths. Often they help, but not this time; the door still wouldn't give.

The lock was nothing special, a standard, brass-plated lockset with a center tumbler. Probably half the kids at Boston Latin could have gotten through it faster than they could have said a Hail Mary, but not me. I circled the house again.

On the side overlooking the lake, the cabin rose to a half-story over a screened-in porch. A pair of dormer windows peered out at me.

A rickety sawhorse got me started, and by using the framing around the porch and more arm strength than I knew I had, I was able to hook a knee onto the roof, and was up.

I scrabbled crab-fashion over to the first of the windows. It was hinged at the top and seemed to be fastened at the bottom. I smacked it with the heel of my hand and the warped wood moved. I smacked it again and it opened with a rheumatic squeal.

It was a matter of thrusting my feet through while lying on my back, then writhing my way in while managing not to strangle myself between the window and the ledge. I probably looked like a quadruplegic limbo dancer, but nobody was awarding style points.

My contortions brought me out in a small room that held a couple of camp cots, a dresser, a table, and a musty odor. I dusted myself off, then pushed the dead wasps and flies that I had dragged in under one of the cots where they'd feel at home. My watch said that barely half an hour had passed since I'd left Rachel; it seemed much longer. I headed down the narrow stairs to the transecting corridor at the foot.

The main bedroom lay to the right. On the left the hall passed a bathroom, then opened onto the living room.

The desk, like the rest of the furniture, was Early American by way of Sears—reproduction Adirondack chairs, antique student lamps made in India last year, a corner cupboard flayed with a chain to look two hundred years old, then slathered with an acrylic coating to give it the warm patina of a bowling alley.

There was a lovely Parker double-barreled shotgun over the fireplace, but the effect was spoiled by a couple of pseudo–Currier & Ives prints and a four-foot, gilt-covered American eagle over the desk, completing the decorative touches. The man had the taste of an engineer.

I started with the bottom drawer of the desk. Mother Hubbard's cupboard. I pulled open the next one. Nothing. The third, and last: three strikes. I pushed in the drawers and opened the slant top. Georgio Armani catalogue; back issue of *Esquire;* thermometer set into a piece of varnished pine, "Souvenir of the Great Stone Face"; assorted bills and miscellaneous pencils, pens, and paper clips, the whole, meaningless assembly laid out with geometric precision. There were some canceled checks and a bank statement from the Mount Chocorua National Bank. I riffled through these. The checks were for ho-hum payments to local merchants, but the statement showed a balance of almost six grand. Platt knew how to stay liquid.

I was going to have to toss the place in a systematic fashion, and that could take hours. I wandered back to the bathroom under the stairs. A tiny window above the toilet looked over the lake. I tried to put myself in Platt's mind: Where would a megalomaniacal engineer with the incredibly bad taste to (a) toss over Rachel and (b) put that tacky eagle on the wall, hide his future? The kitchen. Engineers like kitchens, even though they only eat to keep the machine going. They like the clean, hard, inanimate lines of a kitchen. That, and the fact that appliances work at the push of a button—you don't have to speak to them.

I flushed. No flush. I jiggled the handle. Still nothing. It would not do to leave my spoor. Platt would know it wasn't his—engineers are taught to flush when they're two weeks old, which is why they become engineers. I lifted the stack of *Business Week* off the tank top and followed with the top. I reached down to play plumber.

Where does an engineer hide his future? What is even harder, cleaner, less animate than a kitchen?

I reached in the dry tank and withdrew the package. It was a tight fit but I worked it out without tearing anything. I turned the valve under the toilet. In a minute the tank filled and I flushed. I replaced the lid and let myself out the door.

CHAPTER 14

We were back at the motel in just under an hour, sitting on the bed while Rachel unwrapped the documents. She sat with them in her lap for a minute, staring at the stack. I could see the legend in the lower right-hand corner of the top sheet: ZOLTEC PROPRIETARY: DO NOT COPY.

"I've given this a lot of thought, and I can't think of anything better to do than put the data back where it was when I first started trying to get it to work. It'll take them at least a year to get set up, six months to figure out they've got a big problem, and then God knows what they'll think." She held the stack up and shook it at me like a party favor. "I'm going to enjoy this. Get my briefcase, will you, Nase?"

She pulled out a bunch of graphs and notes, and a calculator. "This is going to take a while, Nase, if you want to watch television or something." She picked up a red pencil. When I pulled the door shut she was tapping it against her teeth.

The first bar near the center of town that had a parking space in front of it looked as good as any other for killing time and thirst. It had Molson's on tap and candlepin bowling on the tube, so it couldn't be too bad.

One of those lean young blond clones that do all the work around ski resorts pulled my beer. I immediately put a question of some weight to him: "Say, buddy—you don't happen to know how the Sox did last night, do you?"

He gave me a spread of white teeth: "Gee, I'm sorry, mister —I don't follow baseball."

A communist. I gave him the look I reserve for people who try to press leaflets into my hand at airports.

"Got beat."

I swiveled around. The only other man in the place, a middle-aged rustic with a John Deere cap and a righteous gut, shook his head dolorously. "Ay–uh. Eleven-six. They was up six-o in the eighth, then Hroman loads the bases. So McCormack goes to the bullpen, brings in Javier."

He finished his beer, yawned, and delivered a belch that shook the walls, " 'Scuse me." He gestured for another. "Bullpen my ass—Gahd damn pig pen more like it, pahdon the expression. Might as well bring in Lyle Huckins, septic tank fella down the road, fling shit at 'em."

He shook his head hopelessly. My heart went out to him— the annual fall loss of innocence for Sox fans. I nodded in sympathy and went to the pay phone in the back.

"Hanrahan."

"I hear the long slide has begun, right on schedule. Do I deliver, or do I deliver?"

"Nase—where are you, boy? I've been trying to reach you."

Where I was was not something I was ready to share. "Hither and yon, and other beguiling byways. But now you have reached me—what's your pleasure?"

"God damn it, Nase, will you please tell me what the hell's been going on?"

" 'Fraid you're being a tad cryptic, Buckleberry; what *has* been going on?'' Bucky's ordinarily as low key and laid back as any other red-faced, two-hundred-and-fifty-pound Irishman. Now he sounded the way he did when he heard an English accent after a dozen Jamesons.

"What's been going on is that it's all over the street that your client's just lost a very valuable asset—to wit, the technology for making a new superchip. Is it true?"

"Why do you ask me, Buckminster?"

"Because if it is, Zoltec just went from prime beef to hamburger, dolt. First place to no place. Just one of the gang. Get it?"

He had mixed at least three metaphors, but I caught the thrust. "So?"

"So on the strength of that, the institutional investors have been selling off the stock like you could get the clap from it. We dumped ours fifteen minutes ago, at a hell of a loss, and it's still heading south."

He slipped into a petulant, wheedling tone. "Nase, come on —I picked up a couple thousand shares on my own account after our tête-à-tête the other night; I haven't dumped it yet. Please—tell me I haven't just blown eighty grand."

How the hell did it get out? I couldn't tell Bucky to ignore the rumor, not without jeopardizing the whole program. I calmed him as gently as I could: "You asshole, I never told you to buy into Zoltec; for all you know, I'm working for a competitor. If you heard Zoltec's got a problem, act on your instincts."

"What do you mean?"

"Jump out a window."

"Thanks, Nase. I knew I could count on you. Take care of Dierdre and the kids, will you?"

"Hey, Bucko—kidding aside, sorry I got you into this, even if it is your own greedy fault. You okay—financially, I mean?"

"Shit, Nase—you think I'd put serious money into some-

95

thing you're involved with? Gimme a break. It's a matter of pride, that's all."

"Great. Well, then, stop your whining and take it like a man, my mewling Hibernian. Oh, and Buckwheat?"

"Yeah?"

"See if you can find out where this story started, will you?" Zoller might like to know whose loose lips had been responsible for knocking a few trillion dollars off Zoltec's market value —a little extra service, no charge.

"You know, Nase, you're the only guy I know got a negative net worth, still manages to maintain his own full-time financial adviser."

"Yeah, well, if my financial adviser could pick anything except navel lint I wouldn't have a negative net worth."

We did some more male-bonding and rang off. I got another beer and mulled things over. This was a bad development all around, but the more I thought about it the more I decided it didn't have a lot to do with me or with the job that had brought me to New Hampshire. I drained my beer, called for another, and settled back to watch some serious candlepin bowling.

Rachel was still laboring at the typewriter when I rolled in a few hours later, and barely looked up. "Oh, hi, Nase. Just give me a few more minutes; I'm almost done."

She turned back to her task. The tip of her tongue parted her lips. She bent over the keyboard until her hair grew slack on the table, staring intently at the page. She struck a few keys. Sitting up again, she studied the product, swiveling her head to look at an adjacent sheet. She tore the paper from the typewriter and beamed. "I'm in the wrong profession; I should have been a forger." She picked up the page on the table, then handed them both to me. "What do you think?"

I looked from one to the other, then back again. There were

columns of numbers, meaningless to me. I ran my eyes back and forth over both sheets, but couldn't spot any differences. I shook my head and handed them back. Rachel added the one she'd been working on to a stack on the table.

"The laser modulations are off by a fraction. You see, the process is temperature-sensitive. Everyone knows that."

I grunted.

"Well, everyone in the business. Anyway, they'll be expecting the burn rates to decrease in a linear relationship to temperature—they always have, before. What we discovered was that it doesn't work that way. The relationship is semilinear, with certain discontinuities. Nothing works unless you adjust for that. But these readings here—" she tapped the pile— "make it look like everything works the way they'd expect."

Rachel saw my eyes assume their technobabble glaze. "You don't understand a word I'm saying, do you?"

"I'm a big-picture man. Leave the details to you bean counters."

"The point is, they might as well use the plant they build to make chopsticks." She chortled. "Now just let me finish copying the pages I made changes on and we can get this stuff back."

She walked over to the copying machine and I followed her. No games this time. She flipped the switch and positioned the paper. Click, flash, and hum. Two copies added to the stacks. Then the next sheet. I stared at the little counter on the machine. Rachel had done an awesome amount of work in my absence; she'd copied a couple hundred pages. I suppose she saw it as the Lord's work. The pulses of eerie green light washed over the shadowed walls of the room, flattening its features and giving Rachel's movements a jerky, old-time movie quality. Suddenly I felt terribly tired. The metronomic advances of the counter hypnotized me, and I wandered over to the bed to lie down. I shut my eyes, but the flashing light came through anyway, beating at my brain.

"How long'd you say before they figure they better get out the warranty?"

"Sorry, Nase—didn't hear you. What'd you say?"

"I said, when is it you think they'll know they've got a problem?"

Rachel looked up, her hand resting on the cover of the machine. "Oh, I don't know. I'm not a production person, so I'm only guessing—but I'd say a year or two. They'll have to build a plant first. It'll be a while." She stabbed a button and the light flashed again.

After a few seconds I voiced the thought that had been nagging at me the night before at the restaurant; beer wasn't as good at keeping it at bay as the serious drinks had been. "Friend of mine was in the FBI. Told me about a case he worked on once. Some little clerk got a hankering for bigger things, started selling Navy Department secrets to the Russians. Thing was, he was such a pipsqueak he didn't really have much to sell." I lifted my head off the pillow. Rachel was still feeding sheets into the copier. "Are you listening?"

"Uhuh."

It didn't sound like 100 percent attention, but it would have to do. I went on: "So this little snook can't bring himself to say 'Sorry, comrade, save your money—I'm tapped out.' You know, no more trips to Atlantic City, no more little baubles, keep the old lady's bitching down to semi-tolerable level, no more thinking that you're not just another one of the drones."

"Nase, what *are* you talking about? You're not making any sense at all. Did you go drinking?" She raised her voice to be heard over the sounds of the copier.

"Just hang on." My voice sounded strange, muffled, but I pressed on. "So after this guy ran out of inventory, he decided to move into production, since his previous supplier, the Navy Department, wasn't keeping him stocked."

"You mean he . . . ?"

"Exactly. Son of a bitch started making up 'secrets.' Not big stuff like the name of our guy on the Politburo or anything like that. He made up little 'secrets,' and got a little money. Went on that way for quite some time."

"And then the FBI caught him? Really, Nase, I don't see what . . ."

"No, no; you miss my point. The FBI didn't get this guy." I laughed, but it sounded wrong. "They screwed around, figured he couldn't do 'em much harm, wanted to see if anyone else was in it. Finally they got a warrant, went to pick him up at his apartment."

"And?"

"And they discovered some very bad guys had done some very painful things to him before they slit his throat."

"God damn it, Nase, that's . . ."

"That's what crooked people sometimes do to people who play games with them, Rachel. What if Platt's customer doesn't like getting clipped? What if the Japanese come back to Platt next year, the year after, tell him they just figured out they got snookered, and now they want to turn him into sushi?"

"Nase, that's ridiculous. These are businessmen, not Russian spies. They don't go around *killing* people."

"These are crooks, Rachel—or they wouldn't be dealing with Platt. Crooks, by definition, have their own moral code. Who knows what a pissed-off, face-lost Japanese crook does. Maybe he commits suicide—or maybe the person who got him that way is the one who committed suicide."

"Are you saying we should just forget about this whole thing —what Bruce did?"

"We could go back to the original plan, Rachel; we've got the documents now, anyway. We could just forget about it. Bruce comes back and spends the rest of his life wondering what happened. Isn't that enough?''

I had rolled over on my side and opened my eyes so I could see her reaction. For a long count of ten there wasn't one.

She jabbed the button and the machine sprang to life. Then she took up another sheet and turned back to the copier.

"Bruce is ready to sell out his country. What we're doing is going to help this country. Don't you think that's worthwhile?''

"I think that's fine. I also think maybe you're more interested in getting back at Platt for the way he hurt you than you're letting on." It slipped out before I could stop it and I was sorry halfway through.

She thought about it a long time. When she answered it was without anger. "That's not true, Nase."

I stared at the ceiling. "I shouldn't have said that. I know you're not like that. Forgive me?"

The bed sagged, then Rachel's fingers were tracing my forehead. "I don't want anything bad to happen to Bruce; I'm not vengeful. I don't want him to get away with this, but that's all. But they're not going to think Bruce tricked them, there's no reason why they would. Maybe they'll think the process really doesn't work, or maybe they'll decide they just don't know how to make it work. I mean, this is advanced technology, Nase —even with the right plans there aren't many people skilled enough to actually make the chips. Let's finish what we started. It's been going so well."

Her guess was as good as mine, maybe better. After a minute Rachel rose. The copier stopped and I heard the door close.

I woke when the door opened. My watch said I'd slept almost two hours.

"Feeling better?" Rachel perched on the side of the bed and passed me a container of coffee.

"Hundred percent. Thanks."

"I've been thinking about what you said."

"Forget it—I got carried away. Saw *The Bridge On The River Kwai* too many times when I was a kid."

"No." She rested her palm on my forehead. "No, I don't want to go through with it if you think . . ."

"Thanks." I took her hand and squeezed. "But it's okay. I was just doing my Hamlet number."

"Sure?" There was concern in her voice.

"Sure." I pulled on the coffee and jumped up. We had the car loaded and were on the road in half an hour.

It was evening by the time we pulled into Platt's turnoff, and I knew as soon as I saw the dark building that Dr. Platt was still off showcasing his sample.

We had rewrapped the documents in their plastic covering. I closed the valve on the toilet and flushed it. When the tank drained I replaced the package. I put the top back on, then the magazines. A last look around to make sure I hadn't left any calling cards, then out the door. The whole thing had taken ten minutes. I turned on the radio as we pulled onto the highway. The Sox were down, 7–0, in the second. Back to manageable anxiety.

CHAPTER **15**

It was just past seven when the sound of metal on metal drifted up from the street, messing up the hundredth rerun of the missed-exam dream. I was back in my own bed, and alone. I'd let Rachel off at her apartment the night before. She told me she'd report to Zoller, and then she had to visit her father for a few days.

I went to the window and looked out. A Saab, plastered with peace stickers, had locked horns with a *Boston Globe* delivery truck. The two drivers were standing in the middle of the street discussing the ethical issues raised by the situation. The Saab driver had the more powerful argument because he had a tire iron in his hand. From time to time he would brandish it, turn, and shout an obscenity at the growing line of cars. Horns blared.

I lowered my window reluctantly. I hated to leave the morning prelude to the Theater of the Damned, since I'd be making my own entrance shortly; the streets of Boston are no place for the unready.

The water was boiling when I got out of the shower, so I

ground the last of the coffee and tuned in the public radio station for my daily three-minute hate. Perfect timing—the announcer's portentous, bass voice oozed out of the box, each syllable delivered as though it had been rented and our doyen of cultural pretense was determined to get his money's worth.

He was doing his best to trash the Mozart they were about to play, babbling on about its "naive, Dionysian rondo." His fatuous twaddle lasted several minutes longer than the Mozart. By the time I poured my coffee and spread jam on a piece of bread I was *cranked;* if I could have reached through the speaker and gotten my fingers on the pompous twit's mellifluous gullet I would have given him the world's first digital laryngectomy. I was ready to face the rigors of another day in Boston.

First, though, curiosity wouldn't let me duck the task I had put off as long as possible. I started the answering machine and lit a cigarette.

"Okay, Mr. Nichols—don't say I didn't warn you. This is to give you notice that there will be a hearing in the Middlesex County Probate and Family Court, Courtroom Twelve, next Wednesday, at nine-thirty in the morning. At that hearing you will be invited to show cause why you shouldn't be jailed for nonsupport."

Ms. Lukacs-Skizenta paused, then continued in a more normal voice, if something that sounded as though it came from the lower register of a Moog synthesizer could be called a voice: "Mr. Nichols, I suggest you bring your toothbrush, because I don't think you're going to be able to show cause. Judge Tyrone doesn't like male pigs who think they can use women and then walk away. I think she'll put you where you can learn about sexual exploitation. I think . . ."

I almost ripped the switch off. A 3 A.M. call from the Zebra Killer would have been more welcome. I needed a lawyer, had to fight this. I had a payday coming from Zoltec; I'd spend

103

every nickel of it on legal talent before I'd see a cent go Brenda's way. Holtree? No way; a thousand-pound great white shark like Lukacs-Skizenta would eat him alive. I needed my own scum-bucket, and it better be female, or better yet, androgynous, so all bets would be covered.

Another chore that would have to wait; other business came first. Washington information got me Butch Tenaki's home phone. We spent a few minutes catching up with each other, another couple reminiscing about those wonderful Eliot House parties we'd starred in a hundred years before, and then I confirmed the key point: *Harvard Magazine* had not lied when it reported that my one-time classmate was Assistant Director of the Japan Desk of the State Department's Commercial Affairs Section.

"Correct, except they made me sound as though I were an Oriental Dean Acheson. It's not that big a deal."

"It sounds big to me, Butch. More to the point, it sounds like you might be able to tell me a little about a Japanese gentleman with whom I may have some business dealings, in a manner of speaking. Kind of like a credit check?"

"Sure—I know all one hundred twenty million Japanese personally. Who we talking about?"

I gave him the name I'd gotten from Fesco—Haroki "Harry" Matsami—and his employment particulars.

"Fujima, huh? What'd they do now?"

"What do you mean?"

"Fujima's a major pain in my ass; I've got half the American electronics industry hounding my office to do something about them: dumping, fixing prices in Japan to subsidize below-cost sales here, ripping off our technology—you name it: Admiral Yamamoto in corporate form."

"Well, what do you do about it?"

"Off the record? Not much. Not much we can do."

"But . . . ."

"Look, Nase—ninety percent of the bitches we get come from lazy, overpaid executives and union reps, or their pet congressmen, who expect American consumers to subsidize their incompetence and soft lives by buying crappy, overpriced domestic goods instead of imports. They act like anybody who isn't a sucker is disloyal. So I start off skeptical."

"But you said . . ."

"I said ninety percent fall into that category. Ten percent are legit beefs. The fact is, some Japanese don't share our beliefs about trade; we say win-win, they say win-lose. Some Japanese companies *do* dump their products until they've wrecked our industry, some figure the best R & D is the stuff the other guy did. Plenty of American companies do the same thing. The difference is our government frowns on it, whereas the Japanese government winks at it because they don't think World War Two ended with Hiroshima—it just changed to a battleground more to their liking. And Fujima's one of the real kamikazes of this go-round."

"And we just take it?"

"Tell me what Fujima's done now. If it checks out, I'll have the Secretary send a strong note to the Japanese government; that'll be easy, since I got stacks of 'em in blank. The Japanese government preprints its responses, too: 'So sorry, and fuck you very much'—all in diplo-talk, of course."

"I see. I'll pass, thanks."

"Hey, look at it from my perspective: my great-grandfather comes over to work on the railroad, busts his ass to make a better life, gets treated like a subhuman 'cause he's short and yellow and has slanty eyes. Granddad puts together a little truck farm outside L.A., just in time to get thrown in a concentration camp because a bunch of crazies he never heard of bomb Pearl Harbor. Incidently, how many German-Americans got locked up? Anyway, Dad goes off, fights in a Nisei battalion, gets a Bronze Star when he's blinded taking Monte Cassino.

You'd say maybe we'd paid our dues, right? Now the know-nothings in this country are baying about the Yellow Peril again, and the Japanese government is playing right into their hands by defending indefensible policies and renegade companies like Fujima. Is velly, velly flustlating."

"Sorry—I get your point. What about this Matsami guy, works for Fesco. Can you find out about him?"

"Maybe. I'll have to contact the embassy in Tokyo, they'll have to make inquiries with the Japanese Foreign Office—it could take some time."

"Whatever you can do. And thanks—I appreciate it, Butch."

"That's what I'm here for, Nase—to help my country. It *is* my country, you know?"

The day was fine—crisp and clear. I wandered around the building calling Magellan's name. He could have been hurt somewhere, so I forced myself to duck into the dark basement recesses. A few rats scurried, but no dog. I didn't see McGinty. He'd probably run off with the rats.

When I came back out, O'Malley was writing parking tickets and shoving them under the windshield wipers of cars parked illegally in front of the building. "You seen any sign of a little dog, sort of terrier-like? Gray?"

He pulled off his hat and scratched his head, then shook it. "I didn't know you owned a dog."

"I don't. It's for a client."

"You don't say." He let out a long whistle. "Lost doggies, huh? You're moving into the big time, Nichols. What's next—stolen bicycles?" He brayed like a donkey with emphysema.

"You do a good job on the parking tickets, O'Malley, they may let you move up to serious felonies. Jaywalkers, even."

His face fell and I regretted my jibe. O'Malley wasn't a bad fellow. He'd made one mistake years before, arresting some hack politician for drunk driving. He'd be passing out parking tickets until he drew his pension.

"I'll keep an eye out for the dog."

"I know you will. Thanks. Hey—" I pointed to a fire hydrant —"that car's a little close, don't you think?"

He looked where I was pointing. "Yeah, I guess it is. But Nase—ain't that your Scout?"

"Why, so it is. But neither fear nor favor, O'Malley, neither fear nor favor. Help you make quota."

"Ah, you won't pay it anyway."

"Well, of course not. Does anybody?"

He shook his head mournfully. "Few tourists, maybe, don't know any better." He looked down at the gutter. Half a dozen old tickets lay in the leaves, the writing washed away.

"That's not the point, O'Malley. The point is, you haven't quit. You show people there are still standards. You can't help the other end of it, but as long as you do your duty, civilization, however imperiled, lives on."

"Jeez, I hadn't thought of it that way." He walked over to the Scout, scribbled a ticket and shoved it under the wiper. "Thanks, Nase."

"No—thank *you*, Officer O'Malley." I took the ticket and climbed into the cab. O'Malley gave me a little salute as I pulled out, and I returned it. Out of deference to O'Malley's feelings I waited until I got around the corner to throw the ticket in the back with the others.

I tooled the Scout over to the North End and spent the morning haggling with toothless Italian women over the price of the last local vegetables of the season. By one o'clock I was famished, so I popped into the Union Oyster House and slurped bivalves and a pair of beers and felt sorry for myself. Rachel had left town for a couple of days and already it seemed like an eternity. I needed her desperately and was thinking like a teenager in rut.

I finished canning the peach preserves and started on the bushel of cucumbers I had picked up at the market. By the time I had sliced them, peeled the onions, and soaked them all in salt, it was evening, so I called Hanrahan at home.

"Jambo, Bwana."

Shit. Hanrahan was into at least his third mart; information would be hard to extract in any coherent form. "And how is my fine, fat, Fenian financier faring?"

"The Hanrahan is hungry. Hungry and horny."

"Glad I asked, but since I'm neither your cook nor your mistress I'm not . . ."

He rolled on: "Soon the Hanrahan will sup. A fine bit o' brisket, soft and sweet as a maiden's breast. Lashings of brown gravy. New potatoes, drowned in butter. Boiled onions, and perhaps the odd wedge of cabbage. The whole, toothsome repast washed down with three or maybe four Harps, depending if the Hanrahan is thirsty."

"Bon appétit. Now . . ."

"Having supped, the Hanrahan will gather his loving wee brood about him for a bit of evening prayer and a cuddle or two. Then the Hanrahan will rise to his full majesty, bid the covey grow still, and declaim as follows: 'God love you, each and every one of you, and peace be upon you; for your sainted mother and I withdraw to our quarters, there to repose ourselves, and plumb the joys of holy wedlock, a sacred state, by laying pipe half the night, to the end that, if God wills it, you shall know the blessing of yet another sibling nine months hence.' How's that shound? Sound?"

Make that at least four martinis. "Well, Motherbucker, it sounds delightful, and good of you to ask me, but I'll have to take a rain check. But say, Big Fella—what word of Zoltec?"

"Who?"

I was having a hard time hearing Bucky, whose voice could pierce granite. It sounded as though the Battle of the Boyne were being reenacted in his living room. "Not who, what. Zoltec's a what. Don't you remember?" I wondered if I should send help; even Hanrahan shouldn't have five martinis.

"Oh, yeah. Zoltec. Sorry, Nase—little hard to hear. Just a sec." I was hammered by a noise like an F-15 hitting mach two: "Listen—the next one of you little bastards that makes a sound is going to find his picture on the back of a milk carton. Now clear out! Where were we?"

"Zoltec. Have you heard anything about where the, uh, rumor about its trade secrets started?"

"Negative, although I've got my tendrils out. But I can tell you, that stock has pancaked; off about forty percent in three days. Of course, Nase . . . ?"

"Say wha?"

"If the rumor weren't correct?"

"If the rumor weren't correct?"

"Anyone buying now would stand to make a hefty gain when the stock goes back up."

"That's a true fact."

"Well?"

"Well, what?"

"Ah, fuck it. You ungrateful . . ."

A blood-chilling shriek cut him off. "Just a second." I was still trying to clear the ringing in my ears when Bucky got back on the line.

"Sweet Jumping Jesus, Buckman, what was that? Did someone take a live round?"

"It was Padraic. Coleen put him in the dishwasher. He blew his cool."

"Blew his cool! Is he all right?"

"Oh, yeah. First time he's been clean in days. Think I'll put 'em all in there."

A dark thought came to me. "Buckfucker—where's Deirdre? Is she at home?" Deirdre ran a tight ship; Bucky was just tight.

There was a long pause. "Ah, shit, Nase. I didn't want to tell you."

"What?"

"Deirdre's left." His voice was barely a whisper.

"Left?" It didn't compute.

"Left. Walked out."

"But . . ."

"She 'needed space.' 'Time to think' is what she called it."

"But you and Deirdre . . ." It was like hearing that Heloise had served papers on Abelard.

"We'd been having a few problems, but I just thought it was the normal husband-and-wife stuff. Then all of a sudden, a few days ago, she calls me into the bedroom and shuts the door. She's got a suitcase packed and she tells me."

"Tells you what?" I was having a much tougher time with this than I ever had with Brenda's exit.

"I told you."

"She 'needed space'? What the hell . . . ?"

"Don't ask me. Anyway, she's at some support group. Some consciousness-raising, sisterhood bullshit: 'Women Opposing Male Bondage.' She's been gone three days. Lasts another four. Then she'll be back." His voice trailed off. "Maybe."

"WOMB."

"Huh?"

" 'Women Opposing Male Bondage'—WOMB."

"Oh." The sounds of gears meshing, barely. "Oh, yeah. I missed that. Jesus, it makes you want to puke, doesn't it? Married fourteen years, seven lovely kids, great relationship, good sex. A few spats, every couple has those, but we were close, Nase—real close. Weren't we?"

"Of course you were. Are. Why, I bet . . ."

"All of a sudden she flings a book at my head, some crap about the penis being the oppressor's stave, shit like that, tells me she needs 'space,' goes off to spend a week having a bunch of wackos tell her how 'exploited' she is. Costs me fourteen hundred bucks so my wife can hear what a pig I am. What the fuck's going on, huh?"

I tried to picture it, couldn't. "Wow."

"You might say."

"Uh, Brenda's and my relationship is a little . . . dicey these days, but I imagine Brenda would be willing to call . . ."

Bucky was starting to sniffle. "Negative, good buddy; not something I could discuss with her. Brenda probably put the idea in her head, anyway."

"Um." A possibility. Brenda and Deirdre had been thick as thieves. I wondered if I could get Brenda quarantined, like Typhoid Mary. "What about the brisket, the night of marital bliss?"

"TV dinners and self-abuse." He was blubbering.

"Buck up, Buckbush. No woman can long resist that great shillelagh you've got. She'll be back."

"You really think so?"

"Wagging her tail behind her."

I rang off, after getting Hanrahan's promise to keep working on finding the source of the all-too-close-to-true rumor about Zoltec. Help keep his mind off his troubles. It shook me to see a fine broth of a man like Bucky brought to such a pass by The Great Sex War, but in these times perhaps it was inevitable. The day was not far away when we of the male persuasion would tread the streets of Boston in Kevlar jockstraps or not at all. I poured the first of several scotches and settled back to brood.

CHAPTER 16

I turned to canning the next morning and kept at it until late afternoon, with a few breaks to continue the hunt for Magellan. I was going through the motions, putting off the moment when I'd have to tell Mrs. Serafina it was hopeless. I wasn't looking forward to that, so I thought about dinner instead. Butch Tenaki called around four, just when I had it down to bad Greek or mediocre Mexican.

"Your friend Matsami's a real charmer, Nase. Want to hear what just came over the embassy wire from Tokyo?"

"Shoot."

" 'Tokyo Prefecture police report that Haroki Matsami is a *jiageya* long associated with Fujima Electronics, Ltd. Reportedly left Japan approx. 01/06/92, after police called him for questioning following reports that subject had been threatening owners of property in area sought by Fujima Electronics, Ltd., for new facilities.' Did you say you were thinking of having *business dealings* with this guy, Nase?"

"I may reconsider. What's a *jiageya*?"

"A *jiageya* is roughly equivalent to a mafioso—muscle for

hire. Quite a few Japanese companies use them from time to time; we use lawyers, they use *jiageya*—you pick. Anyway, they're real sweeties. Cross a psychopathic samurai warrior with Al Capone, pump him up on angel dust, give you some idea. Fujima must have shipped this one over here because things were getting a little hot back home. I'll alert Immigration, but if he isn't actually wanted in Japan, and he's got a valid visa, there isn't a lot we can do."

"You've got to like a company that's loyal to the help."

"Nase, these guys cut off their *own* fingertips, they fuck up. That's how crazy they are. Imagine what they do to the guy who makes 'em look bad, costs them a couple knuckles?"

"Rather not, thanks. Gotta eat soon."

"You do not want to have anything to do with this guy. I mean, *nothing*. Having him on the payroll tells you all you need to know about Fujima, too. I mean, stay far, *far* away from both of them. These are seriously un-fun people."

"Sounds like good advice."

"Best I got—hope you follow it."

I thanked Butch and went back to work, but after fifteen minutes put the spoon down and turned off the burner. It was time to bail out of Zoller's little joke on the competition. Platt was a fool—a fool and a slug—and he deserved to go to jail, but he didn't deserve whatever else might happen, not for hawking gibberish. Rachel's analysis might be right, but I didn't feel up to playing God, not with my credentials. I had to call Platt, tell him it was over.

My vestigial sense of honor told me I had to let Zoller know what I was going to do, so I called him at his office. His secretary put me through right away.

"Mr. Nichols—it is a pleasure to hear your voice again. I congratulate you on your success. Dr. Ornstein informed me when you got back. It is a fine thing that you have done. You have certainly earned your fee—and my gratitude."

"Well, that's what I'm calling about, Doctor." It wasn't easy to get out, and Zoller must have heard something in my voice.

"There weren't any problems, were there? Dr. Ornstein said everything went exactly as planned."

"No, there weren't any problems. There is one now."

"Oh? Perhaps you'd better . . ."

"Perhaps I'd better. I can't go through with it, Doctor. I mean, I can't let Platt walk into what he may be walking into if we go through with this. You've got your stuff back, and now he doesn't have anything. I think we should leave it that way."

"And what is it you anticipate Platt may be exposed to if we allow matters to stand where they are?"

I summarized my thinking, bolstered by Butch's information. There was a long pause when I finished.

"I would not have expected so much solicitude for a thief. I'm surprised you care what happens to him."

"Don't misunderstand me—Platt deserves to be punished. But what he did isn't a capital offense. Let's turn him in to the police."

The line was quiet so long I wasn't sure Zoller had heard. I started to speak, but Zoller cut me off. "I see. Evidently our standards of justice differ, Mr. Nichols. Perhaps mine are more . . . old world? It does not matter. I don't think, Mr. Nichols, the police could add much at this point—merely some unnecessary publicity for Zoltec. What is it we would claim Dr. Platt had?"

"What is it . . . ?"

"What would you propose to tell the police—that Platt had some worthless scribblings that resembled something of ours? That he had had something of ours until we took it back?"

"No—I guess . . ."

He spared me further embarrassment: "As you say, we have not really been hurt, have we?"

"I'm sorry."

"Well, I have learned from a long life that circumstances often make us do things we would rather not do. You must do what you must do."

"Yes." There wasn't anything else to say. I hung up.

The maid had ushered me into the library off the foyer, then retreated, shutting the door with a soft click. There was a fire in the fireplace and the light thrown by the flames danced on the walnut paneling and the gleaming copper fender.

"Bitsy Truscott, Mr. Nichols. So nice to meet you." Her voice was soft and girlish, barely more than a whisper, with a hint of the near South in it.

"It's nice to meet you, too, Mrs. Truscott, but I'm sorry to interrupt like this." Her hand had a pliancy that came from being more worked on than worked with.

"Not at all; Zachariah was delighted you called. I'm afraid he'll be a few minutes, though. He had to pick up our daughter at her riding lesson." She walked over to a butler's table piled with cut-glass decanters, Waterford tumblers, and a silver ice bucket. "Won't you have a drink?" She stood between me and the fireplace, her slim figure outlined by a dress that moved against her as though it had been made from butterfly wings.

"Thank you, but I don't want to trouble you any more than I already have."

"Oh, it's no trouble. I was just going to mix myself something. Please join me. Scotch?"

It came out "thcotch," and I realized that the appealing quality of Mrs. Truscott's voice was owed to an almost imperceptible lisp. "Thank you."

Her fingers brushed mine as she handed me the glass. Bitsy Truscott radiated a vulnerable femininity. Her eyes were blue and clear, and darted away as soon as she caught me looking. I had adjusted to the light and I could see the furnishings well

115

enough to confirm that Truscott had been right about his wife: she liked to spend money. She did it well.

"I won't take much of Zach's time; there's just something I have to fill him in on, and it couldn't wait."

"That's all right. I'm used to Zachariah's business not being able to wait. That's why I'm used to waiting." She smiled to say it didn't bother her. "Anyway, we have to go to a benefit later on. I'd love an excuse to be late." She laughed, a gentle, pealing sound. "I'd love an excuse not to go at all. Did you bring me that excuse?"

Once again she fixed me with a direct stare, a half-smile on her face, but this time she swayed fractionally and it occurred to me that Bitsy Truscott might have started drinking ahead of me. "I'm afraid not; I just need a few minutes."

"Oh." Her face fell. She wore her emotions the way most women wear makeup. It gave her a childlike, open quality. "I don't really like parties. I was hoping . . . Oh, well." She drained her glass. "Another?"

"Thank you, no—I've still got mine."

The decanter chimed against her glass. She poured an inch, looked at the glass, frowned, added another, then dropped in an ice cube. "Cheers!"

I raised my glass in return. "Lovely place you have here."

She looked around as though seeing the room for the first time, then seemed to ponder the point. Finally she said, "Yes, I suppose it is," in an uncertain tone.

It was starting to be heavy going, but I was charmed by the gentle quality of her soft voice, and hoped she'd keep talking. I tried again. "Did you do the decorating yourself?"

"The what?"

"The decorating. Did you do it yourself, or did someone else do it?" I gestured vaguely, although I didn't think it was that difficult a concept.

"Oh—the decorating."

"Yes. A lovely job."

She looked around the room again. "Thank you. I'm glad you like it. I'm never sure people will."

"I'm sure everybody does."

"I hope so. I'd like that—for Zachariah."

A large doll's house sitting on a table against the wall caught my eye, and I walked over to it. It was too perfect to be a child's toy. "I bet you did this, too." It seemed a safe guess.

She came and stood beside me, staring fondly at the model of a Victorian Gothic mansion. It was almost three feet high and at least as wide. The back, which faced us, was open, revealing a dozen rooms and hundreds of tiny pieces of period furniture. Heavy brocade curtains lined the windows. Each room held tiny dolls—some sleeping, some standing, some sitting. "Oh, yes—I did my house." She put the slightest stress on the "my."

She reached down and shifted a tiny chair a half-inch to the left. "Do you think it's silly?"

"Not at all. I've never seen one like it. May I?" I reached toward a tiny porcelain figure standing, arms apart, behind a little music stand next to a miniature grand piano. It wore a ball gown.

"Oh!" Her hand started out, then stopped abruptly, as though about to do something shameful. "Why, of course. She's—she's always been my favorite, too."

"Perhaps I shouldn't?"

"No, that's all right. Please."

The little creature looked lost in my palm, but small as it was, every human feature had been included, from eyebrows to a freckle on the right cheek. It was a beautiful face. "I can see why she would be your favorite. I've never seen a doll so realistic." I stared at it, wondering what to say next, when she reached over and stroked it with her finger.

"That's my mother."

"Your mother?"

She laughed. "Well, not really, of course. I meant that it's a model of my mother. All the dolls are real people. Modeled after real people, I mean."

"You're kidding." I looked more closely at the other dolls and realized that they all had distinct features.

"No, really." She laughed again, nervously this time. "And the house is a model of the house I grew up in. In Nashville. It was my grandmother's house."

"It's incredible. Where are you?"

The shy smile flitted over her face and she shook her head. "There isn't one of me. It's the others I want to remember. Not me."

"Oh?"

"My mother loved to sing. She had a beautiful voice. And that's my grandmother playing the piano. She could have been a professional. There wasn't anything I could do like that. There isn't anything."

"You could be a decorator."

"You're very kind, but dressing up a doll's house isn't like running a real business, the way Zachariah does. Or you do. What you men do is hard. I'm just . . . playing, I guess you could say." She started toward the drink table but caught her heel on the carpet and stumbled. I reached out and grabbed her forearm to steady her. Her drink splashed onto my sleeve.

"Oh—I'm so sorry. I've got you all wet." Panic swept her face. "You didn't drop her, did you?" Her eyes swept the floor.

"I didn't drop her. Look." I held up the figure of the little woman, then replaced it behind the music stand.

Mrs. Truscott reached out and touched it, as though to satisfy herself it wasn't an illusion, then smiled. "Let me get a napkin. There's one around here somewhere." She turned this way and that, and more liquid slopped out of her glass, this time onto the floor.

118

"Maybe you better sit down." I took her elbow and guided her over to a wing chair.

"I am sorry. I'm so clumsy. I don't know what came over me. I'm always dropping and spilling things." She pronounced it "thangs." Her accent was growing stronger as she drank, even as her lisp had almost disappeared.

"Don't think anything of it. You tripped, that's all."

"Would you mind terribly getting me another drink, please?"

I started to ask if she thought that was a good idea but she'd just told me it was, and I wasn't there to play nursemaid so I mixed a light one for her, and while I was at it, a stiff one for myself. I handed her her glass and she took it eagerly.

"Thank you." She took a sip, then another. "Do you work every night?"

"I beg your pardon?"

"Do you always work at night? Like you are now, I mean."

I glanced down. Mrs. Truscott was staring up at me as though intensely interested in my answer. The large chair swallowed her so that she appeared much smaller, and much younger, than she had while standing. Her glass dangled loosely from her hand.

"No. Not often."

"We do. Zachariah does, anyway. I'm not much help to him, I'm afraid. Do you work with your wife?"

"I'm sorry?" The conversation was taking on the randomness of a video game. I prayed Truscott would arrive and bail me out.

"Does your wife help you in your work? What do you do, anyway?"

"I'm not married, and I'm a . . . consultant."

She nodded, no doubt having met many consultants. "It's better that you're not married. Sometimes I think Zachariah would have been better off if he hadn't met me."

"Oh? I'm sure that isn't . . ."

119

She brought the glass to her lips without moving her head, so that I could see the skin on her neck drum as she drank. "Zachariah works at night. He'll be working with you, and he'll be working at the benefit. All those people, and you have to smile, and be glad to see them, and chat about this and that. Tonight, tomorrow night; always another. He's good at it, but I'm not. I wish I were, but I'm just not. Maybe that's why I enjoy the dolls."

"I see. Well, maybe he . . ."

"I'm not much help to Zachariah in his business, I'm afraid. Or in any other way, I think." She said it clinically, without self-pity.

"Oh, I'm sure that's not true."

She looked up and smiled, a gentle, knowing look. "Yes, it is. I just can't keep up. But Zachariah's very sweet. He never says anything. He's never said how disappointed he is."

I started to reassure her but stopped; I had no right to patronize her. Without thinking, I reached down and patted her shoulder. "I think maybe I'd better be going." I sidled backward.

"Mommy?" A small blond head peered around the door.

"Why, come in, Sugarplum, and meet Mr. Nichols. He's a friend of Daddy's. And mine, now. Did you have a good lesson?" Mrs. Truscott held out her arms and the little girl stepped into the room, gave me a shy smile that was an echo of her mother's, then ran to her mother and gave her a hug. She was wearing jodhpurs and a hacking jacket.

Mrs. Truscott rested her cheek on the blond curls. Her eyes were shut and she gripped the child as if she'd never let go. I was watching when Truscott came up behind me.

"Hello, Nase. You've met Bitsy, I see."

I turned with a start. He was wearing a dinner jacket. "Oh, yes; she's been taking good care of me."

He beamed at his family. "I'm not surprised—Bitsy loves

company." He walked over to the chair. "Bitsy, honey, I think
you better go up and get ready. We'll be late." He reached down
and patted her head.

Mrs. Truscott looked up, started to say something, then
looked confused. "But what about Melissa's dinner? Shouldn't
I fix her dinner?"

The little girl laughed and reached for her mother's cheek.
"That's silly, Mommy—Maria fixed my dinner. You know
Maria makes my dinner."

"But . . ."

"She's right, honey—Maria's fixed her dinner. You go on up
now and get ready. I'll send Maria up to help. The pink Ungaro
would be lovely."

The child climbed off her mother's lap and took her hand in
both of hers. "Come on, Mommy—I'll pull you up." She tugged
with all her weight and Mrs. Truscott rose to her feet.

"Good-bye, Mr. Nichols. It was a pleasure to meet you. I have
to get ready now." She stuck out her hand and I took it.

"I enjoyed meeting you, too, Mrs. Truscott." Truscott had
gone over to the drink cart and was building himself a highball.
I took the moment to lean toward his wife. "She looks just like
you." I nodded in the direction of the little girl. "Like the two
of you; she's a tribute to both of you."

She thought a second, then gave me the sweet, sad smile.
"Thank you."

We watched them leave, the little girl leading her mother by
the hand. Truscott stepped to the door, watched for a moment
longer, then pushed it shut. There was a smile on his face when
he turned back. "Bitsy loves parties. She gets so keyed up
sometimes when we're going out to a big do I don't think she
knows what's she's doing. Freshen your drink?"

"I'm fine, thanks."

Truscott gestured toward a club chair and I collapsed into it.
He sat across from me in the chair his wife had vacated and

leaned forward expectantly. "Well, what's up—I take it you've got a lead?"

"Let me be sure I understand what you're saying." Truscott pushed himself to his feet and poured himself another drink. He didn't offer me one. Then he walked back to the chair but remained standing.

"Right now, as we stand here, we have our technology back, and Platt has a bunch of junk? Is that what you're telling me?" His voice was low, incredulous. He loomed over me, forcing me to peer up at him. I wondered if it was a trick he had learned at business school.

"That's right."

"Has he lost his mind?"

"He? You mean . . . ?"

"Zoller. Is he nuts?"

"I . . ."

"Jesus Christ! Zoltec is a public company; he can't run it like his private fruit stand. He's been acting more and more irrationally; I really wonder if he's lost his mind." Truscott took a hard pull on his drink.

"I can't speak to that. All I know is that I agree with you—it was a bad idea."

Truscott got a faraway look, and when he looked back down at me his hands were clenched and he spoke in a low, slow voice. "The other night—in the restaurant—you had already agreed to do this, hadn't you? You knew where the documents were, but you told me you hadn't found them."

It was a question I'd been hoping we could pass. I nodded, unable to meet his stare.

"You lied to me?"

There was no answer, but I forced myself to look at him. For a second I thought he was going to hit me, and then he seemed to sag. He lowered himself into the chair and rubbed his eyes.

We sat like that for what seemed forever, although no more than a minute could have gone by before I realized that Truscott was making a strange sound and no more than a few additional seconds before I recognized the sound and relaxed; Truscott was laughing.

"You know, this is really rich." He chuckled again, then let it turn into a rich fullblown unforced belly laugh. "That old bastard. That conniving, dishonest, devious old bastard. You really got the stuff back?"

"Absolutely."

"We can announce the new process?"

"For sure."

"Right away?"

"This minute."

"And Platt hasn't a clue?"

"What do you mean?"

"What do you mean, 'what do I mean'?"

"What do you mean, 'what do you mean, what do I mean'?"

"Nase, come on—this could go on forever." He put his hand on my arm and smiled. "Platt doesn't know anything, right?"

"No. Nothing."

"You're sure?"

"He hasn't a clue. Yet."

He slapped his knee. "Well, that's terrific. I'll never forgive Zoller, but I've got to admire the old goat—he's got balls. How about another?" He stood and reached for my glass.

"Yet. He hasn't a clue—yet. Why does it matter?"

"Yet? What's that mean? He hasn't a clue yet?"

We were not communicating. "You better sit down. I haven't finished."

He slid back into his seat, quizzical and uncertain.

"Platt doesn't know anything. But I'm going to tell him. Hence I say, 'He doesn't know anything—yet.' "

"Is this something Dr. Zoller . . . ?"

"Definitely not. This is pure Nason Nichols."

"Maybe you better explain."

That line again. I did, as best I could. Truscott listened quietly until I finished. When I did he leaned toward me, forearms resting on knees. A lock of hair fell over his forehead.

"Nase. Listen to me." His voice was low and hoarse. "Don't do this. Please. This thing—it was crazy. Zoller was out of his mind. But it's worked. Maybe that's what makes him a genius, I don't know. But it's worked—don't screw it up now."

I started to answer but he reached out and grabbed my wrist. "It's all over the market that we've lost a valuable asset, Nase. I don't know how it got out, but it did."

"I heard something like that."

He nodded. "Do you know what that means? Can you imagine?"

"I imagine . . ."

He cut me off. "You can't imagine. Our stock's getting the stuffing kicked out of it. God knows how long it'll take for it to recover. My options aren't worth the paper they're written on. None of this would have happened if we'd just gone ahead with the original plan, taken the materials back as soon as we found them, but it's too late to do anything about that now. Let's at least salvage *something* from this mess."

He stared at me intently, and I felt the way I had when I'd let down the one teacher who'd been in my corner. "But telling Platt now isn't going to change things. I mean, you can still make your announcement, deny the rumors; won't the stock go back up then?"

"Hah!" He waved his hand dismissively. "A little, sure. But it won't recover completely, much less gain on where it was before this, until the market sees that we're telling the truth, and that we're leaving the competition in the dust. That means Fujima. Zoller's right; they're always on our tail. This will give us a big lead. A big, big lead. I think that's the least we deserve."

"And when they figure things out—what happens to Platt?"

It was Truscott's turn to look away. "Don't you think you're being just a shade melodramatic, Nase? Don't get me wrong—I think your concerns are commendable, but a little . . ." He searched for the right word.

"Exaggerated?"

He nodded vigorously. "That's right, exaggerated. I mean, whatever they may do in Japan, how much risk could there be here?"

I stood, so that now I was looking down at Truscott. "I don't know, Zach; that's why I've got to tell him. I don't want to spend the next couple of years asking just that question."

He started to push himself up out of his chair until I stopped him with a hand on his shoulder. "I'm sorry, Zach. For all of this. I've enjoyed meeting you, and I'm sorry it has to end this way. Really sorry."

He called to me when I got to the door. "It's not money, is it? It's not that you want more money, Nase?"

I turned, my hand on the knob. "I wish it were, Zach. I'd love more money."

"Well, then . . ." I didn't hear the rest because I shut the door and left.

CHAPTER 17

Beer nuts and a Narragansett. The end of expense-account living. I hadn't been paid by Zoltec, and now I wouldn't be, even though I had accomplished the original assignment, as I saw it. I meandered to the back of the bar, looked up Platt's number, and dialed.

No answer. I got two dimes back when I hung up and figured it was time for bed; the day could only go downhill.

The next morning I called Platt's office. The receptionist answered on the third ring.

"Is Platt in?"

"*Doctor* Platt is engaged elsewhere. Who's calling?"

"This is Mr. Werkins. When do you expect him?"

"I don't know. I expected him yesterday. He was only going for . . . Say, what did you say your name was? Aren't you the man . . . ?"

"I am the man, lamb chop. What do you mean, you expected him yesterday?"

"That's not my name. Anyway, I really don't see that it's any of your business."

"He wanted me to call. Set up a meeting, talk about employee benefits. Pensions, stock ownership, maternity leave, day care. Family planning. Things like that."

"He didn't say anything to me about that."

"He wanted it to be a surprise."

"That's sweet of him. Isn't it?"

"Angel cakes, the man has a heart as big as the whole outdoors. Do you know where he is? Try hard."

"Well, he went away on business."

This I knew.

"But he told me before he left he'd be back yesterday for sure. I mean, like when he said it he didn't say yesterday, he said Monday, but that was yesterday, if you know what I mean?"

I assured her I could relate to what she was saying. "Let us speak no more of little things, dear heart—do you have any idea where he can be reached?"

"No." Her voice turned plaintive. "I've called his house, and the hotel where he was staying in New York said he checked out Sunday. You know, the day before yesterday. I even called his home in New Hampshire. I can't imagine where he could be; he always lets me know his schedule. I mean, I've only worked for him for a few days, but he did. Let me know his schedule, I mean. In case anyone, like, wants to see him."

"Wayward laddie."

"You know, you talk kind of funny. Poetic, like,"

"Had a hairlip operation when I was but a youth. Does that to you."

"Oh. I didn't know that. It's kinda sweet."

"I'm priapic with pleasure."

"I'm glad. Say, mister?"

"Unburden yourself."

"If you find Bruce—Doctor Platt—will you ask him to call me? I'm . . . lonely."

"But of course. Au revoir, Daughter of Venus." I rang off.

The traffic on the way to Platt's condo was fierce, and it took the better part of an hour to make it to the wharf. No Porsche at the condo. I checked the mailbox. The mailman had given up trying to wedge stuff in it and had left it piled on the floor. I buzzed Platt but didn't expect a response and didn't get one. Only one more place I could think of looking.

Some clown had managed to have his car die halfway through the Callahan tunnel, so I ate carbon monoxide for half an hour and drove the rest of the way to New Hampshire with the windows down to limit the brain damage. There had to be brain damage or I wouldn't have been tooling back to Liberty for the third time in a week.

Platt had taken his sample to New York and shown it off while I was using his plumbing. He'd nailed down the deal, then left on Sunday. Since he hadn't returned to Boston, he must have gone straight back to his cabin to retrieve the goods for delivery. I pulled off and let his phone ring again while I gassed the car, then pushed on.

It was almost ten when I pulled into Platt's clearing. I saw the Porsche and relaxed, because even though I wasn't relishing the moment it would be done in a minute.

Platt didn't answer my knock so I opened the door and entered. He'd left a half-eaten steak and a glass of wine on the kitchen table. I called out his name, then walked down the narrow hall to get it over with.

CHAPTER 18

The soles of his shoes were looking at the ceiling because the shotgun blast had blown him across the bed and he had landed on the floor with his legs straight up. It wasn't a graceful position, but a shotgun load in the gut isn't a graceful kill, either.

Whoever had done it had caught the bed with a few pellets, which was too bad because Platt's waterbed had burst like a giant blister. There was water all over the floor and it had mixed with Bruce's juices, and for a second I was going to add anything I had left to the mess, but I got it under control by doing the mouth-breathing routine.

The blood on the walls had congealed and darkened. I touched a drop and it barely stained the towel covering my hand. I went over the body as quickly as possible. It would take an autopsy to tell for sure, but my guess was he'd been dead about a day—which would have put the shooting some time Monday night.

I looked around quickly, but all I learned was that Platt favored Ralph Lauren shirts and had been halfway through the autobiography of a car salesman. There was no sign that Platt had used his dying moments to write the killer's name in blood on the wall—probably because a shotgun at close range doesn't leave much of a dying moment. My guess was that Platt never knew what hit him. I hoped so. I moved to the living room.

This time the desk proved more fruitful than it had before. There was a new checkbook behind the tilt-top, from Platt's Boston bank. I riffled the stubs; a $10,000 deposit jumped out. Going more slowly, I spotted two others: one for $35,000, the other a mate of the first one. They seemed to be spread over the last year, but I didn't take time for study; it went into my pocket.

The rest of the room got a quick once-over, but all I turned up was an appointment book on a table. I took it too. By this time I was hyperventilating and the room was singing to me and I knew I had tampered with all the evidence I could handle for one day—until I saw the gun.

The Parker twelve-gauge lay on the hearth under the mantel. Using the towel, I broke it open, and the empty cartridge ejected. I picked it up and the acrid smell of fresh powder confirmed my guess. I reinserted it in the gun, snapped it shut, and had turned to put it back where I'd found it when the man spoke from just inside the kitchen.

"I was cutting across to my place and saw the door open and wondered if everything was all . . ."

He was dressed in a red Goretex hunting jacket with a Day-Glo orange cap and his eyes were saucers because I'd whirled and the barrel of the gun was pointing at him, six feet away.

"Jesus Christ, Mister, don't!"

"Huh? Oh, no, it wasn't me. I just . . ."

But I don't think he heard because as soon as I lowered the barrel he was out the door. I decided to follow, fast.

I made myself stop by the bathroom and look in the toilet tank. Empty. One way or another, Platt had made his delivery.

I took the road out of town toward Maine, then cut over so

I'd pick up the Boston road well south of Liberty. It had been dark in the clearing and the Scout had been on the far side of the cabin, but the law would be out soon and I didn't want to be in the neighborhood.

It was past three when I slipped into my apartment, and I could have kissed the floor. First stop was the bottle of Laphroig. Once I was sure it would stay down I refilled the glass and examined my take.

The checkbook showed regular bimonthly deposits of about $2,500 apiece: Platt's salary from Zoltec. The same neat hand had also recorded nine deposits, one about every six weeks, beginning January 15. The smallest was $7,500, the largest the one for $35,000, which was also the most recent. I checked a calendar—the big deposit was made two days after Platt gave Zoltec his notice. In all, slightly under $200,000.

I scanned the disbursements. They displayed the predictable array of life's necessities—grocery store, shoe repair, Jordan Marsh, oil companies, New England Bell. Six weeks ago Platt had transferred $30,000 to an account for The Platt Group. I fanned through the leaves one more time, and my eye caught a single entry buried between mortgage payments and electric bills: Winston Quarles was the payee, $2,000 the amount, September 20 the date. Why was Platt paying the fat little technician two thousand dollars? A birthday present? That was one worth asking.

I turned to the appointment calendar and fanned through it quickly. The last two weeks were blank. Platt had been moving on a straight enough line not to need maps, these last days. The final entries were before he left Zoltec: "conf. Bingham"; "call Robertson"; "visit Newmarkt. plant."

There were several Friday evening entries, women's names mostly, sometimes with an address or coupled with the name of a trendy night spot. At first I blocked over the "Meet W's" spread over several months, until I saw "W.Q.—Dinner, Anthony's," and realized "W" could be Quarles again. A $2,000 check and a series of dinner dates; what an unlikely couple.

Odd couples. I free-associated to Rachel. What did I tell her? That the thing I'd warned her about had happened? It would hit her hard; I didn't want that, wished there was some way to spare her. I loved her. There—it was out, the L word, the one I'd put away when things fell apart with Brenda, put away for good, I'd thought. It was a little scary so I put it aside to play with later.

I refilled my glass, missing Rachel wrenchingly, and was glad the engagement book didn't go back far enough to rub those entries in my face. I put the bottle next to the bed, stuck a scratchy Ella on the stereo, and lay back to stare at the ceiling. God, I was tired of being alone.

CHAPTER 19

"Where are you, Nichols?" The question pierced through the fog of sleep, and for a confused second I thought it was one of those metaphysical conundrums from sophomore philosophy class. Then I realized it was Hanrahan, and that I had the phone pressed to my ear. I sat up in bed and looked at my watch: 8:00 A.M.

"What do you mean, where am I? Where the hell should I be? Where are you?" I leaned back against the headboard and red flames shot up behind my eyes. I leaned forward again and stared at the empty bottle on the floor.

"I'm at Tasty's at Harvard Square, meeting you. I left a message on your machine."

"Didn't listen—wasn't sure I could handle the weight of human contact last night. What's the message?"

"The message, my ill-begotten chum, is that I have a very interesting tale to tell, and you were to be here at seven-thirty to hear it told. Which you aren't."

"Tell me."

"Bullshit. I got my ass down here to fill you in on something you wanted to know. I'll wait exactly fifteen more minutes, and then you'll never know what I know." He hung up.

I threw some water in my face, took a quick pass at the teeth, and tossed on the clothes I'd scattered the night before. As I half trotted, half ran the six blocks to Harvard Square I prayed Hanrahan had something really good so I wouldn't have to kill him; I was godfather to his children.

Though it was not yet eight-thirty, the Square was going full bore, and the throngs forced me to a walk. The marketplace of contemporary values clamored for my attention.

Shaven-headed, saffron-robed Krishnas were already syncopating, kids from New Rochelle only a mantra or two away from nirvana. It was a little early for the Trotskyite Youth that had come to picket Cardullo's because the wrong Mexicans had picked its grapes, so they were chatting with a pasty couple. The young man was denouncing the Canadians for killing baby seals; his companion was agitating for abortion rights. A few feet away a woman in army fatigues was ranting about something we were doing with some banana republic dictator, either a good dictator we were being mean to or a bad dictator we were being nice to, I couldn't tell. A long-haired boy with a guitar was standing in the entrance to the Coop, croaking some Weavers ditty about scabs and union-bashing, eyeing the work-bound bourgeoisie to fling a little change into his hat as a sop to their guilt. The kid's father had probably stood in the same spot twenty-five years before, making his own statement about the evils of capitalism. Now he made it by purging his portfolio of South African stocks.

The entrance to the diner was blocked by militant peace-lovers questioning the wisdom of a nuclear war. I took a last look around; it was a close call, but they were probably right. I pushed my way in.

134

Bucky was in the last booth, newspapers spread before him. He didn't look happy.

He spoke without looking up as I slid into the seat across from him. "They did it again. Sweet suffering Jesus, when will it end? I could stand it if they stank all the time, like Cleveland; but the Sox are the baseball equivalent of a pricktease—just when they got you thinking you're going all the way, it's 'wham, bam, forget it, Sam.' " He stared at me. "You look ugly enough to be a student. Have you re-enrolled?"

"Most droll. Now, about this information . . . ."

"Not so fast. First, the Hanrahan must eat." He turned to the slattern waiting to take our order. "Let's see, darlin' . . . ." The grease-covered menu might have been the Book of Kells from the way he pored over it. "A bowl of oatmeal to start, I think. Give the colon a good scrubbing. Stewed prunes, too—for the regularity in them. Then a couple of rashers of bacon and a pair of farm-fresh eggs, reposing on the bosom of buttered scones—English muffins to you, my dear. Potatoes, it goes without saying. Any kippers today? No? Tsk, tsk. Then a side order of sausage will do nicely. Several gallons of coffee—dark as your eyes, hot as your blood. And darlin'—" he flashed a smile the size of a dinner plate—"present the check to my companion here."

The waitress added my order for coffee and dry toast and withdrew, mumbling to herself and sucking a tooth. I grabbed the *Globe* and scurried through it, looking for the headline: "Hub Man Homicide Victim; Local Vagrant Sought for Questioning," but there was nothing. Either the papers hadn't had time to get it in the morning edition or there had been enough shootings, stabbings, and stranglings right in Boston to satisfy even the *Globe*'s insatiable appetite for gore.

"Particular story you're following, Nase? Never seen you so taken with the press."

"No, no, nothing special. Didn't sleep too well, that's all.

Now, for God's sake, what's your news? I've paid my dues." I sounded like Jesse Jackson.

"Aye, lad, I suppose you have, at that. Very well." He paused while the waitress flung a dish of prunes at him. "You were curious to know the source of the word that Zoltec had lost an irreplaceable asset. I've been making discreet inquiries. As you may imagine, rumors, by definition, lack a pedigree." He took a slug of coffee and looked off thoughtfully: " 'Rumors lack a pedigree.' Hmm. Anyway, I finally got lucky."

"And?"

"And, near as I can tell, the first person to tell that tale, at least to someone outside Zoltec, is a gentleman named Leon Altschuler."

I looked blank. "So what? I mean, who's Leon Altschuler?"

"Leon Altschuler is very old, very smart, and very rich. He serves as an investment manager for a handful of very old, very rich men and a few big trust funds."

"So?"

"Wait. Just hang on a minute, will you?" He inhaled a prune. A pit rocketed back into the dish and circled like a ball in a roulette wheel. "A week or so ago he's playing bridge with a guy I know. Altschuler's a grand master or something. Anyhow, they take a break and Altschuler and my guy hit the head." He spooned up half a bowl of oatmeal. "They're standing there, weenie-wagging, making a little chitchat. You know, the way you do, two guys got their shlongs out, foot apart."

The image distracted him, made him stare at a sausage like a hawk eyeing a crippled rodent. Then it was gone. "The guy I know says something about Zoltec, what a great company it is, and how he hears they're working on a new process, gonna really make some bucks. But Altschuler, who's been hitting the schnapps pretty heavy, and making a lot of stupid mistakes at the table, gets kinda flustered and blurts out, 'Not if they had had an accident.'

"So my guy says, 'Whataya mean, an accident?' And Altschuler stands there, holding his old thing and looking at it like he wonders what it's for, and mumbles something about what if other companies had found out how Zoltec did the new process, like if some guy had stolen the technology. Then Altschuler realizes what he's said, claps his hand over his mouth —the other one, I assume—and makes my guy promise to forget he heard anything he said. My friend, being an honorable guy and feeling sorry for a grand old man who's maybe slipping a tad, says certainly, forget all about it, never heard anything. So of course the next morning, soon as the market opens, my honorable friend dumps his Zoltec, clues in a customer, who clues in another, and there you are." Bucky scraped out the last of the oatmeal, then tongued off both sides of the spoon.

"What the hell? You mean some older geezer says 'what if,' you guys run out and sell stock? Why not study the entrails of a chicken? I could've been in bed instead of listening to this shit."

"Callow fool—Leon Altschuler isn't *any* old geezer. Look here." He pulled a copy of a magazine article from his briefcase and pushed it across to me. It was old and brittle. The caption read: "Hub Industrialist, Financier Boyhood Friends." I scanned the story, which was the Algeresque tale of two young men from the same eastern European village who left war-torn Europe together to find wealth and fame in the Athens of the new world. The picture showed them lounging on Altschuler's porch in Lincoln, "in a rare moment of relaxation and reminiscence." Even fifteen years ago Zoller had looked like the Swiss foreign minister.

"Ah ha."

"Ah ho."

"Interesting."

"There's something else, too."

"That being?"

"That being, Leon Altschuler is on the Zoltec board. Ergo, when Leon Altschuler speaks of Zoltec, us moneygrubbers assume he knows whereof he speaks."

"Indeed." My brain wasn't due to come on duty for at least another hour, but I implored it to waive union rules just this once; I needed to think.

Bucky had more. "You know, after I heard this story I went to the firm's library. Pulled everything ever written about Altschuler. Fascinating guy. One little detail from a story about five years ago. Want to hear?"

"You bet. What's the little detail?"

"Leon's a teetotaler—'Secret of a long and wealthy life,' or some bullshit like that. I'd rather die broke in a ditch."

"So?"

"Sweet Jesus in the morning, what kind of detective are you? I told you—Altschuler was supposed to have been in his cups when he spilled the story about Zoltec."

"So maybe he fell off the wagon."

"Maybe. Hard to imagine an old pro like that letting something slip, though—drunk or sober."

Nothing was computing. "That oatmeal's gone to your brain. Why would Altschuler intentionally put out word that Zoltec's most valuable asset had been lost? If it had been," I added.

Bucky gave me a hard stare, all buffoonery gone. I refused to meet his look. "Beats me. Thought you might know."

It was my turn for head-shaking. "Makes no sense at all."

Bucky stood up. "Well, bro, thanks for the breakfast. Time for me to make some money." He turned to leave.

"What do you hear from Deirdre?"

He turned back. "I called last night. Wasn't supposed to, but I had to know how she was."

"And?"

"She said she was 'getting in touch with her feelings.' "

"Huh?"

"And she's got a friend. A good friend. 'Someone very special to her.' " He turned and shambled out.

CHAPTER **20**

A third cup of coffee and a smoke rounded out breakfast. I wasn't going to win any clean living awards, but the way things were piling up it wouldn't matter. How the Zoltec loss had gotten out was an interesting story, but not nearly as interesting as the one I'd have to tell if I didn't want to get tagged for Platt's murder. Shock had kept me from dwelling on it the night before, but now it was obvious: a Japanese hood wasn't going to be some cop's prime candidate for a quick solution to a messy homicide; that honor was reserved for me.

Common sense told me to call the police and tell all. After all, I hadn't offed Platt—I had merely been looking for him, using a phony name, after getting very friendly with his former girlfriend, and was the only person known to have had access to him around the time he was hit. They couldn't tie the murder weapon to me, except that some local yeoman saw me holding it. Common sense also told me that cops like simple solutions, and usually they're right. I was the simple solution.

The more I thought about it the nastier things looked. Even if the guy who'd surprised me at Platt's cabin last night hadn't spotted my license number—and I had to assume he hadn't, or I'd be talking to a public defender instead of myself—there was a good chance someone in Liberty would remember seeing a Scout with Massachusetts plates three times in as many days. The cops would get around to questioning the local motels, they'd get license numbers for everyone who'd registered around the time Platt was killed, and sooner or later they'd be asking me questions I wasn't going to be able to answer very well. They'd get onto Rachel, too, through the motel registrations. I didn't want that. She'd be in the clear on the killing, but she'd never be able to keep her involvement in the trade-secret swap out; they could even try to tag us on a conspiracy rap. Two, maybe three, days to develop something I could give the police when they came. I decided to pick at the only loose thread I had.

There was a pay phone in the back. Quarles answered after five rings.

"Ah, Dr. Quarles. I'm glad I caught you in. This is Nason Nichols."

Quarles paused so long I thought he must have forgotten who I was. "Oh, yes. Mr. Nichols. Of course. How are you?"

"Peachy. Fit as a fiddle. And you?"

"I—I've a slight cold. I'm staying home today."

"Good idea. Lousy day out. Say, Dr. Quarles—I'm still working on . . . you know what, and I wondered if I could stop by and get a little information?"

" 'You know what?' Oh—you mean . . ."

"Exactly. I'd just be a minute. Wouldn't dream of imposing, but you understand the urgency. Dr. Zoller is terribly . . ."

Zoller's name had the desired effect. "Well, if you think it's really that important." He sounded as eager as a man who had just been advised to have exploratory surgery in the next couple of minutes.

"Wouldn't dream of bothering you if it weren't." I got directions to his house, picked up the Scout, and was underway.

Arlington's a middle-middle-class community just past Cambridge, which means that for three hundred thousand dollars you get a three-bedroom frame shack no self-respecting Mississippi tenant farmer would live in. Quarles's was the last on a dead-end street lined with them, distinguished from the others only by being in even worse need of paint. I pulled in behind the six-year-old Chevy wagon, staggered over a bicycle that had been left to snare me, and rang the bell.

A woman answered the door. She stared at me indifferently from bleary eyes sunk in fat. A curl of smoke rose from the cigarette in the corner of her mouth. It was the face of a woman who would never again be surprised by life.

"Uh, Dr. Quarles was expecting me, Mrs. Quarles. I'm . . ."

A hand emerged from a stained caftan and took the cigarette, then used it to point toward a door on the left. Even in the half-light of the hall I could see that the nails were bitten, thick, and yellow. She left without a word.

Dr. Quarles was sitting on a sun porch behind a cramped, dark living room. He had the blinds drawn against the wan fall day, but enough light got through to let me see that he really did look ill. I remembered the sagging jowls and disheveled hair, but the gray skin and rheumy eyes were new.

Quarles made a halfhearted attempt to get up from a sagging easy chair, and he sank back gratefully when I stopped him.

"You really aren't looking well, Doctor—it was good of you to see me. I'll be brief."

"I want to cooperate. I wouldn't want anyone to think I wasn't cooperative. Have you made any progress?" His voice was raspier than I remembered.

"I think so. We've learned a lot about Platt and his activities in the last few days. We're closing in."

"Have you found out what he did with the documents?"

"Not yet, Doctor. I was hoping you could help there."
Quarles's hands were a study. He had them splayed across the
ends of the chair arms. Nine of his pudgy fingers lay calmly,
but the tenth—the ring finger on his left hand—beat a silent
tattoo on the upholstered material.

"I really don't see . . . I don't know . . ." Lank strands of oily
hair fell over his forehead as he shook his head. "I mean I
want . . . "

"You want to cooperate, I know." He nodded rapidly. "Exactly. That's why I came to you. I understand you got to be
quite good friends with Dr. Platt in the last year or so. Do you
know where he got that money?"

"I beg your pardon? Money?"

"You were Dr. Platt's closest friend, weren't you?"

The one-two jolted him. Quarles appeared torn between the
desire to distance himself from Platt and the need to glory in
the role of somebody's best friend. Vanity won out, as it usually
does. "We were good friends, yes. I'd like to think I served
Bruce's cerebral needs. At least that's what he said."

"What did he mean you 'served his cerebral needs'?"

"You make it sound unnatural. It wasn't anything like that.
It's just that I listened to Bruce. He's a brilliant man, in spite of
what he did. I listened to him, understood him. I offered sympathy, encouragement, if nothing else."

"And what did he offer you?"

The finger had come to rest, and the voice grew quiet, calm.
"Attention. He paid attention to me. Not often, but more than I
was used to."

It took courage to say that to another man. I hoped Quarles
wouldn't have too much courage. I tried him: "And the money?
Did he tell you about the money?"

His serenity had been a fleeting thing. "What money?" The
voice was rasping, unsure again. "I don't know anything about
any money."

143

"Come on, Doctor—you were his best friend. It can't have escaped your attention that Dr. Platt came into a bit of good fortune this last year. The Porsche, the condo, the two-thousand-dollar gifts. I just want to know where he got it."

It took a second to sink in. "Why, that's not, that wasn't . . . " He gave it up. "I didn't do anything for it, you know. You have to believe me."

"Of course I believe you, Doctor. Question is, will the police believe you? Will Zoller? What did he want you to do for it?"

"Do they know?" His voice was a horrified whisper.

"No."

"Do they have to?"

"Maybe not. I have a job to do; *how* I do it isn't of much interest to Zoltec."

"You see, I can't lose my job. I can't. It just can't happen, do you see? I'll tell you what I can, but I mustn't lose my job." The finger started its dance again.

"Tell me. I don't have to tell anyone. I just want Platt, no one else."

He was eager to please, then, and his sad little tale came pouring out. Platt had bought him a cup of coffee from time to time, let Quarles listen to him carry on, but that was all until one day near the end of February. Quarles had been tired, despondent. Rachel had been assigned to work on the new process full time in January. Quarles had seen it as a rebuke, a reflection on his abilities; one too many. Now Bingham and Zoller paid even less attention to him than they had before; it was as though he'd been dropped from the team. Platt had approached him, said he seemed depressed, suggested a drink after work. They met at a bar, talked. Quarles poured out his troubles, his conviction that the new process would never work, that Zoller was losing it, growing desperate. Platt asked good questions, made appropriate observations. Then he made what was, to Quarles, a brilliant observation: Maybe it was a good thing the new process wouldn't work.

Quarles broke his monologue, stared at a spot on the wall only he could see: a window into a bar as it looked one night, months before. I brought him back. "What did he mean, 'Maybe it was a good thing the new process wouldn't work'?"

"I didn't understand at first, either. I had never realized that Dr. Platt and I were sympathetic, politically. I'm a liberal Democrat, Mr. Nichols. Does that surprise you?"

He made it sound like he had just walked into the Union League Club and announced he was meeting Bakunin for lunch. "Doctor, this is the only state in the country that went for McGovern. You want to shock me, tell me Nixon turned you on."

I'd meant to reassure him, but had only belittled his shaky claim to individuality. "Well, it hasn't always been easy, in a company that does a lot of defense contracting. It's done my career no good."

"I'm sorry. I didn't think." If that's what he needed, who was I to take it from him? "Anyway, you and Platt were on the same wavelength?"

Quarles gathered himself together. "Well, he just pointed out that it seemed pointless spending all that time and money just to stay ahead of our competitors. If we succeeded, all we would do is enable big business to replace more people with computers and machines, and then the others would try to pass us. It seemed so futile."

"And?"

"And nothing. We talked about that, and about lots of other things. That was all."

"What about the money? What about the two thousand dollars?"

"A few months later Bruce suggested we get together after work. For a few drinks, dinner. He said he'd treat. I accepted.

My wife and I, we don't go out a lot. We went to Anthony's Pier Four. I'd never been there before. I had cocktails, some wine. I'm not much of a drinker, I guess. We talked about the project. Dr. Ornstein was working like a madwoman, and she's terribly good. I mentioned that for the first time I had begun to think it might work after all. Dr. Platt said something again about maybe it shouldn't."

"The thing about putting people out of work?"

"Yes. That, and . . ." His voice trailed off while he decided whether or not to shed all his clothes. His need for humiliation won out. "And he could tell I was jealous. That I didn't want her to succeed where I couldn't. She was Zoller's pet, his protégée. They were together constantly. He didn't know I was alive, treated me like a lab assistant. And Bingham was ecstatic that she had been assigned to the project. I wanted her to be a failure, too. Failures hate successful people. Perhaps you didn't know that?" He leaned back until he was almost prone. I couldn't tell if his eyes were open.

"I know enough about failure. Then what?"

"He suggested . . ." Quarles gulped noiselessly. "He said maybe we should make sure it didn't work." The fat little hands kneaded the arms of the chair.

"And you said?"

"Nothing, at least at first. Then he asked me what I thought, and I didn't know what to say. I thought it must be the kind of joke I used to hear in school, so I laughed, like I had when I heard those jokes. Then he laughed, and the whole thing was over. I thought it was a joke, don't you see?"

"Did he say anything more along those lines?"

Quarles wiped his forehead with the back of his hand. "No. At least not for a long time. We'd go out for a drink after work every now and then, and I'd tell him how things were going, but he never said anything more about . . . you know."

"Until?"

Quarles squeezed his eyes shut and shook his head, as though trying to resist the memory. "Until two months ago. Bruce suggested we go to the Boston Garden to see a prizefight. He had some tickets. I'd never seen a prizefight."

"Well, you being a liberal and all . . ."

"It was disgusting, but . . ."

"But fun to sit with a buddy and a few thousand other guys, suck beer, and watch a couple stiffs whale away while you scream for 'em to kill each other." Quarles's priggishness was too tempting a target.

"No!" I met his self-righteous stare until he dropped his eyes. "I guess maybe so."

"And while you were sitting there Bruce came back to the project, and the idea of trashing it?"

"He never said that!" Quarles drew his hands up into fists and brought them crashing down on the chair arms. Flecks of dust hung in the half-light.

"But this time you knew what he wanted."

"It was different, this time.

"How so?"

"He asked how it was going. I told him that she seemed to be getting it. Dr. Ornstein, I mean. I said we might be just a few weeks away. And he said it didn't seem right—I'd worked so long on the project, done most of the work, and yet she'd get the credit and Zoltec would make millions off it if it worked and I wouldn't get anything. He said we should share in the profits, and at the same time help stop this crazy competition."

"He suggested you steal the technology."

"No! He said we should share it. That's not the same thing as stealing it. At least I didn't think so then." He sat up and looked at me for reassurance.

"And you agreed, and that's when he paid you the money."

"I didn't! I never agreed. I changed the subject. Each time, I changed the subject."

"Platt paid you two thousand dollars for changing the subject?"

"No! You make everything sound so dirty. We stopped off for a drink at some bar. I had had too much to drink. I told him some things—personal things. I had money problems, other problems. Bruce came right out then, asked me if I'd be willing to help him . . . share the project. He said there were people who would pay for that."

"And you agreed?"

"Damn you, I told you—I never did! I told him I wouldn't, I couldn't. I was afraid. I didn't want to lose his friendship, and I didn't want to lose my job. I said I wouldn't say anything, but I couldn't do what he suggested." Color flooded into Quarles's porcine face. Anger became him, but it faded too fast.

"The day after the fights, I came back from lunch, opened my desk, there was his check. I didn't know what it was for, I couldn't imagine. I went to Bruce, asked him what it meant. He said he had inherited a lot of money, more than he needed, and he wanted to help me. It made him feel good. I said I couldn't keep it. He said I'd been a friend, listened to him sound off, hadn't said anything to anyone, now he wanted to do something nice for me."

"It was hush money."

"He was just trying to help me!" His eyes dropped again. I hadn't seen such self-deception since I'd left Harvard. "I suppose you could look at it that way."

"And so you didn't say anything to anyone."

"Not because of the money. I wouldn't have . . . ."

I didn't get to hear what he wouldn't have done because a boy of around ten ran in and flung himself on Quarles, who wrapped his arms around him and buried his face in his neck. "Oh, Jimmy. Jimmy, Jimmy, Jimmy. Did Daddy's boy have a good nap?"

The boy mumbled a reply but it was too muffled to make out.

I looked at Quarles, but he had forgotten I was in the room; all his attention was focused on the child snuggled in his lap. He murmured the silly things parents exchange with their children until the boy realized there was a stranger in the room and squirmed around in his father's lap to face me with an intent, happy stare.

"This is Mr. Nichols, Jimmy. Can you say hello to Mr. Nichols?"

Jimmy tried to say hello but it didn't come out too well. He seemed pleased with himself for the effort, though, and his father praised him. "That's a good boy, Jimmy. Can you find Mommy now? Find Mommy and tell her you want breakfast. Something to eat? That's a boy."

The child climbed down and waddled out of the room. He had the Quarles build and was the spitting image except for the Down's syndrome.

I called, "Nice to have met you," although I'm not sure he heard me, or would have understood if he had.

Quarles made it easy for me. "It costs a lot, having a Down's child. A special school, terrible medical bills. Helen—that's my wife—it's been very hard on her. She hasn't had enough energy for both of us. Jimmy and me, I mean. I've been lonely for a long time. The doctors tell us Jimmy will probably die sometime in the next ten years or so. Maybe then Helen and I . . . Anyway, there are a lot of expenses. I can't lose my job. I should have told someone what Bruce wanted, I know I should have, but I can't lose my job. For God's sake, I'm begging you; please don't tell anyone I knew what he planned. I didn't, don't you see? I really didn't." Tears coursed down his fat face.

I wanted to leave as badly as he wanted me gone, but there was one more thing I had to ask. "There is one other thing, Doctor."

"What? I've told you everything I know, I promise I have."

"This is something else. Something I asked Dr. Bingham during our meeting the other day. Remember? I asked if Platt had been a careless man, since leaving that sheet of paper behind was careless. Without it, we probably would never have gotten onto him. Bingham brushed it aside. What do you think?"

He snuffled again, then thought for a second. Then he shook his head, decisively. "No, you're right. Bruce was meticulous. Everything in place. I was surprised, too."

"Well, we all make mistakes. I'm going to forget about yours. I hope you feel better soon."

I started out, until he called softly to me, "You know, he was still my friend. He asked me out for a drink again even after I said I couldn't help him. He wasn't just using me—he *liked* me."

I let myself out and drove off.

CHAPTER 21

Rachel picked up her phone on the second ring, and I was as tonguetied as I'd been the time I'd asked Cynthia Foreman to the Princeton Triangle. Rachel took the pressure off by ordering me to be over in ten minutes or risk the consequences. I made it in eight, using every second of it to try and figure out how I could tell her.

The door opened, and I pushed the ugly need aside as soon as I saw her. "Howdy, stranger. Like my new outfit?" She struck a gunfighter pose, hands on hips, legs apart.

"Ulp." She moved into my arms. She was naked. Then we both were.

Afterward, Rachel started to talk before I was ready for the other thing. "I don't know—I just feel so . . . free. Seeing my father this time was so much easier. I found myself really talking to him, for maybe the first time in my life. Putting the past behind me at last. I haven't felt like this in years. Ever, really." She snuggled against me. "I thought of you the whole time I was with him. It's because of you he seemed so much more like a person, a lonely old man who loved me, not a symbol I despised."

"You're getting used to lonely old men who love you?"

Her hand stroked my cheek. "Silly man. I mean that thanks to you and these last few days, I was able to see my father, really see him. Before, I was always Rachel Ornstein, woman of purpose. Everything serious, relentless, analytical—including my attitude toward my father. Then you came along."

"Pretty incredible, huh?"

"Pretty weird. But nice. Easy. Ever notice how people around Boston seem to put so much . . . *thought* into living? I mean everything—jobs, politics, relationships. Everyone's so *earnest.*"

"Constricted sphincters."

"Huh? Oh! Yes, exactly. Well, anyway, you're not."

"Better that way."

"Much better. I don't ever want to go back to the other way. Let's go on having fun together, Nase. Let's go on being together?"

I stared into her eyes. The fun time was over. "There's something I've got to tell you."

"That I'm the most sensuous, desirable, beautiful woman you know?"

"That too, but something else." I cupped my hand behind her head. Her breast rose and fell against my forearm. "Something not so nice."

Her face fell and she took her hand away. "What, Nase? What is it?"

I told her, leaving out only sorry stray bits that she didn't have to know. When I finished, she was crying. I brushed away the wet under her right eye.

"When did it happen?"

"I found him yesterday. Last night. I think he was killed the night before."

She clutched at me and let out a long, low moan that cut deep. "I killed him. You were right to want to tell him. You warned me and I didn't listen and I killed him." She circled herself with her arms and started to shake.

"No! Stop it!" I squeezed her neck until the shakes subsided into slow, rhythmic gasps. "No way, Rachel. You can't blame yourself. I know what I told you, but that's not what happened. A customer didn't kill Platt."

Her head shook me off. "How can you say that? You told me . . ."

"Because it doesn't fit." I pulled away, slowly, then leaned back against the headboard, rubbing her shoulder. "First, why would the buyer kill Platt now? The Japanese hadn't had time to find out they had been ripped off, even if the sale had gone through, which we don't know. Second, if this Matsami wanted to kill Platt, to cover his tracks or avoid having to pay for the stuff, he wasn't going to rely on finding a shotgun on the wall. He'd have come prepared."

She looked up slowly. "But then who did shoot Bruce? What do the police think?"

"I don't know what the police think. I haven't talked to the police."

"You haven't told . . . ?"

"What can I tell the police? That after I stalked the man for several days, using an assumed name, I burglarized his cabin, then came back to say 'Gotcha' and there he was, dead, and I just happened to be holding the murder weapon in my hand when that guy walked in?"

She wiped her nose. "But it's the truth, isn't it?"

"Honey, there's scientific truth, which is what you look for, and then there's cop truth, which is what I know about. Your truth is pure—you *want* to find problems with your theories. You scientific types want them to stand up under all conditions. A cop's different. He works with makeshift truth: if it looks guilty, walks guilty, and smells guilty, it *is* guilty. Problems with the theory, a few inconsistent facts? Hey, defense lawyers gotta live too, don't they? Let them worry about the holes. It doesn't have to be true in some metaphysical sense; it only has to close a file. I'd fill the bill just fine. If I were still a cop, I'd bust me."

"But why would they think *you'd* want to kill Bruce?"

"We're here, aren't we? Jealousy, revenge, who knows? Cops make connections. You and me in bed together, that's connection enough. And you can't imagine how they'd come after you. I've got to keep you out of it."

"You don't have to think about me. I made my choice."

"Wrong. Anyway, I've got to keep me out of it, which is job enough. My ex-wife is depending on me." I reached across Rachel and snubbed out the smoke. "That's why I'm going to get the person who did do it."

"Are you serious?" She sat up, stared for a second, then nodded. "You are serious."

"Cross my heart."

"But how?"

"I've been trying to find out more about Platt's activities these last few months." I told her about the checkbook and Quarles's story.

"But what does it mean?"

"I don't know. Maybe nothing. Maybe just that Platt had his own agenda all along. And maybe, just maybe, someone else was in on that agenda. Someone who paid Platt a lot of money. Someone who didn't want your project to succeed. Someone who didn't want Platt to talk."

The back of her hand brushed her eyes. The dead look was gone. "Don't you think maybe you're getting a little paranoid?"

"Well, as I see it, I'm the most likely perpetrator of a homicide. I've never been in this position before, but it does tend to make one paranoid. Which is why I decided I better take this case."

She sniffed and a smile broke through. "Okay, let's do it." Her arms reached for me.

I pushed her away. "Negative, negative, negative. You stay out of this. As far away from me as you can get."

"Wrong, Nase." Rachel pulled me back. "Positive, positive, positive. No farther than this. Ever. We'll do this together."

"Why, damn it? Why do you want to get involved?"

"Umm." Rachel's teeth were sharp at my ear. "Because I *am* involved. You said the police would come after me." She pulled me over onto her. "And because I love you."

CHAPTER 22

Rachel's furnishings were simple but uncompromising, the surroundings of someone who had done without, would do without again, before accepting the second-rate. It was a comfortable apartment that said the tenant was comfortable with herself.

I joined her in the kitchen and poured us each a glass of wine. She had showered and tied her hair back with a ribbon and looked sixteen in a pink satin robe. I hated the idea of going back out, but time was something I didn't have a lot of. I told her what I had in mind, and that it was something I had to do alone.

"No way. I'm going with you, and that's final."

"Damn it, you're not. It's too risky."

"Risky? You didn't mind when I helped you burglarize his cabin. How's his office any different? Besides, what about his condominium? What's the point of searching his office if you're not going to search his condo? Tell me that."

"I just have a hunch, that's all. After you've been in this business as long as I have, you get pretty good at developing hunches."

"That's the craziest . . ."

"Besides," I admitted, "I figure I can crowbar my way into his office and no one will know until tomorrow, if then. I'd be caught in two seconds if I tried that at his condo."

"So that's it! Some hunch. I thought you guys were supposed to be able to open a door with just a bobby pin or a toothpick or something. And you only search places if you can kick the door down?"

"I never got very good at lockpicking. It's harder than it looks on TV. Anyhow, I just think the office makes sense. I've got . . ."

"I know, I know—you've got a hunch." She snickered. "So do I." She got up and walked into the bedroom.

"You're not coming, you know," I called out. "I don't care what you say. And there are lots of detectives who can't pick locks. Lew Archer couldn't pick locks. Hercule Poirot couldn't pick locks, for Chrissake."

I could hear her bustling around the bedroom. After a few minutes she came out dressed in a dark wool sweater and jeans that fit like the skin on a seal.

"Now look—I told you . . ."

She extended her right arm toward me, her hand in a fist. "I just remembered I had this. Look." She opened her hand and I reached out and took the key that lay on her palm.

"What's this?"

"The key to Bruce's condominium. He gave it to me just before we . . . he . . . broke it off. I never used it."

"Well, great, babe." I tossed it up and caught it. "Of course, you're still not coming."

Rachel's hand snaked out and caught the key at the top of the second toss. "Then no key."

. . .

"Don't blame me if you wind up in the Woman's House of Correction." I pulled the Scout into Platt's parking place.

"Don't you see? This is perfect. If someone does come along, we entered perfectly legally. I can tell them I came to get something I left with Bruce."

"The only thing you tell them is you want a lawyer. Then start saying the Rosary."

We didn't pass anyone on the way up. The key was rough, but after a little jiggling it turned and we were in. I locked the door behind us.

Rachel started to feel around on the wall for the light switch but I stopped her until I found the cord to the curtains and pulled them shut. The first thing I saw when the lights went on was the LeRoy Neiman over the phony fireplace and I didn't have to turn around to know what the rest of the place looked like.

"What are we looking for?"

"Something that will tie Platt in with somebody else. Letters. Checks. Something like that. I don't know what, to tell the truth. We'll know it when we see it." We were both whispering. "I'll take the bedroom. Why don't you start with that?" I gestured toward the bookshelves on the far wall. There was a pull-down door in the center.

I drifted into the bedroom. After half an hour I had been through every drawer, bedside book, and the closet.

Platt was a fan of self-improvement tapes of the "Power Over Others in Just Sixty Minutes" sort, which he apparently listened to while poring over the philosophical rantings of Ayn Rand. None of it surprised me. Nor did it make me a whit wiser. I retreated to the living room. Rachel was curled on the couch, reading.

"Found something?"

"I don't know. I don't know what all this means."

She handed me a handful of flimsy paper forms from a local

brokerage house. They were written in cramped computerese, all acronyms and abbreviations. At first they were as inscrutable as hieroglyphics. Then I noticed something. "Hey—what's Zoltec's symbol on the stock exchange?"

Rachel looked up from her stack. "ZT, I think. Why?"

"Look—is that it?"

She stared for a minute, scrunching her eyelids. "Yes, I think so." She took the form. "But what's it mean? Was Bruce buying Zoltec stock?"

"According to that key at the bottom, this shows a sale, not a purchase. This one's from last February; see if there are any earlier ones, where he might have been buying the stuff."

Rachel leafed through the pile, then looked up and shook her head. "They're all the same, from last winter through April —all sales, if that's what that means."

I took the stack and flipped through it. A hundred here, two hundred there—four, five thousand dollars at a crack, but the total was only eleven hundred shares, coming to slightly more than forty-five thousand dollars; that was a lot more than I had ever seen at one time, but substantially less than Platt had had in his bank account.

"These all?"

She nodded.

"Let's get out of here." I jammed the stock forms into my pocket and we slipped out.

CHAPTER **23**

I shook him by the shoulder, but might have been prodding a dead walrus. He finally opened eyes as latticed with veins as an old man's calves.

"Come on, Buckbean, wake up—you've got company." He was slumped in a spavined armchair in the basement, a volume of medieval Irish poetry open across his lap. From the looks of the bottle of Jameson on the table next to him, that wasn't the only volume he had consumed.

"He's been doing this every night, Uncle Nase—ever since Mom went away. We're worried about him." Moira, Bucky's oldest daughter, stood in the doorway.

"Well, he's not a pretty sight, I'll grant you that, but he's got the constitution of a bull moose, and I don't think whiskey can hurt someone of Irish extraction." Bucky started to nod off again and I slapped his face lightly a few times. "Don't worry about that, honey," I said to Moira. "That's how the Irish show affection." I patted him again.

"What you need, Buckeen, is something to take your mind off your troubles. Dr. Ornstein and I—" his eyes started to close

160

again, and I clapped my hands next to his ear—"have brought you that something."

He lurched to his feet, shaking his head violently, and made a sound like rhinos rutting on the veldt. Then he noticed Rachel and segued into a bow. "Good evening. You're known by the company you keep, you know. Bucky Hanrahan." His immense hand swallowed hers.

"Rachel Ornstein. So I've been told."

He lumbered to a slop sink in the corner and stuck his head under the tap, then slurped a gallon. He turned back to us, water and hair cascading over his forehead. "To what do I owe the honor?"

"We've come to plumb your vast knowledge of the securities markets."

"Bit late in the evening for picking stocks, don't you think, Boyo? Or is it Ms. Ornstein who's hankering to take a flyer?" He drew out the "Ms." so it sounded like a bee in flight.

"It's Dr. Ornstein, Buckshot, although I'm sure she'll consent to Rachel if you'll tell us what we want to know, which has nothing to do with picking stocks."

"I see, I see. Well, draw near and give head. 'Scuse me— heed." He drew up two chairs, then plunged back into his upholstered ruin.

"The question is, Buckeye, what're these?" I handed him the sheaf from Platt's apartment.

He fingered through them slowly, his large lips mirroring some inner conversation. After a few minutes, and without looking up, he reached out and grabbed the bottle of Jameson. When he passed it over it was an inch lower.

Finally he looked up. "They're confirmation slips from a brokerage house."

"We can see that. What I mean is, what's all this gibberish mean?" I pointed at the rows of numbers and symbols on the top sheet.

Bucky fanned through the stack, then looked up.

"Some guy named Platt's been active, in a small way, in Zoltec. So what? Why're you interested in this guy?" He looked from me to Rachel, then back again.

"That gentleman is no longer among us." I took a pull on the Jameson bottle, then passed it to Rachel, who started to refuse, then shrugged her shoulders and took a belt.

"Oh, yeah? Too bad. He won't get to enjoy the money."

"How do you know he made any money on these sales? Don't you have to know what he bought the stock for, first? He could have lost money, couldn't he, depending on what he paid for it?"

"Fool—who said he paid for it?"

Rachel and I exchanged glances. "Forgive us, Buckberry. Are you saying he stole this stock?"

"Of course I'm not saying he stole it; I'm saying he sold it short. He borrowed Zoltec stock from the broker, shares one of their customers had in his account, and had them sell it, betting that it would go down and he could cover by replacing it at a lower price. Done all the time. Completely legit."

"Come again?"

"Beejasus—there must be Albanian shepherds who have a better understanding of the economy. Selling short is very simple. You think some company's stock is going to go down in the not distant future. Call the company Ace Widgets. Selling at ten bucks a share. Okay? With me so far, Nase?

"Doesn't matter why you think Ace's going down, mind you —maybe you think their earnings'll be lousy, their CEO's a bum, anything. So you go to your broker. 'Harry,' you say, 'I'd like to short a little Ace Widgets. Say, ten thousand shares?' 'No problem,' says Harry, 'got 'em back in the vault.' If Harry doesn't, he just borrows them from a broker who does. Got it?"

Two nods prompted him on: "So Harry the Broker takes ten thousand shares of Ace Widgets, which some customer owns

162

and has left with Harry, and Harry sells them. Now since I know, Nase, that you gotta take off your shoes to count to eleven, let's walk through this. Ten thousand shares. Sold for ten bucks a share. What's that come to, Nase? And no cheating, now."

It was his party. "A hundred grand."

"Good. Very good. Top-drawer mind, young Nichols is. Here." He thrust the bottle over.

"So then Harry takes his commission and gives you the change, to do with as you please. Say, ninety-five grand, okay?"

Rachel cut in: "But when do you pay it back?"

"Ah—the hundred-thousand-dollar question. But first, what is it you owe?"

"Why, one hundred thousand dollars."

"False!" A fine mist of Irish whiskey settled on us. "You don't owe money. You didn't borrow money. You borrowed *stock*, and you *owe* stock. To be precise, you owe ten thousand shares of Ace Widgets to Harry, who in turn owes them to their owner, his customer. Nobody cares how much you have to pay for them. Except you, that is—and you care plenty. That's the whole point."

"I get it," said Rachel. "You're betting that the stock's going to go down before you have to replace it. Your profit is the difference between what you sold it for and what it costs when you replace it." She beamed the way she must have the day she mastered the Second Law of Thermodynamics.

The veil lifted. "Hey, that's pretty neat. Why, I could try . . ."

"Don't even think it. It works the other way, too."

"Huh?"

"Old saying in the trade: 'He who sells what isn't his'n, buys it back or goes to prison.' See, when you shorted the stock, you also agreed to replace it any time ole Harry asks for it. No reasons given, no excuses, no ifs, ands, or buts."

"So?"

163

"So say you guessed wrong. Instead of going down, Ace announces unexpectedly good earnings. All of a sudden everybody wants some, and the price goes up. Say to twelve bucks?"

I nodded, beginning to get it. "And so the broker calls and . . ."

"And so Harry the Broker calls, shmoozes you a little, asks about the kids, the little woman, tells you the one he just heard about the elephant and the ant. You know, ant's walking through the jungle . . ."

"Thirty seconds, you're a dead man, Buckshot."

"Okay, okay. So then Harry lays it on you. 'Good buddy, I love you like a brother, but I got this nervous feeling, see, Ace is maybe going up for a while, not down, like you thought. We let this ride, and pretty soon you're gonna hafta sell your house, you wanna replace ten thousand shares Ace Widgets. So how about covering now, only lose about twenty grand. Plus commissions, of course. No hurry, I trust you, know you're good for it. This afternoon will be plenty soon. Have a happy day.' Get it?"

"I guess that's your way of saying there's a little downside risk, huh?"

"Cover at fifteen, net loss of five. Cover at twenty, net loss of ten. Cover at thirty . . ."

"All right, all right; I get it."

"Short selling is for the big boys, or at least the brave ones. Stick to something safe, like no-limit poker. With short sales you guess right, you make a bundle. But you guess wrong, and oh, Momma, somebody's gonna own your fillings."

"How can you tell he was selling Zoltec short?"

"By the bowels of Christ, man—are you blind? It says so, right here." He stabbed at the middle of a form with a meaty forefinger. All I saw was a bunch of initials that could have meant anything. I took his word for it.

"And I'll tell you something else; the late Mr.—" Bucky glanced down at the papers—"Platt picked well."

"How's that?"

"Faith, it's no wonder you don't have two nickels to rub together." He squinted at Rachel. "He told you that, has he? That he's one step away from food stamps? Now I, on the other hand, could care for a fine-looking woman like yourself in the style to which she is entitled." His eyelids settled in a hooded leer. "And I have need of a woman."

"Buckberry—remember yourself, old lad. What do you mean, he picked well?"

Rachel was tugging at my sleeve and whispering we should leave. Bucky laid a large paw on her forearm. "No, no—that's all right; a momentary lapse." He patted gently. "Don't you see? He sold these shares short last winter and spring, while Zoltec was way up. Now he, or his estate, seeing he's among the departed, can go in and cover—pick up the shares he owes the broker, to replace the ones he borrowed and sold short— for a song, since the stock's collapsed after that rumor got out. Nice little bit of change on the swing. Lucky widow."

Moira came in with coffee. "So that's it," said Rachel. "Don't you see?"

I didn't see much, and said so.

"This explains everything. Bruce had done this shorting thing with Zoltec. He probably read about it in some get-rich-quick book. It's just the kind of thing he'd love. Then he got worried the shares were going to go up because of the new process, so he tried to get Winston Quarles to sabotage it. When that failed, he stole it." She beamed at us both.

I ignored Bucky's glare. Now he knew I had left him hanging out to dry. "And then, because the whole thing had worked so well, he killed himself?"

Rachel's face fell. "Um—I didn't think of that. But couldn't it . . . ?"

"God damn it, Nichols, what the hell's going on? What was stolen? Who killed himself? What the hell are you two talking about?"

I shook my head. "There's more to it than that, I know there is. What about Altschuler?"

"Nase, honey, who's this Alt—?"

Bucky broke in. "Have you lost your mind, Nichols? This morning you said Altschuler didn't mean diddly. Now you're saying he does? Does that mean Zoller's tied in to something? What's . . . ?"

I pressed on. "Anyway, Platt didn't get that condo and that Porsche on this money; no way. Buckass, can you do us a favor?"

"Oh, what's the use? I'll be on my deathbed and you'll be asking me for favors. Sure, sure; what do you want?"

"Is there any way you can find out if these are the only shares Platt shorted? That's all."

"That's all? For Christ's sake, when will you tell me what's going on?"

"Soon, Buckbasket—soon. Promise. Now, you'll do this little thing for me? Tomorrow, maybe?"

He nodded resignedly. "I'll try. I'll ask around. No promises."

"What a sport. Seriously, Buckhorn, I appreciate." I dropped my voice. "Things haven't improved with Deirdre, huh?"

He couldn't look at me. "She's left that group. She and her friend have gone to the Berkshires. There's a commune there, something like that. She wants more time to sort things out."

I patted him on the shoulder, then gave him a hug before either of us realized it. As we left the room he called softly, "They're vegetarians. It's a vegetarian commune. Vegetarians and . . . lesbians." We were almost out the front door when I heard the old Bucky roar: "God damn it, she always loved meat!"

CHAPTER 24

Early the next morning I had the broker's forms laid out on Rachel's dining table, next to the appointment calendar and checkbook. I'd pushed away the breakfast dishes, taken a piece of paper and drawn three columns, which I'd headed "Trades," "Appointments," and "Deposits." Down the left-hand margin I'd written dates, starting in January. When I had every piece of data entered I started looking for a pattern. I couldn't see one. Rachel brought me a fresh cup of coffee and stood looking over my shoulder. I threw down my pencil in disgust.

"I've got to be leaving for work, Nase—how's it going?"

"Nothing. The only connections I see are the sun-coming-up-after-the-rooster-crows kind."

She looked at the sheet for a minute.

"Nase, honey?"

"Um?"

"What's that you've written across from January twelfth?"

I read it off: "See A—seven-thirty. Forty-seven Brighton Ave."

"But that's Dr. Zoller's address."

"Dr. Zoller?"

"Sure. That's where he lives. Forty-seven Brighton Avenue."

The penny dropped.

"Nase? What is it? What are you thinking? And what did your friend mean last night when he asked you if Dr. Zoller was tied in to something. Something to do with someone named Altman, Almond, something like that? What's going on?"

I looked up. Rachel was staring at me.

"You aren't going to like this."

"Let me decide."

"You'll think I'm silly."

"We're already there."

"You'll accuse me of jumping to conclusions."

"You just did. Enough. Let's have it."

"You're sure?"

"I'm sure."

I leaned back and shut my eyes. "All righty. You asked for it." I took a deep breath. "I think Zoller's a bad man. A very bad man. I think he's up to something with Zoltec stock."

" 'Up to something'—what does that mean?"

"I'm not sure how he's playing it, but he's got some scam going, illegal trading, that kind of thing."

"Nase, that's ridiculous."

I told her about the Zoller/Altschuler connection and the leak about the stolen technology.

"But that doesn't mean Dr. Zoller did anything wrong."

"I think he's involved in an insider-trading scheme, Rachel. That's a felony."

"Dr. Zoller? You are talking about Armand Zoller?"

"The same."

She settled into the chair next to me and put her arms around my neck. "I see. Care to tell me how you got there?"

So I did. I strung everything together, seeing where the pieces fit, thinking out loud and trying to see where it all went. Rachel stared at the floor, a half-smile twitching her lips.

"Let me be sure I get this. You think Bruce went to Dr. Zoller's apartment Friday evening, January twelfth. On Monday, January fifteenth, Bruce makes the first of several large bank deposits. Ergo, they're connected? The rooster crows and the sun comes up?" She flapped her arms like wings: "Cock-a-doodle-doo!"

"Okay, try this one—would Zoller have had Platt over after work? Were they friends?"

"No, but that doesn't mean . . ."

"Altschuler's the key. Why would he have leaked the news about the technology being stolen if Zoller weren't behind it? And if he is, then he's sure as hell playing a game the rest of us aren't in."

"*If* he did, *if* he did. You'd make a terrible scientist—you're always leaping to conclusions."

"I told you you'd say that."

"Well, it's true."

"Damn it, I've . . ."

"Dr. Armand Zoller, world-renowned head of Zoltec, paid Bruce Platt to try and wreck the most important project his company has underway. When that fails, he has Bruce steal Zoltec's technology, then sets up an elaborate scheme to get it back, meanwhile leaking the fact that the secrets were gone, through some man named Altschuler? And he does this to make money, even though he cares less about money than any man I've ever known?"

"That's the broad outline."

"And why did he want to wreck the project, then have the secrets stolen? How does that make money?"

169

"Well, I told you I haven't filled all the holes yet."

"You know something?"

"What?"

"You *should* be worried about the police—compared to Dr. Zoller, you look like the Boston Strangler."

"That bad, huh?"

"Nase, Dr. Zoller's a . . . a scientific saint, for heaven's sake. Zoltec's his life." Her voice softened. "Besides, he's a kind man, Nase—a good man. He's been wonderful to me. Like a . . . well, like a father, I guess. I don't believe for a moment he'd do anything dishonest. It's just crazy. You're way off base."

"But . . ."

"And anyway, do you want to know something?"

"What?"

"I don't care if he did do something with Zoltec's stock. It's ridiculous, but even if he did, it didn't hurt anyone, did it? Leave it alone, Nase—please?"

"You're thinking with your emotions, Rachel. You're letting your . . ."

"My hormones—is that it, Nase? Going all soft because I'm a woman? God damn it, just because a woman tells a man he's full of shit doesn't mean her emotions are . . ."

"All right, so you don't think much of that one. Try this out. Suppose he did hurt someone, Rachel? Suppose the stock thing was just the beginning."

"What on earth are you talking about?"

"Suppose securities law violations are the least of Zoller's sins. Suppose he murdered Platt. Should I leave that alone, too?"

She pulled as far away as the chair allowed. "You've lost your mind. That's even more insane."

"You heard me. I think he murdered Platt. Killed him. Blew him away, to keep him from talking."

Rachel uncoiled, started to climb out of the chair. I grabbed her wrist, pulled her back, hard. "Rachel, are you going to tell me Zoller couldn't have gotten my call, decided he couldn't risk Platt talking to me, then gone up there and killed him?"

She snatched her arm away and rubbed her wrist. "Don't, Nase—don't do that. Ever again."

"I'm sorry." I reached for her hand. She started to pull it away, then let me take it. I rubbed the soft spot between her thumb and forefinger while I pulled her to me. "I am sorry. But you can't tell me that. Because he could have. Because he did. I'm going to prove it. I'm not going to take the rap for him."

"But he couldn't have. . . ."

Her shoulders quivered while I turned her to face me. "Stop. Think. Forget what you think you know about the man. Tell me why he couldn't have gone to Platt's place and killed him. Tell me you know he was bowling with the guys Monday night. Tell me he had Sox tickets. Come on, Rachel—forget about how much you care about him, tell me why it's impossible."

She kept her eyes locked on her lap. "Because . . ."

"Because why?" I lifted her chin until our eyes met.

She started to speak, bit it off, dropped her eyes again. "No, I can't tell you why it's impossible. It's only 'my emotions.' Just a woman's emotions. That's the way we are, isn't it?"

"Stop it—you know I don't think that. All I know is, last January Platt went to see Zoller, and a lot of things started then. Platt comes into money, gets a new car, a new apartment. He takes up with Winston Quarles. And he tells you . . ."

"Yes, Nase, he tells me. Believe me, I remember."

"A lot of strange things, Rachel, and I think they began with Platt visiting Zoller, and ended with Zoller visiting Platt."

We looked at each other, then came together. "Let's find out, Rachel. Let's find out what happened then."

She buried her face in my shoulder. "If you think we should; if we have to." She let me rock her until the tears stopped.

CHAPTER 25

They came for me at my apartment while I was shoving clothes into a bag to take to Rachel's. There were two of them, and I would have known they were cops even if they hadn't double-parked their squad car out front. The black one looked like he was about twelve; the other was the size of a Cape buffalo and looked as friendly.

"Mr. Nichols? Mr. Nason Nichols? Cambridge Police." The big one flipped a shield. "We've got a warrant for your arrest."

My options could be reviewed quickly because there were none. I let them in, then assumed the position against my living-room wall. I wondered what they knew, and what I could say without implicating Rachel.

After a few minutes my arms got tired and I looked back over my shoulder. The black cop was looking through my record collection; his partner was staring at a Blake engraving on the wall.

"Hey, guys?"

Neither looked around. I tried again, louder: "Uh, gentlemen, please—may I put my arms down? This is tiring."

The Blake admirer spoke without looking around. "That's

really something, huh? I always did dig the Romantics. Bet that
Blake was doing some kinda drugs, wouldn't you say?" He
looked over his shoulder. "Say, why're your standing like
that?" Then it dawned on him. "Oh, Jeez—you thought . . ."
He turned to his partner, who had slipped a record out of its
jacket and put it on the turntable: "Adrian. Hey, Adrian! You
know what Mr. Nichols thought? Why, he thought we was
gonna brace him." He drifted over as his partner lowered the
tonearm. "What'ya got?"

"Shhh, Wally—listen to this!" Paul Robeson's voice filled
the room. I went back to the kitchen, made a cup of coffee, and
read the personal ads in the *Phoenix*.

They got through "Mammy's Little Curly-haired Boy" and
"Joe Hill" before Adrian wandered back. "Boy, he had some
kinda voice, didn't he? Criminal what they did to him." I nodded.

Adrian started poking through my cookbooks, humming
"Water Boy."

"Think we ought to go?" I asked. It took a few minutes to pry
him loose, but finally I had my coat and toothbrush and escorts.

By the time we pulled up in front of the courthouse I had
decided to get hold of Bucky, get him to front the funds for a
good criminal lawyer. After that I'd decide if my best chance
was full disclosure, saving only what I had to hold back to try
to keep Rachel out of it. I hoped that would be doable.

The arraignment judge was an Irishman with a purple face,
who was taking pleas and setting bond for the sea of pimps,
hookers, shoplifters, and generic scuzzballs with as much passion as a supermarket clerk stamping prices on cans of peas.
"Calling Jose Fonseco. He here?"

"Come with us. We'll get you in next." Adrian beckoned to
me and started elbowing his way to the front. He wore an
apologetic smile as he pushed aside the throng of derelicts
crowding the bench.

"They don't mind if we go ahead—they'd rather be here than out on the street." I nodded reassuringly; cops in Cambridge carry a heavy load of guilt. Finally we stood before the bench and Adrian handed up the warrant for the judge to read.

The judge skimmed the arrest warrant. "Okay, next up is Nason Nichols. Mr. Nichols, you're charged with a violation of Title Seven, Massachusetts Revised Code Section 5-904, a misdemeanor in the third degree; how do you plead?"

I started to respond, then realized what he had said. "A misdemeanor?" A misdemeanor in the third degree carried a maximum sentence of thirty days; Platt might not have been a model citizen, but I couldn't believe that the Commonwealth was willing to let me waste him for no more time than I'd do for peeing on the sidewalk. "Beg your pardon, your honor, but what was that charge?"

He glared at Adrian and Wally. "Didn't you men show him the warrant and advise him of his rights? You know what that can cost you?" The courtroom stilled. The two policemen looked crestfallen.

"No, no—they did all that; it's just I . . . forgot."

"You're not on drugs, are you? Or hallucinating? Do you want a doctor?" His Honor looked distressed.

"No. I'm fine. I just forgot what I'm charged with. Could you remind me?"

The judge looked dubious but opened the warrant again. He cleared his throat. "It says here you owe for back alimony. You're charged with criminal nonsupport." His mouth drew into a scowl and his wattles shook as he read down the page. "Oh, Jesus—you gotta go before Judge Tyrone. You poor bastard. You're not going to take off, are you? I gotta set bail." The judge couldn't have looked more sympathetic if I had stood before him with a terminal disease.

"No, I won't take off."

"You better plead not guilty, get a good lawyer. I dunno,

maybe you can cut a deal." He made it sound improbable, but I nodded and he wrote something on the warrant.

"Right. Pleads not guilty. Trial will be held before Judge Tyrone." He leaned as far over the bench as his girth would allow. "You sure you don't want to take off? Maybe go visit friends in another state for a while, something like that?" His great bulk shivered.

I shook my head. It was doubtless good advice, but not an option.

"O–kay." He sounded even more uncertain of my sanity. "Released on your own recognizance. You've been notified of your hearing date. Next!"

Adrian and Wally gathered around me outside the courtroom. "Hey, thanks for covering for us. We sure blew it." Adrian seemed ready to cry.

"No big deal."

Wally looked uncertain. "The judge was right, you know; that Judge Tyrone really has it in for men. Not that we don't deserve a lot of it," he added. "I mean me and Adrian, all the cops, we gotta take these gender-sensitivity classes. Like, we've been chauvinists and all, and we gotta learn better. But still, Judge Tyrone . . ." He sucked in his breath. "Do you think she maybe goes too far?" His warm eyes looked at me as though I were already but a memory.

Adrian and Wally drove me home in silence. As I was shutting the car door Adrian made a sudden, jerky gesture with the fingers of his right hand. At first I thought it was a vulgar gesture; then I realized it was the sixties' peace sign. They were a pair of relics, and I was touched. "Peace, brothers," I murmured. I raised my fist.

"Right on!" They were smiling as they drove away.

. . .

Bingham thrust his hands into his lab coat and pursed his lips. "I really won't be able to talk very long; I've several meetings today, one in just a few minutes."

"Good of you to make time at all, Doctor. I have just a few questions."

"Very well. I suppose we should step in here." He turned into an empty office just off the anteroom and flicked on the overhead light.

"I take it you've made no progress?"

Bingham's tone was offensive but his question reassured me; it meant Zoller hadn't told anyone I was off the team. "Not yet. I was hoping you could give me a little information that might help."

"I'll see. What is it you wish to know?"

"I wonder if you could think back to the beginning of the year. Did you notice any changes in Dr. Platt around then?"

"Any changes?"

"Right. New clothes, different attitude, change in personal relationships; that sort of thing."

"I really don't see . . ."

"Please, Doctor; it's too complicated to explain, but it could be important."

"Oh, very well. Last January?"

"Right."

He stared at a spot on the wall behind my head for a few seconds, then shook his head. "Not really. You must understand, Platt was never a particularly pleasant person to have around; he had a better opinion of himself than his performance warranted. I always regretted hiring him. But changes? Last January?"

"Or thereabouts."

He gave it another few seconds but I didn't think his heart was in it. "Not that I can recall."

"Oh. Too bad."

"Is there anything else? I really must be going."

"Particularly busy day?"

"Every day is a busy day, but Dr. Zoller's out, so I have to cover a meeting I hadn't planned on, in addition to everything else. If you'll excuse me?"

I was almost out the door when Bingham caught up to me. "One second." He looked over his shoulder at the receptionist, then beckoned me over to the wall. "You asked about changes in Platt, early last year?"

"Right."

"Well, I do remember one thing. I don't know if it's the sort of thing you mean, or what it could have to do with anything."

"Yes?"

"It was in February. Your mentioning January threw me off." He glared at me as though I'd tried to trick him.

"Sorry. Please go on."

"I remember because it was Washington's Birthday. One of the technicians who had been with the company since the beginning was retiring, and we gave a little party for her. Platt was there, and Dr. Zoller took time off from work to look in. There was champagne, Dr. Zoller and I said a few words, that sort of thing."

"Yes?"

"I'm getting to the point. Anyway, Platt got up and gave a toast. Just a few words, but they seemed to be directed at Dr. Zoller, and I thought they were quite insulting."

"How odd. What did he say?"

"Something like 'how lucky we should all feel that the grand old man of science and industry would tear himself away from his new toy to come play with mere mortals.' It didn't make a lot of sense, really, but the insolence was obvious. I wanted to fire him on the spot."

"Did you tell Dr. Zoller that?"

"I did."

"I take it he didn't agree?"

"He said Platt must have had too much to drink and it wasn't worth making an issue of."

"Very charitable."

"Very. In hindsight, regrettably so."

The guard I'd met on my first visit was back in the gatehouse. "How you doing, Gene?"

The big man lowered his newspaper and looked down at me through the open window. "Just about able to sit up and take nourishment, I reckon." He chortled. "How about yourself?"

I unclipped my visitor's badge and handed it up to him. "Don't ask."

"You do look a little tuckered. Gotta watch those late nights, Mr. Nichols."

"Wouldn't trade my hours for Dr. Zoller's, tell you that."

"You can say that again. Phew—ee; wouldn't work his hours, no sir."

"Guess he deserves a few days off every once in a while."

He glanced at the wall clock and pulled the visitors' register over, then wrote in the time opposite my name. "Why, sure. Sure he does. Don't take many, I can tell you that." He passed the register down to me to sign and I pulled it through the car window. "Got a pen, Gene?"

He turned and I dropped the register on the floor. "Damn." As I bent over to pick it up I flipped back three days, to Monday. "Sorry—got stuck under the seat."

"No problem."

There it was—"Dr. Z," out at 4:42. I turned the page and signed next to my name. "Here you go. Got a little dirty. Sorry."

"No problem."

He pressed a button and the electric gate opened. "You take it easy now."

"You can say that again."

"Okay—you take it easy now." He slapped the counter and bellowed. His big face beamed at me as I pulled out of the lot.

So I'd been right: I'd called Zoller, and he'd left within half an hour. I pulled into a gas station and called Hanrahan, but his secretary refused to put me through. Bucky had been looking "a little peckish" and was catching Zs on his office floor. I exacted a promise that she would deliver him to me at Jacob Wirth's at five o'clock.

Rachel would be at work for several more hours. That left a hole in the day until I got together with Bucky. The best way to fill that hole was by seeing if I could trace Zoller's movements after he left Zoltec on Monday. I drove back into town and swung down Washington Street.

CHAPTER 26

Tony was propped against a wall next to a placard. When I got near enough I could read the hand-lettered caption under the cutout of a busty, naked woman: "The Scarlet Whore of Boston." Underneath, in similar letters: "Boston the Great, the Mother of Harlots and Abomination of the Earth (Rev. 17:1–7)." A tin dish holding change rested on the sidewalk. Tony was wearing a dirty off-white clerical collar over a black T-shirt and was waving a Bible that said "Provided by the Gideons" on the cover. The penguins were gone.

"Hey man, fugya been?"

"Not too bad, Tone—yourself?"

"Ah, mezzo-mezzo, like the guineas say." He extended his right hand in a rocking motion, palm parallel to the ground and fingers splayed, as though playing boogie-woogie. He wore gloves with no fingers.

"When'd you get religion? What happened to the penguins?"

"Fuggin' penguins. Wasn't for the numbers, I'd fuggin' have ta eat 'em. So I start thinking, see, all these white dudes got a religious hustle, like? See 'em on the tee-vee, preachin' and a-prayin' an' tellin' folks to send 'em money?"

"Yeah?"

"Yeah. So I figure, what the hell, same folks doin' all that prayin' Sunday morning down here, fornicatin' and whorin' an' lustin' after the flesh the res' of the week, this ole black boy gone get hisself a little of that action, know what I mean?"

A coffee-colored hooker in red satin short shorts and white, calf-high boots twitched by and gave us the look. Tony caught her eye: "Repent, ye sinner, ye who whore after other gods. Repent or be damned!" He waved the Bible in the air.

"Hey, baby—how you been?" The hooker cocked a hip and gave us a smile.

"I be livin', Lucille; youself?"

"Gettin' by, gettin' by. Where them toys you had? I likes them."

"I outta that business. I in the sin business."

"Oh, honey, you ain' in the sin business. Us girls in the sin business. You an ama-ture. Now I gotta go do some a that business. Be seein' you."

We watched her saunter into a bar, under a sign promising "Girls—Completely Naked—Live Sex Acts."

"She may have a point there, Tone; even Jesus would have found this a tough crowd to work."

"Shee–it." He picked up his dish and shook it.

"How'd you like to move your operation for a day or two? Be fifty bucks in it for you?"

"Hey, man, what'ya tryin' to move? It's cool, know what I mean—smoke, books, iron, I don' give a shit. 'Cept smack. Won' truck with that shit. Jus' another way honkies got to kill black folk."

It was nice to know Tony was a man of principle. "Nothing like that, Tony. It's perfectly legal." His face fell. "I need to find out if somebody was out and about Monday night.

Thought maybe you could poke around, see if he stayed home. Maybe the guy keeps his car in a garage someplace, you could find out when he brought it in. Or just find me his garage, I can do the rest. That sort of thing."

"Hey, I'm not exactly built for speed, know what I mean? Think I oughta bring a piece, case he spots me?"

"I don't think that'll be necessary, Tone. I've seen how you get around. You could run circles around this guy—he's got a few years on you."

"What's it all about, man? Guy puttin' it to somebody's ole lady?" The thought of sin lit his eyes; maybe he *had* found his vocation.

"Can't tell you, Tone—it's on a need-to-know basis, if you follow me? Came to you because you're one of the few guys I know can handle this kind of thing quiet like. Want to do it?" I threw him a wink.

"Hey, yeah—tha's cool, man. Tomorrow morning." He thrust out his hand and we shook.

I pressed twenty dollars on him for cab fare, gave him Zoller's name and address and Rachel's phone number. He promised to call as soon as he knew anything.

I looked back once. Tony was shouting at a sailor and his woman: "Give yourself up to Jesus, before you burn in hell . . ." He saw me looking and gave me a thumbs up and a grin.

I beat Bucky to the bar. I had time to kill and gambled a quarter to see if I could run down another connection. It took a little doing but I finally got through to Hairston at the police station.

"Hal, my man, my main man—how you doing?"

"Not too bad, Nase—how about yourself?"

"Just about able to sit up and take nourishment." I did my best imitation of the Zoltec guard's chuckle.

"Huh?"

"Never mind. Hey, speaking of eating, how'd you like to take the little woman out to dinner—on me?"

"What, you gonna pay your tab, I can take her to McDonald's maybe?"

"Hal, Hal—always the kidder. Hundred bucks, take her to Hugo's, Legal Sea Food. Whatever."

"Wendy don't like seafood."

"Jesus Christ, Hal. Take her to the Hilltop, feed her beef until she gags, I don't give a shit. Point is, I need a little favor, there's a hundred bucks in it for you."

"A hundred bucks? I dunno. What's the favor?"

"Nothing. Got a couple of phone numbers, want to see if they made any long distance calls the last few days. Piece of cake."

"How the hell do I know?"

"Hal, ever thought of being a meter maid?"

"You want me to call the phone company, huh?" He sounded hurt.

"Bingo! Give that man the hundred-dollar first prize."

"How do I explain it? Suppose they let someone here know I asked?"

"Never happen."

"Yeah, but what if?"

"So you think maybe Wendy's getting some on the side, you want to see if any of these guys been calling your house. Make something up."

His voice fell, then strangled in his throat. "Hell, Nase— how'd you know?" He sobbed. "Did Kevin say something? He swore he'd never . . ."

"Huh? Oh, Jesus, Hal, I didn't mean—Christ, I'm . . ."

His whinny cut me off: "Gottcha, asshole. Now, what're the numbers?"

"Terrific, Hal—you ought to be on Carson." I pulled out my notebook and reeled off the phone numbers for Zoller, Zoltec, Platt's condo, his office and cabin, and Altschuler.

"You said a couple numbers. That's six, and one of them's in New Hampshire."

"So sue me. A hundred fifty bucks."

"I'll hafta call New Hampshire, don't know if they'll cooperate."

"Threaten them. Two hundred. That's the limit, you bloodsucker."

"What're the dates? An' don't tell me the last five years."

The last year would have been perfect, but quick and dirty would have to do. "Say, Monday and Tuesday. That should do it."

"This could take a while."

"I'll call back tomorrow."

"How about settling the tab?"

"The check is in the mail."

"Screw you."

"Love to Wendy."

I walked back to the bar. Hanrahan was propped against it, reading a folded copy of the afternoon paper. "Afternoon, lad. You're looking chipper."

He turned a weary eye on me. "Softly, softly—I think I had a stroke last night."

"Nonsense, my man. All you need is a liquid restorative, and I'm just the man to provide it. *Garçon!*" I snapped my fingers for the bartender. "Gin, and plenty of it—with a whisper of vermouth. My friend needs therapy. Make it two while you're at it."

I turned back to Bucky. "Well, big guy—got anything for me?"

"Just a second." He waited until the martinis arrived, then drained his. He shuddered, and for a second I was afraid he was having a seizure. Then he snatched my drink and tossed it after the first. Another spasm shot through his body, and he shook like a dog having a nightmare. "That's better. Wow!" He gestured for another set, then hoisted himself onto a stool. "Oh, my. Now, what was that?"

I climbed up beside him. "You remember what we were discussing last night?"

"Of course I do. Just 'cause the machine hurts, doesn't mean it doesn't work. You wanted to know how big your guy was into Zoltec."

"Well, have you found out? Did he buy any more than we knew about?"

"He didn't *buy* Zoltec stock. I told you that. He sold it short —borrow it, sell it, eventually replace it. Think you got that?"

The new martinis arrived and we each took a pull. "Just get to it, Buckler—had Platt done any other selling, buying, whatever? I don't give a shit. What else had he done in Zoltec?"

He gave me a calculating look. "Oh, what the hell. No, the late Mr. Platt hadn't done anything else in Zoltec stock, least as far as I could find. Does that satisfy you?"

So Platt hadn't raised his money, at least most of it, by selling other people's Zoltec. I drifted off in thought.

"I found out what he did buy, though."

"Huh? What?"

He slid over a copy of the *Globe*, tapping a two-inch squib at the bottom of the second page. "The farm. You didn't tell me this guy bought the fucking farm two days ago. What the hell are you dragging me into?"

"I told you he was dead. '*New Hampshire State Police seek unknown assailant in slaying of Hub resident . . . burglary apparent motive . . . Dr. Bruce Platt . . . solid leads but no suspects. . . .*' "

"You told me he was dead. You didn't tell me how he got dead."

"I didn't want to weigh you down with details. Besides, I don't know how he got dead." *No suspects.* That had a nice ring to it. *Solid leads* didn't.

"Details! You got me calling all over Boston, trying to get an angle on this guy, you say it's a detail I'm inquiring about a stiff whose killer the police are looking for? I cashed molto chips for you today, and what do you think the guy I call thinks when I start asking questions about his newly wasted, ex-customer? He's probably on the horn to the cops right now."

"Let me read this, will you? I've got to think." It didn't read any better the second time.

A taunting voice reached me. "I can tell you who *has* been getting a lot of action in Zoltec, though. A whole lot of action."

It snapped me back. "Who?"

"Uh–uh, uh–uh, uh–uh. No more free ride. First you tell Uncle Bucky. Everything."

"I gotta hand it to you, Nase; only a man of exceptional talents could have gotten into the shit like you have. I mean, it takes real skill to get hired to do a little routine industrial security work, then turn it into a race to hang a homicide on one of Boston's preeminent scientific entrepreneurs before the cops hang it on you. And pro bono, too—nobody's paying you a nickel. I feel proud to know you. Look sharply, my man!" He rapped his glass on the bar: "Another round for my stellar friend here. And, so he won't be drinking alone, one for me as well."

"What I'm hoping, my loyal chum, is that a few pieces will fall into place and I'll be able to nail this down. Something stinks with Zoller. I just can't prove it—yet. And now you owe me, remember?"

"Me owe you! That's wonderful. But what the hell—we've never kept score, have we?" He leaned over so that he could whisper to me, "I didn't find out about any more trading this guy Platt did, but I did find out an outfit called Bahamian

Holdings, Limited, shorted a *lot* of Zoltec over the last year or
so. I mean a *ton*."

I didn't see why it mattered what some company I'd never
heard of had been doing, but Bucky cut me off when I said so.
"Wanna guess who the partners are in Bahamian Holdings?"
He hunched his head down and gave me a sly look.

"Come on!"

"Yep—the boyhood pals themselves."

"But how. . . ?"

"You'll see. Anyway, this partnership of Zoller and Altschuler made megabucks when the stock pancaked. Nase, they
knew it was going down. But do you know what's really beautiful?"

"What?"

"Yesterday Bahamian Holdings started *buying* Zoltec. *Huge*
blocks of it. Nase—they rode it down, and now they're riding
it back up!"

"I don't get it."

"Don't you see? They shorted it when it looked like this new
process wasn't going to work. Then they tried to make sure it
wouldn't. Now they're buying it up because they know it *does*
work, after telling the market it *doesn't*. They're stone, fucking
geniuses!" He put his face inches from mine.

"But how do you know this Bahamian Holdings has anything to do with Zoller and Altschuler?"

He nodded. "See, anybody can guess right, short a stock
that's on the way down. But when I heard the same group's
buying it back, while the rest of us can't get out fast enough—
that starts me thinking, that's somebody with more balls than
brains, or it's somebody who knows something. It's somebody
who know something, who could that be? Zoller and Altschuler, they'd be in a position to know something—better'n anybody. So I decided to test that theory."

A nervous feeling crept up my spine. "What do you mean? How'd you test your theory?"

"Easy—I asked Zoller."

The hand reaching toward the martini jumped, knocking the glass to the floor. The old bartender silently mixed another and pushed it across.

"What do you mean, you asked him? Are you totally round the bend?"

"Well, I didn't exactly ask him point-blank; would've been a little too pushy, don't you think? Nope, I was a *little* more roundabout." He spun on the barstool, doing a three-sixty to face me again. "Like that!"

"Listen, Hanrahan, I'm . . ."

"I called him, and we had a nice chat. He was very forthcoming. A fine gentleman." He started to giggle, mostly silently but with bursts of spray. I was losing him fast.

"Please, Buck; just hold on for another minute. Exactly what did you do, beside let Zoller know I'm on to him?"

"Y'know, Nichols, your problem is you're a solecist." He thought for a second, then shook his head. "Naw, that's not right. I mean, you think everybody's thinking about you." His upper body started rotating around the axis of his barstool like a gyroscope running out of steam.

"Solipsist. *Now what the fuck did you say and what the fuck did he say?*" It was the way you'd ask someone in a coma where he hid the money.

"Don' need to shout, Nase." His huge left arm did a round-house and landed across my shoulders, sandwiching me against the bar and almost forcing out lunch. "You're my buddy. Always have been, always will be. Only guy I can trust. Only person." He started to go lugubrious, then snapped back. "I called him, tol' his secry—secretary, I was calling from Bahamas. Like this: 'Doctor Armand Zoller, please; Reggie Fynch-Jones heah, Bahamian Ministry of Commerce.' "

It wasn't what I was expecting and I almost jumped out of my skin; it sounded like Olivier playing Othello. Bucky laughed: deep, pealing chuckles, and then I got it—it was the black guy who did the "un-cola" ads a few years ago, a pure Islands sound.

"Sure, and the Irish have a gift for mimicry. But get this—it worked!" Bucky belched. " 'Scuse me. Anyhow, Zoller comes on the line and says, 'Zoller here.' " Suddenly, ersatz Kissinger was sitting next to me, as basso and guttural as the real item.

" 'Fynch-Jones, Doctor. Commerce, don't y' know—matter of Bahamian Holdings. Sorry to bother, what?' See, Nase, I kept dropping my voice, wiggling the cord so I gotta lotta static, played my dictating machine next to it—musta sounded like I was calling from Antarctica. Had the old kraut shouting by the time I finished."

He drew up his chest and went back into character: "Mere detail . . . course, old boy . . . required to confirm . . . bloody great nuisance, really. . . .

"Vat? Vat? I can't hear you. Vy are you calling me?"

"Question of registration fees, some such, hem? Chappies from tax section thought you gents might want to prepay; save a few quid, all that. Mean to be helpful, 'spose, but more trouble than it's worth, hem?"

He broke off. "Whad'ya think, Nase—your old buddy Bucky gotta future as a dick?" He ruminated a second. "My dick gotta future?" A scowl flitted across his face, then vanished. "Get ready, my man, 'cause here comes the high note. Whad'ya think your client said next?"

"Whatever you say, Buckmeister—you've got the floor."

"Betcha ass. He said, 'I've nothink to do with that. Call Altschuler.' And he hung up on me! 'Call Altschuler!' Get it? 'Call Altschuler.' See wha' that proves?" And for a second he looked positively happy, just before his head hit the bar.

CHAPTER 27

I wondered when Tony would call, or if he would; he wasn't exactly Mr. Reliability. I kept these pointless thoughts going while I putzed around Rachel's apartment, then made my own call.

"Top o' the mornin' to you, Buckup. Well rested, I trust?"

"She's coming home." He spoke in the dolorous tones of a priest at a baby's funeral.

"Who? Deirdre? Hey, that's terrific. When?"

"She called this morning. She wants to come home Sunday: 'To share in the pain of her sisters, striving for self in the midst of a misogynistic reality.' Sounds like fun, doesn't it?"

"Oy."

"My very words. I'm considering self-immolation. What can I do for you beforehand? I assume you want something; you always do."

"Nothing that's not within your power to give. In return, I'm going to tell you how to become a rich man."

"I've already done it."

"Done what?"

"Bought twenty thousand shares of Zoltec—in a street name, of course. What did you think I'd do, after what you told me last night? Did it first thing this morning. We'll make a tidy pile in a few months or so. Isn't that what you were going to suggest? Of course, if you have some scruples about the securities laws, let me know. I'll keep it all for myself."

My last felonies had been for Zoltec; Zoller owed me one that was all my own. "As always, I'll be guided by your sage financial counsel. But since I've shown you the way to riches, the least you can do is call back to your friend at the brokerage house. One teensy factoid missing." I told him what I wanted to know. He bitched and moaned, but agreed to give it a shot, then get back to me.

"Thanks, bubba. It'll work out with Deirdre."

He paused. "I don't think so."

" 'Course it will. Give it a little time, spend some time together. Take a trip someplace. Just the two of you."

"That may be difficult."

"Why? Moira can take care of the younger kids. Hell, I'll take them."

"The kids aren't the problem."

"Well, what is, for Christ's sake?"

"She isn't coming alone."

"What?"

"She's coming with her 'friend.' It was take it or leave it. I'm supposed to move into the spare bedroom. What could I do? The kids need to see her." He paused. "I need to see her. I just didn't need to see her 'friend.' " He rang off.

I sat down and stared at the phone. If Deirdre had taken a running start and tried to place-kick them over the goalposts at Harvard Stadium she couldn't have done a better number on Bucky's privates. Why? Men and women had fallen out of love for a million years; all of a sudden boredom had to have an ideological underpinning? I shook my head in bewilderment.

Why had I escaped, found a woman content to see me as a symbol of . . . nothing? Just a person, not a metaphor or a cause, not a member of a class, not a historical way station? It seemed so unfair, holding a person to account for the real or imagined iniquities of an entire group, when we all have a full-time job just paying for our own.

By the time I finished these musings I had worked up a savage rage: at Brenda and Deirdre, at the scabrous Lukacs-Skizenta, at the judges who handed out people's justice as defined that week, at Boston's whole rabid rat pack of humorless, obsessed ideologues who viewed every human activity or relationship in political terms, and who had as little feeling for the individuals who failed the litmus tests as Lenin had.

There's nothing like a fully consummated morning hate for kicking the adrenal gland into action; when the phone jerked me out of my reverie I was ready to eat the receiver.

"Is that you, Nase?"

"Of course it's me. Why are you whispering?"

"This line secure, Nase? Ya check it for bugs?"

"Huh? Oh, yeah; it's okay. I just swept it. Whatya got, Tone?"

"I couldn' find out if this dude was home the other night, Nase; kind of neighborhood he live, I start askin' folks his whereabouts an' I be in the slam *quick*, you dig?"

"Sure. I didn't think of that. Thanks anyway, Tone."

"No—wait, man. I found it, Nase. Found where the old guy keeps his car. Don' know whether he in or out that night, but maybe you can?" He gave me the address.

"That's great, Tone, great. You follow him?"

"Never saw him. So I cruise aroun', stop in every ga-rage near his place. Tole 'em I was looking for this ole white-haired guy, name Zoller, bought some books from me and drove off without payin'. 'Wha' kinda guy steals from a vet, lost his legs servin' his country?' I say. That gets a listen, see? Some guys ast wha' kinda car he drive, I say I dunno, seein' as how I'm

192

legally blind from the same round what blew my pins across a hootch. Dumb fucks never say, then how come I know wha' the old guy look like, see, 'cause guys don' like to embarrass crips. Finally I come to this one place, pull my number on this dude, he say 'Missa'—thas how he talk, Nase, swear ta God— 'Missa Zoller, he too uptight have truck with trash like you.' An he laugh. I couldn' bee-lieve that nigger, Nase—mofo field han' laughing at me, calling me trash? I shoulda fragged him. You gonna waste that mutha, Nase?"

"Not unless he gets rough with me, Tony. Hey, thanks a lot; you did your job."

"Shee–it, I doubled what you gave me, Nase; all them guys wanted books. Same with them hot little honky broads comin' outta school. I may set up there regular; don' have to worry 'bout bein' hassled by that sumbitch Reilly, know what I mean?"

The first storm of winter was moving in and I pulled my coat around me as I inched my way through the gloom of the garage toward a tiny office in the back. A large black man almost filled the room as he sat staring at a four-inch television screen. A red-hot electric heater sat on a bench next to him.

"Excuse me."

The man didn't lift his eyes, but after I tried a few throat clearings, he grunted, "Uh?"

"I'm looking for a car. Got in a little scrape. Supposed to do an estimate." I pushed an insurance adjuster's card through the slot at the bottom of the ticket window.

The attendant finally looked over, first at the card, then at me. "Don' know nuthin' 'bout that. Wha' you wan'?"

"Gentleman named Zoller. Keeps his car here. Gotta check the fender damage."

"Whassis name?"

193

"Zoller. Armand Zoller. Z–O–L–L–E–R. Older gentleman, white hair."

"Don' know if they be anybody heah by tha' name." Now he was looking at me. I reached into my pocket, pulled out a ten and plopped it next to the card. It disappeared into his hand as he swiveled to look at a clipboard. He swiveled back to me. "Green Buick Cent'ry. Number seventy-six."

I made a show of wandering back to find stall seventy-six, but of course Zoller's car was out. I walked back.

"You sure Dr. Zoller parks his car back there?"

"Tole you so." He didn't look up.

"It's not back there."

"Never say it was."

"Supposed to have been in an accident Monday night. His car out Monday night?"

"Would'n' know."

"You keep records of when customers bring their cars in and out?"

He cast a last look at the screen as it faded into an ad for soap, then turned toward me. "You the Man?"

"If I were the Man, would I have given you the money?"

He thought about this. "Naw, you ain' the Man. Wha' you wan', an wha' you gimme?"

"I want to know when this guy Zoller brought his car in Monday night, and I'll give you twenty bucks." I pushed the money through.

"Worth more than tha'."

I turned to walk out. I was almost to the garage entrance when I looked back. He was fiddling with the television, his face a few inches from the screen.

"Thirty."

He waited until he had the fuzzy picture just right. "Fifty. Fifty dollar . . . Boss." It wasn't a bad smile.

CHAPTER 28

A titan of industry, me
But not yet as rich as can be,
So out of my flat,
And shoot Dr. Platt,
And back in my bed by three!

Ta-dum. It took most of the drive back to Cambridge, and a little poetic license—Zoller had logged in to the garage at 3:12, but twelve's a bitch to rhyme, so I was pleased with my ditty when I accelerated past a fatally hesitant Peugeot and slid into the last parking space on my block.

The girls were out in the quadrangle again, their rosy cheeks witness to the edge of winter that had slipped in overnight. A football had taken the place of the Frisbee, and the little white dog wasn't around. On an impulse inspired by my run of luck, I crossed the street and approached the girl closest to me. My "excuse me" brought her to a wary halt, eyeing me and the others and ready to bolt if I started to act like the kind of man her mother had warned her about.

"Yes?" The others stopped where they were, laughter fading to a nervous silence.

"Sorry to bother you. My name's Nichols; I live across the street." I pointed over my shoulder.

"Yes?"

"I think I saw you out here the other day with a dog. A little white one?"

Her poppy-blue eyes widened and a smile spread across her freckled face. "Oh! Have you seen her? Have you seen Madame Bovary?" The other girls stepped forward eagerly, faces lit with expectation.

"Madame Bovary?"

"Professor Englander's dog. The little white dog that was out here the other day. Isn't that the dog you meant?"

"Oh—I see. I didn't know her name. Yes, that's the one."

A tall, redheaded girl said, "She teaches French literature." I assumed she meant Professor Englander and not the dog; even at Harvard there are limits to affirmative action.

"Where is she? Did you find her?" Blue Eyes again.

"No. I'm sorry. I haven't seen her." The choral "Ohhh" sounded like Fenway when a Sox rally dies in the ninth. "I'm looking for another dog. A little gray one. I thought they might be . . . friends. Maybe you've seen them together?"

"I'm afraid not, at least I don't think so." Solemn headshakes all around.

"When did Madame Bovary disappear?"

"Last week, while Professor Englander was in class."

The others chimed in: "From her pen." "In the back of Rawlings House." "There was a hole dug under the fence." "Friday, maybe."

"She was penned up because she went into . . . heat." The blue-eyed girl blushed and I wanted to hug her but settled for "I see."

"You're looking for a little gray dog? Sort of . . . like, ratty-looking?" It was a tiny girl in a fatigue jacket, who'd been sitting reading on the dorm steps.

"Like, real ratty-looking." Titters of appreciation for this bon mot. "Have you seen him?"

She twirled a lock of stringy hair and thought for a second. "I think maybe so."

Collective skepticism: "Oh, Claire, you're just . . ." "You have not . . ." "She's always . . ."

Her hand dropped. "I did. I saw him last Friday." Claire looked smug.

"How can you . . . ?"

"Yes, I'm sure—I remember now." Her look turned inward. "I was coming back from Charlie's." Thin lips drew up into a smile.

"Well, *of course*."

"Yecch!"

"What time *was* it, Claire?" Many snickers.

Claire's pug nose thrust higher. "The dog was trotting around the corner there." She pointed toward the dorm.

"Near Professor Englander's . . . ?"

"Like he was heading back there."

"How can you remember?" The blue-eyed girl's voice held wonder, but no disbelief.

"I saw the dog and . . . it reminded me of something." Claire looked at me uncertainly, suddenly shy.

"What?" The blue eyes grew as big as plums.

The stringy-haired girl looked around and a defiant look settled on her face. "I saw that ratty little dog walking back there like he owned the world and I thought . . . I thought, why, that's the way Charlie struts when he's, you know, walking into the bedroom." She shrugged.

"*God*, Claire."

"Make me *puke*."

"I'd rather be a nun."

197

I thanked the girls and left. The last thing I heard was the blue-eyed girl's sweet voice: "What's it really like, Claire?"

I was slamming the pieces into place like Willie Mosconi running the table. The phone was ringing as I let myself back into my apartment, and I knew it was Bucky even before I picked it up.

"You got it right, buddy; Bahamian Holdings was organized just when you thought—last February. The Bahamians are tight-lipped, but that's a matter of public record. That must be when they started shorting Zoltec, huh?"

"Bet on it." I was breathing hard, and not just from the dash to the phone.

"How'd you know?"

"Lots of things happened last winter; busy time for Herr Zoller."

"What next?"

"One more call, I think, do things up brown."

"And then?"

"Pay the gentleman a visit. Lay things out, give him a chance to take his best shot at them."

"Poor choice of words. Why not just call the cops?"

"Will, if I don't get anything from Zoller. Fact is, the case against Zoller still contains a lot of surmise. I can prove opportunity, and we've got some idea of motive, but it would take a lot of solid police work to fill in the gaps. You know, haul in Altschuler for questioning, look for people who might have seen Zoller's car in New Hampshire, that sort of thing. The cops going to roust two of Boston's leading citizens when they got me at the scene, murder weapon in hand?"

"I'll serve as a character witness."

"Exactly. I think I better get Zoller to 'fess up, instead."

"Hope so; hate those all-night vigils by prison gates. Need anything from me?"

"I think not, but thanks."

"A first. Not wanting anything from me, that is." His voice softened. "Kidding, buddy. You've helped me keep my mind off things. Thank you. You might also be careful." Then there was just a buzzing.

Hairston was still on duty, and after a few false starts I got through to him at the precinct house. "Hey, guy, what's the word—got what I want?"

"Who? Nase?" His voice dropped to a whisper. "Nase—is that you?"

"None other, pal. You practicing obscene phone calls again?"

He stayed with the whisper: "Nase, what the hell have you done?"

"Hey, come on—everybody gets behind on their alimony."

"Nase, whattaya talking, alimony? I'm talking homicide, Chrissake. It just came over the wire. Pick you up, suspicion of. That guy in New Hampshire."

This was not good news. "Little misunderstanding, Hal. Now about that favor . . ."

"Nase, are you nuts? Where are you? You better come in."

"Look, Hal, I come in now you're going to be sending me Christmas cards at Concord quite a few years to come. I'm no killer. You know that. I think I know who is, but I need that information to tie it down. Please?"

"Nase, you gotta be nuts. I gotta report . . ."

"Hal, you've got nothing to report. I'm off this phone in thirty seconds, either way. But I'll make you a deal; you do this for me, within twenty-four hours I'll either turn over the man who did it, or surrender myself to your custody. Either way, you're a hero. How about it?"

I was just about to hang up when he bit. "There a bunch of 'em. Got a pencil and paper?"

. . .

There wasn't time to stop and talk to Mrs. Serafina, since I could expect visitors any second. I pulled my .38 out from a drawer, slipped it into the shoulder holster, and slipped on an old sport coat.

I was reaching for the handle of the front door when I glanced through the glass panel and saw McGinty talking to two men in a beige Ford idling in front of the building. Then McGinty pointed toward the building, and after a few seconds the car slid into the open space by the hydrant. McGinty stepped back onto the tree lawn and glanced up at my front window.

The men, trailed by McGinty, marched in tandem up the front walk. They did not look like they'd have much interest in my record collection.

I bolted for the steps off the lobby that led to the basement, then hid in the stairwell until I heard footsteps going upstairs. I was out the door and hailing a cab on Mass. Avenue three minutes later.

A few unfriendly grunts settled the cabbie back into sullen silence while I looked over the numbers Hairston had read off.

Both Zoltec and Altschuler generated a lot of long-distance calls. Hairston had given me almost seventy, but when I got done circling the ones I'd been looking for I felt as though I'd been there when they were made.

I'd called Zoller about four-fifteen. The thought of Platt's reaction when I told him what we'd done had thrown Zoller into a panic. There it was, Zoltec to Altschuler—the sixth number down.

Then the next call, a few minutes later, *to Platt in his cabin. Got to talk to you, little problem.* Four-thirty. Then Zoller had left Zoltec.

The final call, nine-twenty Tuesday morning: *Zoller, back at*

Zoltec, to Altschuler; everything's under control. They hadn't needed to make any more.

As the cab pulled up in front of the car-rental agency I didn't have much doubt I had the picture pretty well filled in. It was time to talk to Dr. Zoller.

CHAPTER 29

"I won't waste time. I haven't so much to waste, I think. You want money, I suppose? That seems to be what most people want. I have never understood why." The voice, a few days before so rich and compelling, sounded diminished, halting.

I'd told Zoller's secretary that I needed to talk to him about business opportunities in the Bahamas. That had won a visa back to the conference room.

"I wouldn't knock it; for a guy who learned to covet mammon late in life, you haven't done badly for yourself." I advanced on the bar and found a light switch. "Mind if I have a drink, Doctor? I've been on the go a lot recently." I poured a scotch.

He waved his hand dismissively, whether at my comment or my request I couldn't tell. I lifted the glass in his direction. "Nice. Want to tell me about it?"

"It gives me no pleasure; you tell me." He lowered himself into an armchair and waited impassively. In the faint light from the bar his head seemed cadaverous, the skin tightly drawn. It was an old man's head.

"Fair enough. You hired me, you're entitled to my report." I retrieved a crumpled pack of cigarettes, lit one, and hiked myself onto the directors' table.

"A year ago or so you figured Zoltec was played out. The company was losing its technological lead, about to become just another one of the gang. You'd been working for a breakthrough, but it wasn't there. Maybe you were tired of living like a monk; maybe you just decided you were a burnt-out case, a has-been, and you'd get some while the getting was good. Doesn't matter." I watched the smoke play in the light from the bar.

"You had this old buddy, Altschuler. Your only real friend, I'd guess?" Zoller nodded, almost imperceptibly. "You shared your fears. He listened, he sympathized, and then he suggested a way you could recover your feeling of control. You'd get rich. If you can't be smart, be rich. Hell, a lot of guys think rich is better than smart. You can buy smart; you can't buy rich."

"Leon had only my interests in mind. He wanted nothing for himself. He is my family." Zoller spoke softly, the tone that of a father gently correcting a precocious son.

"Sell Zoltec stock short. That was Altschuler's suggestion. Borrow a bunch of stock, sell it short, make a bundle when the company settled back into the pack."

"So many men profited from my abilities; was it so wrong that I should seek something for myself as those abilities faded?"

"Let's leave right and wrong alone for the time being, Doctor."

"Very well. We will leave right and wrong alone, as you say. Please continue."

"Anyhow, you and your buddy were shorting Zoltec like hell wouldn't have it when the unexpected occurred: Dr. Ornstein got put on the project, had her own reasons for needing to make it work, and it started to look like she would. If she did, Zoltec's stock would go up, not down, and you and your 'family' would be looking at big liability. How am I doing?''

He gave a rasping chuckle, deep in his throat. "Go on." Once again the dim light deprived him of substance so that I felt I was hearing from a shade.

"You knew you couldn't just stop the project, couldn't cancel it just when it started to show signs of hope, or Truscott or Bingham and the others would wonder what was going on. So you decided to hire a monkey wrench—Bruce Platt."

"He was such a . . . contemptible man. His hatred of me was so obvious, yet he was so ready to take my money when I offered it to him." Zoller's voice grew thinner, as though he were disappearing around a corner. "I could never see what . . ."

"You could never see what Rachel saw in him? I never knew the man, Doctor, but there's no figuring human chemistry."

I got up and poured a little more in my glass. "You had Platt pay you a visit, and he agreed to do what he could to torpedo the new process. And he was as good as his word, wasn't he? Got all palsy with poor, pathetic Dr. Quarles, tried to get him to intervene. But Quarles turned out to have a little character —not a lot, but enough—so that didn't work." I looked around for an ashtray, then ground the butt out on the bar.

"All of a sudden it was short-strokes time; you couldn't stall any longer, and Truscott insisted you had to issue a press release about the new process. That would have blown the stock price through the roof, and you and Altschuler with it. So you paid Platt to steal it."

Again Zoller's mouth opened to reply, but instead of the words I expected there came a wheezing, asthmatic "hnnng, hnnng, hnnng."

"Are you all right, Doctor?"

The wheezing slowed, although the death's-head grin remained plastered to his face. His hand fluttered with a hint of the former imperiousness, and I took it as my cue to continue.

"Of course, it wasn't enough for him to steal the secrets; somebody had to *know* they were stolen, so that the new process couldn't be announced."

Zoller started to say something, then shook his head and waved me on.

"The irony is that it was Platt's greed that put me onto you. If he hadn't decided to take a little flyer short-selling Zoltec stock himself, even though you were already paying him generously, I probably never would have stumbled onto what you and Altschuler were up to. Has that occurred to you?"

The eerie wheezing once again poured out of Zoller's mouth, but I realized it was cackling laughter I was hearing, an old man's mirth that bordered on hysteria. It rolled on and on, peals of it, echoing through the cavernous room. "Oh, Mr. Nichols, Mr. Nichols—I just can't let you go on this way. It isn't fair of me. Here I thought you knew. You know nothing, nothing."

"You have a nice sense of humor, Doctor, but the joke escapes me. Maybe some more of your fine whiskey will help." I dipped into the bottle again.

Zoller brought himself under control. "Help yourself, Mr. Nichols, help yourself, but you won't find the explanation for my amusement in there. I assure you, I knew nothing about Platt's investment activities. I'm amused because you have such a limited view of irony. You don't begin to appreciate the possibilities."

"Why don't you tell me about them, Doctor? I'd love to expand my sense of irony. It's been pinching recently."

"Very well, Mr. Nichols. First, though, I'll join you in a drink." He rose slowly and advanced toward me and the bar, his feet slipping across the floor in the moon walk of the very old. Dr. Zoller had gotten very old, very fast. He poured a glass of sherry, then lifted his glass in a mocking toast. "To you, Mr. Nichols; you have contributed the perfect ending to a farce." He chuckled once, offered a bow, and sipped.

"You were going to tell me about irony, Doctor?"

The tight, white skin crinkled into a laugh that collapsed into a choking cough. "Oh, Mr. Nichols—there's no way to go on with this without letting you into the whole secret. You simply cannot appreciate the . . . symmetry of nature without hearing the rest. You are nowhere near reality." He stopped and sucked in air through pursed lips, as though in pain, then shuffled over to the nearest chair and lowered himself into it. The laughter had drained him, and he began taking shallow, panting breaths. His eyelids fluttered as though two moths had settled on his face.

"You think I did these things, sold this stock, for greed. Do you know why I find that amusing?" His voice cracked and I had to lean forward to catch his words.

"Come on, Doctor, it's late and I'm tired and drunk and I believe you may be dying. No more enigmas. Please."

His head flopped back against the chair back and his eyes closed so I wasn't sure if he had heard me until he whispered, "As you say: no more enigmas."

His voice strengthened and took on the tone of someone telling a story. "I reached old age having known only one love, Mr. Nichols. That love was science. Knowledge, learning—call it what you will. We courted, flirted, mated, yes—procreated —for fifty years. I had no others. And then do you know what happened to me?"

I shook my head.

"Think. What so often happens to old men with fickle wives? And no wife is as fickle as inspiration, Mr. Nichols. It will be your constant companion, your loyal helpmate for decades, and then—one day it's gone. To another, younger man. Because you see, we age, but insight, inspiration—it doesn't. It is always young, always looking for someone young enough, strong enough, to enjoy its favors."

"Where's this . . . ?"

"Please, Mr. Nichols. There is a point, I assure you. One you will find most amusing, I think." I settled back, realizing he wouldn't be hurried.

"For many years I had had in mind a new kind of computer chip, a quantum leap over everything that had gone before. A few years ago I committed all of Zoltec's resources to it. We got nowhere. Months passed, and there was no progress. Always before I had been able to advance the science, develop the technology, and others could only imitate. Now I started getting reports that others, competitors, were gaining ground, closing the gap."

He winced and pressed his hand to his chest. A fine sheen of sweat had broken out on his forehead.

"Do you want anything, Doctor?"

"Only to finish, thank you." I waited while he took shallow, panting breaths.

"I gradually realized that the fault was mine. Things that had been easy for me before, connections, observations—they were not happening."

He paused, panted some more, then lifted the glass to his lips and took a bird sip. "Now we come to the ironic part. You are a student of irony, so I think you will enjoy this, Mr. Nichols. Because it was just at this moment, just as I realized that I was becoming like a man who is impotent with women, that a woman came into my life. A real woman, Mr. Nichols. A young, beautiful, real woman."

A long sigh escaped, and he sat motionless, eyes shut, a half-smile across his face. He looked like an old man asleep in the sun, lost in the land where we're all still young, where possibilities still roam.

"Rachel Ornstein was that woman, Mr. Nichols. I'm sure it

took weeks, perhaps months, but for me it happened one day. She had been working on the project part time, a little here, a little there. I had been aware of her as a Zoltec employee before, but then, one day, I was aware of her as a woman. And then I missed my first wife not at all."

A look of utter peace passed over his face. "But there was a problem, as there must be when an old man falls in love with a young woman. Two problems, really. The young woman already had a young man, and the old man had nothing to offer her. Oh, she admired me, respected me, looked upon me as a father figure, perhaps. That was all. She is brilliant, you know; perhaps as good as I was, once. I could see in her eyes that she knew my time had passed."

"I don't see what this has to do with anything." Zoller's story was grotesque.

"You will, Mr. Nichols, you will. You were interested in irony, I believe?"

"Go ahead."

"I had the young man come to my apartment." Zoller's voice grew remote, as though he were describing something that had happened to someone else. "I told him I wanted Rachel working with me full time. That their relationship would distract her. He understood what I wanted. He said there were some projects he could pursue if he had some money. I gave him the money—all I had. He agreed to sever his relationship with Rachel."

I got off the table, went and stood before him. He seemed to be shrinking before my eyes. "Let me get this straight, Doctor —you *bought* Rachel from Platt?"

"Yes." I could barely hear him.

Zoller's eyes met mine. He had left shame behind long ago. "Then what?"

"I assigned Rachel to work on the project. After a few weeks, I wanted more. I . . . wanted her, wanted her to want me. As a

man. I decided I needed money, a great deal of money. I saw
her love of science, of research. I thought that if I could endow
a great research foundation she would want to join me there; it
would be my gift to her. A gift she couldn't refuse, Mr. Nichols.
I was not thinking very clearly, I know that now, but I projected
onto Rachel what I would have wanted had I been she. I
wanted her to love me, Mr. Nichols. I thought if she needed
me, that was the same as loving me. I knew so little of these
things, you see?"

"So you approached Altschuler, and he suggested selling
Zoltec short—in February?"

"I asked him to lend me money. I told him why I needed it.
He said there was a better way to get the money, that I didn't
need to borrow it. He said that if the new project really was
going nowhere he could make us all the money I needed, and
that no one had a better right than I to that money. He said no
one could know, that he would set up some company in the
Bahamas to do the business. I did not care about the details. I
don't understand these things, but I trusted Leon, and he
brought me a great deal of money."

I pulled out the last cigarette, tossed the empty pack on the
floor, and walked back to the bar cart for a light. Zoller looked
so empty that I could not sustain anger. Pity took its place.
"And then Rachel threatened the whole scenario, because she
started to make the process work."

Zoller just stared.

"Do you know what she told me, Doc? She told me she threw
herself into the work so hard because it was the only way she
had to salvage her self-respect because Platt had tossed her out.
And he had tossed her out because you *paid* him to."

"You see, Mr. Nichols? You are beginning to appreciate the
endless permutations of irony."

I sank into a chair next to the old man. "You poor bastard.

You poor, poor bastard. You're right—if there were a hall of fame for irony, they'd retire your number."

I had no desire to torture him further, but we had to get to the end: "So you gave Platt more money to try and get Quarles to help sink the project, and when that didn't work you paid him to steal the technology. I get all that, but I do have two questions. After paying Platt to steal the technology, why did you hire me to get the secrets back, and why did you kill him?"

His eyes were closed, his breathing shallow. His hands lay on his lap, and for the first time I noticed age spots on them. The sherry glass had slipped to the floor.

"Come on, Doctor—finish it. You'll feel better if you do."

The faint smile returned. His eyes fluttered open and he turned his head toward me. "It is finished. I assure you, everything is finished."

"No, it isn't. Not until you tell me why you changed your mind, then killed him. We've come this far; let's wrap it up. Did he threaten to blow the whole thing? Did he get too greedy?"

Flecks of foam appeared on liverish lips. When he spoke, it was in the voice I'd thought had gone forever. "I did not kill him, Mr. Nichols. Nor did I pay him to 'sink' the project, as you put it. Rachel had put her life's blood in that project—do you think I would have let that scum steal her work? If I had known he intended to, I would have killed him, but I did not. I wish I had."

"Come on, Doctor—it's a little late for games, don't you think? You had to prevent the new process from being announced, so you got Platt to steal your know-how. When I told you I was going to tell him what we'd done, you panicked and killed him."

"As you say—it is much too late for games."

I lurched to my feet. His serenity was a taunt, and it was all I could do to keep from hitting him. "God damn it, you killed

210

him. Monday night. You called him, then you went to his place and shot him. You were out until after three in the morning. Plenty of time to drive up to New Hampshire and back."

"I'm sorry, Mr. Nichols. Believe me, I know what it is to have an elegant theory destroyed by an inconvenient fact."

"What's the inconvenient fact, Doctor? Seems to me I laid out the facts." I willed my hands to unclench, so that they dangled uselessly at my sides.

"Don't—just let it go, Mr. Nichols. For your own sake, and hers. Especially hers."

"You care so much about Rachel, let me tell you something: she blames herself for Platt's death, for her part in your little scheme. Tell the truth, so she doesn't go through life carrying that weight."

"Mr. Nichols, Rachel knows I didn't kill that man."

"I know—she thinks you're too good to have done something like that. But we know better, don't we?"

"Rachel knows I could not have killed him because she was with me the night it happened." He said it softly, without satisfaction, and I knew it was true.

"But . . ." Bile rose in my throat. I staggered to the couch across from him and sank into it.

"When she called to tell me that you had succeeded in altering the papers Platt stole she said she was going to take a few days off. I asked her to be with me Monday night. There was something I wanted her to see." His voice softened even more: "Something I wanted to ask her."

I felt numb, and there was a ringing in my ears. "Go on."

"She agreed. I left work early to meet her. We had dinner. I took her to see the building I had commissioned. The Zoller Foundation." He rolled the words mockingly, a palsied hand jerking dismissively at the drawings on the director's table. "My great dream, Mr. Nichols. The dream I dreamed she'd share. The reason for everything I'd done."

"She told me she was with her father."

"She had been. She came back early, as a favor to me. Maybe it seemed as though she were still with her father."

"But I asked her if she could tell me where you were the night Platt was killed. She said she couldn't."

"She couldn't. She loves you, Mr. Nichols. I thought you understood. I thought you understood the irony. Mr. Nichols —you are the irony."

"What are you talking about?"

"I asked her to marry me. To share my dream. My fantasy. But she told me she'd fallen in love with you! That's the joke, Mr. Nichols—the perfect joke. An old man conceives a beautiful child with a young woman, it is kidnapped, and the young woman falls in love with the man hired to get it back. You appreciate irony—you must appreciate this."

"You asked her to marry you? What in hell made you think . . . ?"

"Mr. Nichols, don't. She loves you—isn't that enough?"

I bolted across the space between us and grabbed him by the throat. "She lied to me—why, God damn it?"

His wheeze throbbed against my fingertips. "'Don't do this— don't do this to her!"

"Tell me, or I'll make her tell me. I'll tell her how you bought her from Platt—I swear to Christ I will! She'll hate the very thought of you." His dull eyes looked at me and saw that I meant it.

"I think she was afraid you'd want to know why she had agreed to meet me, why I would have presumed to dream that she would accept my offer."

"And why did she? What gave you the idea that she would ever . . . ?"

"Don't. Let it go. It does not matter."

"Tell me. Tell me, or I'll make her tell me."

"Don't do that to her."

"Then you tell me. Now. Tell me, old man. Why did you ask her? Why did she lie to me?" I could feel the faint pulse in his throat.

"You are a fool, Mr. Nichols. She didn't want you to find out that we had been lovers. She was afraid it would repulse you to think of her with me. With an old man."

I shut my eyes and tried not to think, but it was no use. My hands dropped. Zoller sagged back.

The voice that remained was more breath than speech, and hardly enough of that to stir a flame. "It was only for a few months. Do not judge her, Mr. Nichols. What she gave me was gratitude, kindness. A young woman's warmth. She never gave me love."

I looked down at a shrunken figure, less a man than a cadaver. I stumbled to the door.

CHAPTER **30**

I have a hazy memory of pisspot bars and cheap liquor, of sweat and vomit, of flashing neon and garish whores, of zircon love and Washington Street. I wear the memory of a high-stepping pimp who left the imprint of his teeth on the knuckles of my right hand, and of a half-sized man who pulled me out of the gutter where the pimp and his friends threw me. After that I have no memories, which was what I wanted. No memories, no images, no more hurt.

Before there was consciousness there was a caress, bidding me open myself to the cool, insistent touch. I was back in her bed, and she was kneading away the bruises, the stiffness, the tender parts where they'd kicked me, the all-over hurt where she had kicked me, and for a few seconds, that moment between the nothingness of sleep and the pain of memory, it was all forgotten, and I reached for her.

And screamed, screamed with the power of a man who has seen the Serpent itself, because I had. The dappled light that broke through the torn shade played with the bands on the creature, broke them into disjointed segments, so that it might

214

have been twenty reptiles, instead of one, that were wrapped around my leg, forty hoodless eyes staring up at me from my groin, instead of two black, unblinking pinpricks. But two were enough, and I might never have stopped screaming if the light hadn't come on when Tony pulled the string that hung to the floor.

"Fucksa matter, Nase—you'll scare him. Ya never see a snake before?"

I clawed at the thick body. "Get it off! Get it off!" The head never took its eyes off me, but bobbed away from my grasp like a contender in a warm-up with a palooka. I pawed at the thick, dry body, as big around as my arm, circling my right calf, undulating in place.

"Awright, awright. Don't hurt him. He jus' a baby." Tony skated across the floor until he was alongside the couch. His right hand shot out and caught the beast's neck just behind the spatulate head. "Come on, Scooter, come to Poppa. Nase don't want you messing with him." He talked in a low, monotonic murmur, and after a few seconds the pressure on my leg eased as the snake slowly slithered up Tony's outstretched arm.

It took forever and there were several feet of reptile coiled around Tony's neck before I sat up. As soon as I did, the room spun and I had to fight the urge to lose everything.

"Hey, Nase—don' go sleep. Ya gotta get up. Yo' fren's on the phone."

I tried not to answer, just to lie there and not breathe. "Come on, Nase, he waiting."

"I don't care. Go away, leave me alone."

"You want I should put Scooter back in bed with you?"

I staggered into the next room. The receiver hung by its cord from a wall phone. Light streamed in the open window, searing my eyes. "Top o' the mornin' to you, lad!" Bucky's voice tore through my shattered head.

"What is it, Buck?"

215

"What is it? What do you mean, what is it? Is it Zoller? Is that what drove you to this little celebration?"

"How did you know I was here?"

"Tony called me last night. Said you'd been tangling with Cong, your position'd been overrun. Wanted to know what to do with you. I suggested selling you to Harvard Med School but he seemed worried. So I told him to let you sleep it off, give me a call in the morning. I repeat: Is it Zoller?"

"No. Not the big part, anyway."

"Huh? What are you talking about? What do you mean, 'not the big part,' anyway? Who . . . ?"

"I don't know who. I don't care."

"Nase, what the hell . . . ? You sound like forty pounds of shit in a ten-pound bag. Is that all hangover, or is there something else? What's going on?"

"Let's leave it, Buck. Zoller didn't do it. It doesn't matter. None of it matters. I'm through, out."

"Nase . . . "

"I got to go, Buck." I hung up. When the phone started ringing again I picked it up, set it down, then picked it up again and left it dangling while I staggered over to the sink and threw water in my face. I drank some, fought back the stomach spasms, and drank some more. When I turned off the water Tony was behind me, looking up. The snake was gone.

"You all right, Nase?" I nodded.

"You want some breakfast, somethin' to eat? I think I got some hot dogs roun' here somewhere."

I fought the dry heaves. "Thanks, Tone. I don't think so. Where's the snake?"

"Scooter? I put him back in his cage. He musta snuck out last night, lookin' for rats. He do that. You see any rats?" He swept his arm around.

"No. Looks great."

"I'm telling you, Nase, you should get a python. Ain' nothin' like 'em to live with. Clean, keep the rats out, don' bother ya none. Fuggin' druggies won' go near 'em, either. Don' hafta worry about gettin' ripped off, know what I mean?"

"I ever find a place to settle, maybe I'll get one."

"Whataya mean, Nase?—you gotta place. Oh . . ." His face fell. "You mean you're . . ."

"I got to be pushing off, Tone. Thanks for taking care of me last night. I appreciate it."

"Shit, I didn' do nothin'. Ya sure ya gotta split?"

"That's the only thing I am sure of."

I was pulling the door shut behind me when Tony called out. I looked back and he pulled himself across the cracked linoleum until he was a foot or two away, then thrust his hand up. I held it.

"Scooter an' me, Nase—we got sumpin' in common."

It took a few beats but then I nodded.

"Tha's what I like about snakes, see. One of the things, anyhow. People, they look at me like I'm . . . I dunno, somethin' ugly. Or they don' look at me at all, like maybe I'll just go away, they don' see me, know what I mean?" I nodded again.

"But you never made me feel . . . you know. You look at me." He dropped my hand and turned away. "Thanks, man."

"Bye, Tone."

The door was almost shut when Tony called out again: "Hey, Nase—ya' know what else I got, same's Scooter? No balls! Way you was talkin' last night, I think maybe I'm lucky, huh?"

I'd lost the rental car somewhere in the Combat Zone, so I grabbed the MTA to Cambridge. It took fifteen minutes to pack the things I needed. McGinty could steal the rest. I remembered that I'd left my checkbook at Rachel's. I cursed, then dialed her number, ready to hang up if she answered. After a dozen rings

I put the receiver down, picked up my bag, and walked out. I didn't lock the door.

There was one piece of business I had to finish before I left the neighborhood, so I pulled on some sunglasses, turned my collar up, and tugged a cap down over my eyes before stepping out of the building and hurrying over to a pet shop on Shephard Street.

"Nase, is that you?"

I pulled off the sunglasses. "It's me, Mrs. Serafina. May I come in?"

"Sure, you come in. You don' look so good. Come in, sit down, I give you something to eat." She swung the door wide and gestured for me to enter.

"Nothing to eat, thanks." The thought of Mrs. Serafina's sweet, heavy desserts made me retch.

She looked at me closely. "Some whiskey, then. Tha's wha' you need; good shot of whiskey, egg in it."

My stomach turned over and I fought for control. "I don't think I could . . ."

"Yes, you can. Don' you think I know how to fix a man up, got hisself a hangover like he going to die?" She pressed me back into an overstuffed armchair and bustled off into the kitchen. In a few seconds she was back with a glass full of something ugly. "Drink this." She pressed it into my hand.

"Oh, God . . ."

"Drink it! Is wha' I always make for my Ferd'nan', he come home drunk. Night before, he the worl's greatest lover. Wake up next day, he moan and groan like he a dead man. I know wha's good for a man, either way."

I took a deep breath and tossed it back. It yo-yo'd between my mouth and my stomach a few times, then settled. After a few seconds I did feel better.

"Thank you."

She took the glass and set it down. "Hair of the dog, Nase, hair of the . . ." Her face fell. "Nase, now you feelin' better, you heard anything about Magellan? He gone, huh?"

I nodded. "He met a friend, Mrs. Serafina. A lady friend. I think they're on their honeymoon." I told her what I'd learned across the street. Halfway through, she sat down across from me and a smile broke ear to ear.

"He a lover, Nase. I always knew he a lover. A lover, an' a traveling man. Ran off and left me for a younger woman!" She slapped her hands down on her lap and roared.

"I'm sorry I couldn't find him, Mrs. Serafina. I'm not much of a detective."

"Nase, you a great detective. You made me very happy. They young an' free an' on the road together. I miss him, but . . ."

"I'd return your money but I spent it."

"You crazy! You don' have to . . ."

She stopped when she saw what I pulled out of my backpack. I held it out and her big hands swallowed it.

"Oh, Nase, he a beauty." She held the puppy inches from her nose. His tiny pink tongue darted out and licked it.

"I'm glad you like him."

"Like him? I love him. Gonna name him Vasco da Gama." She bent over and set the little dog on the floor, then beamed at him before looking up at me. "Wha's the matter, Nase?"

"Tired. Got to get some rest."

"I mean, why you get drunk?"

There was no answer, so I just shook my head.

"Nase, you met a woman, din you?"

I nodded.

"She a good woman?"

"I thought so."

"You love her?"

"I thought so."

"The perfect woman for you?"

"I thought so."

"Then you fine out, she maybe not perfect?"

I nodded again.

"So now you goin' to wait for a perfect woman?" She leaned forward and clouted my shoulder hard enough to knock me back against the seat. "Nase, honey, I gotta tell you—I the only perfect woman I know, an' I'm maybe a little ole for you." Her laugh shook the walls.

I looked down at the little dog. It had deposited a present at Mrs. Serafina's feet and was trying to destroy the fringe on the rug.

Mrs. Serafina's eyes followed mine. "See, Nase—Vasco da Gama leave a little mess, cause a little trouble, I don' love him less for that. We all leave a little mess, cause a little trouble. People wha' love us, they come along, help us clean it up, fix it up. Doin' it alone all the time, tha's no good."

The hurt was too raw. I nodded again and stood. "I'll be leaving town for a while, Mrs. Serafina. Don't know when I'll be seeing you again."

She pushed herself to her feet, a troubled look creasing her wrinkled face. "I'm leaving, too, Nase—going to go live with my sister in New Bedford. Can't take no more of this city. But you not leavin' alone, are you, Nase?"

"Afraid so."

"Tha's not good, Nase. Try not to leave alone. Promise me that." She reached up and pulled me to her. Her bosom heaved and we clutched each other. "Promise."

CHAPTER 31

Rachel's apartment was dark when I let myself in, and I tried not to look around as I gathered up my things. I found the checkbook and my clothes and was about to leave when I saw the note with my name on it propped on the table near the door. I peeled open the envelope and let it fall to the floor.

DEAR NASE:

I left this for you because I didn't know where you were. When you didn't come home last night (you see, I already think of anyplace with you as 'home'), I had a chance to think of what you have brought into my life. I know it won't be a life without you in it. For that to happen I have to tell you something that will be very difficult for me. I pray it won't make you hate me.

There's something else I have to do. Something crazy, but right. It means I have to go out of town tonight. I'll be back this afternoon to change and pick up my bag. I have to catch a six o'clock flight but I'll be back Sunday night, and I'll tell you about it then if we don't get a chance to talk this afternoon.

Please, my darling, be here when I get back—and always.

With all my love,

RACHEL

I held the note for several minutes without moving, then reread it. I looked around for a pencil, then pulled out the sheet of paper with the phone numbers I'd gotten from Hairston and tore off the bottom. I started to put the numbers back and then looked at them again. My hangover lifted.

I scribbled, "There's a job I have to finish so I can't be here this afternoon, but it doesn't matter—you've already told me the only thing that matters. It's only home when you're here. Love, Nase."

Rachel's suitcase lay on the bed. I opened it and pushed the note down where she'd find it later. My hand bumped against a package and I pulled it out. The brown gusset folder fastened with an elastic cord. Inside was a three-inch stack of paper, covered with typewritten figures. I didn't need to see the "Confidential" stamp in the lower right-hand corner to recognize Zoltec's documents.

The next hours passed in a dream. I knew what had to be done, but the elation I had felt when I read Rachel's letter was gone, replaced by a sense of necessity, a need to see things finished, to be done with the lies.

It was four when the cab let me off at Bucky's. I'd been careful to put the folder back and close the suitcase before I left Rachel's apartment. My note had gone into my pocket. I'd taken a last look from the doorway; nothing said the suitcase had been touched.

"Will you tell me what the hell's going on?" He dragged me into his den and shut the door.

"Not now. Maybe someday. I just need to borrow a car."

"What's wrong with you? You sound like you've been lobotomized."

"I've got something to do. Will you lend me a car?"

"Of course I will, but where's yours?"

"Too hot."

"Too hot? You mean . . ."

"Yes. They want me. I have to get out of town."

"Just a second." He stepped out of the room for a second, then returned, dangling a set of keys. "Do you need anything else—money, for example?"

I shook my head. "Just the car."

"Where are you going?"

"I don't know."

"Will you let me know?"

"Sure."

"When?"

"Maybe in a few hours."

"A few hours? How far can you go in a few hours? Nase, you're not . . ."

"Good-bye, Buck. Thank you." I let myself out the door and climbed into his car. He was standing in the doorway as I pulled out.

There was a light on in the upstairs window, but there was an empty bay in the garage so I took a chance that the owners were out. I used a pocket flashlight to look for signs of an alarm system. I didn't see any contacts so I broke a pane of glass and unlocked the French doors. I stepped into the garden room and waited.

There was no alarm. Sounds of television filtered down from upstairs but I didn't hear any voices. I stepped into the main hall and across to the library. I shut the door behind me. My flashlight beam caught the house within a house, all the little people asleep.

I swept the light around the room until it settled on Truscott's desk and the walnut filing case behind it. I went over and pulled open the first file drawer.

It didn't take long, because Truscott hadn't been expecting visitors and had been taught to be neat and orderly. Everything had a file, nicely alphabetized: "Altschuler" under A; "Bahamian Partners" under B; "Zoltec" bringing up the rear. I pulled out the Bahamian Partners file and started to read.

The partnership papers confirmed my guess: Altschuler and Truscott—not Zoller—were the partners. The rest of the file was records of the partnership's trading activity in Zoltec stock —short sales up to a few weeks ago, then a lull, and then the big purchases Bucky had heard about. The last purchase was two days old.

Truscott had kept notes of the amount of each short sale that was to be credited to Zoller. It looked as though Zoller had gotten about 10 percent of the proceeds; so much for Zoller's "family." The purchases weren't credited to Zoller; Altschuler and Truscott had no more use for him. I shoved the file into my pack and pulled the next one out.

It took me a second before I realized that the reason the Zoltec file was going to be easier to read than the last one was because the light was on. It took me another second to realize that it was on because Zach Truscott was standing in the doorway with a startled look on his face.

"Oh, hi."

"I don't need to ask what you're doing here. That's obvious

enough." He pushed the door shut behind him and stepped into the room.

"I don't suppose you'd believe me if I told you I'd just come by to borrow a cup of scotch?" I followed his eye to the open file drawer. "No, I don't suppose you would. Why don't you have a seat?" I gestured at the settee across from the desk.

He moved to the desk like a sleepwalker, a puzzled look on his face. He was wearing a dinner jacket again.

"Bitsy wanted to come home early. I guess that's good?"

"I don't see how it makes much difference. It's over, you know."

"I think I'll have a drink. Would you like one?"

"Thanks. A light whiskey, I think."

Truscott busied himself with the drinks, his back to me. "How did you figure it out?"

"Just luck. I was so locked into another theory that I almost missed it. Then I recognized your phone number."

"My phone number?" He handed me the drink, then settled onto the settee, sipping his own. His voice was marginally higher than I remembered it, and he was slightly flushed, but for a man in his position he had a lot of panache.

"Your home number, the one you wrote on your card for me. It showed up on a list of calls from Altschuler and Platt. I was looking for a whole different set of connections and blew it the first time, but once I saw that, the rest was sort of obvious. Which is why I say it's over."

"Do the police know?"

"Not yet. I thought it would be nice to give them those—" I pointed a thumb over my shoulder at the file drawers. "They're kind of understaffed, need all the help they can get."

He nodded, as though I'd just remarked on the weather. "That's really very clever of you. I never expected it."

"I know you didn't. It hurt my feelings when I realized you

had suggested me because you *didn't* want Platt caught. All that stuff about not wanting publicity—that was just a cover, huh?"

"I'm afraid so. I'm sorry."

"You shouldn't have told me that Zoller had recommended me; Zoller said *you'd* given *him* my name. Took me a lot longer than it should have, but the little things do add up."

He shook his head as though he'd prepared a balance sheet and overlooked depreciation. "That was stupid. I am sorry we tried to take advantage of you. It seemed necessary at the time."

"Most things do. But no hard feelings. Mind if I ask a question?"

"Not at all."

"Altschuler filled you in as soon as Zoller came to him last February?"

"We both knew that the company would decline fast without Zoller's intellectual input. When the lovesick old goat came to Leon with his pathetic story it was easy enough to see what the future held if we didn't do anything."

"So you and Altschuler figured you'd make some money on the downside by setting up Bahamian Holdings to short Zoltec stock?"

"I gave up a partnership in a major investment banking house to come to Zoltec. What kind of a future would I have had if the company went belly-up because some hyperglandular old man held on too long? My stock options would be worthless. How was I to know that woman would pull it off? How would I take care of Bitsy and Melissa?"

"Good point. How'd you get onto Platt? I would have thought he was a little déclassé for you."

"Platt was an idiot. We wouldn't have this problem if it weren't for him."

"How so?"

"After a while I started getting reports that the new process

226

might work out after all. Zoller was so smitten with that woman that he'd come in and rhapsodize about her accomplishments. Leon and I realized that something had to be done; we'd bet everything on the company failing, the stock going down. This place—" he waved expansively—"the cars, everything. They'd all be gone. Bitsy would . . ." He shook his head.

"Perhaps you underestimate her."

A smile came over his face, and he shook his head.

"So anyway, you hired Platt."

"When Zoller told Altschuler what he'd done with Platt, it was obvious that Platt wasn't particular about what he did for money. Leon approached him, said he'd make it worth Platt's while to slow things up, that it would help cover some short sales."

"And he bit, started trying to get Quarles to gum up the works."

"Leon's very good. He's spent his life recognizing men's vanities, using them to his own advantage. A little intimacy, some flattery—Platt was child's play. Unfortunately, Platt couldn't get the job done."

"But Altschuler's mention of short sales gave Platt the idea of doing some shorting on his own. Small potatoes compared to you guys, but enough to start me thinking when I found out about it."

"The man was impossible. We never should have . . ." His voice trailed off and he threw back the last of his drink, then rose to his feet as though his knees hurt. "Another?" He lifted his glass.

"I don't think so, thanks, but help yourself. Why'd you kill him?"

His shoulders slumped and he paused, the bottle held in midair. "I know it doesn't matter, but I never meant to. I swear I didn't."

"What happened?"

He resumed pouring. "Platt got greedy. He called Leon, wanted money to keep quiet about the short sales. Leon gave him some, and he went away for a while. Then he came back and wanted more. We realized there'd be no end to it. Then, when Zoller told me the new chip was going to work after all, Altschuler and I had an even bigger problem."

"As soon as it was announced the stock would take off, you'd have to cover, and bye-bye Austin-Healey."

"Bye-bye everything. But I saw a way to keep Platt quiet *and* keep that from happening."

"You told Platt to steal the secrets and sell them?"

"Right. I told him Altschuler and I'd be silent partners of his. He'd sell the technology, we'd each take a third. We really didn't care about that at all, of course. We didn't want to have anything more to do with the man than absolutely necessary."

"So Platt didn't know about the rest of it?"

"That we'd leak word of the loss and cover our short sales?"

"Right."

"Oh, no. He was hopelessly small-time. He hadn't a clue that the real money was to be made by shorting every share that Leon and I could borrow."

"Once he stole the secrets, of course, he wouldn't be able to blackmail you anymore."

"Exactly. I made one more payment. 'Working capital,' we called it."

"Thirty-five thousand dollars."

"Right. Say—you really are good. Just my luck."

"Thanks."

"You're welcome. Yes, thirty-five thousand. To cover his start-up expenses. But I figured that would be it, and then I'd be done with the bastard."

"So as Platt saw it, he'd steal the secrets, but no one except his partners would ever know they'd been stolen. He'd sell them, and no one at Zoltec except you and Altschuler would ever know why the competition caught up so fast. What Platt was too dumb to realize was that the reason you and Altschuler wouldn't care wasn't because you were going to make a million or so selling the technology, but because you and Altschuler were making fifty times as much betting the company was going to hell in a handbasket anyway. But for you to win that bet, the theft *had* to be discovered?"

"Of course."

"So you had to leave evidence of the theft. You planted that piece of paper?"

He leaned back against the bookshelf, a wistful look on his face. "Platt asked for my advice on setting up a company to market his new asset." He turned to look at me. "Can you imagine that?"

"Never had one quite like that at the B-School, I bet."

"Hardly. Anyway, we sketched out a few things in my office. He took some notes but left a page behind. The rest was easy. The day Platt left Zoltec I shoved the notes into his desk, and waited."

"Of course, with the theft discovered, you had to make a show of going after Platt, while you and Altschuler were closing out your short positions."

"Well, we couldn't very well say, 'Forget about it'—for one thing, Zoller wouldn't have stood for it. He wanted Platt caught, the fool."

"Love overtakes reason, I guess."

"What? Oh, yes—I suppose so." A disgusted look swept Truscott's face. "Anyway, that wouldn't have mattered. Bingham and the lawyers had to think we wanted the stuff back. I persuaded them not to get the police involved, because of the risks of leaks. Actually, of course . . ."

"Actually you'd have me, a none too awesome investigative force to start with, reporting to you. If I seemed to be getting lucky, you could just warn Platt to take off. Neat."

"You fouled it up." He sounded vaguely accusatory.

"Well, to be fair, you'd have to say it was Zoller who fouled it up. If we'd stayed with the original program I would have told you as soon as we'd located Platt, and when we went back with the law, your papers would have been long gone. It was Zoller's idea to doctor the papers, and not let you know I'd found them. If you've got a complaint, I'm afraid you'll have to take it up with him."

"Right. Zoller. God!" He shook his head disgustedly.

"I don't think he's too happy, if it's any consolation."

"Oh? Oh, hell, I guess it doesn't matter now, anyway."

I drained my drink. "You certainly showed poise when I showed up the other night with my little surprise. It must have come as quite a shocker."

"Well, considering I'd talked to Platt no more than a few hours before, just to assure him that he was in the clear, you might say so."

"You'd called him from Zoltec?"

"Right."

"Rachel sure had me pegged."

"How do you mean?"

"I mean I jumped to another conclusion—I assumed that call was from Zoller, just because it was from Zoltec and I wanted it to be from him. And those were your calls to Altschuler, too?"

"Sure—we were talking every day; there was a lot to coordinate."

"Especially after my bombshell."

"Well, one thing I've learned in investment banking is that nothing ever goes quite the way you plan it. The good players learn how to react to surprises, turn them to their advantage."

"Did you?"

"I thought so." He pursed his lips and thought for a second.

"Yes. Objectively speaking, I'd have to say my idea was brilliant."

"To take over Zoltec."

He looked at me quizzically. "Very good. Very, very good. I did make a mistake, picking you out of the phone book." He hoisted his glass in my direction, then drained it.

"Nothing to it, really. As soon as you found out that we'd recovered the technology for Zoltec, but the market still thought it was gone, you had the best of both worlds: a company that owned an invaluable asset, and everyone else thought the asset was lost. Ergo, the stock could be bought cheap. Prime takeover target. You did a one-eighty overnight."

He looked back over his shoulder. "We were going to acquire as much as we could in the marketplace. Try not to drive up the price. Then make a tender offer for the rest."

"But if I told Platt about the prank Zoller had played on him, he'd figure he had no more reason to keep quiet about you guys."

Truscott set his glass on the desk, then wandered over by the fireplace. "I called him as soon as you left, told him what Zoller had done. He started to shriek about how I'd ruined him, all kinds of crazy stuff."

"You tried to reassure him."

"Sure. I told him this was an opportunity, not a loss."

"Take advantage of the unexpected."

"Exactly. But the man was insane. He didn't understand anything. He told me I'd better have half a million dollars for him that night or he was going to tell everything. He was unstable. Dealing with him was a mistake, a bad mistake." He stared off into space for a second, at that textbook place where mistakes don't happen.

"So you went north."

"I brought Bitsy back from the party early, told her I had work at the office. I went up to reason with him. I certainly didn't have that kind of cash lying around. Leon and I had tied up everything to raise money to buy Zoltec. Everything."

"He wasn't reasonable, so you killed him."

"I told him we'd get him money, more money than he'd ever dreamed of, but that he'd have to wait. He wouldn't listen. He flung the documents at me, said he was going to call the police right then. He went back to the back room. I thought he was going to call. I had to stop him."

"I suppose you did."

"If only he'd listened to reason."

"Indeed."

"Will you listen to reason?"

"Meaning?"

"Meaning that if we come to an understanding I won't have to use this." He opened a drawer in an end table and pulled out a revolver. He pointed it at my chest.

"It won't work. Don't you see that?"

"Maybe not, but I have to try. After all, the police don't know. I surprised a burglar, he attacked me . . ."

"You want your wife and child to come downstairs to find you've killed a man?"

His jaw tightened. "These things happen. Please be reasonable. I can make you very rich."

"My ex-wife would just take it."

"Get up and come over here." He gestured with the pistol and I did as he said.

"Over here." He pointed the barrel at the fireplace. "Face me. Keep your hands up." His voice was strained and the flush had deepened.

I got up and faced him. The gun, four feet away, held steady on my chest.

"Do you have a gun with you?"

"At my waist."

"Good. That helps." His finger whitened on the trigger. "I'm truly sorry." I believed he was.

"I wouldn't. Mine's bigger."

Truscott whirled to confront the voice in the door and I jumped forward and knocked down his gun hand. He tripped and we fell forward into the doll's house. Wood splintered and then the table collapsed and we both were lying on the floor. Truscott writhed under me and was about to slip loose when I jerked his hand up, then smashed it down against the rubble. I grabbed the gun from the pile of splinters. When Truscott tried to shove his foot into my stomach, I smacked the gun against the side of his head. I struggled to my feet, leaving Truscott lying on his wife's dreams.

"I am glad to see you, Buckmaster. Might I ask why you saw fit to drop in?" Truscott rolled over slowly, then drew himself to his hands and knees, but made no effort to rise further. I looked at his gun, then glanced at the massive .45 service automatic Bucky held. He was right: his was bigger.

"You seemed in no condition for flight, much less fight. I followed you. When you made your somewhat unconventional entrance, I figured I might as well listen in."

"So you heard the whole thing?"

"Pretty much."

"Kind of an ugly story."

"You might say. What . . . ?"

"Zachariah? Zachariah, what's happening? Who are these . . . why, Mr. Nichols—what is this? Why do you have a gun? What's happened to Zachariah?" Bitsy Truscott pushed past Bucky and knelt by her husband. "Oh, Zachariah . . ."

"Darling, I . . ." His voice broke and he started to cry, wrenching sobs that shook his whole body. She sank to her knees and put her arms around him.

"It'll be all right, Zachariah. Whatever it is, it'll be all right. I'll make it all right." She cradled his head and rocked him.

Her head lifted and she looked past him to the shattered doll's house. Her hand reached out slowly and pulled a tiny figure out of the wreckage. The head was a white shard. She closed her hand around it and enfolded her husband again. "Don't worry, darling," she murmured, "we'll see this through together." It came out "thee thith," but it didn't sound silly. She was still holding him when I left to call Hairston.

CHAPTER **32**

There had been no sound until I heard the key in the lock. For twenty-four hours, no sound. The bottle clicking against the glass had made a sound, I suppose, but not one that mattered. The key in the door, the door opening, the light switch clicking—those sounds mattered.

"Welcome home, toots."

"Oh God, Nase, you startled me. Why were you sitting in the dark?" She shut the door and advanced on me, a worried look on her face.

"Is it dark?"

"You look like something that lives under a rock. What have you been doing?" Her eyes lit on the bottle, then the ashtray. "Forget it; I can see. Why Nase? Has something happened?" She stopped: "You know who did it, don't you?"

I nodded. "Truscott."

"Truscott?" The color drained from her face and the muscles in it collapsed, so that it looked as though she were melting. "Then you know it wasn't Dr. Zoller," she whispered.

"Yes. I know that. I know how you knew."

"I'm so sorry."

"Don't be. I understand."

"I was going to tell you."

"I knew you were. I got your note. Thank you."

She started to bustle about, picking up the ashtray, the glasses, the bottle, finding refuge in domesticity. "There's so much we have to say to each other. Do you want to tell me about what happened, or should I tell you about . . . the other thing?"

"There's not much to tell. The other thing doesn't matter. The thing with Platt is what I thought. Most of it. It just wasn't the person I thought."

She came and settled in the chair with me. Her hand cradled my cheek. "What will happen to him?"

"Truscott? I don't know. He'll do time. His wife will get a good lawyer, but his life is over."

"You're so far away from me. Is there any way I can make it better?"

"I told you—that doesn't matter. It did, but I got over it. How was your trip?"

"Don't, Nase. Please don't. I'd rather you'd hate me. Don't shut me out."

"You're wrong." I wrapped my arm around her, felt the satiny smoothness of her under the dress. "I don't care about you and Zoller. I did, but I'm over that. It was when you were ready to tell me about it that I realized it didn't matter. It's that you'd keep a secret from me—not what the secret is. Do you understand that?"

She didn't answer, but after a few seconds I felt her head nod against mine.

"Good. So you'll understand why I want to hear about New York. And Mr. Matsami. How was he?"

She stiffened as though an electric charge had run through her. "You know?"

I nodded. "This was the 'crazy, but right' thing you were going to do?"

Her soft hair rubbed my neck. "How did you know?"

I stroked her shoulders. "The other day I went into your suitcase. I wanted to leave you this."

I pulled the note out of my pocket and handed it to her. A bit of fluff fell out as she unfolded it. She read it, then refolded it carefully. "I'm glad. I'm very glad you wanted to give me this. I'll never forget." She curled against me again.

"As soon as I felt the package I knew. I looked at it, but I didn't need to—I knew. That day in the motel room in New Hampshire? The counter on the copier? There had been so many more copies than there should have been. It stuck, but it didn't register, know what I mean?"

"I didn't know why I made the extra copies; I really didn't think about it. I just made them and put them aside. Security, I guess. It wasn't until you told me what Armand had done that I decided they were mine more than his. Ours."

"It doesn't matter. How much did you get?"

"A million. One million dollars." Her voice grew remote. "Money we earned, Nase; money for us."

"Was he surprised? I mean, to find somebody else delivering the goods?"

"I told him Bruce asked me to bring them. He didn't seem to care."

"I suppose he wouldn't. He will, though, when they figure out what I did." I drifted off, content to hold her like that forever.

It took a minute, but then she pulled away. "What do you mean?"

All I felt now was exhaustion, the feeling that I was outside my body, looking down. "Remember what I told you about the guy who sold stuff to the Russians? Stuff he'd made up?"

"Yes, but what . . . ?" Her hand clenched at my neck. "Oh, Nase—you didn't?"

I couldn't look at her. "I'm not sure I understand it myself, love, but I couldn't let you do it. I'm sure my changes aren't as good as yours were, but they'll do. Pure gibberish, but they'll do. They won't be making much from the recipe you sold them."

"You—*altered* the documents you found in my suitcase?"

"I had to, Rachel—don't you see?"

"But you didn't need . . ."

"I haven't much, you know. I haven't accomplished much. In a city of accomplished people, I'm a nothing."

"Nase, it wasn't . . ."

"That's why it matters to me that I have a little integrity. Not much, but a little. That's the only thing that's in short supply around here. I couldn't let you sell that stuff to them. Zoller was right, that far. They couldn't have it."

"You didn't . . ."

"That's just an excuse; I could have burned them, told you it was over."

I started to ease myself out of the chair but Rachel pulled me back. "But you didn't think . . ."

"I wasn't thinking very clearly. All I can say is, I hurt, Rachel —I hurt so much. Just when I got over the first hurt I found this other thing, and it hurt so much more."

"Oh, Nase—you've got it all . . ."

"A lot of people in this town wouldn't understand this but —I love my country, Rachel. For all its faults, I love it. I couldn't let you hurt it. I wanted to hurt you for being willing to hurt it. I thought you were different. I'm sorry."

She reached out. Slowly she pulled my head to her chest. "Oh, Nase—no wonder I love you."

"You love me anyway?"

"More than ever."

"I don't understand."

"I know you don't." She began to rock me, stroking my neck.

"Rachel, if Matsami catches up to you he'll . . ." I couldn't finish the thought.

"Yes, there is that. Do you think he'll be terribly upset?" I looked up and saw a mother's smile.

"Yes. I think he will be. When they find out they've been taken . . ."

"Oh, well, I knew there was that chance going in." Her hand continued its soft caress.

"You knew?" I jerked upright. "What do you mean?"

Her thumb brushed my cheek. "My silly man. My silly, silly man. You didn't think I'd sell the *real* technology, did you? Do you really think you're the only person in Boston who loves this country?" She pushed my head back down against her breast.

"You mean . . . ?"

She pushed my hair off my forehead, then stroked my cheek again. "Well, of course. I sold the phony technology. That's what I copied. You *are* a silly man."

"Then my changes . . ."

"Absolutely wasted. But wonderful. A wonderful man. You're *my* man. My wonderful, silly man."

My head swam. "I didn't have to?"

"You didn't have to doubt me, Nase—you don't have to, ever."

" 'I'm sorry' seems to be the only thing I'm good at saying."

"You do the right things. Saying the right things is easy."

"Damn. I even used my old Boy Scout code to send a message."

"You did? What did you say?"

" 'MacArthur lives!' "

"Go on!"

239

"Scout's honor." A black thought clutched at me. "It isn't going to take them long to figure out they've been had."

"Well, with my version they wouldn't ever have been sure what went wrong." She thought a second. "You're right, though—with the changes you added, they'll know it's bogus as soon as a halfway competent technician looks at the stuff. You have complicated things." Her fingers brushed at my temples.

"I'm sorry; I'm just . . . sorry. I'm an arrogant fool."

"Well, I'm not sorry—I love you for what you did. For what you are. Even if you are an arrogant fool." Her lips brushed my forehead.

"We could call this guy Matsami, tell him everything, give back the money."

"There's another way, isn't there?"

"I don't think so. What would life be like, always on the run, always wondering, looking over your shoulder? Would you want that?"

"If I were with you."

"You'd want that, after what I was willing to do to you?"

"I told you—more than ever. What you did was right—would have been right, if I had done what you thought. What I did, I did for us, Nase—so that we could be free. So that we could get out of here, out of all this. If that's what you want."

I put my head back and shut my eyes. Her touch followed me, moved to my shoulders, while I saw.

I saw squalid couplings with women unable to surrender enough of self to create a life that was more than self; a city careening into madness, teeming with people too preoccupied with abstractions to care about any real thing. I saw a man growing old, drawing hollow victories from another day survived.

Into that vision swam another: a small man, afraid, uprooted from the familiar, empty as it was; a fearful man, bound only by a prayer. I saw the rootless, errant man my father had promised, my wife had predicted.

I nestled my head in her lap. "Oh, sweet. Maybe life is just the choice of lesser evils?"

Her slow rocking matched her words: "Of course. And I'll choose whichever one you choose."

CHAPTER 33

Mr. Nason Nichols
C/O Zuricher Staatsbank
Pferdstrasse 99
Zurich, Switzerland

DEAR WASTREL:

Hans assures me he will get this to you, and the assurances of a Swiss banker aren't lightly given, so I assume you are, at this very minute, pondering this missive. There is much to ponder.

Truscott's decision to confess all proved a great boon, sparing me no end of nettlesome questions. Nonetheless your abrupt departure, given the circumstances, occasioned a certain amount of consternation among the ranks of Boston's finest, some of whom had the audacity to importune your correspondent, under the misapprehension that I could shed light on your whereabouts. (Two of them appeared to know you and were quite solicitous about your well-being, hewing to the view that they were in some unspecified manner responsible for your absence.)

I deflected these inquiries, of course, with a few deft allusions to the heritage I shared with my interlocutors, coupled with protestations of ignorance. Since ignorance, far more than the Ould Sod, is the common bond of our gendarmerie, I have had few problems.

Herr Zoller's self-imposed departure from this planet is no longer the subject of much remark in the popular press, being attributed, with unintended accuracy, to business reverses. Apropos of which you will be pleased to note the steady recovery of Zoltec shares in the nation's bourses, as even those touts less able than I have come to realize that perhaps the old man's company will survive, and even thrive, under the steady, if colorless, guidance of the assiduous Bingham.

I have gradually begun liquidating our holdings—with the utmost discretion, needless to say—and have transferred your share to your account, for Hans to re-convey. You should find yourself in comfortable circumstances as long as you live—no humor intended.

The home front is, how shall I say, quirky but, in its own way, stimulating. After the inevitable awkwardness of our reconciliation Deirdre and I have reached an accommodation: I satisfy her need for stability, warmth, support, money, and a home for her 'friend'; she satisfies the children's need for a mother and my need for self-degradation; and the 'friend' takes turns satisfying our respective needs for orgasmic release at least every other day. When I think of the contemporary hazards of random congress, I can only be grateful that circumstances brought these fine ladies back to the marital bed!

The hideous hyphenated harridan came baying about once or twice, hot on your spoor; Deirdre finally smacked her upside the earhole and she slunk off, though I doubt she'll ever be truly off your case. You were wise to see that a Japanese hit man was the preferred alternative. Beware the fanged huntress!

Well, Rolling Stone, I must be off. God willing, time will reunite us. Until then, I'll hoist a cup of Bushmill's to your name, bid you stay three steps ahead of the dark ones, and wish your lady my warmest regards.

Oh Jesus, Nase—I ache for your company.

Your brother in Christ,

THE HANRAHAN

I looked up as a conga drum heralded the start of another night of tropical debauchery. I tried to remember how many there had been, but gave up when I spotted a small figure dancing through the throng of near-naked bodies that crowded the beach. I lowered the letter, squinting against the setting sun. Rachel wore only the bottom of a string bikini. As she drew closer, I knew it wasn't time to run yet, and was glad.

SILENT WITNESS

For Gill with love.
Without you I could do nothing.

SILENT WITNESS

Nigel McCrery

ST. MARTIN'S PRESS ☙ NEW YORK

A THOMAS DUNNE BOOK.
An imprint of St. Martin's Press.

Library of Congress Cataloging-in-Publication Data

McCrery, Nigel, 1953-
   Silent witness / Nigel McCrery.
      p.   cm.
   ISBN 0-312-18178-7
   I. Title.
PR6063.C365S5   1998
823'.914—dc21   98-16364
                                                                    CIP

First published in Great Britain by Pocket Books

First U.S. Edition: June 1998

10 9 8 7 6 5 4 3 2 1

My thanks to **Helen Witwell,** Home Office Pathologist and my inspiration, for all her help, advice and patience; **Bernard Knight,** Home Office Pathologist, for all his help, time and advice; **Peter O. Rose,** for his advice on ivy and the use of his learned book, *Ivies*; **Mike Lucas.** (Mike Lucas Yachting) for his advice on knots and use of *The Ashley Book of Knots*; **The National Training Centre** for Scientific Support to Crime Investigation, Durham; **Peter Ablett,** Director; **Keith Fryer,** Assistant Director; **Sue Thornewill,** Head of Fingerprint Training; **Sandy Bushell,** Instructor; **Dr Z. Erzincglioglu,** entomologist; **Amanda Burton**; actress; **Vicki Featherstone,** script editor; **Catherine Reed,** book editor; **Kevin Hood,** writer; **Ashley Pharoah,** writer; **Caroline Oulton,** executive producer BBC Drama; **Tony Dennis,** producer BBC TV; **Patrick Spence,** script editor; **Nick Webb** of Simon and Schuster; **St John Donald** of Peters Frazer and Dunlop; **Sue Hogg,** executive producer, BBC TV; **Colin Ludlow,** producer, BBC drama. And for all those who may not have been included, many thanks.

PROLOGUE

Nothing ever happened in Northwick. It was that sort of village; quiet, predictable. A place you passed through en route to somewhere more enticing without even registering its existence. Even its church, in a county famous for its churches, was dull and uninteresting, and attracted few visitors.

After months of drought the storm, when it came, was a welcome relief. The heavy droplets bounced off the red, slatted roofs and gushed along the drains and gutters, dragging with them the soot and dirt which had built up over the summer months, before finally spilling out on to the roads and pavements and reflecting the street lamps in pools of shimmering light.

PC Morris Jay stood impassively under an ancient yew whose branches stretched out over the cemetery wall, offering him a temporary sanctuary from the relentless downpour. As he watched the water drip from the tip of his helmet, the church clock struck the quarter hour. He looked down at his watch; one forty-five. There was just enough time to check the last few shops on the high street before making his way back to the station to dry out and investigate the mysteries of his sandwich box.

Despite working shifts for almost twenty-five years PC Jay still hated nights, there was something unnatural about them. Nights were meant for warm beds and soft women, not hard roads and wet feet. As the lightning forked across the sky and the thunder rolled overhead, he pulled the collar of his raincoat tightly around his neck, secured his helmet strap, and left his leafy refuge.

Any energy Mark James had left in his body was knocked out of him by the fall. He lay on his back, peering through the rain, letting it splash over his face and along his lips, taking in deep gulps of air, his rib-cage rising and falling with each rasping breath. Fear had dried his mouth and he was suddenly very thirsty. He licked his lips, picking up the droplets on the end of his tongue and letting them trickle to the back of his throat, providing momentary relief. He needed time, time to think, time to sort out what had happened. Everything had gone so well. How had he been found out so quickly? He wondered now whether he had made a grave error in crossing Bird for a second time. He normally knew when to quit, but this time he seemed to have made a big mistake, gone too far, and now he was running for his very life.

He had felt no sense of apprehension when the car had arrived. It had followed the agreed procedures to the letter. Stopped, flashed its lights twice quickly and then once slowly, just as arranged. The only thing he had found a little unusual was the location. He was a bit of a moth and liked to hover around the bright lights of the city.

Despite living in Cambridge all his life he'd never heard of Northwick. It was a cold, isolated place in the middle of nowhere, the kind of village to which people came to retire and die. He hoped he'd never see it again. Still, the man must have his reasons, and whatever they were it was fine by him.

When the initial approach had been made Mark had been surprised, the man didn't seem to be the type to be involved in the drugs trade but then, who was. The merchandise was top quality, though – the best he'd seen in a long time. It was cheap too, so he expected to be able to move it on quickly and still make a tidy profit.

Feeling secure, Mark had stepped out of his hiding place and made his way through the rain towards the vintage sports car. Nice car, he'd thought, big and old-fashioned. Mark liked old cars, he'd owned an ageing Spitfire for years and, although its seats were ripped and its bodywork falling apart, he loved it.

He had been only yards away from it when its engine suddenly roared back into life, and the car accelerated towards him. He had leapt sideways, narrowly avoiding the nearside wing, and crashed into a row of dustbins. The car's reversing lights had flashed on and, realizing the driver was preparing for another attempt to squash him against the nearest wall, he had scrambled frantically to his feet and made a dash for an ancient sandstone wall. Half climbing, half jumping, he had begun to scramble over the wall when the car, still desperate for its prey, collided heavily with the sandstone blocks sending Mark crashing to the ground on the other side.

Recovering quickly, Mark wiped the rain from his eyes and tried to focus on his surroundings. Strange dark shapes seemed to rise unnaturally from the ground, silhouetted for a instant against the black sky as the lightning turned night into day, before disappearing again into the darkness. With a sense of overwhelming dread, Mark realized where he was; a cemetery. His mind raced as he tried to calculate his next move, his eyes searching for his best line of escape. His concentration was broken by the sound of his pursuer beginning to scale the wall. Whatever he decided, he would have to act quickly. He forced himself to his feet and made his way deeper into the graveyard, slipping and falling on the wet grass and mud, as he made his last frantic bid to escape. Finally, exhausted, he threw himself behind a tall, flat headstone, pushing his back into the smooth slate monument, trying to blend into his surroundings and hiding his face in his hands in his desperation not to be seen. Mark had no choice but to sit and wait. He was disoriented and too breathless to do anything else. Fear had robbed him of rational thought, but he knew his life was important to others and he was determined to survive, if only for their sake.

He tried to focus his mind, to rationalize his situation and understand where it had all gone wrong. Instinctively, for the first time in his adult life, he prayed.

✻　　✻　　✻

4

PC Jay's radio suddenly crackled into life. 'Control to 784, over.'

PC Jay fumbled through his clothes trying to get to his radio.

'Control to 784, over.' The message came over the radio again, only this time the voice was more impatient.

Jay was annoyed at their persistence. 'Hold your horses,' he thought. 'Bloody office men, what do they know about life at the sharp end?' Finally, forcing his raincoat to one side, he got to his radio. '784 to control, go ahead, over.'

'There's a Mr Typhoo at the police station to see you. He says you've got to deal with him.'

'Yea, ten-four control, I'll be right in.'

He recognized the shift code. It meant the tea was in the pot and the cards were on the table. Only one more building to do, he would have to be quick.

He was late and Frances Purvis was becoming concerned. She glanced at her watch again. The last train had gone and the station had become a strange eerie place.

A couple of drunks had ambled past a short while before, their carrier bags stretched to capacity with numerous cans of strong lager. They'd settled themselves down on one of the porter's trolleys and quickly began to drink the contents of their bag dry. They'd made a few lewd comments, but so far hadn't bothered her unduly. However, she wasn't sure how much longer that situation would last. It wasn't the kind of place a solitary girl should hang around late at night. She began *to wonder if she hadn't asked too much of Mark. He wasn't the brightest of people but his devotion to her was touching, and he was the obvious choice when she had felt so desperate. Perhaps Bird, or one of his strong-armed employees, had got hold of him, then she would be in trouble. She'd have to deny everything, of course, and hope Bird believed her. Just five more minutes, she thought, and then she'd have to make her way back to the house and hope she got there before Bird returned. She'd pretended to be ill, making her excuses not to go to the club. As soon as Bird had driven off, she'd packed and caught a taxi to the station. It had seemed the logical place to meet, but now, in the dark, with the two drunks becoming bolder with their comments she wasn't so sure. Where on earth was Mark?*

Mark looked up towards the sky, as if to ensure his prayer would be heard. It was then that he saw her, looking down at him, smiling, her face white and beautiful, illuminated for a moment by the moon, as it found a brief gap between the rolling clouds. One arm stretched out towards him while the other pointed to heaven, as if offering an escape from his torment. In the madness of desperation, Mark found himself reaching out to her, and grasping at her small, white, marble hand. Then, without warning, something struck him full in the face. The force, although not great, sent him crashing backwards, screaming with terror and thrashing out with his hands as he tried to ward off the unseen presence attacking him. The cat had been perched, hidden, at the angel's feet, sheltering beneath her marble shroud. The storm had frightened it and, seeing Mark, she had jumped into his outstretched arms, searching for some human comfort. He looked down at the giant black shape which was now lying across his lap, its green eyes glaring up at him. Mark normally liked cats. Frances had two and he always made a point of playing with them when he was visiting her. But he didn't like this one; this one had probably killed him. He grabbed the cat violently by its scruff and threw it away from him, watching it land awkwardly several yards away before it disappeared quickly into the darkness of the cemetery.

Mark strained his ears for the sound of approaching footsteps, there were none. Perhaps his pursuer hadn't heard his screams, perhaps he'd stopped searching and Mark was safe after all. He got to his feet slowly, peering over the top of the headstone for any sign of movement.

The sheer power of the blow that struck him down from behind sent him sprawling into the wet grass and mud of the cemetery. He lay there for a second clutching the back of his head, searching for the source of the pain which shot through his neck and down his spine. He didn't wait for the second blow to arrive, nor did he look behind to see who his assailant was, too afraid of what he might see. He began to run, almost on all fours, using his arms to keep his balance as his feet slipped on the wet earth. He tried to keep low, running stooped and hoping to use the other headstones as cover, in an attempt to shake off his pursuer. He ran quickly towards the safety of the village's street lights. He knew once he reached them he would be safe.

Finally, he reached the cemetery gates, his last obstacle to freedom. He pulled at the handles and shook them violently hoping they would give way, but although the iron gates rattled loudly against his assault, they remained firmly locked. Looking out along the village street for any sign of help he saw him, his saviour, his knight in blue armour. Mark had never thought he would be pleased to see a policeman, but now he was. He smiled with relief, forced an arm through the gate's railings and drew breath to call out.

PC Jay crossed the road towards the post office. Pulling his torch from his pocket he shone it through the shop's front window. Everything seemed to be in place, nothing tipped over, nothing broken and the windows were all intact. He walked over to the front door, grabbed its handles tightly and gave them a firm shake. They were locked, it would take a bulldozer to get through those doors. PC Jay breathed in deeply with a sense of relief, it had been a quiet night, and those were the ones he liked best. He was already visualizing himself sitting in the police canteen, his feet up, eating his sandwiches while his uniform dried out over a hot radiator. He turned deliberately and started to make his way back towards the police station.

Mark knew his mouth was moving. He could feel it, couldn't he? His mind told him he was shouting, but he heard nothing. The policeman didn't react either, just pulled on a door, and flashed his torch into a building. He tried again, his eyes bulging and his face reddening with the effort, but now he felt far away, his world spinning towards the bottom of a long black tunnel and there was nothing he could do to stop it. He realized he could no longer feel his mouth, his tongue would not react to the messages from his brain. As if a great weight was pushing him down, his legs buckled and he fell heavily to his knees. He tried to steady himself by grasping the gates, but his arms felt heavy and his strength was gone. Finally, he fell sideways on to the grass. Sheltered from the street by the cemetery wall, Mark lay motionless, looking up at the sky through the leaves of an ancient yew. He felt strangely calm, almost as if he were at peace with himself. He began to wonder what Frances would think when he didn't turn up; it would be the first time he'd ever let her down in his life. A dark shadow moved slowly across his face and Mark realized his nemesis had arrived.

The commotion disturbed PC Jay. He turned and stared back through the rain towards the church but could see nothing. He looked at his watch, five to two, if he went back now he'd be late, they'd start without him, and the tea would be stewed. He convinced himself there was nothing wrong; probably an animal of some sort, it nearly always was. Nothing serious had happened in the village for years, not even a burglary, so it was unlikely to be anything important. He stared along the street towards the church one more time, just to salve his conscience. Then he saw it. Its large black shape jumped quickly on to the cemetery wall under the tree where he had been sheltering, it crouched low and stared back along the street towards him. Jay knew it was the sexton's cat but was surprised to see it was still out, he thought it was cleverer than that. PC Jay smiled to himself, turned and walked away.

Mark James was dragged slowly back into the cemetery. His eyes were still open, allowing the rain to bounce off his unprotected pupils, obscuring the face of his killer, and run along the channels of his twisted face.

CHAPTER ONE

Samantha Ryan looked around the old magistrates court at Ely. It had been over a month since they'd found Andrew Stringer's body at the back of the Cromwell Library at St Steven's College and now she was about to pronounce judgement on his rather bizarre death. She enjoyed her visits to Ely, much preferring them to the make-shift inquests which were organized in committee room number three at the Park Hospital, with its plastic and chrome fittings. Here was a court worthy of the law. Its beamed ceilings and wooden benches oozed justice from every grain, while ancient paintings of long-dead judges hung from the oak-panelled walls, looking down imperiously on the innocent and guilty alike.

Sam scanned the room, looking at the faces of other witnesses. She moved from face to face examining each in detail before moving on to the next. She wondered what part each of them had played in Stringer's life and, more importantly, his death. Detective Superintendent Harriet Farmer was there, next to her was Dr Richard Owen, the police surgeon, followed by Detective Inspector Tom Adams. As her eyes drew level with his, he looked across at her. Their gaze lingered for a moment before Sam looked away, slightly flustered. Adams was amused at her embarrassment and continued to stare at her for a few moments longer.

He had first met Sam when she'd turned up at the Ross murder a year before. It had been a tricky one and if it hadn't been for her evidence they would probably have lost the case. He'd never really understood why she'd moved from the bright lights of London to a comparative criminal backwater like Cambridge, but that was her affair, and he was sure he'd find out in time. He'd liked her from the moment they'd first met, but she'd always kept the relationship strictly professional, and at times was even offhand towards him. The squad called her the 'ice maiden' but he wasn't convinced. She wasn't stunning in the 'accepted' sense, no long, blonde hair or silicone-enhanced breasts but there was something about her. Some women, he thought, simply possessed an indefinable attraction. She wasn't tall, but she was slim and beautifully proportioned, with an attractive face and the most memorable, soft, brown eyes he'd ever seen. She was also intelligent and he'd always found that appealing. He'd attended one of the old secondary modern schools in which intellectual ability was underestimated and frequently stifled. Future employment prospects for most of the boys had relied upon one of the many apprenticeships on offer at that time. He hadn't fancied any of those and so had joined the police cadets. He had seen this as a step up, it made him feel middle class, respected, part of the establishment, and he'd always enjoyed the work. The ultimate 'pull' during his school-days had been to go out with one of the grammar school girls and he had, quite often, but it had never come to anything. They had usually gone on to marry the boy who became the local bank manager, accountant or company executive. Still, he thought, he could dream. He'd been ambitious and astute enough to take advantage of the opportunities offered by the Open University since those days, and had found that education was more enjoyable and rewarding the second time around. Suddenly, realizing he'd been looking at her longer than he'd intended, he turned his head and focused his stare back into the court.

George Allan's firm voice suddenly cut across the court, 'Dr Ryan, would you like to give your evidence please?'

Sam, still feeling slightly disconcerted and annoyed by Adams' persistent stare, hadn't been paying attention to proceedings and was taken by surprise. She moved quickly, collecting her notes together and walking across the court to the witness box. She knew the procedure well. Picking up the Bible she read the oath aloud. She had done this a hundred times before and needed no prompting. When she'd finished, she looked across at the coroner, he nodded and she continued.

'Dr Samantha Ryan. I am a Bachelor of Medicine, and a member of the Royal College of Pathologists. I am the holder of a diploma in medical jeoprudence, a consultant Home Office pathologist and senior lecturer at Cambridge University. I am currently employed at the Park Hospital as a consultant in forensic medicine.'

Allan looked across at her, 'Thank you, Dr Ryan.'

He studied his notes for a moment before peering back at Sam over his half-rimmed spectacles. 'The police surgeon, Dr Owen, has stated in evidence that because of the advanced state of rigor mortis, he concluded that the deceased must have been dead between . . .' As if forgetting his lines, he looked down at his notes again and, reading from them, continued, 'between six and eight hours.' He looked back at Sam. 'I see from your notes, Dr Ryan, that you don't entirely agree with Dr Owen's findings. Perhaps you could elucidate?'

He sat back and waited for Sam's reply. She opened her notes and began to give her evidence. She didn't really need them, it was one of those cases which she was unlikely to forget easily. In her fifteen years as a forensic pathologist, Andrew Stringer's death was probably one of the most bizarre and difficult cases she'd had to deal with.

From the moment she arrived at the scene she'd felt the sense of disquiet amongst the investigating team. She'd arrived early for once, which was unusual for her. The time needed to arrive at a scene could vary considerably, depending upon the time she was contacted, where she was, what she was doing, where she'd left her car keys, and, most importantly, where in the county the body was located. Just travelling to a scene could sometimes take over an hour. This time she was lucky, the body had been discovered behind one of the old colleges, close to The Backs, making it easily accessible, especially during the early hours of the morning. Despite her punctuality, however, everybody still seemed to have arrived before her and there was the normal commotion and organized chaos which seemed to accompany every murder scene she attended. Uniformed and plain-clothed police officers scurried to and fro, while white-suited Scene of Crime Officers, SOCOs, carried both mundane and suspicious-looking objects away in a variety of plastic bags. The whole area was illuminated by high-intensity mobile lights which gave the scene an almost surreal perspective. Parking her car on the grass verge behind St Steven's College she left her car keys with a surprised PC on the main gate, before making her way the hundred yards along 'Fellows Lane' towards Old Bridge and the back of the college. Half-way across the bridge she noticed two CID officers talking to a couple of bowler-hatted porters. Both looked pale and shaken, and she assumed they had been the ones to discover the body. As she reached the far side of the bridge she turned left, crunching her way across the gravel path running between the River Cam and the Cromwell Library, and made her way towards the murder tent.

At first she had thought it was some kind of peculiar joke but the faces of Farmer and Adams told her it wasn't. The victim was sitting bolt upright on a wooden bench, his body and face turned slightly to one side. A small stream of blood ran from beneath the bench forming a sticky pool by the victim's feet. She walked around to the front of the body, bringing the man's face slowly into view. It was alabaster white, the half-open eyes staring blankly ahead. His mouth was wide open and fixed in a giant, soundless scream. A large metal-handled knife protruded from the left side of his chest about six inches below his armpit, twisting his arm unnaturally upwards as if someone had forced a coat hanger inside his T-shirt. Sam stood back for a moment. Murder it certainly seemed to be, but there was something about the entire scene that puzzled her.

'When you're ready, Dr Ryan?'

The coroner's inpatient voice interrupted Sam's thoughts and she began to give her evidence.

'For rigor mortis to have advanced to such a degree I would have expected the body to have been both stiff and cold. However, the deceased's body was still warm and had, in fact, hardly cooled by the time I arrived at the scene. From that, I concluded that the deceased had only been dead for a short time.'

Allan interrupted her, 'About how long is "a short time"?'

'It's impossible to be absolutely precise about these things, but I would certainly have thought less than two hours. I also examined the deceased's legs and found no evidence of hypostasis,' – Sam glanced across at the press gallery and noticed several reporters looking up at her expectantly; she took the hint – 'the settling of the blood downwards due to gravity after death.'

The journalists started to write again. Allan noticed the glance and was irritated by what he interpreted as Sam playing to the gallery. He continued with his questions.

'How, then, do you explain the presence of rigor mortis, Dr Ryan?'

Sam waited for a moment, scanning her notes to make sure her explanation was clear and accurate.

'It wasn't rigor mortis. Well, not in its true sense, anyway.'

Allan suddenly sat up with renewed interest. He knew Sam well, and was aware of her professional competence; he even found himself looking forward to her evidence. It was always clear, precise and well presented with no flights of fancy. This was certainly a deviation for her and he was already intrigued.

'It is a condition known as cadaveric spasm.' Sam looked across at the press gallery again. 'The instantaneous contraction of the muscles at the time of death.'

Allan pulled her attention back to him. 'I'm well aware of what cadaveric spasm is, Dr Ryan, but in fifteen years in this court I have never before come across a case of it. Are you sure of your facts?'

'Yes,' Sam replied firmly.

'In fact, isn't there a certain school of thought which believes that the condition doesn't even exist, or if it does, it's only likely to be found on battlefields and the like?' This time *he* looked across at the press gallery and, with a certain amount of satisfaction, watched them note down his every word. 'But you clearly think it does exist?'

'Yes, I do.'

'Then how do you think he died?'

Sam looked into his face, waiting for his reaction when she made her announcement.

'Suicide. It is my belief that Andrew Stringer took his own life. We know that the emotional state of a person in

17

these circumstances is important. We also know that the deceased was in a highly charged state due to the recent engagement of his former girlfriend, and had, in fact, threatened revenge. This, I believe, was his revenge.'

'That's a bit elaborate, don't you think?'

'Not if you wanted the authorities to think you were murdered.'

Allan, leaning back in his chair, waited to see how her arguments developed. Sam continued, confident of her facts.

'We now know the knife he used was stolen from his former girlfriend's flat some days before he died. It is my belief that he arrived at the college fully intending to kill himself and hoping the blame would fall either on her or her fiancé. Sitting on the college bench, he carefully positioned the knife between the top of the bench and the soft tissue area under his left armpit. This would explain the unusual position of his arm at the time he was discovered. At first I thought he might have been trying to pull the knife out, but he wasn't, he was trying to ensure it went in. The scratch marks found on the top slats of the bench were consistent with a metal-handled knife being scratched across the surface of the paint. Once the knife was in position he pushed his body back on to it with such force that the knife passed between the deceased's sixth and seventh ribs before penetrating both his heart and one lung. Death would have followed almost immediately.'

The court was now totally hushed and Sam continued with her evidence.

'The pain and the shock of the knife entering his body, combined with his emotional state at the time, almost certainly brought on the spasm. Had it not been for the spasm, preventing the body falling to the ground, an innocent person might now be facing a murder charge, and the deceased would have had his bizarre revenge.'

Although captivated by her testimony, Sam had stepped beyond the bounds of her expertise and Allan interjected quickly, 'I think that's for the court to decide, don't you, Dr Ryan?'

Sam, also realizing she might have gone a bit far, nodded and closed her file.

Reg Applin had been the church sexton for as long as anyone could remember. He enjoyed the status, but knew his time was short; rheumatism was stiffening his knees as the ageing process took its inevitable toll. If he'd been in any other job he'd have been retired by now, but the parish, not surprisingly, were having problems finding a replacement and had asked him to stay on for 'a while'. He had hoped they'd buy him a mechanical digger to take the strain out of the job, but there wasn't enough money in the parish fund. They bought him a new type of spade instead, by way of compensation, but it wasn't much use. The new spade had a sort of lever at the back and was supposed to take the effort out of the digging, but it broke after a week and he was forced to use his old one again and that had finished his knees off. And the work wasn't as rewarding as it once had been. People either didn't tip him or if they did, it was hardly enough to buy a couple of pints at the Black's Head. Besides, most people wanted to be cremated these days and there was nothing for him in that job. It was funny, really, he'd known most of his 'clients' when they were alive; they all thought themselves better than him, but here he was still alive and throwing dirt on to most of them. He'd already picked out his own spot and been promised it by the vicar. It was under the old yew tree at the back end of the cemetery. He liked it there, it was cool and shaded from the extremes of the weather and the kids seldom ventured that deep into the cemetery, so he hoped to be safe from the vandalism which had desecrated so many of the graves in recent years. He propped his bike up against one of the numerous old tombstones which littered the graveyard, unravelled his bag from the handlebars and, with his terrier, Scruff, marching by his side and his spade over his shoulder, made his way into the cemetery to start preparing another grave.

Sam emerged from the court into the daylight. It was mild and muggy and the air lay heavily over the town. The sky was black as the storm clouds began to roll in from the east. Stretching her shoulders, she looked out across the old town's roofs towards the cathedral. Although much of the building was hidden, it was a majestic sight all the same. The great mass of stone rose above Ely like a forbidding glacier, its amber, grey and pink colourings standing out against the black sky, illuminated by the final rays of the rapidly setting October sun. She visited it from time to time, wandering around the various chapels and reading the inscriptions to the great and the good. She felt that it helped to add a spiritual dimension to her otherwise clinical life, even though she wasn't sure about God any more. She used to be, when she was child, but that was before her father died.

She had seen it happen, had watched as one moment he waved goodbye and the next exploded into a ball of flame and light. They never caught the people responsible, they seldom did, it was all too political. He knew he was under threat, a Catholic and a policeman was an almost certain recipe for disaster. Dozens of his friends had already died or been seriously injured, which was why he had been such a careful man. He normally checked everything at least twice and she could remember playing with the mirror on the long pole which he ran under his car every time he went out. She'd being playing with it on the day he died. She had left it at the end of the garden when her mother called her in for lunch. Her father had been called out in an emergency and had taken a chance. The IRA were blamed, but later when Sam was old enough to ask questions of her own she had doubted that conclusion. Catholic policemen weren't trusted. All her daddy wanted was a peaceful Ireland. She knew his death was her fault, her mammy had told her. Mammy had stood by his grave holding Sam's sister close to her and refusing to acknowledge Sam's presence. So God and the church had become Sam's scapegoats and all her anger was directed at them as her mother's had been directed at her. Fifteen years as a pathologist had only confirmed her atheism, exchanging what remained of her spiritual awareness for the cold clinical analysis of the dissecting table and the laboratory.

Now, for some inexplicable reason she found herself being drawn slowly back, examining all her past assumptions. The cathedral had been the first church she had entered for over twenty years. It had been a difficult process and she had found herself hanging about outside the main entrance trying to summon up the courage to enter, walking up and down and looking at the door as if it were the gateway to hell. Finally, tagging along with an organized group, she had been swept anonymously into the vast interior.

Her thoughts were interrupted by the police surgeon, Richard Owen. 'Quite magnificent, isn't it?'

Sam looked at him, confused for a moment.

'The cathedral, magnificent.'

She collected her thoughts. 'Yes, it is.'

'I always like to come to the cases I've been involved with, especially when they're heard at Ely. It's such a beautiful place.'

Sam nodded. 'Yes, it's lovely, isn't it?'

'You were quite brilliant in there. Made me look a bit of a chump though.'

'That wasn't the intention, Richard. It's an extremely rare condition, it's the first time I've ever seen it. There's no reason why you should have spotted it.'

'*You* did. If I'd bothered to take his temperature properly then I might have realized something was wrong. It just seemed so obvious.'

She looked into Richard's face and found herself feeling quite sorry for him. 'Well, you'll know for next time,' she said awkwardly.

'Yes, I certainly will.' He paused for a moment.

'Listen, Janet and I were wondering, if you have a spare evening over the next few weeks, whether you'd like to come and have some supper with us. Give you the chance to get to know her, you're about the same age. I'm sure you'll have a lot in common. Perhaps we could swap a few ideas as well?'

It was the first time Owen had really spoken to her since she'd come to Cambridge a little over a year ago. They'd swapped notes occasionally but it had always been on a strictly professional basis, she wasn't even sure he liked her very much, so she was surprised by the invitation. She was pleased that her display in court hadn't alienated him. Owen was one of the old school and set in his ways. He'd been the local police surgeon for almost thirty years and had been dealing with murders while she was still in pigtails and running around in blue serge knickers. The problem was that he was finding it difficult to adjust in a rapidly changing world.

'I'd love to.'

Owen appeared pleased, 'Good, good. I'll ring you next week to make arrangements.'

Their conversation was interrupted by the approach of a young girl. She was about twenty-two years old, slim and pretty with a sweep of long blonde hair. Sam had seen her in court. She spoke to Sam.

'Dr Ryan? I wonder if I could have a word with you?'

Richard Owen took the hint. 'Look, I must be going, I'll catch up with you later.'

Sam smiled, nodded and watched him leave. She returned her attention to the young girl.

'I'm Rebecca West, Andrew's old girlfriend. I'd just

like to say thank you for what you did. I knew Andrew was a mad sod, that's why I left him. I just hadn't realized how mad.'

'Well, he certainly won't be causing you any more problems.'

'No.'

Sam noticed a young and rather handsome young man standing a few yards along the street, watching them intensely; they clearly belonged together.

'He looks nice.'

Rebecca glanced at him and smiled, the boy smiled back as only young lovers can.

'He is, best thing that ever happened to me really.'

'Fresh start.'

The girl smiled broadly at Sam. 'I hope so. Well, thanks again.' She put her hand out. Sam took it and gave her a gentle squeeze. She'd been through a difficult ordeal for one so young and Sam found herself hoping that everything would now work out for her. She watched with a certain degree of jealousy as Rebecca rejoined her boyfriend and they disappeared hand in hand along the road. She envied their youth and their fresh start.

'Penny for them?'

Detective Inspector Tom Adams' question made her jump. She turned around and looked up at him.

'They're worth more than a penny.'

'I expect they are. Well, that's another one we've lost.'

Sam was irritated by the remark. 'You didn't lose it, you never had it in the first place.'

'Try telling Superintendent Farmer that, she's chalked it up as lost glory and guess who she's blaming?'

'She can suit herself,' Sam replied.

'Clever stuff though. I was very impressed.'

Sam felt flattered and slightly embarrassed. She was attracted to Adams, who was tall and broad with a crop of dark black hair that seemed to enhance his blue, twinkling eyes. He was different to most of the police officers she had to deal with, and although he was a bit rough around the edges she always felt he was only playing a part and that in fact there was far more to him. He never gave the impression that he considered women to be in any way inferior to him. His manner suggested that he was at ease in and comfortable with the company of women. A very attractive trait, Sam thought. Their conversation was interrupted by a call from the opposite side of the road. Superintendent Harriet Farmer was standing by the side of her dark blue Escort, staring across at them. She seemed annoyed.

'Do you want a lift back or are you walking?'

Sam glanced across at Farmer. She looked every inch the police officer. Although tall and slim and not unattractive, she had a hard face which expressed years of struggling, not only against criminals, but also against a system which had difficulty dealing with career-minded women. Her hair was long and brown and she kept it in a smart ponytail. This she pulled back so tightly that it seemed to stretch her skin like a cheap face-lift. Sam always imagined that when she let it out at night her face would crumple into a thousand crinkles and lines. Farmer was watching the two of them impatiently, waiting for Adams to break off his conversation and join her. Adams looked down at Sam. 'Got to go, conspiring with the enemy and all that.'

Sam looked across at Farmer. 'She who must be obeyed.'

Adams laughed quietly before turning on his heel and walking off. As he did, the two women's eyes met for a moment before Sam finally turned and made her way towards the cathedral.

It was late, and the storm was raging overhead. Reg was sheltering under the branches of the old yew, sitting on his spade and watching the rain bounce off the church roof and pour down its walls. If they didn't get the drains repaired soon, he thought, there'd be no more St Mary's. It was the season for storms, and this was the second bad one in a month. He reached into his bag and retrieved his flask. Pouring the last of his tea into a small plastic cup he slurped it down. It was almost cold, but he didn't care. The grave he had just finished was already an inch deep in water and he wondered if the deceased had realized he was going to be buried at sea. He was exhausted. All the digs seemed far longer and harder than they used to. He'd have finished this job hours ago if he'd been younger and fitter, then maybe he would have missed the storm. He would have to stop, they'd have to find a younger man, he wasn't up to it any more. One day, he thought, they'd find him dead inside one of his own graves and then they'd have some explaining to do. He stood up, secured the cup on to the top of his flask and emptied the contents of his sandwich box on to the ground before slipping on his jacket and slowly making his way through the rain towards his bike. It wasn't until he reached it that he realized his dog was no longer with him. Probably sheltering under some bush or headstone, Reg thought, he wasn't stupid. He glanced at his watch, the pub had already been open over an hour and he was keen to get in out of the wet. He called out, 'Scruff, where are you, boy, time to go, come on, pub's open!' He peered through the rain for any sign of his dog. Suddenly the small terrier came bursting through the wet grass and ran towards him. As the dog came closer Reg noticed that he was holding something firmly in his mouth.

'What you got there then, boy, eh, what you got there?'

He crouched down and tried to pull the object away from him but Scruff was keen to hang on to it and fought fiercely for his prize. Finally, Reg managed to tear it free, leaving only a small part in the dog's mouth which he chewed and swallowed quickly, fearful of losing that as well. Wiping the rain from his eyes, Reg stared down at what he'd retrieved. At first he wasn't sure what it was and thought it might be just a piece of rotten meat, or perhaps the remains of an animal. However, as his eyes began to focus, he realized it was none of those things but was, in fact, a person's hand, or rather what was left of one. Half of it was missing and three blackened fingers dangled loose from a disembodied palm. Scuff had brought a few bones back in his time and that was bad enough, but a human hand, and one that hadn't been dead long, shocked and surprised him. Almost instinctively, Reg threw it across the graveyard, not wanting the object near him. It travelled for several yards before colliding with a headstone and splashing into the mud in a crumpled, blackened heap. Scruff, having lost his prize, raced back into the cemetery looking for another. Reg, shaken, called after him, 'Scruff! Come on, lad, let's have you, I'm getting soaked!'

Normally, he would have left him in the cemetery and let him find his own way back. It wasn't the first time he'd disappeared, but he was concerned about how Scruff had come across the hand and fearful of what his dog might bring back next. Reg hung his bag over one of the old headstones and pushed his way through the wet grass following the sound of his dog's barking. The trail led him into one of the older, overgrown sections of the graveyard. He looked around. The barking was coming from the seventeenth-century tomb of Sir Jasper Case. He knew the tomb well. It was one of the more interesting in the cemetery, but it was old and falling apart. He'd done what he could, but as fast as he repaired it the bloody kids came in and smashed it again. It was a sort of contest and the kids were winning.

'They've no respect for nothing these days,' he mumbled.

The lid, like the rest of the tomb, was broken and a large piece was missing. It was clear that Scruff had managed to squeeze inside the tomb and had got himself trapped.

'Silly beggar,' Reg shouted at his dog. 'Should have more sense.'

He peered into the darkness of the tomb searching

for his dog. As the sky flashed cobalt blue he was just able to make Scruff out. He was sniffing around something lying in the bottom of the tomb. The light wasn't good enough for Reg to see what it was so, in the half light, he leaned in and, cupping his hand under the dog's stomach, started to pull him clear of the tomb. The job, however, wasn't as easy as Reg had hoped and Scruff was resisting. Pull as he might he just couldn't seem to move the small dog. He looked down into the tomb searching for the cause of the problem.

'Come on, you daft beggar, we'll be here all night.'

He pulled again with no result, so he waited for another flash of lightning. He didn't have to wait long, a particularly powerful fork crossed the sky lighting up everything for a moment in a brilliant blue flash. Reg looked deep into the tomb. It was only then that he realized he wasn't holding Scruff. The head twisted towards him in his hand, causing the face to stare up at him. It was only half there, the flesh dropping from its bones. The lips had already disappeared, exposing the teeth and producing a sort of grizzly smile. One eye was missing, leaving a black void, and the other bulged out of the skull, red and bloated, the skin surrounding it having been eaten away. Reg screamed and dropped the head, staggering backwards. He looked down and noticed that part of the scalp had stuck to his hand. Shuddering, he frantically wiped it off on the long wet grass and ran from the cemetery.

*   *   *

It had been the same dream, the one she'd had for the past month. The one that woke her in the middle of the night leaving her body and bedclothes soaked with perspiration. She lay there for a moment trying to come to terms with it, staring into the darkness of her bedroom, her chest heaving up and down as she strove to recall the images that only moments before had invaded her dreams. As usual, however, they were gone, like will-o'-the-wisp, disappearing into the dark recesses of her subconscious only to reappear the following night to terrify her again. She knew her dreams were vivid, she did have momentary flashes of them, all in glorious Technicolor. But the faces were alabaster blank and smooth, appearing and then disappearing again, floating off into a void. The ringing of the phone by her bedside finally brought her back to reality. She propped herself on one elbow, turned on the bedside light and picked up the phone, almost dropping it as she brought it to her ear.

'Hello, Dr Ryan.'

She fought against the slurred tiredness in her voice but it was impossible. The voice on the other end of the phone was young, confident and awake. These facts alone told her it was a policeman.

'Sorry to bother you, Dr Ryan, but they've discovered a body at St Mary's Church and we were wondering if you could come out. It's a bit of a dodgy one.'

Sam couldn't help but be impressed by his clinical interpretation of a suspicious death as being 'a bit of a dodgy one'. He must have got that from one of the many police series which had invaded TV of late. Besides, what did they expect her to say, 'No, sorry, it's my day off and I'm going shopping'? She could feel her bad mood and she tried to control it.

'I thought Dr Stuart was on call?'

The answer came back crisply, 'Yes, he is, but we can't find him, he's not answering his bleeper. That's why we're a bit late phoning you.'

Probably interfering with his love life, Sam grumbled to herself. She was beginning to recover.

'Yes, of course I'll come . . . just a moment, let me grab a pen.'

She leaned across the bed and opened the drawer in her bedside cabinet. Fumbling around inside she found a small, black notebook and pen. She sat up, resting the book against her legs, trying to focus on its clear white pages. 'OK, I'm ready now. Where is it?'

His voice was so sharp it made Sam wince. 'St Mary's Church, Northwick. It's just off the B381, about twenty miles outside . . .'

Sam cut in, 'Yes, I know where that is, thank you.'

He was only trying to be helpful but she didn't need his efficiency right now.

'There'll be a policeman on the gate to direct you to the scene. Superintendent Farmer is already there.' He said it as if it were some form of warning for her to hurry. She wasn't about to be intimidated by Farmer or anyone else. 'Yes, thank you. I'll be about an hour.'

She put the phone down and looked at her alarm clock, twelve twenty-eight a.m. She made a note of the time in her book before dropping it on the bedside table and swinging her legs out of bed. She calculated that, by the time she'd got dressed and ready, it was going to take her longer than an hour to get there. Northwick was on the other side of the county and not the easiest place in the world to reach, but the police liked a time, it gave them something to look forward to.

Shuffling across the room to the window she pulled back the curtains and threw open the window. The storm had passed, but she could still hear the distant sound of thunder as it rolled on across the county. The mugginess that had seemed to linger for weeks had gone and been replaced by fresh, clear air. It raced unchecked across the East Anglian countryside from the North Sea before pouring through her open window, cooling and reviving her naked body. The heavy rain had filled the air with the smells of the night and she loved those. It reminded her that her sense of smell was still intact and hadn't, yet, been totally destroyed by the aromas of the mortuary. She looked down into her garden. The storms had been a welcome break from the long hot summer the county had just experienced. The garden had burst into life again as it drank deeply. She looked forward to the season's work. Closing the window and securing the latch she made her way back across the bedroom towards the shower.

She was surprised to find herself musing with some pleasure that if Farmer was dealing with this case, Adams was almost sure to be there too.

Samantha was late as usual. She'd managed to lose her car keys yet again and was finally forced to use the spare set which she kept for just such an occasion in a kitchen drawer. She imagined Farmer pacing up and down, waiting impatiently for her to arrive and pass judgement on the deceased. She turned into the village. The church wasn't difficult to find, she only had to follow the blue flashing lights which were illuminating the whole area. The press were there already, milling around the graveyard looking for their lead story. They were only stopped from invading the cemetery and destroying the scene by a thin piece of yellow and black police tape and a single police officer's vigilance. The press always seemed to find out quickly about major cases, tipped off no doubt by some friendly detective within the murder squad. It wasn't strictly allowed, but it always happened. She drove through the throng of reporters slowly, masking her face with her hand from the camera flashes and ignoring the numerous taps on the side-window of her car.

As she approached the church she was stopped by a young constable who shone a torch irritatingly into her face. He looked cold, but then he'd probably been there several hours already. By the time every police officer and his dog had travelled out to the scene and expressed their opinion on the situation, it could take hours before somebody finally made the decision to call out the pathologist. She flicked open the glove compartment and rummaged through the collection of chocolate papers, discount vouchers and maps which littered the inside, searching for her identity card. Finally, locating the piece of drab plastic, on which was an even drabber photograph of herself, she held it up for the constable's inspection.

'Dr Ryan, Home Office Pathologist.'

He nodded, and after making a few quick notes on the pad he had secured to a clipboard, directed her to her parking place by the side of the church. She thanked him, dropped her ID card back into the mess of her glove compartment and drove steadily along the road towards a small gap in an apparently unending line of police cars.

The police swarmed around the site. Some in uniform, with their black woolly hats pulled tightly around their ears, carrying long poles, the SOCOs in their white boiler suits, and the CID wandering around talking earnestly to each other but not, apparently, doing very much.

She climbed out of her car and made her way through the church gates, following the taped path to the scene. Half-way along the path she was approached by the crime scene manager who handed her a white boiler suit. This, of course, was for the protection of the crime scene, preventing contamination of the evidence, but it was also invaluable for protecting her own clothes. She was always careful about her appearance. Smart but practical, with just a hint of make-up. She remembered turning up to one scene looking like death warmed up. She'd been out to a late dinner the night before and hadn't bothered making her usual effort after the phone had rung at five in the morning. Her greatly reduced concentration had been focused on getting to the scene. Unfortunately, the press had been tipped off and were everywhere. Newspaper reporters, photographers, television crews, the works. She had found herself pushing through a wall of flashing lights and unanswerable questions before emerging into the field in which the body was lying. She'd seen herself the next day on both the national and local news looking dreadful, like a bag lady, pale faced and scruffy. But most humiliating were the phone calls from friends who had also seen her. Farmer, on the other hand, had looked her usual cool, confident self, dressed smartly in trousers and a rather expensive-looking black winter coat. Sam had made a promise to herself that she would never be seen in that condition again, even if it did mean turning up at a scene a few minutes late.

She was approached by Richard Owen. He looked every bit the prosperous country doctor in his dark wool blazer and unprotected green wellingtons, which, after all, she thought, is what he was. A police surgeon's main function in life, as far as Sam was concerned, was to pronounce life extinct, and that at a suitable distance if possible. Some, she found, fancied themselves as latter day Sherlock Holmeses, and would often interfere far beyond their brief and, more irritatingly, their competence. Owen had learned, when dealing with Sam, to keep his opinions and diagnoses to the minimum. She was surprised and a little annoyed to see that he wasn't wearing his white protective boiler suit and wondered how he'd managed to get around the crime scene manager, as they were normally sticklers for procedure. He greeted her with a half smile, 'Evening, Sam. Managed to fight your way through the circus, then?

Sam nodded. She rubbed the edge of his jacket between her fingers. 'Nice smart jacket, Richard, very in keeping with the situation.'

Owen looked down at his uncovered jacket and brushed it with his hand.

'Do you like it? Present from the memsahib. Got to show willing, haven't you?'

'You could have covered it up with a set of white overalls. It's the first thing I teach my new students.'

Richard remained unrepentant. 'Hardly worth the effort, I was in and out in a trice.'

Sam did her best to hide her annoyance at this lack of procedure but found it difficult. 'Have you never heard the saying, a person can be murdered once, but the scene can be murdered a thousand times?'

Owen changed the subject. 'Thought Trevor Stuart was on call?'

'He is, but they couldn't find him; probably stuffed his bleeper under some unfortunate's mattress.'

'Perhaps they should have tried some of the female student blocks, always a good bet during his student days.'

'Well, it's time he grew up. Anyway, what have we got?'

'White male, late teens, early twenties, been dead a few weeks I would think.'

Sam listened politely but took little notice, preferring to make up her own mind about what she found at the scene.

Owen continued, 'Church sexton found him a few hours ago; he'd been strangled. The cord's still around his neck. He's in a bit of a state, I'm afraid, animals got there before we did.'

'No identity on him?'

'No, nothing. He's naked and there's no sign of his clothes at the moment.'

Sam considered what he had just told her for a moment. 'Sexual motivation?'

'Not sure, but then you're the expert on these things, not me. I'm just a jobbing police surgeon.'

Knowing he was aware of her feelings on police surgeons, she smiled across at him.

'I've told them they can take the body out of the tomb if that's all right? Wasn't enough room to swing a cat in there.'

As much as she disliked people 'mucking about' with the body before she got to the scene, Sam knew he'd made the right decision and it would certainly help her get on with the initial examination. She nodded, acknowledging his help. 'No, that's fine. I suppose I'd better go and see what I can do. Thanks for the help.'

Picking up her bag and looking back across at Owen, she couldn't resist having one more swipe at him about his failure to follow the rules. 'Hope the smell hasn't stuck to your jacket, Richard, or Janet will be upset, won't she? See you later.'

Sam turned and walked away along the taped path towards the centre of the cemetery, a wicked smile across her face. Owen waited until she was out of sight before grabbing the bottom of his jacket and bringing it up to his nose. He winced, Sam was right, the smell of the body seemed to have clung to every fibre, it would have to be cleaned. He dropped the jacket back into place and, shaking his head, made his way towards the cemetery gate.

The body wasn't difficult to find, broadcast by the presence of arc lights and the commotion surrounding it. Sam spotted Farmer and Adams, surrounded by SOCOs, standing by the side of a tomb. One SOCO was already inside the tomb taking various samples while others combed the surrounding area and yet another took photographs. They all looked cold and Farmer and Adams were drinking steaming coffee from cardboard cups. She made her way towards them.

She noticed that the lid from the tomb had been removed and now lay in three pieces on the wet grass. The body lay next to it on an opened-out bodybag. Owen had been right, the tomb was small and she certainly couldn't have worked inside it. Farmer looked up as she approached, clearly surprised at her presence.

'I thought Trevor Stuart was on call?'

Sam was becoming tired of the question. 'They decided this one should be done properly,' she snapped.

Farmer and Adams looked at each other, detecting a problem. Sam crouched down by the body, opened her medical bag and searched through the array of bottles and instruments for her dictaphone. It wasn't there. Then she remembered. She had been using it at the Park Hospital to copy up some notes and had left it on her desk. She took out her pad but was unable to find the pen. Awkwardly she asked, 'Can anyone lend me a pen for a moment?'

Farmer and Adams exchanged an amused glance before Adams felt inside his pocket and handed Sam a biro.

'Make sure I get it back,' he joked, 'that's how I got it.'

Sam thanked him but was too annoyed with herself

to smile. She jotted down the time and location of the initial examination of the body into the book, as well as a list of those who were present at the scene. She looked down at the body, it was a mess, there wasn't much she could do with it at this stage. Owen seemed to have been right about most things. She began to make her notes.

'The body is that of a white male, probably in his late teens or early twenties. It is badly decomposed and naked. The right hand is missing . . .'

Adams spoke up, 'We've found that; the sexton's dog had it.'

'There are also three fingers missing from his left hand . . .' She looked up at Adams. 'Don't suppose the dog has those as well?'

'No, sorry. We didn't find his hors-d'oeuvre.'

'Half of one foot has disappeared and there are superficial injuries to both arms and the torso. The injuries to the torso seem a little unusual. They consist for two cuts, one vertical and one horizontal. The cuts intersect at the lower stomach, in an approximation of an upside-down cross.' Although intrigued by the injuries she knew there was little more she could do until she had the body back at the mortuary. 'A ligature has been twisted tightly around the victim's neck. There is a small metal pole on the left side of the neck to which the two ends of the ligature have been attached and which was clearly used to twist the cord tight, forming a garrotte.'

Sam turned her attentions to Colin Flannery, the Crime Scene Manager. 'Have we got the air temperature yet?'

Colin had been with the scene of crime department most of his working life and found himself resenting the question. It was almost as if Sam was challenging his competence. He nodded. Sam continued.

'What about inside the tomb?'

Colin nodded again.

'We'll need to get on to the weather bureau to establish the mean temperature for the last few weeks.'

Colin could feel himself becoming annoyed. He disliked the feeling, it didn't sit well with the cool, calm image he liked to project at any scene.

'It's all in hand, Dr Ryan, you don't have to worry.'

Sam wasn't sure what it was, the tone of his voice or the sharpness of his reply, but she realized she'd offended him.

'Telling my grandmother how to suck eggs here, aren't I, Colin?'

He gave a sort of half nod but didn't respond. Sam returned to the body. The maggot infestation was extensive and seemed to make the body move as they wriggled to and fro just below the remaining skin. An average fly could lay more than three hundred eggs each and this body had been visited by a lot of flies.

'I'd like samples of these maggots. Have we sent for an entomologist yet?'

'We're still trying. Having trouble getting hold of one.'

'Would there be any objection to me taking a few?'

Colin shook his head. 'I'll get you some formalin.'

The samples would be important if there was to be a chance of establishing, with any accuracy, the time of death. Contrary to popular perception, establishing time of death is a very inaccurate science and she would need any help she could get, insect or otherwise. Sam delved into in her bag and emerged with a small specimen jar. Plucking several of the small white creatures off the body, she dropped them into the glass container before sealing it and handing it to one of the SOCOs.

Colin quickly returned with a second jar containing the formalin. He crouched down beside her and plucked several more maggots off the body before dropping them into the jar, watching them sink slowly to the bottom. Sam then took the thermometer from her bag and shook it before pushing it into the mass of maggots which surrounded the body's neck. She had to establish the temperature at which the maggots had developed. The cooler the temperature, the slower they would develop, the warmer the faster; it all helped. When she had finished she asked Colin to roll the body carefully on to its side. He did this quickly and professionally, taking care to cause the minimum of disruption to the remains. After a quick glance along the back of the body, and seeing no further injuries, it was rolled back into place. Sam looked at her watch and stood up.

'Initial examination concluded at one fifty-eight a.m.'

Farmer and Adams examined their watches and nodded.

'PM at ten a.m. if that suits everyone?'

They nodded again.

'Right, well, see you there then.'

Sam began to walk away from the scene, followed by Farmer and Adams. Farmer spoke first.

'What can you tell us?'

'Not much more than you already know. He was certainly strangled and there appear to be other injuries to both his body and arms. But whether they were caused by our killer, or because he's been out in the open for a while, I won't know until I get him cleaned up at the mortuary. Have his clothes been found yet?'

'No, not yet, we're still looking for them. Do you think there could have been a sexual motive, being naked?'

'It's going to be difficult to tell after all this time.'

Farmer continued with the cross-examination. 'How long has he been dead?'

Sam shrugged. 'A few weeks maybe. I'll try to get it as close as I can but don't hold your breath. I might have a better idea when I've finished the PM and the entomologist's had time to do his dirty work.'

As Sam began to peel off her white boiler suit, Farmer looked across at her. 'Dr Owen did a bit better than that.'

Sam, annoyed at having her judgement challenged, snapped back, 'Really? Well, as far as I'm concerned if you want it any closer ask a gypsy.' She finally kicked off the boiler suit and handed it to a passing SOCO before making her way towards the cemetery gate, leaving Farmer impotent and annoyed.

CHAPTER TWO

A s Sam reversed her car into her allotted spot she
noticed that the hospital had finally managed to
erect a name board officially reserving her place. It
had only taken a year, she thought, not bad. The
board was dark green with black lettering informing
uninvited guests that this was her space. **RESERVED.
DOCTOR SAMANTHA RYAN. PATHOLOGY.**

She parked her car and clipped the anti-theft device
around the steering wheel. It was only there for show,
she'd lost the keys months ago, but still, she hoped, it
might put people off.

Climbing out of her four-wheel drive Land-Rover,
Sam stared down the long, dark alleyways of the concrete maze they called a car-park. It was a forbidding
place, even during the day; badly lit with pillars and
alcoves which cast irregular shadows across the concrete
floor. At night it assumed an almost sinister quality,
making even the short trip from the lift to her car an
unnerving experience. She'd often complained about
the security but it made little difference; other priorities
claimed the hospital's limited budget and the general
consensus was that it would take a rape or murder

before any changes were made. Sam hurried across the car-park to the lift, fingering the anti-rape alarm which she kept concealed in her coat pocket. She wasn't sure how effective it would be against a determined attacker, but it was the one small concession made by the hospital to help calm the female staff's increasing concern.

Stepping out of the lift at the fourth floor, Sam began to feel relaxed and comfortable again. Here it was warm and light and full of people. As she approached her office door she noticed her secretary, Jean Carr, making her way purposefully towards her. In one hand she held a steaming cup of coffee, while in the other was the rest of Sam's week, cunningly concealed inside a large brown desk diary. Her strong Norfolk accent caught up with Sam first.

'Morning, Dr Ryan!'

Jean was a short, stocky woman with a large face and deep-blue eyes which were exaggerated by a pair of heavy-rimmed spectacles sitting uneasily on her nose. She was always smartly dressed, if a little old-fashioned, but had always resisted Sam's attempts to bring her wardrobe up to date. Jean had worked at the Park Hospital for over twenty-five years, with only a short break to bring up her family. She was one of the great unrewarded assets of both the department and the hospital and Sam was aware that life would be impossible without her. As Jean finally caught up with her, Sam lifted the mug of freshly brewed coffee from her hand and began to sip at it, smiling wickedly with her eyes.

'Thanks, Jean, mother's milk, my caffeine level is right down.'

Realizing that any protest would be useless, Jean just sighed and shook her head. She liked Sam and was fiercely protective of her. It was the first time she had worked for a woman and despite Sam's persistent attempts to try and change her, she was enjoying the experience. They entered Sam's office together. It was a large room with a homely feel engineered by the inclusion of numerous pot plants and a discriminating selection of prints adorning the walls. It contrasted sharply with her grey, clinical office in the mortuary which was about as appealing as the interior of a prison cell. At the far end of the office behind her desk was a large window which looked out over the back of the hospital and gave her a clear view of the mortuary. This allowed her to keep an eye on its various comings and goings.

As Sam reached her desk Jean's interrogation began. 'What's all this about you being called out last night? I thought it was Dr Stuart's turn?'

'So did I. Haven't seen Trevor this morning, have you?' There was a casualness about Sam's voice that Jean often found a little irritating, as if her mind was elsewhere and not concentrating on the present.

'No, I don't think Dr Stuart's in yet. Probably still in bed.'

Sam looked down at the pile of paperwork and unopened correspondence that littered her desk and casually flicked through it, searching for anything new or unusual which might stimulate her interest. There was nothing. Finally, her curiosity satisfied, she looked up and returned to the conversation.

'Probably, but with whom?'

Jean was aware of Trevor's predilections and had a reasonable idea where he might have laid his head.

'I'd check the female student blocks if I were you. That's where he normally turns up when he goes missing.'

Sam smiled. 'Jean, whatever are you implying?'

'I'm implying nothing, I'm stating. A middle-aged man like that. I don't know what they see in him.'

Sam was amused. Jean was probably the straightest person she had ever known, and although as aware as other women of Trevor's attraction, she heartily disapproved of him. Jean returned to the point.

'Where did they find the body?'

'The graveyard at St Mary's Church.'

'In Northwick?'

'Yes, do you know it?'

'I was married there.'

'It's got a lot to answer for then.'

Jean frowned at her but the mischievous look on Sam's face quickly calmed her and she smiled back.

'You've had quite a few messages.'

Sam slumped into her seat taking a final sip of her stolen coffee and awaited the onslaught. Jean opened her diary and began to outline the messages.

'Your sister called, it's your mother's birthday and she expects to see you this evening, but call first to say what time you're coming.'

'What? Oh God, it can't be a year.'

'I ordered a "With much love on your happy day" bunch of flowers which should be delivered this morning.'

Emerging from behind her hands, Sam looked up at Jean with a sense of relief. 'Thanks, Jean, how could I forget?'

'You're busy. The bill's on your table, they'd appreciate an early settlement. Nothing was too good for your mother, I thought.'

Sam picked up the bill and looked at it, her eyes widening when she read the price.

Jean continued. 'The Murphy case has been brought forward to . . .'

Sam interrupted. 'Not the Murphy case? I thought that had been sorted out.'

'Apparently not, so you've got to hold yourself in readiness for Crown Court.'

'Which one?'

'Norwich, I think.' Jean flicked quickly through her papers, searching for confirmation of her last statement. 'Yes, Norwich.'

'Who's defending?'

Jean ruffled through her papers once again. 'Mr Atkinson.'

'Not "I put it to you, Dr Ryan",' she intoned in an affected upper-class accent. 'He hates me. I'll be in the box for hours. Better get the file out, I'll have to be ready for that one. Anything else?'

'Mr Chambers of Walter, Chambers and Pilkington wants a meeting about the appeal as soon as possible. Their client's case is going to be heard at the end of the month and they want to make sure they agree on some of the more salient points of the case.'

'They do, do they? I don't know why I bothered

becoming a pathologist, it would have been easier to be a barrister, I spend enough time in court.'

A short, sharp knock on the office door interrupted Jean before she had time to finish her list. The two women looked up to see Trevor Stuart's smiling face appear around the door.

'I hear I owe you one?'

He strode into the room as confident and as dapper as ever. Although short, he was slim and wore an attractive air like an expensive suit and looked younger than his forty years. He was one of those men to whom women are inexplicably attracted and he knew it, using his attraction to its best advantage and taking great care with his appearance, from the tip of his Gucci shoes to the top of his carefully styled head. The one woman who had exhibited no sign of succumbing to his charm, however, was Jean Carr and today was no exception. She glared across at him before turning back to Sam.

'I'll give you the rest of your messages later, Dr Ryan,' she looked pointedly at Trevor Stuart, 'if you're not too tired.'

As she left the room she eyed him icily, but Trevor was not intimidated.

'Morning, Jean, any chance of a coffee?'

His cheek made Jean's mouth drop for a moment but she quickly composed herself and, making her displeasure clearly felt by the tone of her voice, she responded with a curt, 'I'll see what I can do,'

When he felt it was safe to do so, he turned towards Sam. 'Exit the Demon Queen. Don't think she'll put anything in it, do you?'

'Bromide if she's got any sense. Have you come to apologize?'

Trevor smiled and sat uninvited on the opposite side of Sam's desk. He liked Sam and had been attracted to her since she'd arrived. He thought she quite liked him too, she certainly flirted with him, especially with those eyes, but he wasn't sure if this indicated any serious intent or whether she was playing him at his own game. Although these doubts made him keep their relationship as professional as possible, he was always looking for opportunities to take it further.

'Sorry about last night. Spent the night at a friend's and my bleeper didn't go off.' He unclipped his bleeper from his belt and waved it in front of Sam in a feeble attempt to prove his point. 'Jap crap.'

Sam was singularly unimpressed. 'I thought it was your sense of smell you'd lost, not your hearing.'

'I'll take over the PM if you like, give you a chance to finish your list.'

Sam was having none of it. 'No, it's all right, Trevor, I'll do the PM, *you* finish my list.'

Trevor nodded reluctantly. 'Where did they find him?'

'Graveyard at St Mary's Church, the one in Northwick.'

'Body found in cemetery. There's a novelty. Natural causes?'

'There was nothing natural about this one. Strangled, been dead a few weeks too.'

'Anything else?'

'Not much. He was naked, there was no sign of his clothes and no identification on him. So we've got absolutely no idea who he is.'

'No old wounds, tattoos?'

Sam shook her head. 'Nothing obvious, but there was an odd-shaped cut down the front of his body. A sort of upside-down cross.'

'Naked men in graveyards with crosses cut into their bodies. All sounds a bit kinky to me. What time's the PM?'

'Ten.'

'Really? You'd better get a move on then, it's ten past now.'

Sam glanced quickly at her watch, jumped up and made for the door. 'Damn!'

As she opened the door she looked back at Trevor who was flicking casually through her private papers. 'Don't forget to do my list. All of it.'

Trevor nodded, holding his hands up reassuringly. Sam wasn't convinced. 'It'll be "Bobbit" time if you don't.'

Trevor winced and moved his hand between his legs. Sam smiled and shook her head before closing the door firmly behind her.

The trip to the mortuary, which was situated in the hospital basement, wasn't a long one. A short descent in the lift, followed by a brief walk, the whole exercise taking no more than five minutes. Today, however, the lift appeared to be stuck on the sixth floor and after slamming the lift-call button several times, Sam finally gave up and ran for the stairs, jumping down them two at a time. She could smell the remains as she descended the stairs. Despite an efficient extraction system, the smell still seemed to escape from the mortuary and drift its way slowly through the lower floor of the hospital. To be fair, the hospital had done what it could, but the foul smell of a rotting corpse was very pervasive.

Finally, hot, out of breath and flustered, she arrived at the mortuary fifteen minutes late. Sam changed quickly into her green surgical gown before scrubbing her hands and snapping on a pair of protective latex gloves. When she entered the dissection room it was already crowded; SOCOs, various detectives, and Mr Palmer, from the coroner's officer, were all there awaiting her attendance. The mortuary at the Park was always very bright with powerful ceiling lamps bouncing their light off the white tiled floors and walls which reflected back into the room. Sam noticed Superintendent Farmer standing with Adams glaring across at her disapprovingly and glancing pointedly at her watch. Sam ignored her and looked across at Fred Dale, her mortuary technician.

'Everything ready, Fred?'

Fred had been with Sam since she had arrived at the Park a year before and she trusted him completely. He was both efficient and loyal and seemed to guess her next move on every PM they did together. A gentle giant of a man, he stood six feet two inches in his stockinged feet with a large, round face which seemed to have a permanent grin playing over it. He was also a natural clown with the darkest sense of humour she had ever known, but which lightened the atmosphere of even the most harrowing occasions, and there had been plenty of those. Although younger than her, he looked years older. A former corporal in the Royal Green Jackets, he'd been badly wounded in the leg during a riot on the Falls Road in Belfast in which several of his friends had been killed. The wound had left him with a slight but permanent limp which had ended his career prematurely. After spending some time on the streets selling copies of the *Big Issue*, he had drifted through several civilian jobs and eventually ended up at the Park. He'd found a sort of contentment surrounded by death and, despite his appearance, Sam had noticed how gently, even reverentially he treated the bodies he worked on. It was probably his association with the troubles in Northern Ireland which made her feel close to him, an experience which, although never spoken of, was still shared.

Sam walked across to the long, black, plastic bodybag lying across the grey, stainless steel table. She nodded to Fred who began to unzip it, slowly revealing the decomposing body concealed inside. As he did so, the SOCO photographer stepped forward and began to take the first of a series of photographs which he would continue to take throughout the PM. Fred gently rolled the body on to its side and Sam pulled the bag carefully from underneath it before passing it to one of the SOCOs who folded it and placed it in a large plastic exhibits bag. Sam and Fred then stepped back while the radiographer X-rayed various parts of the unknown corpse, conducting a full skeletal survey as he searched for any unseen fractures, foreign bodies or wounds.

The body, or rather what was left of it, was now lying

black and naked in front of her. Fred placed the head on to a curved wooden block and removed the black plastic bags covering his feet and one of his hands. The other hand, which had been retrieved from the sexton's dog, lay twisted in a plastic bag by the side of the body. This was also unwrapped and laid carefully at the bottom of the arm. It wasn't going to be an easy PM due to the advanced state of decomposition and clues, if there were any, were going to be difficult to spot. She began to speak her way through the PM.

When Sam began any PM, especially a forensic one, her concentration was total and her world closed in around her. It was as if her consciousness changed in both time and space and nothing existed or mattered except the body on the table.

'The body is that of an unknown, white male in his late teens or early twenties. It is well developed and nourished. One eye is missing and his hair is fair, although it seems to have been dyed, the roots being either black or dark brown.'

Sam picked up a chart from the end of the bench and read from it. 'The body is sixty-eight inches long and weighs a hundred and forty pounds.' Despite all the recent changes, Sam still preferred to work in inches and pounds when it involved the larger measurements, only reverting to centimetres for the small marks and injuries she found on the body. 'The remains are in an advanced state of decay as a result of lying out in the open. The maggot infestation is severe. I am going to take several more samples for examination by the entomologist.'

Fred, picking up Sam's direction, held out a small, dry glass tube.

'Pity I'm not a fisherman, I could clean up.'

Sam scowled at him but Fred, undaunted by this silent reprimand, smiled back and labelled the two maggot-filled jars before passing them to the exhibits officer.

Sam continued with her examination. She lifted the right arm. 'There is a crude, possibly self-inflicted, tattoo on the right arm. Fred, could you clean this up a bit?'

Fred stepped forward with a bowl of warm water and a small sponge and cleaned the area of the tattoo quickly. Warm water was the only thing he could use at this stage; any form of chemical could destroy evidence secreted on the body. Sam returned to the table and measured the tattoo.

'The tattoo is six centimetres long and consists of seven letters.' She spelled the letters out as she identified each one, 'F.R.A.N.C.E.S. Could we have a photograph of this please?'

Sam held the arm while the photographer took several photographs of the tattoo. When he had finished, she put the arm down and examined the rest of the body for other tattoos, marks or injuries that might help identify the anonymous corpse. There were none. She moved on.

'A cord has been pulled tightly around the deceased's neck continuing around the neck for a full 360 degrees, without a gap, before being tied off on the left side of the neck to a hollow metal tube, forming a garrotte or Spanish wind-lash. This tube has been twisted tightly, possibly causing stangulation; will confirm later in the PM.'

Without prompting, Fred passed Sam the scissors from the steel tray by the side of the body. Sam cut the cord, taking care to avoid the area around the hollow tube. As she gently eased the cord away from the neck, a layer of decomposing flesh came away with it. The cord and the pieces of flesh were dropped together into the exhibits bag which was being held out by one of the many SOCOs littering the mortuary. Sam returned to the body, and took swabs from both the mouth and nose, forcing the swabs deep into the body's nasal cavities before passing them to Fred. It wasn't an easy job as the nose had been all but eaten or rotted away. She moved down the body.

'There are superficial and unusual injuries to both the chest and abdomen. These consist of two linear incised wounds. One running vertically from the base of the neck to the suprapubic region. The other running horizontally across the abdomen forming a cross, an upside-down cross.'

Fred passed her a tape measure and she took the measurements of the injuries.

'The vertical cut measures forty-two centimetres and the horizontal cut twenty-eight centimetres.'

She passed the tape back to Fred who exchanged it for a dissecting knife. Pressing down firmly with the scalpel, she opened up the two cuts.

'The cuts are superficial, and not deep.'

She looked across at Fred and nodded. He rolled the

body gently on to its side and Sam ran her eyes carefully over the body.

'There appear to be no obvious injuries to the rear of the body.'

Sam nodded again and Fred lowered the body back into position. Picking up the dissecting knife once again she began to cut into the body.

'I am now commencing my internal examination.'

Adams knew what was coming next, the cutting of the liver, removal of the bowel, samples for toxicology. He'd already seen enough and looked away as the first incision was made.

Frances looked at her face in the mirror, paying special attention to her left eye, examining the fading bruise that had only just calmed down sufficiently to be covered with make-up. He'd never hit her before and she was determined that he would never do it again. He'd apologized but, although it was completely out of character for him to do so, she was still very wary of him.

It had been a month since her failed attempt to leave Bird. She'd finally given up waiting and had just reached the war memorial at the bottom of Station Street when she'd heard the familiar roar of a sports car engine. At first she had thought it was Mark and was angry and delighted at the same time. Dropping her suitcases on the ground she'd jumped up and down waving wildly at the car lights as they approached. The car had come to a sudden halt in front of her. She couldn't see the car clearly through the lights, but she had smiled broadly at the windscreen. The car door had clicked open and the dark shape of a man began to emerge.

'You took your time, didn't you?'

'I'd have been here earlier if I'd known.'

It wasn't Mark's voice. Frances had felt her body freeze as Bird's tall figure emerged from behind the lights and walked towards her.

'Remarkable recovery. When I left, you were at death's door, now look at you, all fit and well again. Amazing what a couple of aspirin can achieve, isn't it?'

Frances had just looked at him, not daring to move or speak. He moved his arm quickly, grabbing her face in his large hand, squeezing her cheeks against her teeth, forcing her to cry out.

'Hasn't he turned up then, your lover?'

The menace in Bird's voice had terrified her and she could only look at him, waiting to see what he would do next.

'When will you ever learn, you stupid bitch? He didn't want you, he just wanted the money and now that he's got it you'll never see him again. Nobody crosses me and gets away with it, not you, and certainly not James.'

The blow, when it had come, was not held back or controlled. The back of Bird's hand hit her full in the face, knocking her backwards and sending her sprawling across the road before she felt her body hit the concrete with a thud. The next thing she remembered was waking up back in Bird's bed the following morning.

It was odd really, he'd never mentioned Mark or the money since that night. She knew Mark had stolen it and managed to get out of the club via the fire escape at the back, just as they'd planned; the staff told her that much. But nobody had seen hide nor hair of him since. Probably living it up on some beach in Spain, she thought. She couldn't understand why he'd taken the money and left her behind. If anything, she'd have thought it would have been the other way around, given how he felt about her. She obviously didn't know him as well as she thought, but then, she considered, she had always been a poor judge of character; how else would she have ended up with Bird?

That money was hers and the baby's. Bird had always made it plain that he had no interest in children and there would be little chance of him paying maintenance, so she'd decided to take a small advance against the baby's future and Mark had offered to help her.

Staying with Bird despite his behaviour was her only real option at the moment. She'd visited a local women's refuge but that was worse than staying with Bird and she really didn't fancy bringing her baby up under those conditions. She was unsure of her father's response if she suddenly turned up now on his doorstep looking like Little Nell with an illegitimate bundle. She wasn't sure she would be able to take her father's rejection as well, especially after Mark's.

Bird's behaviour towards her had been impeccable, although he'd also made it quite clear that if there was one more incident like the one with Mark she'd be extremely sorry, and she believed him. She looked down at her tight-fitting evening dress, which had become a little tighter-fitting recently as her stomach began to swell. She would have to tell him soon or find somewhere else to hide. Bird shouted up the stairs.

'Come on, Fran, it's time to go!'

Grabbing her bag from the bed she made her way down the stairs to meet him.

The day had passed quickly, that was the way of it when the work was interesting, which it wasn't always. As usual, the police were screaming for her report and had actually sent, at great public expense no doubt, a traffic car to collect it as soon as it was finished. She moved the cursor to print and clicked the top of her mouse, sending her printer humming into action. As she watched the paper emerge from the other side of the machine something was bothering her. She'd gone over and over the report but still, she felt, there was something amiss, something she had missed, not realized. As she bit into her tuna sandwich, which had to suffice as lunch, a voice from behind broke through her thought pattern.

'Finished already?'

She didn't need to turn around to know who it was, the voice was familiar enough.

'Twice in one day, Trevor; this *is* an honour.' She turned to face him. 'And what can I do for you?'

'Just thought I'd pop in and see how things were going.'

Sam turned back to her word processor. 'OK. There are a few odd points, but I'm sure I'll resolve them, *without any help*.'

Trevor nodded and eyed Sam's spare sandwich. 'Is

that sandwich going spare? I'm absolutely starving, no breakfast.'

She looked at him for a moment and, despite her better instincts, found herself giving in. 'Go on. Perhaps you should consider having an affair with someone who can cook?'

Trevor took the sandwich and bit into it. 'I heard *you* were a bit of a Delia Smith.'

Sam ignored the comment, though she was flattered by it.

'Discovered who he is yet?'

Sam shook her head. 'No, his clothes are still missing, and there wasn't enough skin left on his fingers to get any prints.'

'Odontologist had a look at him yet?'

'He's just about to have a look. Depends whether there are any dental records to make a match, of course.'

She picked up the photographs which were lying by her side and handed them to Trevor. 'What do you make of those?'

Trevor stopped eating for a moment and picked them up. 'You've got your photographs back already, you're obviously well in.'

Trying to retrieve PM photographs was a bit of a standing joke amongst the pathologists at the Park. If they came back at all they came late and usually ended up in someone else's in-tray. Trevor examined them casually. 'Decomposed corpse of a young male, been dead a week or two by the look of him.' He bit into his sandwich again, flipping the photographs on to the desk.

'Look harder at his torso, can't you see it? Look at this one.' She handed him a close-up photograph of the body's torso and a magnifying glass. Trevor put down his sandwich and studied the photograph under the lens.

'I see now. You want me to confirm your theory about the cross. Mmm, might be a cross I suppose.'

'What do you mean *might be*? That's the last sandwich you get off me.'

'Might be lots of things.'

Sam could feel herself getting annoyed with him. 'Like?'

'Defence wounds, or perhaps he was tortured before they killed him; it happens.'

Sam felt that he was being deliberately awkward. 'Since when do you get defence wounds on your stomach?'

Trevor shrugged. 'You might have a signature killer on your hands, somebody who wants you to know it was them. It wouldn't be the first time. Happens quite a lot in the States apparently.'

'It's the first one they've found.'

'He's got to start somewhere. Worrying isn't it?'

Sam nodded. 'I thought there might be some sort of ritualistic element to it, otherwise why a cross, why not something else?'

'Like what?'

'I don't know, I'm just grabbing at straws I suppose.'

Trevor contemplated her for a moment. If there were two things he'd learned to trust during the time he'd known Sam, it was her judgement and intuition.

'Can I have a look at the body?'

'If you think it will help.'

The two pathologists left the office and made their way into the mortuary. The body had already been laid out on one of the many mortuary slabs. Fred was standing outside the door while Dr Clive Gilbert, the department's odontologist, X-rayed the skull. Sam and Trevor waited while he finished.

Although not routinely used, the PM radiography would reveal details unavailable by any other means: root structure, arrangement of sinus cavities, structure of any bony areas and such like, and it was therefore very useful when identification was difficult. It was certainly one of the most accurate and reliable methods of identification, but still relied, like fingerprints, on a comparison with ante-mortem information. More recently a new development in X-ray technology, xeroradiography, was being used. This produced an image of both soft and hard tissue on the same exposure. By this means, non-metallic invading bodies such as wood, plastic and glass could be seen. The principle behind it was quite simple. Charged selenium particles, when exposed to the X-ray beam, become photoconductive, producing an electrostatic image. Since they had miniaturized the equipment, making it practical for use in forensic dentistry, it had become the eighth wonder of the world in that field. Sam was pushing hard for the funding to enable her to have the new technology available in the mortuary but had, as yet, met with little success. Under certain circumstances, and to make it easier for the odontologist to make his examination, Sam would remove the entire jaw and put it to one side. In this case, however, she hadn't had the chance, but Gilbert was coping.

Gilbert finally finished and left the mortuary without a word. Sam had always found him a bit of an odd fish but good at what he did, which was all that mattered, really. Fred began to pack away the equipment while Sam and Trevor walked across to the body and began to examine its unusual injuries.

'Very peculiar, it's certainly a cross and it's definitely deliberate, single-stroke incisions. I can see why you think there's an occult angle to it.' Trevor walked to the top of the table and looked down over the body. 'On the other hand he might have been tortured or it might have been done as a warning to others. I understand street gangs and drug dealers do that sort of thing to each other?'

'This is no Colombian necktie, there's far more to it than that. Upside-down crosses, graveyards at midnight.'

'Like I said, it all looks a bit kinky to me. Told Farmer yet?'

'It's in the report, but God knows what she'll make of it. "By the way, superintendent, I think he might have been murdered by a witch." I don't think she'll be impressed.'

'Yes, I see your problem.' Trevor paused for a moment. 'Could be a religious nut, there are plenty of those around.'

'Trouble is, they all work for the church.'

Trevor laughed out loud. 'True enough. There might

be someone worth talking to, though. A chap I know, Simon Clarke, he's a psychologist, a fellow at St Steven's. I met him at some dinner or other, he specializes in serial crimes and killers, especially those with an occult angle to them.'

'Do you think he'd talk to me?

'Oh, he'll talk to you all right. This is right up his street, probably end up writing a paper on it. I'll ring him, get it arranged.'

'Dr Ryan?' Jean Carr's voice, recognizable but muffled from the opposite side of the mortuary door, broke into their conversation. 'There's a police officer outside your office, says he's waiting for your report.'

Sam looked across at the door. 'It's ready, you can come and get it if you like, Jean.'

'No, thank you, I'm quite happy where I am. The smell's quite enough, but you'd better hurry, he seems in quite a rush.'

Trevor and Sam looked at each other smiling secretly.

Farmer scanned the faces of the expectant reporters in front of her like a teacher overlooking her class. It was a good turn-out with a number of national newspapers there as well as the locals. She was surprised that the nationals were taking an interest in such a local murder, there were so many of them nationwide these days. She hated the press and considered them social parasites. If they weren't after you for a story they were trying to turn you into one. Still, she considered, they did have their uses and this was one of them. They'd had the body just over a week now and were no closer to establishing its identity than they had been on day one. They couldn't take his prints and couldn't find a match for his teeth. The missing-from-home files had been checked for every force in the country but had proved fruitless. This really was their last chance.

Farmer looked at the E-Fit which had been developed from a photograph of the corpse's face and marvelled at the technology which could produce such a realistic image. The Electronic Facial Identity Technique used computers to create a full-colour image and was a huge advance on the old photo fit technique. She looked across at Adams, who was sitting at her right, before standing.

'Ladies and gentleman,' the sharpness of her voice stopped the general chatter that always accompanied these occasions and brought the reporters' attention back to the desk at the front of the room. 'First, I'd like to thank you for coming this morning. I am Detective Superintendent Harriet Farmer and the gentleman to your left is Detective Inspector Tom Adams.' Adams nodded. 'As most of you already know, the body of an unknown male was discovered in St Mary's churchyard in Northwich just over a week ago. Due to the body having lain out in the open for several weeks and the absence of any clothing or other means of identification, we have not been able to establish who he is, despite extensive enquiries. What we can tell you about him is that he was a white male, in his late teens or early twenties, approximately five-feet eight-inches tall, and weighing ten stone. Although his hair was fair this wasn't its natural colour which was dark brown. Probably the most important clue to his identity is a tattoo on his right forearm. This tattoo consists of seven letters in blue ink and spells the name Frances.'

One of the reporters suddenly stood up. 'Peter Bushby, the *Sun*. Is it true, Superintendent, that the murder of this young man has some sort of link to black magic? Especially with him being found naked in a church at midnight?'

Farmer was slightly unbalanced by this question. 'The body certainly wasn't discovered at midnight . . .'

Another reporter jumped to her feet. 'Claire Hargreaves, *Cambridge Evening News*. We understand that ritualistic markings were carved into the front of the victim's body, can you elaborate on that?'

Farmer could feel herself becoming angry. 'There were a number of injuries to the body, whether they were ritualistic or not is open to debate.'

A question came from the right of the room.

'Helen Blackmore, *Daily Mirror*. If it wasn't some sort of black magic killing how do you account for the presence of a dead cockerel and four black candles?'

'As far as I'm aware there were no . . .'

'Can you confirm for us that there is a connection with black magic?'

The room errupted with a cacophony of shouted questions. Adams had to raise his voice to its full volume to be heard above the confusion.

'I don't think we have anything more to say at this time. PC Gill Warren will hand out a brief press pack as you leave the room which will give you all the information you need on our unidentified body. Thank you.'

The two detectives left under a torrent of further questions from the reporters.

Farmer was fuming. 'Where the fuck did they get all that information from!'

Adams tried to calm her down. 'Most of it was wrong.'

'Some of it was right though. How the hell did they find out about those cuts?'

'Could have been anyone. Half the squad go drinking with the local press.'

'This is that bloody pathologist's fault, her and her half-baked ideas. You can bet your life that's where it's come from!'

'I can't see Dr Ryan getting herself involved with the press, she's far too professional.'

Farmer glanced up at him, surprised by his defence of a person he knew only slightly.

'Well, whoever it was, I want them found and found quickly!'

Frances looked at the clock beside the bed. It was ten to one. Early really, their days didn't usually start until two. They hadn't left the club until three that morning and when they finally did get home Bird had been keen to demonstrate his manhood. She was off sex but daren't admit this in case he started to ask difficult questions, so she had been obliged to make all the right sounds to reassure him of his sexual prowess. She wasn't sure how much longer she could hide the truth from him. She'd been lucky with the morning sickness and managed to explain it away, but now she'd started to put on weight and her normally flat stomach was expanding. He'd already mentioned it once, insisting she go on a diet, and had taken her to his training centre to get her back into shape. Frances knew she'd have to tell him soon. She had no idea what his reaction would be and that caused her further anxiety. She threw her legs out of bed, slipped her short satin dressing-gown over her naked body and staggered towards the kitchen.

She picked up the kettle and shook it, it was empty so she filled it from the tap while switching on the transistor radio on the window sill. While she waited for the kettle to boil she examined her face in the kitchen mirror. The bruising had almost gone and she wouldn't need quite so much make-up in future. She remembered the punch with a shiver, how it hadn't broken her jaw she didn't know, she must be tougher than she thought. The kettle began to steam and she walked across to the fridge to collect the milk. The one o'clock news began; she was only half listening to it when she heard the item.

'An appeal was made by the police this morning for help in identifying the body that was discovered in St Mary's churchyard, Northwick, just over a week ago. The body is that of a white male in his late teens or early twenties. He was about five-feet eight tall and weighed approximately ten stone. Although his hair was fair that was not its natural colour which was dark brown. Probably his most distinguishing feature was a small tattoo on his right forearm which spelt the word "Frances . . ."'

She hadn't really been listening up to that point, but

she recognized the description of the tattoo straight away. She remembered the pride on his face when he'd shown it to her. The report staggered Frances almost as much as Bird's punch had. She grabbed the side of the sink to try and steady herself, but the milk bottle slipped from her hand and smashed, sending glass and milk spraying across the kitchen floor. Frances' vision became cloudy and her stomach churned with shock as the realized for the first time why Mark hadn't been there that night. Bird had murdered him.

Bird's voice broke through her thoughts. 'Fran, what the bloody hell's going on out there!'

A sense of self-preservation now took over. She hadn't realized until then how dangerous her situation actually was. She would be a very important witness and Bird would be aware of that. There was also another feeling, one much more basic, one that she hadn't felt until now, the feeling of a mother protecting her unborn child. She ran quickly to the door, grabbing Bird's car keys before making a dash to his car.

Bird lay in bed for a moment collecting his thoughts. He called out again but still there was no reply. Suddenly the sound of the engine of his sports car being over-revved spurred him into action and he rushed into the kitchen to see what was happening. In his anger he'd forgotten that it had been the sound of smashing glass which had first woken him and as his naked feet reached the kitchen floor the glass cut deeply into them, making him scream out and grab the kitchen table to stop himself falling. Although in great pain, he managed to stagger to the wide-open kitchen door, his feet trailing blood behind him. He watched as he saw his beloved Porsche jump off the drive as Frances struggled with an unfamiliar gearbox. Finally managing to select the right gear, she sent the car roaring off along the suburban street and disappeared from sight. Bird watched her departure before falling to the floor to begin plucking large slivers of glass from his bloody feet.

Frances could not master the Porsche's gear-lever, the car was just too complicated and powerful. Her only experience of driving had been a rather shabby Ford Escort which spent more time in the garage than it did on the road. Her eyes were still red and bloated and tears streaked along the smoothness of her skin. She was also cold and the thin satin dressing-gown offered little protection. The combination of this and the shock of hearing of Mark's death made her shake uncontrollably. She couldn't stop thinking about him or blaming herself for what had happened. She'd played with him, toyed with the feelings that she knew he had for her, kept him at her beck and call like a pet dog she could whistle for at any time. He'd been worth more than that. And now, because of her selfishness, he was dead, murdered by her boyfriend. She wasn't sure she would ever get over the shock.

She brought the Porsche to a jerky halt at a set of red traffic-lights, pulling the gear-lever into neutral as she did. Almost as soon as the car had stopped, the lights changed to green and the cars behind began to rev their engines loudly, keen to get on. She fought to push the gear-lever back into first, pressing her foot down hard on to the clutch pedal, but despite her efforts, the lever would not drop into place. Several of the drivers behind her became impatient and sounded their horns, encouraging her to move on or get out of their way. Finally, with one last desperate push, the gear-lever slotted into place and the Porsche began to move forward. The sudden shock of the gearbox complying to her wishes took Frances by surprise and the car staggered forward into the junction before stalling. As it did the lights returned to red and cars from both her right and left began to move into the junction. Now, in a total panic, Frances fought to get the car started again but she flooded the carburettor and, try as she might, the car wouldn't start. Under a barrage of horns and the voices of angry drivers, she finally collapsed across the steering wheel and cried inconsolably.

Standing at the front of the lecture theatre, Sam scanned the faces of her young students and wondered how many of them would eventually become forensic pathologists. Probably not many, most of these were Thatcher's children and far more interested in the glittering prizes and bank balances which came with the various forms of surgery now on offer. She nodded to a student sitting at the back of the room and with a quick click of a switch he threw the lecture theatre into darkness. Sam pressed the start button on her remote control and a beam of light immediately pierced the darkness throwing a photographic image on to the wall behind her. She turned to face it. It was a photograph of a large sitting-room; on the sofa were the remains of a man. The left side of his head had been blown apart and large sections of his brain, skull and flesh were slashed across the wall behind him. The man's body was leaning slightly to the right and what remained of his brains hung flaccid from the skull's cavity. The right side of his face, the side still intact, held an expression of shock and surprise. It was a terrifying spectacle. The control she was holding emitted a small red light which she used to point at the various areas she was describing on the photograph.

'Crime scene, well, maybe. We see here,' she pointed to the victim's head with her red light, 'extensive head injuries. Anyone got any idea what might have caused them?'

After a few moments' silence, a voice broke through the darkness, 'Gunshot.'

'Good, any idea what kind?'

The same voice answered again, 'From the blast damage it looks like a shotgun.'

'Right, very good. Can anyone see any sign of the shotgun?'

The room remained silent.

'Then what do you think we might be dealing with here?'

A different voice this time, 'Murder.'

'OK, let's see.'

Sam pressed a switch on her hand control and the photograph changed. This time the picture was of the same room but taken from a different angle. Leaning against the side of a door was a double-barrelled shotgun. Sam pointed to it with her light.

'Here we have the "murder" weapon. A double-barrelled, Purdy shotgun. It's about ten feet from the body. Now, what do we think it is?'

This time several voices spoke up, 'Murder?'

'That's what the police thought and spent at least three weeks investigating it as a murder, they even had a suspect. But it wasn't a murder, it was a suicide.'

Expectant and muffled whispers filtered out from the dark.

'Anyone know how?'

'Shot himself and then staggered back on to the sofa?'

'After putting the shotgun neatly against the wall? And don't forget most of what's left of his skull has been blasted up against the wall directly behind him.'

Sam clicked the hand control again. This time the smiling face of a uniformed police superintendent appeared on the screen and Sam continued, 'Anyone recognize this man?'

The room was silent.

'You're lucky. He's retired now, probably the best thing he ever did for the police force. Superintendent John Munrow. Divisional Commander of 'A' division where the killing took place. Shortly after the body was discovered Munrow arrived at the scene. He entered, telling the hapless PC on the door not to book him in or out because he was only going to be a moment. The PC, not wanting to find himself posted to the outer reaches of Cambridgeshire, did as he was told and kept quiet. Meanwhile, friend Munrow, being a bit of a gun buff, recognized the shotgun which, by the way, was still being held by the deceased. So he decided to pick it up and examine it. After satisfying himself that it was indeed a fine example of a Purdy, he left the room, carefully leaning the shotgun against the wall in case it was damaged further.'

Whispers of disbelief filtered from the floor. Sam touched the button on her remote control again and a close-up picture of the man's thumb was thrown up on to the board.

'What made the pathologist in this case suspicious was the position of the man's thumb. As you can see,' she circled the man's thumb with her red light, 'the thumb is in an unnatural position, twisted around; in fact, in the kind of position you would have expected to find had we been dealing with a suicide. After this was pointed out to the investigating officer, a few more enquiries were made. This time a bit closer to home. Three weeks after the man's body had been discovered, the young PC who had been on the door finally admitted that Munrow had been in the room and the full story came out. Munrow retired on a medical pension a few months later.'

Sam flashed her light to the back of the room. One of the students switched on the lights and Sam continued, 'So what does this tell us about our profession?' She looked at the students, waiting for an answer. One spoke up.

'Never assume the obvious?'

'Good. Anything else?'

Their faces remained blank.

'No matter how good, or how clever the science, never ignore the possibility of human error, and always build it into your equation when dealing with any crime scene or corpse. So remember . . .'

The orchestrated voice of the students replied, 'Never say never, never say always!'

'Right.'

Frances finally managed to arrive at her destination; a large Georgian townhouse. For a while she had thought she wouldn't make it, but the sight of a beautiful young girl, scantily clad and in some distress, had brought the male drivers of Cambridge to her rescue in droves and thus she'd managed to limp her way here. She looked up at the impressive building. Here, contained within these bricks and mortar, were all her happiest memories. Here she had grown up happy and secure with her mother and father. She longed for those times to return. She'd been stupid, immature and selfish. She remembered how, at seventeen, she had screamed at her father to stop treating her like a child and to give her some space. When she finally left, she knew she was causing her father pain, but she was young and more than a little stupid. She considered that she had managed to hurt just about everybody who loved her. She desperately wanted to go home, but she wasn't sure if she would be welcomed back.

Suddenly, there was a loud knock on the driver's side-window. Startled, Frances looked quickly towards her right. She saw her father's familiar face, large and strong, though time had certainly taken its toll on his hair, which was receding rapidly. As he opened the car door Frances just looked at him, scared to move, like a naughty child waiting for its punishment. Suddenly, she was unable to stand it any longer and she threw her arms around her father's neck and sobbed, 'Oh, daddy, I'm in trouble, I'm in so much trouble.'

Her father did not say a word, just patted and stroked her back gently before lifting his dishevelled daughter from the seat and carrying her into the safety of the house, closing the door quietly behind him with his foot.

CHAPTER THREE

H e parked his car a good distance from the entrance of the large double-fronted house. Although it stood back from the road it still managed to dominate the local area. He was always careful and had been watching the house for about a quarter of an hour; the last thing he needed was to be caught before his work was finished. It was still very early but the world had begun to stir and people on the early shifts, their collars turned up against the wet and the cold, were already making their way to work. A battery-powered milk-float hummed and clattered its way into view, the driver stopping every few yards to deliver his white cargo to customers' doorsteps. As the float drove past he pushed himself deeper and lower into his seat, trying to keep himself from view, but he needn't have worried, the driver was far too busy checking his next drop to pay any attention to him. Adjusting his scarf so that it covered both his nose and the bottom part of his face, and making sure his hat was pulled low over his forehead to completely obscure his face and hair from view, he picked up the large, brown paper parcel lying on the passenger seat next to him, opened the car door quietly and made his way towards the building.

Although he was dressed warmly against the weather, the cold seemed to penetrate through every layer of clothing and bite deep into his body almost as soon as he stepped from the car. He was thankful though. Had it been mild, he might have looked out of place and people would have remembered him, but on a morning like this he was just another cold person making his reluctant way to work and covered up against the weather. After only a few minutes he'd arrived at the front gate and made his way along the path towards the door. Fortunately, the door was surrounded by a large wooden porch which protected it against the extremes of weather. The parcel was far too large to go through the letter-box, so he placed it against a wall, covering it with the door mat. Content that it was out of sight and secure he turned and made his way back to the car. Although his journey had been short and only taken minutes he was still surprised that he hadn't seen another living soul. He began to realize the truth, that this was a holy mission, that God was on his side and clearly wanted him to finish the work he'd begun.

Sister Veronica Butler had been at the convent now for three years. She enjoyed the work but was ready to move on. She hoped this time she'd get her long-awaited posting to Africa. There, she thought, she was really needed. Running a home for single and destitute mothers was all well and good but none of them was starving or suffering from the multitude of rare and unpleasant diseases which seemed to plague Africa.

Despite their sad situation, they and their children were well fed, well clothed and would eventually do all right. The people in Africa, on the other hand, had nothing, not even a Christian belief to sustain them through their hardships. There was a lot to do and she felt that she was the woman to do it. Still, she thought, those decisions were in the hands of others and if God did not want her to go, then she would have to be content with what she had. She picked up the mail from the floor and flicked through it, bills and unsolicited advertising mainly, as if they hadn't got enough to contend with. She opened the front door and picked up a bottle of milk. There were twelve bottles in all but she only wanted to make herself a quick mug of tea and would bring the rest in later.

She almost missed it, concealed as it was behind the doormat. But the corner of the brown paper envelope poking out from one corner of the mat caught her eye and, pulling it to one side, she found the large paper parcel. Why the postman hadn't knocked as he normally did when there were large parcels to deliver, she didn't know, probably a new boy who wasn't aware of the system. Lucky it didn't get stolen, they were like that around there. She looked up and down the street as if to reassure herself that she wasn't being watched and then stepped back inside, closing the door behind her. She carried the parcel into the kitchen and dropped it along with the other letters on to the table before going across to the kettle and switching it on.

'That smells good.'

Sister Veronica turned to see Father Edward Farrar smiling across at her.

'There's no smell yet, it's only boiling water.'

'Ah, but there will be and I'm full of anticipation.'

She laughed. 'So I'd better make it tea for two then.'

'Very kind and not a single hint dropped.'

Sister Veronica turned and continued to make the tea while Father Farrar picked up the mail and began to flick through it.

'Bills, bills and more bills. Here's an interesting one and addressed to me.' He opened it, pulled out its contents and read it with amusement. 'Ah! All our troubles are over.'

Sister Veronica, pouring the tea, looked across at him quizzically.

'According to this I've won £10,000, a trip around the world and a sports car. All I have to do is fill out this small form, send it off and the riches of the world will be mine.'

'And what would you want with a sports car?'

'To help me carry the £10,000 to the boat for the around the world cruise.'

She handed him the tea and took the letter out of his hand. 'Sounds like wishful thinking to me. Oh, I see, all you have to do is subscribe to a year's worth of dull magazines.'

'Our girls might like them.'

'Not unless it was *Just Seventeen* or *Cosmopolitan*.'

'They're not still reading *Cosmopolitan*, are they? And us with a library full of the great classics. Modern times, modern times.'

'It would take a miracle before anyone in this place was given something for nothing.'

Father Farrar looked at her sadly. 'I'm sure you're right, sister, and miracles, like money, don't grow on trees. See you later.'

Putting her mug of tea down on the kitchen surface Sister Veronica began to open her mail. She'd been right, they were either bills or circulars. Finally, she got around to the large parcel she'd found behind the mat. It had been well wrapped and needed to be cut open with a large pair of kitchen scissors. Finally, the top removed, she emptied the contents on to the work surface.

Her scream could be heard all over the convent. It was loud, piercing and unrestrained. Father Farrar was the first on the scene. Having heard the scream and thinking one of the girls was being murdered he ran the length of the house into the kitchen. When he arrived he saw Sister Veronica, her hand clamped firmly over her mouth and pointing at the kitchen surface with a trembling finger. Father Farrar's eyes followed the direction of her hand. Lying across the kitchen surface and spilling out on to the floor were hundreds of five- and ten-pound notes. Father Farrar looked at them in amazement as he picked up the typewritten note which had also fallen from the large envelope.

'I thought this might help the convent's good work. A Well Wisher.'

Father Farrar picked up a handful of banknotes and looked up towards the ceiling. 'That was quick. Now, about this sports car.'

When he finally returned home it was light. Parking his car in the garage he made his way quickly to his study at the back of the house. Although the study door looked wooden it was, in fact, a security door made of tempered three-inch steel. He unlocked it and pushed the door slowly open before slipping inside and locking it firmly behind him again. Walking across to his desk he opened one of the side drawers and pulled out a large blue cardboard file which he quickly began to flick through. The first photograph he came to was one of Mark James standing by his beloved Spitfire. Next to it was a brief synopsis of James' life and a day-by-day account of his movements. Across the front of both the synopsis and the photograph, a large red cross had been drawn. He lingered on it for a moment smiling, content at a job well done, before turning the page and examining the next photograph. This time it was of a beautiful young girl. She was walking along a Cambridge high street peering in at the shops. He looked across at her profile and her day-by-day activities before running his finger across her name at the top of the sheet, Frances Purvis.

Samantha Ryan made her way briskly along the grimy corridors of the forensic science laboratory in Scrivingdon. The large glass windows facing out into the corridors gave Sam a clear view of most of their interiors. Each of the rooms was characterized by white-topped benches punctuated to a greater or lesser extent by various pieces of high-tech equipment. Ghost-like, white-coated scientists and technicians drifted between the benches or sat hunched over a particular experiment. Scrivingdon was one of six regional laboratories scattered around the country and dealt with most of the forensic investigations in the eastern region. Tucked carefully away amongst the trees at the back of the local general hospital, Scrivingdon not only dealt with forensic evidence from its particular area but also with firearms enquiries from all over the country, making it possibly the busiest and most prestigious in the group. Over recent years it had become more independent and, although still controlled by the Home Office, now also accepted work from the prosecuting and defending side of an investigation. This change in attitude had been manifest when the board, displaying the helmet badges from every police force in the country, mysteriously disappeared from the laboratory's front entrance hall where it had been proudly displayed for many years.

Sam finally arrived outside the door she had been looking for. She knocked and peered into the lab through the glass panel, searching for her friend, Marcia Evans. She finally spotted her at the far end of the room, her eyes glued to a Nikon microscope, while her right hand delicately adjusted the focus as she changed each slide. On hearing Sam's knock she turned and looked up at the window. She quickly recognized her friend and, smiling, beckoned Sam in before returning to her microscope. Sam pushed down the grey handle of the door and entered the spotlessly clean, white lab. Marcia heard her come in but didn't bother looking up again.

'To what do I owe this honour?'

They had been friends since Sam arrived in the county a year before. Although Marcia was much younger than Sam, their friendship was strong and was matched by the mutual respect of fellow professionals. Marcia had only been qualified for a few years but she was naturally gifted with a quick, analytical mind and an even faster eye. Because of her ability she had already been marked out for early promotion but had so far resisted it, preferring life in the laboratory to one of paper-pushing bureaucracy.

'I thought I'd come and see how the workers were coping. And see if you were free to join me for lunch. I want to pick your brains about a new hairstyle, I'm fed up with mine.'

'A new hairstyle? Do I detect a romance? Is there a new man in your life you haven't told me about?'

'No such luck, Sherlock, I just need a boost to my flagging ego.'

'Flagging ego? That'll be the day, but a change of image does sound interesting, perhaps I'll join you.'

'Great. In the meantime, have you discovered anything interesting?'

Marcia gave a wry smile. 'Not much to go on without his clothes and they're still looking for those. I've found a couple of interesting bits on the body though. Want to have a look?'

Sam nodded and they walked across to the far desk where several binocular microscopes sat impassively on the top of a long white work-bench. Marcia lowered her eyes on to the top of one of them and adjusted the focus slightly to create a sharper image before looking up again. 'Take a look at that.'

Sam peered into the microscope. Under the glass she observed a single, dark blue fibre. The scale pattern on the fibre presented itself as a series of parallel wavy lines which made it a natural fibre, probably wool, she thought. Increasing the magnification from two to four hundred, she looked deep into the central core of the fibre to examine the broken black bands of the medulla. The bands were formed as the hair grew and the dying scales were replaced by minute air pockets which showed up as small black blobs. Sometimes the medulla could be very distinctive but this was not normally the case with wool.

'Dark blue, natural wool fibre.'

Marcia was impressed. 'From?'

'Either a blue jacket or pair of trousers.'

'That's what I think it looks like, but you have to be a bit careful with the colour. Under this intense artifical light it reveals its real colour, a very intense, dark blue. However, under normal circumstances and to the woman in the street, it looks black. So any potential witness would have seen our killer in a black jacket or trousers, not blue.'

Now Sam was impressed. Marcia continued. 'I'll be able to tell you a bit more about the colours when I've done the chromatography and spectrophotometry tests.'

Sam's eyes returned to the top of the microscope. As she looked, her mind was drawn back to the murder scene and her conversation with Richard Owen.

'Where did you find it?'

'Attached to the cord around James' neck.'

'Find any others?'

'A few. Why do I get the impression there's something you're not telling me?'

'Richard Owen was wearing a woollen jacket at the scene, it looked black to me. You'll have to get some fibres to be completely sure, but I bet . . .'

'What, Owen the police surgeon? Didn't he have a protective suit on?'

Sam shook her head. Marcia was furious. 'Well, that's it then, the police surgeon did it. Case solved!'

Sam frowned at her in mock seriousness. 'I don't think so, he's no street fighter. A bit too respectable to get his hands dirty.'

'Where the bloody hell was the crime scene manager? Has Owen never heard of Edmund Locard: "Every contact leaves a trace." This is bloody ridiculous, I thought I was on to something there.'

Sam interjected quickly, calming Marcia down. 'I'll have a word with him, you know what an old woman Owen is, bit set in his ways.'

'That's not the point, God knows how much time we could have wasted if you hadn't noticed his jacket.'

'You said there were a couple of fibres?'

Marcia changed the slide under the microscope, adjusted the focus again and Sam peered in. This time the fibre was long, coarse and dark, possibly brown, and had been cut at both ends.

'What's the magnification?'

Marcia took a quick glance at the microscope. 'Hundred and fifty.'

Sam nodded, increased it to two hundred and adjusted the focus to compensate. It made little difference. She still hadn't a clue what it was.

'You mean you don't recognize this one?' Marcia leaned down by her side. 'I feel secure again. Owen didn't have a horse with him, did he?'

Sam looked up, confused.

Marcia continued, 'It's a horse's hair, I found a few of them. All on his . . .' She picked up a clipboard lying by the side of the microscope, 'Right arm and hand.'

Sam looked back into the microscope. 'Unusual. How do you know it's horsehair?'

'By its look and structure mostly. It's too thick to be a man-made fibre, no uniformity to it. As you know, hair consists of three layers, the outer cuticle, the cortex and the inner core, the medulla. Have a look at the medulla. If you look closely you'll see that it is continuous. In human hairs the medulla is generally absent or at least fragmented except, that is, for mongoloids where it's continuous. Animals, on the other hand, tend to have differing and quite complex medullary structures but it's the cuticle of this hair which reveals it's animal and not human hair. Stop me if I'm boring you. Rabbit hair is pretty easy to identify through the medulla, but I had to check the structure of this one and then compare it with the pigment granules in the cortex. I compared the lot against some of the reference samples we keep in the lab. It could have been one of a few animals but I decided it was closer to horse than anything else.'

'Why horse?'

'Because the hair has been deliberately cut at both ends I think it's had some commercial use, stuffing for chairs, mattresses, that sort of thing. I know it's not used quite so much these days but horsehair was once used a lot. We'll have to have a good look around, see if we can't find a match for the hair. If the police could find his clothes it would help.'

Sam looked up at her, she was impressed with Marcia's meticulous analysis. 'They will. What about the cord and the tube used to garrotte him?'

Marcia walked across to a large table at the centre of the lab and opened one of the plastic exhibits bags lying on the top. She held up the metal pipe by the string which ran through a small hole at the top of the tube. 'It's a wind chime, I think it's been cut away from a group of chimes and then converted into a garrotte.'

'Any prints?'

'No, it's been out in the open too long. Odd thing to murder someone with though.'

Sam nodded, intrigued. 'Yes, it is.'

Marcia held the chime up and hit it with her pen, sending a high-pitched ring around the room. 'For whom the bell tolls?'

'Beware, it may toll for thee.'

Marcia smiled and shrugged. 'Well, I haven't "tolled" enough yet, so I'll see you later. Shepherd's at one and the drinks're on you.'

'Aren't they always?'

Marcia quickly put the chime back into the exhibits bag, and returned to her microscope, waving goodbye over her shoulder as she returned to her work.

Frances' bedroom hadn't altered, it was as if time had stood still in this small corner of the world. Her bedspread was turned down as if in readiness for bedtime and the assortment of fluffy bears, rabbits and dolls still sat on her pillow just the way she'd left them. Even her slippers sat neatly by the side of the bed where they'd always been. Frances looked up at her father.

'It's just the same, you haven't moved a thing. It's as if I'd never been away.'

Malcolm Purvis stared into the room. 'You haven't, not really, you're as much a part of this house as your mother was and she's still here, keeping an eye on things. I knew you'd come back one day, just a matter of waiting.'

Frances put her arms tightly around her father. She had hurt him deeply, yet he'd never stopped loving her, never stopped wanting her back. For the first time in a long while, and despite all her problems, she felt completely safe, even happy. She felt she could cope with anything.

'We have to talk, Daddy. I've got a lot to tell you.'

'I'm sure you have, but there's plenty of time for that. Get yourself a shower and get changed. I've kept all your old clothes in the wardrobe; they might be a little out of fashion now, not what you're used to, I expect, but they'll do until we can buy some more. If they still fit.' He ran his eyes along the length of his daughter's body, 'I think you've put a bit of weight on.'

Frances looked down at herself and a shadow of concern passed over her face. Her father noticed, 'Don't worry, it looks good on you, you were far too skinny.'

As he said it Frances could feel herself biting her lower lip anxiously, trying to stop herself from blurting out the truth. She'd have to tell him eventually, but this didn't seem the right place or time. At the moment she was daddy's little girl again, and she rather liked that. He was in charge and he would look after her. If she told him of her pregnancy it would break the illusion. She needed time to think, to calm her mind and allow her father's welcome to seep through her and strengthen her before becoming an adult once more.

Her father finally kissed the top of her head and walked back down the stairs. 'I'd better call the police and ask them to move that heap of rubbish outside the house. We don't want a little Bird calling, do we?'

Frances looked down at him, watching him descend the stairs, before turning and walking into the warm, friendly comfort of her old bedroom.

Wyn Collins pulled the curtains across her large sitting-room window, taking care to make them overlap in the centre, effectively shutting the outside world away for another evening. The nights were drawing in rapidly and the cold night air seemed to seep through every gap and crack in the frame. She turned back to her mother who sat uncomfortably in a large easy chair at the other end of the room. It was her mother's sixty-fifth birthday and Wyn was determined she should enjoy herself. Her trips downstairs from her bedroom, like her grasp of reality, were becoming less frequent. She'd dressed her mother in her favourite skirt and blouse and hired a mobile hairdresser to come and style her hair; the old lady had seemed to enjoy that. The girl who came couldn't have been much older than twenty, but she was kind and her mother had taken to her straight away. When the girl finally left Wyn used what limited skill she had to brighten up her mother's ageing and lined face with make-up, finishing off her efforts by placing a small colourful party hat on top of her head and pulling the elastic strip under her chin. The effect was to make her mother look like some grotesque clown, but she didn't seem to mind, only smiled inanely into the mirror which Wyn had propped in front of her.

'Well, Mum, what do think? You don't look a day over . . . sixty.'

The old lady smiled into the mirror and stroked her hands through her hair, she obviously liked what she saw. Wyn looked at her watch, 'There's no sign, so I suppose we'd better start without her.' Wyn placed her hand on her mother's shoulder, 'Never mind, too busy with her career I expect.'

Wyn walked into the kitchen and lit the candles on the birthday cake she'd spent the week preparing. She was proud of it. Mixed fruit in the shape of a giant sixty-five, topped with white icing and over thirty multi-coloured candles. She was determined to make this as normal a birthday celebration as possible, realizing that there would soon be little point in making any special effort on her mother's behalf. She had hoped that Sam would come and felt disappointed and annoyed that she hadn't rung.

She pulled a box of matches out of a kitchen drawer and lit each of the candles in turn. When she'd finished she carefully picked up the cake and walked back into the sitting-room singing, Happy Birthday. She put the cake down on a small table in front of her mother before kissing the old lady on the cheek. Her mother looked up at her and smiled but there was no recognition in her face, just mild confusion.

'Come on, Mum, we'll blow out the candles together.'

The old lady spoke for the first time that evening, 'Is your Dad back from work yet? Probably doing some overtime for Christmas. Do you still want a bike?'

Wyn shook her head gently. Her father had been dead for twenty years, but it didn't seem fair to remind her.

'No, Dad's not back yet, I think we'll have to start without him. Ready, one two three, blow . . .'

As Wyn began to blow out the candles, the front door bell rang. Wyn blew out the rest of the candles quickly not daring to leave her mother so close to fire, no matter how small, before answering the door.

Sam stamped up and down on the porch mat, trying to keep herself warm. A dense, freezing fog was descending over the area and it was becoming very cold. The front door suddenly opened flooding the porch with light and warmth from the house. Sam looked into her sister's face, 'Sorry I'm late, last-minute problems.'

Wyn found it hard to disguise her anger, 'I thought you weren't bothering. I told you to ring.' Wyn moved away from the door reluctantly and Sam stepped into the entrance hall.

'I've been really busy. I'm dealing with that murder at the church in Northwick.'

Wyn was not impressed. 'Really. Want a cup of tea?'

'Please, I'm frozen. Where's Mum?'

'Sitting-room.'

'Did she get the flowers?'

'I'm amazed you remembered.'

Sam felt a sudden pang of conscience but said nothing. Her sister continued, 'They're in a vase in her bedroom, they were very nice. You and your flowers, you're as bad as Dad was.'

Sam smiled, she liked the analogy. 'How is she?'

'Not one of her better days.'

Sam nodded and took her coat off, hanging it over the bottom of the stairs before walking into the sitting-room to see her mother. The sight which greeted Sam was not the one she had expected. With Wyn away her mother had decided to start without them and scooped out great portions of the cake with her hands in an attempt to feed herself. Unfortunately, she had managed to get most of the cake all over her. Sam looked down at her and smiled, 'Oh Mum, you're going to be popular.'

Her mother smiled up at her totally unaware of what she had done. 'Hello, dear, back from school already?'

Sam called into the kitchen, 'Wyn, can you bring a cloth out, Mum's decided to start without us!'

Wyn's anger didn't have to be spoken, it was written all over her face as she walked into the sitting-room and began to clean the mess from her mother's head and clothes with the cloth.

'It's worse than having a baby in the house.' Wyn grabbed her mother's face and looked at her, 'Do you know how long it took me to make that cake for you? Any idea how much it cost?'

Sam looked on, alarmed at her sister's treatment of

her mother. 'Take it easy, Wyn, she doesn't know what she's doing.'

Wyn was in no mood to be reasonable; she'd had such hopes for this evening and it had fallen apart so easily. She was tired and disappointment made her rub the cake off her mother's face all the harder as if she had a point to prove. 'She knows all right. Anything to make my life a bit harder.' She looked deep into her mother's eyes, 'True isn't it, anything to get at me?'

Sam interjected, 'That's rubbish.'

Wyn rounded on her instantly, 'Don't you tell me it's rubbish. When you start to pull your weight around this family *that's* when you can tell me it's rubbish. When you have to live with her day and night, week after week, listen to her constant moaning and insults while changing yet another soiled bed, that's when you can tell me it's rubbish!'

Wyn started to pull the large lumps of cake from her mother's hair while Sam, upset, and more than a little taken aback at her sister's verbal assault, struggled for a reply, 'I'll increase your allowance if that would help?'

It was the wrong thing to say.

'Everything's money with you, isn't it? No, I don't want any more of your money, I want you to take more responsibility for Mum. If it was Dad and not Mum who's still alive it would be different, wouldn't it?'

'That's not fair.'

Sam knew there was some truth in the allegation, but still, it hurt. She had always been closer to her father in much the same way as Wyn had seemed naturally closer to her mother. That was just the way things were in their family. She'd always been her father's 'good and clever girl'. When he had died, even though she was still young, the experience had shattered her. Most of her life since then seemed to have been spent trying to assuage her feelings of guilt and prove to his memory what a 'good and clever girl' she was.

Wyn turned angrily on her sister, 'Isn't it? Look, I've been on my own now for three years since John pissed off back to Ireland. I've got two kids and only a three-bedroom house. I've got her,' she pointed angrily at her mother who was picking off the last pieces of cake from her dress and eating them, 'who needs more attention than a baby and Ricky – who was seventeen last week by the way, thanks for the card . . .' Sam had forgotten and had no excuses. Her sister's onslaught continued, 'and who is sick of sharing his bedroom with his brother and wants his own space and seems to think it's fun to cause me as much grief as possible in an attempt to get his own way . . .'

Sam cut in quickly trying to calm the situation, 'What about a nursing home?'

'What about you taking her off my hands for a while!'

'I can't, you know that.'

'Interfere with your social life, would she, not quite nice enough to show to your middle-class dinner guests?'

Sam could see that Wyn was in no mood for compromise. 'I'd better go.'

Wyn folded her arms angrily and nodded. Sam leaned down and kissed the head of her rather dishevelled mother.

'Happy birthday, Mum, I'll come and see you again soon.' She stroked the old lady's hair gently and got her hand covered in fruit cake. Wyn handed her the cloth. 'Thanks.' She wiped her hands quickly, made her way into the hall and slipped on her coat. She turned to her sister, 'See you next time then.'

Wyn nodded, still angry.

'Tell Ricky I'm sorry I missed his birthday. I'll make it up to him.' Sam turned, opened the door and walked back along the path. She heard the front door slam behind her.

Wyn's attitude annoyed her. She'd never really been close to her sister, not even when they young, they were so different. It was sometimes hard to believe they had the same parents. To hear her talk you'd have thought she was the only one to have made sacrifices. The only reason Sam had left London was to be closer to her mother, Wyn seemed to have forgotten that. The allowance she gave her sister was generous too. Wyn certainly couldn't have coped without it, although she was reluctant to admit it. Despite Sam's anger though, they were all the family she had, and no matter how frustrated she might get, her sense of family loyalty was strong, so she would have to make the best of it.

Malcolm Purvis had just cracked another egg into the frying-pan when Frances entered the kitchen. He spoke to her without turning, 'Fancy some breakfast? I thought we'd have a fry-up.'

The smell of the greasy food made Frances feel worse than usual. 'No thanks. Shouldn't you be at work?'

'Taken a couple of days off, they'll survive without me. It's all legal aid stuff anyway.' He turned to look at his daughter. It was as if the past couple of years had never happened. She was wearing a white T-shirt and a long, blue denim skirt. He remembered it was the last thing her mother had bought her before she died.

Frances noticed the way he was looking at her and looked down at the slightly dated clothes. 'It's not the height of fashion but there wasn't a lot of choice.'

'I haven't seen you in that since . . .'

Frances cut in, 'I was twelve?'

'Not quite, I remember your mother buying it for you from C&A. You'd moaned about having one for weeks.'

Frances looked back at her father and judged the moment right. 'I'm pregnant.'

The short silence that followed seemed to last an age. Her father put down the pan and walked across to her, taking her hand. 'Are you sure?'

Frances nodded, 'Yes, I'm pretty sure. I'm getting morning sickness quite badly.'

'So did your mother. Sorry about the fry-up.'

'Are you angry?'

'Angry? How could I possibly be angry? My daughter's back home and she's about to make me a grandfather.' He hesitated for a moment, feeling presumptuous. 'That is, if you want to keep it?'

'Yes, I do,' she said vehemently.

Malcolm smiled and nodded back, 'What about the father? I take it it's Sebastian's?'

'I don't want him to know.'

'I think he might find out.'

'It'll be too late by then, he'll be in prison.'

'What for? He didn't hurt you, did he?' Malcolm asked in alarm, confused by his daughter's last remark.

'Not me. Do you remember Mark James?'

'Of course I do, I defended him, didn't I?'

'Do you know he's been murdered? It was on the news. The body they discovered in the graveyard, it was Mark.'

'Have you seen it?' Frances shook her head. 'Then how can you be so sure?'

'He tattooed my name on his right arm, did it with a pin and some ink. The body in the cemetery had the word "Frances" tattooed on its right arm. It's Mark, I know it is.'

Malcolm put his arm around her. 'Have you told the police yet?'

Frances shook her head.

'Don't you think you ought to?'

'It's more difficult than that. I know who killed him, it was Sebastian.'

Malcolm Purvis looked into her face, 'Are you sure, absolutely sure?'

Frances nodded. 'I'm frightened, I think I might be the next on his list.'

For a moment Malcolm was stunned and unable to think clearly, then he pulled his daughter to him and hugged her as if he would never let her go. 'No one will ever hurt you, not Bird, not anyone. We're back as a family and that's the way it's going to stay, I promise.'

* * *

Frances sat with her father in the interview room opposite Farmer and Adams. Farmer eyed her for a moment. Although she'd never met Frances, she knew her father, Malcolm Purvis QC, well. He'd both prosecuted and defended cases she was concerned with, and he was good. She passed Frances the E-Fit they had prepared for the press conference.

'Is that Mark James?'

Frances stared at the picture long and hard before making up her mind. 'It's very like him. The face is slightly the wrong shape and the nose is a bit big, otherwise I think it's him.' She pushed the photo-fit back towards Farmer. 'His eyes were blue by the way, dark blue.'

'Tell me about the tattoo.'

'He did it himself with a pin and a bottle of blue ink; trying to impress me, I think. He wasn't a bad person, just a bit stupid sometimes, that's all.'

'Has he got any family?'

'Not that I know of. His parents were killed in a road accident when he was young. He was brought up by his aunt after that, but she didn't really want to know. Anyway, she died a couple of years ago and left him on his own. He had his own flat . . .'

'Where?'

'On the Histon Road, number seventy-nine, I think. He let it go though, moved out on the day we were supposed to run away together.'

'From the little I know about Mark he doesn't really seem to be your type.'

'It wasn't a sexual thing, well not on my part anyway.

More like brother and sister. We've known each other since we were at junior school together, just great friends.'

'But Mark wanted to be more than "just friends"?'

'Yes, but he knew how I felt. He never tried it on, not in all the years I knew him.' She paused, 'Have you found his car yet?'

'What kind of car did he have?'

'A clapped-out old Spitfire, but he loved it.'

Adams turned to Farmer, 'There was a report of a burnt-out car being found just outside Northwick a couple of weeks ago, I think that was a Spitfire. There wasn't enough left to trace the owner with. The assumption was that it was down to joyriders again.'

'Everything he owned was locked inside that car, his entire life.'

'So why were you running away?' Farmer continued.

'I'm pregnant. Sebastian made it clear he didn't want children and I was frightened he might force me to have an abortion. He was becoming violent too.'

'He hit you?' Men who beat up women were Farmer's pet hate and she could feel herself becoming angry.

'Yes.'

'Often?'

'Just once, the night Mark went missing, but it was enough. It always starts with the first punch, doesn't it?'

'So why did you decided to run away with Mark?'

Frances looked across at her father, 'I thought he was the only friend I'd got left.'

Malcolm leaned across and took his daughter's hand. 'My daughter and I haven't seen eye to eye for a while, but I think we've sorted it out now.'

'It was Mark who stole the money, was it?'

'Yes, but I put him up to it. He'd do anything for me and I used him. Not a very nice person, am I?' she said sullenly.

'Why did you need the money?'

'It wasn't for me, it was for the baby. I knew Sebastian wouldn't pay any maintenance and it was his child, after all. I didn't want to bring it up in some slum.'

Malcolm spoke up again, 'I'll pay back any money Sebastian might have lost as a result of what's happened, just let me know the amount.'

Farmer nodded and continued with the interview. 'You say you never saw Mark that night?'

'No, he never turned up.'

'But Bird did?'

'Yes, we thought we would be safe at the station. It seemed like a good place to meet, out of the way, no chance of any of Sebastian's friends spotting us.'

'What makes you think he killed Mark?'

'He'd obviously been out looking for him and he knew where I was, that was no coincidence. He was in a violent mood too. I've never seen him so angry. I thought he was going to kill me.'

'And that was when he hit you?'

Frances nodded.

'Did he get his money back? They certainly didn't find any with Mark.'

'I don't know. He's never really mentioned it since.'

'So he hasn't gone out looking for Mark or tried to get his money back?'

'Not that I know of. No.'

'Any idea how much Mark stole?'

'Not exactly, but it must have been a few thousand, he took it from Sebastian's safe at the club.'

'Right, well I think we've heard enough. I'll get a police officer in here to take your statement and if you tell her what you've just told me, that should be fine.'

Frances looked across at her father who smiled at her encouragingly.

The queues were as long as ever outside Bird's club. Farmer looked along the line of young faces, recognizing several of them. She decided it looked like a Who's Who of Cambridgeshire's young villains. She glanced at her watch. 'Where the bloody hell are the wooden tops?'

Adams, sitting next to her in the driving seat, looked at the clock on the dashboard. 'It's only just eleven, ma'am, give them a chance.'

Farmer wasn't in the mood to give anyone a chance. 'They're supposed to be professionals which means they should have been here at eleven, not a few minutes past.'

Adams judged she wasn't in a reasonable mood and decided not to continue the discussion, sucking on his cigarette deeply instead and blowing the smoke out of the car's open window, watching it disappear into the cold night air. The sound of a vehicle braking behind him made Adams glance up at his rear-view mirror. A white transit van had pulled up behind their car and a number of large police officers in heavy blue overalls were jumping out on to the street. Adams looked across at Farmer, 'They're here.'

Farmer and Adams climbed out of the car and walked across to the nine Special Operations Unit officers who stood by their van awaiting orders. Farmer walked up to the sergeant, who was quick with his apology, 'Sorry we're late, ma'am. Bit of trouble in . . .'

Farmer cut him short, 'Have you been briefed?'

The sergeant nodded.

'Then let's get on with it, shall we?'

The unit followed Farmer and Adams across to the club. The jeers from the people waiting to get in had already begun by the time they reached the door. Adams, together with two of the SOU officers, walked across to the large wind chime hanging outside the club's main entrance. Adams examined the long brass tubes and quickly discovered that at least two of them were missing. He nodded to one of the officers with him and they began to take it down, dropping it carefully into a large black exhibits bag.

The two doormen had been slow to react, not entirely sure what to do. Finally one of them, deciding that it was his job to stop unwanted intruders entering the club, stepped forward, putting himself between Farmer and the club door. She stopped and looked up into his large imposing face, her eyes meeting his and fixing on them. Despite his bravado he was nervous. She could see it at the back of his eyes. 'Are you going to move, or am I going to have to move you?' He hesitated, uncertain what to do, almost transfixed by her penetrating stare. He stayed a moment too long. When it happened, it happened quickly. For a brief second Farmer's eyes seemed to drop and she appeared to look away from him, it was a relief and he could feel his body begin to relax, it was a mistake. Farmer brought her knee up into his groin with all the power she could muster, making him double up in pain. As he bent over she brought her fist crashing down hard on to the back of his neck sending him sprawling to the floor. His partner made a move to support him, but a fierce glance from Farmer stopped him in his tracks and he thought better of it.

She looked down at the moaning, prostrate figure on the floor. 'Arrest him.'

The SOU officer was confused. 'What for?'

Farmer wasn't used to being questioned and disliked it. 'Breach of the peace. Now get on with it.'

The sergeant gestured to two members of his unit and they dragged the moaning figure towards their van. Farmer and Adams climbed the stairs into the main club with no further opposition and made their way to Bird's office. She didn't bother with the formality of knocking, just pushed it open. When she entered, Bird was sitting behind his large oak desk working on some papers. He looked up.

'Who the fuck are you?'

Farmer walked across to the desk pulling her warrant card out of her coat pocket and showing it to Bird. 'I'm Detective Superintendent Farmer and this,' she indicated to Adams who was standing by the door together with two SOU officers, 'is Detective Inspector Adams. Are you Sebastian Bird?'

Bird looked first at Adams and then back to Farmer. This was his office and he didn't welcome the intrusion. 'What is this, some kind of game? You know who I am. What's this all about?'

'Sebastian Bird, I am arresting you on suspicion of the murder of Mark James. You are not obliged to say anything unless . . .' She droned the rest of the caution out in her normal style.

Bird could feel a rising sense of shock and anger pour through his body. 'This is a joke, right? you're not the police, you're bloody Jeremy Beadle.'

Farmer looked across to the door and nodded. Adams stood to one side to let the two SOU officers into the room. They walked across to Bird and pulled him out of his chair, forcing his hands behind him and clicking on a pair of ratcheted handcuffs. Bird felt unsure of himself and his composure began to leave him. It wasn't a feeling he was used to and he didn't like it. 'This is crazy, I've done nothing, I haven't killed anyone!'

Farmer smiled at him as he was dragged from the office, still protesting his innocence. Adams lit up another cigarette and drew in a deep lungful. He looked slowly around the office. He was, despite himself, impressed by Bird's style. Everything looked expensive and was beautifully co-ordinated; wallpaper, rugs, even the numerous pot plants surrounding the room seemed to blend in with the general look of the office. The only object which looked strangely out of place was an ancient sepia photograph of two black men dressed in Victorian farming garb. The photograph sat above a large, green ivy plant whose vines trailed on to the floor. The two men were standing side by side outside a thatched cottage. Behind them, with a large white beard, was an elderly white man dressed in similar style. Adams studied the photograph for a few moments wondering who the men were before his thoughts were invaded by Farmer barking another order.

'All right, let's have this placed cleared and turned over. I want some SOCOs here as well, let's have the job done properly.'

She glanced across at Adams with a questioning look. Adams understood, he'd seen the look enough times before. He moved away from the photograph and began to search through Bird's desk drawers.

Malcolm Purvis tapped lightly on his daughter's bedroom door and gently pushed it open. Frances was lying on the bed, her hands tucked under her head, staring thoughtfully at her bedroom ceiling. Malcolm walked across to her.

'Saw your light was on. Can't you sleep?'

Frances pulled herself up on to her elbow and looked across at her father. 'No, I can't help wondering if I've done the right thing, going to the police. Perhaps it would have been better left.'

Malcolm sat on the bed next to his daughter. 'You did exactly the right thing. If he did murder Mark, then he wants locking away for a very long time. I know Mark wasn't the most perfect human being but

I quite liked him. He thought the world of you, and he certainly deserved better than that.'

Frances fell back on the bed clearly unconvinced. 'I didn't exactly see him do it.'

'No, but the circumstantial evidence is pretty strong. It's up to the police and courts now, you've done your bit.'

'But what will happen when he gets out?'

'He won't be coming out for a very long time, and when he does, he'll be so institutionalized he won't be a danger to anyone.'

Frances sat back up again. 'I thought barristers could see the good in everyone.'

'That's social workers, different profession. I don't like most of my clients.'

'You liked Mark.'

'Despite my better judgement. Probably because he'd been so good to you.'

Frances smiled and held her father's hand. Malcolm leaned down and with his spare hand searched inside a small plastic bag he had brought into the room. From it he produced a small, blue baby's jacket, holding it up in front of her. 'What do you think?'

Frances giggled, taking the jacket with her other hand. 'It's beautiful but a bit presumptuous, isn't it? How do you know it's going to be a boy?'

Malcolm put his hand back into the bag and this time emerged with a pink jacket which he also handed to Frances. She looked at them both. 'This is going to be one mixed-up kid.' Throwing her arms around her father's neck, she hugged him closely. 'I don't know how you put up with me, Dad, I'm nothing but trouble.'

Malcolm put his arms around his daughter. 'You're my daughter and I love you, that's unconditional. All for one, just like when your mother was alive.'

Large, hot tears slowly trickled along Frances' cheek before dropping down on to the top of her father's shirt.

Farmer spoke into the tape recorder which was on the edge of the table in the police interview room. At the table Farmer and Adams sat opposite Bird and his solicitor, Mr Colin Lane. Bird sat impassively, casually leaning back in his chair.

'I have to remind you that you are still under caution. Do you understand?'

Bird raised his eyebrows in a dismissive gesture of acknowledgement.

'For the tape recorder, please.'

Bird leaned forward, 'Yes.'

Farmer continued, 'I am making enquiries into the death of a man by the name of Mark James. I believe you can help me with those enquiries.'

Bird failed to respond and maintained his impassive stare.

'Did you know Mark James?'

'Yea, I knew him, he worked for me sometimes.'

'What did he do?'

'Barman.'

'How long had he been working for you?'

'Off and on for about two years. It was pretty informal.'

'We've had information that he stole several thousand pounds from you. Is that right?'

Bird nodded, Adams pointed to the tape recorder.

'Yes, that's right.'

Adams asked the next question, 'Why didn't you report the theft?'

'What's the point?'

'We might have been able to get it back.'

Bird leaned forward across the desk and looked straight into Adam's face. Adams didn't move,

'I can't get insurance any more, do you know why? Because my club has been broken into seven times over the past year. I've had over twenty thousand pounds' worth of kit either stolen or smashed up and you lot did nothing. That's why I didn't bother reporting it.' Having had his say Bird leaned back in his chair.

'But you knew who it was this time.'

'I knew who it was the seven times before that but you still did nothing.'

Farmer came back into the interview. 'So you decided to take the law into your own hands and went after James?'

'That's right, I wanted my money back.'

'Is that why you killed him?'

'I didn't kill him.'

'You went after him.'

'Big difference between going after someone and killing them.'

Bird leaned forward on his seat again. 'Frances has been telling you all this, hasn't she? Look, she's got her own axe to grind with me so I wouldn't take too much notice of what she tells you, she's a bit . . .' He indicated with his finger to the side of his head.

Adams joined in the interview again, 'So what happened when you found him?'

'I never found him. I searched, went to all the usual places, clubs, pubs, the streets where the pimps and tarts hang out, but there was no sign. Then one of me mates said that he'd seen Frances walking up towards the station. Well, when I left her she was supposed to be at death's door so I went to see. She was there all right but Mark was nowhere to be seen.'

'What were you going to do if you'd found him?'

'I was going to give him a bit of a slap, he'd got it coming, but that was all. Anyway he never showed, so that was that.'

'So you took it out on Frances?'

'Yea, maybe. I went a bit too far. I didn't really mean to hurt her though, she hit her head. I told her I was sorry, tried to make it up to her. I felt bad afterwards.'

'It wasn't just the money though, was it? You thought he was going to run off with your girlfriend. You'd have lost a bit of face if he had.'

'Nobody kills anyone over a woman.'

'Hundreds do each year, why should you be different?' interjected Farmer.

'Frances is a free agent, if she wanted to run away with the creep then she was welcome to him, they just weren't going to use my money to do it with.'

'Is that why you killed him?'

'You can keep asking the question but you'll keep

getting the same answer. I didn't kill him. I didn't even find him. And if I had found him he wasn't worth doing life for. You've got the wrong man.'

'Why didn't you keep searching for him after you found Frances?'

'I asked around but he'd just vanished. Thought he was sitting on some beach somewhere laughing at me with my money under his arm.'

Farmer placed an exhibits bag on to the desk containing the wind chime and cord they found around James' neck.

'I am showing the accused, Bird, exhibit number twelve, the wind chime and cord used to garrotte James. This was used to strangle James and it's been identified as coming from the wind chime outside your club. Have you got an explanation for that?'

Bird picked it up and looked at it through the clear plastic bag.

'Yea, I might. A couple of the chimes went missing a few weeks ago. They're always going missing. I leave them out all night. Supposed to ward off evil spirits.' He looked into Farmer's face, 'Think I'll get my money back? They clearly don't work.'

A broad smile crept its way across Bird's face as he sat back in his seat and put his hands behind his head.

Bird sat calmly on the bed inside the bland prison cell and smiled arrogantly at Farmer as he watched her slam the cell door against him. The station sergeant chalked Bird's details on to a board by the side of the cell door and Farmer and Adams walked away.

Adams lit up another cigarette and looked across at his boss.

'Think he's going to have it?'

'He'll have it OK. Bloody psycho, just enjoying the control.'

'He isn't going to admit it, his sort never do. Think we've got enough to bang him up?'

Farmer looked back at him. 'Not sure. A few years ago there'd have been no problem, but now . . . Depends on the magistrate, you know what inconsistent bastards they can be. We need a bit more and I know just where we're going to get it.'

Farmer was interrupted by a shout from the station sergeant's office.

'Ma'am, the Chief Super' would like to see you straight away.'

Adams raised his eyebrow quizically, 'Want me to come with you?'

'No, he'll only want an update. He'll accept one of us bull-shitting, but not two. Thanks, anyway.'

Adams watched as his boss walked away from him. He knew the Chief Super' too well to believe that he'd turn out in the middle of the night for an update. He realised Farmer must know that, too. There was trouble and Farmer was going to face it alone. Adams walked back slowly towards the incident room.

CHAPTER FOUR

Detective Chief Superintendent Words slammed a pile of newspapers down on his desk in front of Farmer. Farmer disliked Words at the best of times but now at his arrogant, bombastic worst, she despised him.

'Tomorrow's papers, we're front page bloody news!'

Farmer picked up the well-known tabloid at the top of the pile and read the sensational front page,

BLACK MAGIC SEX SLAYING IN SLEEPY CAMBRIDGESHIRE VILLAGE

The article contained a full account of the investigation surrounding the unidentified, murdered body found in St Mary's churchyard, described in lurid detail, including a photograph sexton holding his dog and a complete description of the circumstances leading up to the discovery of the body by the sexton's dog. The rest of the papers were written in a similar style.

Words roared on, 'It's not good enough, Harriet! It's just not good enough. Where the hell did they get all their information from?'

'Probably slipped the sexton a few pounds?'

'The sexton could only have told them part of it, where's all this stuff about black magic sex slaying come from?'

'Dr Ryan, the pathologist, mentioned it in her report. Well, the ritualistic possibilities anyway, they've made the rest up.'

'Why these bloody people don't keep their bizarre ideas to themselves, I don't know. All we need to know from her is, yes he's dead and this is how he died. Then she should bugger off out of the way. I'll be having words with her Trust about this. So are you telling me that the leak has come from her?'

'No, I can't be sure of that.'

'Then where has it come from? Your team?' Farmer was beginning to get a little tired of his hysterical outburst and accusations. 'I've got no idea where the story's come from. I've got Adams looking into it.'

'Well make sure he does his bloody job. I want this leak plugged and if it has come from your team I want the bastard's balls on my carpet as soon as you know who it is.'

Farmer nodded, she could do little else.

Words continued, 'What about this suspect you've got in. Charged him yet?'

'No, not yet, but it's looking promising.'

'I don't want "promising", Harriet. I want a result and I want it bloody quick. The sooner this nonsense is sorted out and the people around here feel they can sleep safely in their beds again, the better.'

He calmed for a moment trying to make Farmer relax before his final threat.

'I don't want to fall out with you, Harriet, but if this job isn't cleared up quickly and the press don't get off my back, we'll find ourselves discussing your career and how you might look in blue!' Farmer breathed out deeply but remained silent. There was nothing she could do that would pacify him, except charge Bird, and she wasn't sure she was in a position to do that yet.

PC Sandy Wilson sat outside 42 Croft Lane with his partner Philip Troakes. He looked around at the various houses. It was a nice road, modern but nice. All the houses were large, four-bedroomed constructions with double garages and large driveways accommodating top of the range cars. It was just what he wanted, but couldn't afford. It seemed to Sandy Wilson that there was no limit to the price people were prepared to pay for these houses, there was always someone willing to buy them. They must all have bloody well-paid jobs or be on the fiddle to afford these, he thought. He turned to Philip Troakes.

'Think you could live here?'

Troakes, who had been leaning back in the passenger seat of the white Panda car dozing, pulled his cap away from the front of his eyes and looked around. 'Wife-swapping and orgy land? Yea, I'd give it a go.'

'How do you know that then?'

'Try reading the Sundays, there's stories in every week. Middle-class women bored out of their minds. They're gagging for it.'

Wilson shook his head at his colleague. 'You live in a world of your own, you.'

'Look at that murder enquiry at Bradthorpe last year. Middle-class estate right? Two of the lads got sent back to section for drinking on duty, six got sent back for shagging, and one of those was the local bank manager's wife. Caught them at it apparently, he still had his helmet on.' Troakes burst into laughter at his own joke before pulling his cap back over his eyes and sinking back into his seat.

'A real credit to the force.'

Troakes answered without moving, 'Look, it's this great new world of police accountability. We're expected to provide a service, right? Well, we are. Community policing at its best, that's what I call it.'

Sandy Wilson shook his head in disbelief and continued to watch the house. He hated jobs like this, domestics. They always ended in tears and no one ever came out with any credit. There were more coppers killed and injured through being in the middle of some stupid domestic dispute than for any other reason. As his thoughts began to drift towards the weekend and the football match on Saturday, a dark, grey Ford Escort pulled on to Bird's drive and stopped. Troakes, awaking from his slumbers, looked across as a blue-suited man emerged from the car and stared across at them.

'Is that him?'

'No, away colours, probably his brief. Sergeant said he'd be here.'

As they watched, Bird's solicitor walked up the drive to the front door and let himself in. A car drove past them slowly and stopped further up the road. They didn't noticed it. Even if they had, there would have been no reason for them to be suspicious. It was just another car on the road. Their inquisitiveness was satisfied and, as the object of their attention disappeared into the house, they relaxed back into their seats. Malcolm Purvis stepped out of his Range Rover and looked across at the police car. If he hadn't known better he'd have sworn they were both asleep. He slammed the driver's door just to let them know he was there. The two constables sat up with a start and, after adjusting their caps, stepped smartly out of their police car. Malcolm had mixed feelings about the police. He realized that they had a difficult job to do, but he did wish they'd take a more professional approach sometimes, especially when it came to giving evidence in court. He'd lost too many cases to hold many of them in any great esteem. These two seemed big enough and ugly enough to get the job done, though. He hoped they wouldn't be needed. He walked around to the back of his car and opened the boot, removing a large, brown suitcase before following the two PCs along the drive to the front door.

They didn't have to knock, the solicitor had seen him arrive and had opened the door in anticipation. He led them up the stairs into the master bedroom and opened a wardrobe door. Malcolm Purvis nodded his thanks and began to load Frances' clothing into the suitcase he'd brought with him. Bird's solicitor stood over him, watching him closely and making a note of everything he took. Finally, the suitcase full, he closed it and clicked the fasteners shut. Bird's solicitor followed the small group back down the stairs and saw them safely out of the house, not taking his eyes off them for a moment. Once outside he locked the door and waited until he saw both Malcolm Purvis and the police drive away.

As the two vehicles rounded the corner at the top of the road he noticed another car pull away from the side of the kerb and begin to follow the small convoy off the estate. It was the deliberate nature of the car's actions that made him suspicious, as if it had been waiting for them. He wondered if it might be worth a quick but anonymous call to the police on his mobile phone. If Bird's friends had decided to take the law into their own hands he didn't want to be involved. He pulled the phone from its clip at the back of his trousers and pondered his decision. Although the car had been a good distance off he was sure the driver was both white and middle-aged, not the type of person who would readily associate himself with Bird. After a few more seconds' thought he clipped his phone back on to his belt and made his way down the drive to his car.

It was early evening when Sam finally returned home, her car overflowing with plants of every size and variety. Several of them protruded through the car's open windows giving it the outward appearance of a mobile greenhouse. She tried hard to keep her weekends free and, short of emergencies and the occasional on-call, she generally managed to do so. Weekends offered one of the few opportunities she had to shop, clean the cottage, and spend time in her beloved garden. Autumn was a busy time and there was always something to do. She adored the soft sleepiness which descended over nature at this time of year, and the necessary duties of planting, pruning, dividing and general tidying in preparation for winter's icy blanket were her joy and salvation.

Sam lived in a small, two-bedroomed, former game-keeper's cottage. Although she enjoyed its age – it was over two hundred years old – she also enjoyed its upgraded comfort. It retained many of its original features, like the large, open fireplace and the dark-beamed ceiling, but extensive, sympathetic renovation had been carried out to introduce all modern necessities. The only unfortunate thing about it was its name, 'Badger View'. As far as Sam could tell, all the badgers in the district had either been gassed or dug out by baiters long ago and during her year of occupation, despite catching tantalizing glimpses of the district's other wildlife, she hadn't seen a single badger. The cottage was remote and surrounded by woodland and fields with just a small dirt track leading to the front gate. That's why she'd chosen it, that and the fact that it had one of the most beautiful gardens she could ever remember smelling.

Although neglected, the garden had held its own against the invading weeds and was resplendent with old English roses, the scent of which has rarely been captured by modern hybrids, while honeysuckle and jasmine scrambled amongst the rambling roses over the side of the house and the wall which protected the garden from the east winds. Aromatic herbs and varieties of lavender were planted at the rear of the house, along the path leading from the kitchen door into the main body of the garden. Here the sun warmed the plants for most of the day and with each trip into the garden the leaves were lightly bruised, releasing their distinctive and pungent fragrance. Wallflowers had endured many winters and mingled with old garden pinks planted in light, free-draining soil in a raised bed in front of an old lilac tree and, as she was to discover to her continuing delight during her first year in the garden, there was no time of year which did not bring forth the delights of aromatic leaves and flowers in this remarkable garden. Sadly, as is the way with nature, some of the plants were diseased or too old to be rejuvenated and so she had spent both time and money taking cuttings, collecting seeds and searching catalogues in an effort to replace those specimens beyond help.

Her nearest neighbour, the farmer who had owned the cottage, lived over a mile away across the fields and she enjoyed the solitude. It gave her time to think, reflect and prepare for the following week. When not engrossed in the garden, Sam spent hours just rambling through the woods and tramping across the fields, breathing in invigorating lungfuls of the fresh, clear air and admiring the ever changing, living world around her.

She always drove slowly along the rutted dirt track leading to her cottage, pulling her car from side to side to avoid the large, water-filled pot-holes of uncertain depth which always littered the road. An absent-minded miscalculation could result in her plunging into one of the perpetually glutinous ruts from which she might never extricate herself, not to mention the damage it would do to the car. Sam viewed the tricky navigation of this track as a type of 'rite of passage' which separated her cerebral, professional persona from her spiritual, personal self. As she finally pulled her Land-Rover on to the drive she noticed a dark blue car parked just beyond her cottage and facing towards her. In the fading evening light she couldn't quite make out the faces of its two occupants but she guessed they were police officers. Despite their best efforts, police cars, even the unmarked ones, still looked like police cars. Sam walked to the rear of her car and began to unload the boot. The sound of Farmer and Adams' footsteps crunching across the gravel path alerted Sam to their approach. She put down the large witch-hazel she had just wrestled from her car and turned around to face the two police officers, eyeing them suspiciously and hoping they had a good reason for invading the privacy of her weekend.

'Didn't know you made house calls?'

The annoyance on Sam's face was apparent and made Farmer feel slightly uncomfortable, a feeling she didn't enjoy.

'Sorry, we don't normally, but this is a bit of an emergency.'

'You're going to have to talk to me in the garden, I want to get this in before it's too dark to plant.' She indicated the *Hamamelis mollis* sitting on the ground in front of her.

Farmer looked across at Adams, 'Give Dr Ryan a hand would you, inspector?'

Adams was clearly unhappy at the order but realized he had no choice but to comply. Sam looked across at him, smiling mischievously, before walking off with Farmer to the rear of the house, leaving Adams pondering how to lift the large, awkward plant without getting the contents of the pot all over his clothes.

It had been a long walk from the main road to the cottage and it had all been uphill. His progress hadn't been helped by the state of the track. He'd slipped and stumbled on several occasions by the time he reached the cottage and his hands and the knees and hems of his trousers were both wet and covered in thick dark mud. The large, white machine he clutched closely to his chest, rather like a child with a favourite stuffed toy, wasn't helping the situation as it kept him constantly off balance. When he finally reached his destination he was exhausted, and leaned heavily against one of the cottage's antique gateposts to recover. It wasn't until that moment that he noticed the blue Vauxhall. It was parked by the side of the track a few yards in front of him. He didn't pay it much heed at first, assuming it belonged to visiting friends. When the police radio suddenly crackled into life, however, with its familiar beeps and call signs, he began to panic. Abandoning his prized machine, leaning it against the side of the gatepost, he ran headlong into the dense woodland that abutted the cottage, disappearing quickly into the undergrowth and shadows until he felt safe.

Even as winter approached, Sam's garden was still beautiful and had the power to charm. Farmer, who was no great gardener, admired it. She was impressed by the amount of work which had clearly been necessary to create and maintain it. The borders were full and deep and had been planted in such a way that there was colour, shape and form, as well as perfume, throughout the year. At the far end of the garden, separated by a trimmed hedge and well-constructed trellis-work there was a small orchard of assorted fruit trees, the leaves of which had turned and now, even as they died, exhibited a Rembrandtesque blaze of reds and browns.

Sam made her way into the small porch at the back of her cottage and collected a pair of green wellingtons as Adams struggled around the corner with the witch-hazel, searching for a place to deposit it. Sam noticed his discomfort and called across to him, 'In the corner!'

Adams moved, but in the wrong direction. Sam was quick to redirect him, 'No, not that corner, over there.' She indicated to the far end of the garden. Adams glared across at her, clearly tiring of orders and becoming impatient with the menial task he had been given. Finally, reaching the area Sam had indicated and having had the royal nod of approval, he carefully dropped his parcel on to the ground.

Slipping on her pair of size-five boots and collecting a spade and a bag of rotted compost from the shed at the back of the cottage, Sam walked across to where Adams was standing and began to dig a large hole. Still unhappy at the two police officers' unwelcome intrusion and racing against time to get the plant into the ground before the light failed completely, Sam initiated the questioning.

'So, what's so important that it's dragged you two out on a cold, wet Saturday?'

Farmer looked across at Adams and then back to Sam. She found it a little disconcerting trying to interview a moving target.

'Mark James. We've got someone for it.'

Sam looked up but continued to dig, her laboured breath pouring from her mouth like fog into the cold evening air.

'I'm impressed. If you've got someone what do you need me for?' She finished digging the hole and emptied a generous amount of the compost into it, not waiting for Farmer's reply.

'The person we've arrested is a local club owner, a man called Sebastian Bird.'

Sam stopped working for a moment and leaned on her shovel. 'Has he got any sort of interest in the occult?'

'This has got nothing to do with black magic. One villain has fallen out with another and paid the penalty.'

'And the cross cut into James' chest?'

'These aren't nice people, it's the kind of thing they do to each other.'

'Sounds like you've got all the answers, what do you need me for?'

'We know James stole several thousand pounds from Bird's safe, and that Bird went after him on the night we think he was murdered. We've got a witness who confirms those two points. We also know that he was strangled . . .'

Sam interjected, 'Garrotted.'

Farmer accepted her mistake grudgingly, 'Garrotted, by a tube from a wind chime we found outside Bird's club. The trouble is, anyone could have stolen the chime, it hangs outside twenty-four hours a day, and that, unfortunately, is as far as it goes.'

Sam returned to her work. 'He hasn't confessed then?'

Both Adams and Farmer shook their heads in unison like nodding dogs at the back of an old car.

'So where do I come in?'

'I'm not sure we've enough to hold him, it's all pretty circumstantial.'

Sam evened out the compost at the bottom of the hole.

'We,' Farmer glanced briefly across at Adams in an attempt to share the responsibility with him, 'were wondering if you'd found anything else that might help the cause.'

Sam walked across to the garden tap by the side of the shed and turned on the water, dragging the long black hose-pipe across the ground to the hole, and began to fill it with water. She looked back up at Farmer. 'Sounds as if you've already got enough, circumstantial or not. I don't think I can add anything.'

Having watered the hole she turned off the tap and began to wrestle the plant from its holder. Adams, unsolicited this time, crouched down by her side and helped her to lift the plant from the pot and place it into the hole where it finally came to rest with a splash of muddy water.

Farmer, irritated by this domestic scene, persisted,

'With the exception of the wind chime which, considering its general accessibility, is not of much use, we've got no evidence putting him at the scene, nor have we been able to link any of the other forensic evidence we found to Bird.'

Sam looked at Farmer inquisitively and Farmer continued, 'So, we were hoping you might have spotted something.'

Sam wasn't quite sure what she wanted. 'Like what?'

'Anything. Anything that might link Bird directly to the murder scene would be handy.'

'Marcia Evans discovered some fibres on his body, they might be worth a look.'

Adams spoke up, 'We've checked those. We're pretty sure the horsehair came from James' car seat. And Doctor Owen sent us samples from his jacket. They match the ones found on the body. So they're not much help either.'

Sam raised an eyebrow disapprovingly,

'He has been spoken to. It won't happen again!' Farmer snapped. Sam wasn't convinced but allowed Farmer to continue. 'Are you sure there was nothing? Nothing that might perhaps, if it were interpreted in a different way, give us what we're looking for?'

As the sun finally went down, melting into the top of the cottage, Sam shovelled the last few spadefuls of dirt into the hole and heeled it down firmly while Farmer continued her verbal onslaught.

'If we don't find something soon we might lose him. Are you *sure* you didn't find . . . anything?'

Sam couldn't pinpoint what it was, something in the tone of Farmer's voice, the look on her face, but whatever it was, with the waning light came the clarity of Farmer's intention. Sam realized exactly what she was being asked to do, and she resented it.

'I can't find what's not there,' she snapped.

'Perhaps you missed it the first time, only just discovered it. Do you understand me?'

Sam finished raking the ground around the plant and looked Farmer full in the face. 'I understand you all right. You've got my report, everything's in there. I didn't miss a thing.'

Farmer's face flushed with anger as the two women stared into each other's face. The moment was broken, however, by Adams' quick intervention.

'Like me to bring the other plants around?'

Sam looked across at him, tearing her eyes away from Farmer's. 'No, I think I'll do those in the morning. There's been enough *planting* for one evening.' ·

She looked down at Adams' trousers which were covered in mud. 'Sorry about your trousers.'

Adams glanced down and, annoyed, attempted to brush the worst of it away. 'Shit!'

Sam glanced back at him on her way into the house. 'Probably.'

She opened the back door and walked into the kitchen, closing the door behind her and locking it with a decisive click, leaving the two detectives standing alone in the darkening garden.

It was clear from the moment they entered the room

what the rest of the class were thinking. A late middle-aged man with a pretty young girl on his arm, another case of mid-life crisis gone mad. She was young enough to be his daughter, which, of course, she was. Malcolm Purvis sat awkwardly at the back of the class with Frances, feeling a little embarrassed and looking forward to the moment when all could be revealed. The lecturer, a short, plump midwife with a round, kind face introduced herself and then asked each couple in turn to do the same. Each married couple reeled off their names, outlined the stage of their pregnancy and gave a brief family background. When Malcolm's turn came, the whole class seemed to turn and look at him with almost universal disapproval. Their unfounded assumptions caused a flare of annoyance within him and he was almost tempted to make out that Frances was indeed his girlfriend and that the baby was his. However, under the circumstances common sense prevailed and he heard himself blurt out, 'My name's Malcolm Purvis and this is my daughter . . .'

Frances spoke up, 'Frances, who is about to make him a grandfather for the first time . . .'

Malcolm quickly ended her sentence, 'And I'm looking forward to it.'

The class turned back to face the midwife, some smiling their approval, others looking slightly embarrassed by their mistake. Frances saw the contented look on her father's face and nudged him in the ribs with her elbow, smiling as she did.

The darkened figure watched as Farmer and Adams

drove away. He waited until he saw the car's brakelights flash on at the bottom of the lane and then disappear as it accelerated on to the main road. When he was certain they had gone he turned and began to make his way along the gravel path towards the back of Sam's cottage. Sam stood in the kitchen preparing dinner. She was hungry, having had no time to stop for lunch during the day. Bernard, her long-haired tabby, jumped up on to the kitchen worktop and sniffed around the pan. Sam picked him up gently and began to stroke him. Bernard was the only company she really had and she valued it. He'd been lost for a while after they'd moved. Being a city cat, the great outdoors had unnerved him for a while, but he gradually got used to it and now brought home a succession of dead rats, voles and fieldmice. As she put him back on to the floor she heard a tapping on one of the glass panes in the conservatory. She strained her eyes against the darkness but could see nothing. She flicked on the security light and the garden was immediately illuminated in its beam, but there was no sign of life. Slightly unnerved, she slipped on her boots and picked up her garden spade as a weapon. She unlocked the back door and ventured cautiously into the garden.

'Hello, Aunty Sam.'

The voice was familiar but it still made her jump. Sam spun around to be confronted by the smiling face of her errant nephew. Although greatly relieved, she was angry.

'Why don't you knock on the front door like every one else? You'll give me a heart attack!'

'Sorry, I was waiting for your visitors to go.'

Sam couldn't believe the state he was in. 'What have you been up to? You look like the creature from the black lagoon.'

Ricky looked down at his mud-covered clothes. 'Sorry, I fell down a couple of pot-holes on the way up here. It was dark!'

Sam had always loved her nephew but sometimes it wasn't easy. He was tall and slim with the gangling awkwardness that seems to come with the onset of puberty in boys. The one blessing was that he hadn't developed teenage acne, and his handsome face and crop of red hair were his redeeming features.

'Have you eaten?'

'Not recently.'

'Come on, you can share mine. I think there's enough.'

Ricky followed Sam back into the house, kicking off his muddy shoes by the kitchen door as he went. Sam moved across to the stove and examined the contents of the pot. She looked back at Ricky.

'A few more minutes and it'll be ready. How's the family?'

'Gran's much the same. Mum seems to be angry all the time, and David spends most of his time out with his new girlfriend.'

David was Wyn's older son and Sam's only other nephew. Despite Sam's fondness for Ricky, she'd never liked David. He was far too much like his father, self-centred and broody, and he lacked the youthful friendliness of his brother. Although Ricky was far from perfect, there was a basic goodness about him which Sam loved. She was glad that there might be a chance of David moving on. It would certainly give Wyn and Ricky the break they needed.

'We might be having a wedding in the family then?'

Ricky wasn't so sure. 'I doubt it, use 'em and abuse 'em is his motto.'

Sam could feel her hackles rising. It was typical of David. She changed the subject. 'Can you get a couple of plates out, Ricky? They're in the cupboard over there.'

As Ricky got up from the table he took his left hand, which had been concealed since he arrived at the cottage, out of his pocket. Sam noticed that he had wrapped a grimy white handkerchief around it. The handkerchief was covered in a mixture of dried blood and dirt. She walked across to him.

'What have you been up to?'

Sitting next to him, she took his hand and began to remove the make-shift bandage. He winced as she unravelled it, exposing a nasty gash that ran the length of his palm.

'How did you manage this?'

'I cut it on some glass, stupid really.'

She hadn't noticed before but now that her nephew was sitting close to her she could smell his breath.

'Been drinking?'

'Just a couple.'

Sam nodded sceptically and walked across to one of her cupboards, pulling out a first-aid kit before returning to the table. Splashing antiseptic on to a wad of cotton wool she began to clean the wound, making him flinch as she did.

'Sorry. Are you sure this is a glass cut? It doesn't look like one.'

Ricky nodded but Sam wasn't convinced. When she'd finished she wrapped his hand with a fresh bandage before securing it with a safety pin.

'There, that should do it.'

She put two plates out on to the table and began to serve up the pasta.

Ricky started eating almost before Sam had finished serving. Then he looked across at his aunt, trying to look as pathetic as he could. 'Can I stay here tonight? If I go home I'll only have to explain this.' He held up his bandaged hand.

Sam looked at him. 'Nothing to explain, is there?'

Ricky continued eating, talking between the pieces of pasta that filled his mouth, 'No, but try telling Mum that.'

Sam sighed, but her sense of duty and the genuine affection she had for her nephew overrode the irritation she felt at this further disruption of her weekend.

'I'll make up the bed. Better give your mum a ring and tell her where you are.'

Ricky looked sheepishly at her. 'Don't suppose you could . . .'

'No chance, you do your own dirty work and before you do that, you can wash up.'

Ricky leaned back in his seat and breathed out, loudly. Sam didn't really like upsetting her nephew so she decided to add a sweetener, 'Sorry I forgot your birthday, things have been a bit hectic recently.'

Ricky shrugged as if he understood. Taking her purse

out of her handbag Sam handed a twenty-pound note to her nephew.

'Spend it wisely.'

He smiled broadly as he looked at the note. 'Thanks, Aunty Sam, I will.'

She doubted it, but it was good to see him happy.

'How's the new job going?'

Ricky's head dropped and he looked down, morosely, at his food.

'What happened this time?'

'Bad timekeeping. It was a dead-end job anyway. I want to go back to college but Mum won't let me.'

'Well, you didn't exactly shine at school did you?'

'That was different. Anyway the teachers hated me.'

Sam smiled wryly. 'And with good reason as I remember. Do you think college will make any difference?'

He nodded enthusiastically. 'They treat you like an adult not a kid.'

'The question is, will you act like an adult?'

'You sound like my mum.'

Sam stopped eating for a moment. This comparison with her sister irritated her and effectively ended the discussion, and the meal.

'You start the washing up and I'll make your bed.'

Ricky nodded.

'And don't forget to ring your mum.'

Ricky looked uncertain.

'I mean it.'

After initially reacting to them with caution, Malcolm and Frances had become a *cause célèbre* within the group. The other couples were very impressed at the support Malcolm was giving his daughter. There was much talk about how he'd cope *the second time around*, and he and Frances were often called to the front for practical demonstrations. Frances was impressive and had an instinct for the tasks required. He, on the other hand, was hopeless. He dropped the doll at least twice, pricked both his fingers and the baby with a safety pin, and spilled the bath water down the front of his trousers. Frances cried with laughter but found herself loving her father all the more. At the end of the evening and despite his continuing disasters he received the congratulations of all the parents-to-be.

Apart from feeling embarrassed, Malcolm found he had actually enjoyed himself. As they walked back towards his car he was in a reflective mood, going over in his mind all the things the baby would need, making mental lists of the essentials. Frances, her arm locked firmly in his, looked up into his face reading his mind.

'I think we'll have to rely on disposables after your effort with the real thing.'

He looked down at her. 'I think you could be right. Still, it's only money.'

Frances laughed. They were too engrossed in their plans to notice the dark maroon car parked only a few spaces from theirs. The occupant noticed them, however. He glanced at his watch and made a note of the time they left the college before following them out of the car-park to check their route home.

It had gone nine by the time Sam came scurrying down.

The smell of the fried bacon had already registered in her nostrils before she reached the bottom of the stairs. She walked into the kitchen to find the table laid and her nephew standing by the stove preparing breakfast.

'This is nice.'

Ricky turned briefly to look at her. 'A good, healthy fry-up.'

'I don't know about healthy, think what it's doing to your heart.'

Sam grabbed her coat from the peg at the back of the kitchen door. Ricky looked at her.

'What about breakfast?'

She walked across and kissed him, sighing regretfully, 'Sorry, no time, I'm late.'

'But it's the weekend!'

'Work doesn't end for everyone on Friday afternoon you know.'

As Sam moved away from him towards the kitchen door, he called her back, 'Here.'

Ricky held out a bacon sandwich and Sam grabbed it taking a large mouthful.

'Thanks, it's great.'

Ricky watched her rapidly disappearing back.

'What did your mother tell you about speaking with your mouth full?'

'Are you going to be here when I get back?'

'Probably not, better go home and face the music.'

'Good luck.'

She moved to the front door and stooped to pick up her mail. Most of it was circulars, but there was one postcard which she read immediately She was still chuckling over this as she took another mouthful of sandwich and opened the front door. Standing in front of her was Detective Inspector Tom Adams. He was holding a large white cigarette machine on the back of which were large lumps of plaster from where it had been ripped from a wall. Around the edge of the machine its attacker's bloody fingerprints were still clearly visible. Sam swallowed hard trying to force down the last bit of her bacon sandwich. Adams smiled and gestured to the postcard in her hand.

'Family away on holiday?'

'No, just an old boyfriend. Apparently I'm to expect a visit from him.'

Adams' expression changed briefly and he pushed the machine towards her.

'Yours? I found it lying outside your cottage. Didn't know you smoked.'

Sam frowned at him, 'I don't.'

She looked at the blood on the side of the machine and suddenly realized how Ricky had really injured his hand. It was time he was taught a lesson she thought. Even if it's only not to lie to your aunt. Adams put the machine down and quickly disclosed the real reason for his early morning visit.

'Sorry about last night, nothing to do with me. There's a bit of pressure to get a result.'

'And Farmer's passing it down the line?'

'Something like that.'

'I appreciate your honesty. I'll take another look at him if you like, see if I missed anything, but if it's not there . . .'

Adams held his hand up, 'I understand, thanks.'

Ricky, having heard his aunt in conversation at the door, made his way inquisitively along the corridor. Sam, hearing the footsteps behind her, turned to see her nephew approaching.

'Ricky, let me introduce you to Tom Adams.'

Ricky put his injured hand out.

'Tom's a detective inspector.'

Even as she spoke, Ricky noticed the bloody cigarette machine leaning against the side of the door. He half withdrew his hand before beginning to sway awkwardly from side to side.

'He found this in the drive,' Sam indicated the cigarette machine. Ricky tried to look indifferent. 'Looks like a good set of prints to me, should get the culprit. What do you think inspector?' She winked at Adams and he nodded, looking straight at Ricky.

'We anticipate an early result.'

Sam gave Ricky a final smile before making her way to her car. 'Well, must go. I'm sure you two will have a lot to talk about.'

Ricky watched her go with a mixture of disbelief and betrayal. Adams looked at him.

'Shall we go in and discuss your latest "no smoking" campaign?'

Adams picked up the cigarette machine and followed Ricky back into the cottage, closing the door firmly behind him.

Half an hour later Sam was pulling into the small, cobbled car-park at the front of St Steven's College.

She made her way through the gate and into the porters' lodge where she was directed across Grand Court towards Simon Clarke's rooms at the far end of the court. Sam thought Grand Court had to be the most beautiful in Cambridge. A huge space surrounded by three gates and rows of rooms belonging to both students and Fellows alike. To the right of the court from the main gate was the college chapel, a tall impressive building where the great and the good had prayed for hundreds of years and where Roubiliac's masterpiece of the college's greatest scholar, Newton, sat looking out towards the college he never really left. At the far side of the court stood the hall with its beamed ceiling and long, stained-glass windows in which food was still eaten on large wooden tables, served by uniformed college servants to the few individuals privileged enough to be members of this very exclusive club. The focal point of the court and the most charming feature for Sam was the fountain. Erected by Italian craftsmen to an Elizabethan design it dominated the court. Its gently gurgling waters could be heard in almost every room around the court and created the calming, contemplative atmosphere that was so conducive to serious study.

Sam finally arrived at staircase M10 and climbed the wooden stairs which were smooth and worn by years of use. At the top of the stairs she came to a large, green, oak door. The outer door was already open and the white inner door ajar.

As she was about to knock, a voice shouted from inside, 'Come in, come in, I'll be with you in a minute, make yourself at home.'

Sam pushed open the inner door and entered the room. It was dark. The four windows that overlooked the court were covered in dense ivy which forced the light to fight its way through the vines to brighten the gloomy interior wherever it could. The room was dominated by a large Georgian fireplace with a wide mantle on which stood an assortment of jars, statues, and pots of all shapes and sizes. At the far side of the room was a sagging bookcase overflowing with books of all ages, many in a poor state of repair and looking as if they were about to fall apart. In the centre of the room was a wooden desk which was obscured by papers and books. The room had the faint, musty smell of old, damp paper, mingled with stale smoke and an air of having been closed for some time after a hurried abandonment. The walls were lined with pictures and prints depicting everything from the common to the totally weird. One thing that caught Sam's eye was a black death mask which hung precariously from a single nail above the fireplace. Its expression was almost hypnotic and Sam began to find herself increasingly drawn to it. Her concentration was broken by a sharp voice.

'Aleister Crowley's death mask. The great Warlock, the beast of the three sixes.' He marked the air with his finger. 'It's very rare.'

Sam raised her eyebrows and then returned to the mask. 'I'm not surprised.'

'You must be Samantha Ryan, Trevor Stuart's friend. Simon Clarke, pleased to meet you.' He extended a slightly tobacco-stained hand and Sam took it.

'Thanks for seeing me on a weekend.'

'All the same to me, weekdays, weekends, they all merge into one. I seem to work on all of them.'

Simon Clarke was about thirty, but looked ten years older. He was tall and thin with thick, wire-rimmed spectacles and a permanently dishevelled look about him, and smelt strongly of stale tobacco and sweat. He returned to the mask.

'He engaged in every debauchery known to man, and a few that weren't. Died during a drug-crazed orgy in France.'

'With a smile on his face no doubt.'

Simon burst into a quick, sharp laugh before walking briskly across to his desk and dragging off a large leather book. Dropping it on to the floor he sat cross-legged in front of it.

'Why did you choose pathology?'

Sam was a little surprised by his question but answered readily, 'I find the dead more interesting than the living. And they don't squeal so much when you prod them with a sharp instrument.'

He smiled briefly. 'I did three years at medical school; didn't suit me, couldn't get used to the operations, tying up bits of body. Still makes me shudder.'

Sam decided to ask her own question, 'Why criminology?'

'Liberal intentions at first. You know, put the world right, reform criminals, make them worthwhile members of the community, that sort of thing.'

'And now?'

'Just help catch the bastards. Most of them don't want to be reformed; they're quite happy being criminals. So if I can help put a few of them away so much the better.'

'Hang 'em and flog 'em, eh?'

'Bullet in the back of the neck actually; cleaner, quicker.'

Sam was a little surprised at his views. Simon was amused.

'You're shocked, obviously not bitter and twisted enough yet. When someone close to you is murdered or violently assaulted and all the system wants to do is get the perpetrator back on the street as quickly as possible to carry on their carnage, then you'll change. Come back and see me then.'

Sam remained silent and he quickly returned to the point. 'It's not the first time this kind of symbolism's been used in a murder.'

For moment Sam was confused.

'The upside-down cross – it's not the first time it's been used.'

Coming to her senses, Sam joined Simon Clarke on the floor.

'Really?'

Simon continued, 'It all happened around here actually. Well, in the fens anyway. Do you know anything about black magic?'

Sam shook her head. Simon opened the book and searched eagerly through the pages, finally letting the book fall open on the floor. Depicted on the pages were two women about to be burned at the stake.

'This whole area is steeped in it.'

Sam examined the pictures carefully. One of the

women was clearly screaming from the effects of the flames as they licked around her legs and body. The other, her face contorted in pain, her tongue hanging unnaturally out of her mouth, was being strangled by one executioner as the other began to light the fire at her feet. Sam pointed to the second woman. 'What are they doing to her?'

Simon looked at the picture. 'Garrotting her.'

'Why? Aren't they about to burn her?'

'If they admitted their guilt they were garrotted before they were burnt. Quicker, less painful. Merciful lot, weren't they?'

Sam continued to look at the picture. 'Yes, very.' She noticed something wrapped around the left wrist of each of the women and pointed it out to Simon. 'What's that around their wrists?'

'Ivy probably.' Simon grabbed a magnifying glass from the top of his desk and took a closer look. 'Yes, garlands of ivy. It was supposed to prevent the witches from using their powers against their enemies. Ivy's used in a lot of black magic ceremonies. The Romans used to make the Jews pray to it.'

Sam nodded, fascinated. 'But what's all this got to do with the Mark James murder?'

'I was coming to that.' He flicked through several more pages until he came to a picture of two black men in nineteenth-century farming garb. 'Here they are, Charles and Isaac Ironsmith.'

'They're black?'

'Yes, I think they must have been the only black men in the area at the time. They were quite an

142

attraction. People used to come from miles just to look at them.'

Sam took the magnifying glass off Simon and studied the photograph closely. 'A sort of Victorian Ann and Nick.' Simon was confused and Sam reminded herself of his cloistered existence. 'Sorry. I'm just being flippant.'

He nodded and continued with his story, 'They turned up in Little Overton just after the turn of the century. They were only about ten at the time and couldn't talk a word of English. No one seemed to have a clue where they came from. Anyway, Joseph Ironsmith, a local farmer, took them in and raised them as his own, hence their name. He'd lost both of his sons in the Boer War and until these two turned up was desperately short of help on the farm. The association seemed to work well. When the old man died he left the farm to the two of them and although they kept themselves to themselves, there were never any problems that I'm aware of and they ran the farm well enough.'

'Did they ever learn to speak English?'

'Yes and no. No one ever heard them speak English but most people who came into contact with them were convinced they understood every word being spoken and they communicated with the old man well enough.'

'This is all fascinating stuff, but you still haven't answered my question.'

'Patience, I'm getting there. There were a lot of stories surrounding the boys, most of them nonsense but strange things did seem to happen when they were around.'

'Like what?'

'Wax impressions of people were found nailed to the

church door, graves and tombs were vandalized, cattle fell ill, all the usual things and none of them directly attributable to the brothers. I think some of the locals would have burnt them if they'd had the chance but the old man was fiercely protective.'

'Did anyone discover where they came from?'

'There were a few stories, the odd legend. It was rumoured that about a month before the boys turned up at the village a trader from Haiti was wrecked off the Norfolk coast, hence the voodoo connection.'

'Is that true?'

Simon shrugged, 'I've searched every archive there is to search and I've found no record of the wreck but that doesn't mean there wasn't one, not all the wrecks were recorded.'

'It all sounds a bit far-fetched to me.'

'Possibly, but voodoo certainly synthesizes a lot of African beliefs. It also owes a lot to Catholicism. The boys may well have been influenced by it during their early life. It would certainly explain a lot.'

'You still haven't told me what it's got to do with Mark James though.'

'A lot. One of the brothers, Isaac, was killed in a farming accident during the twenties leaving Charlie on his own. The farm was too much to work alone so he sold it to a local landowner and moved into one of the small farm cottages where he lived happily doing odd jobs around the farm until his early demise.'

'What happened to him?'

'He was murdered in the mid-sixties.'

'Murdered!'

'He'd been out hedge-cutting and when he didn't come back after dark they sent out a small search party. They found him on top of Primrose Hill just outside the village.'

'And the connection?'

'He'd been garrotted and a garland of ivy tied around his left wrist.' He looked into Sam's face for a reaction. 'More interestingly,' he paused for effect, 'a large upside-down cross had been cut into his body.'

Sam was relieved that her visit hadn't, as she had begun to fear, been a total waste of time after all. 'Was anyone arrested for it?'

'Not that I'm aware of. The person to talk to is John Shaw. He's been the vicar in Little Dorking for the last twenty-something years. He's a bit of a walking encyclopaedia on local witchcraft and the murder of old Charlie. He might be worth a visit.'

Sam stood up and looked at Crowley's death mask on the wall. 'Look, I don't mean to be dismissive but isn't witchcraft more to do with people having sex in odd places with funny hats on than anything else?'

'To some. But there are over a quarter of a million practising witches and warlocks in the country at the moment and most of them take it very seriously indeed.'

'Ghoulies and ghosties and long-legged beasties and things that go bonk in the woods?'

Simon smiled, not greatly amused. 'There is someone else who might be worth talking to, one of my old students. Wrote his dissertation on the Ironsmith case. Did a good job too, as I remember. Trouble was, he became so obsessed with the story that he forgot about the rest of his work and finally managed to get himself sent down.'

He began to rummage through the mountain of paper on his desk. 'Now what was his name? It's here somewhere.' He finally recovered the piece of paper he'd been searching for and waved it at her with a satisfied flourish. 'That was him, Sebastian Bird.'

Sam stared at him, hardly believing what he'd just told her.

Detective Superintendent Harriet Farmer stormed along the narrow corridors of the Cambridge magistrate's court, her heels clicking against the hard stone floor and echoing around the building. 'Bloody do-gooders, no social responsibility whatsoever. Where did he get those kind of sureties from? It's bloody ridiculous. If he kills again it'll be on *their* heads not mine!'

Adams, hard on her heels, tried to rationalize the situation, 'The evidence wasn't that strong, ma'am, you knew that when you went in. They've imposed conditions and we can always bring him back in later, when we've got a bit more.'

'Try telling that to the family of his next victim.' She stopped for a moment and turned to him, 'I want him followed morning, noon and night. If that bastard farts, I want someone there to smell it. Do I make myself clear?'

Adams nodded and Farmer strode off again making her way out of the building and into the low autumn sunshine. When she reached the top of the steps she suddenly stopped. The movement was almost unnatural, as if she'd walked into an invisible wall. Adams, who was close behind her, had to step smartly to the side, only narrowly avoiding a collision with her stiff, indignant back. Farmer was almost transfixed, staring towards the pavement at the bottom of the steps. Adams followed her gaze. Sebastian Bird was standing by his red Porsche, his solicitor by his side. They were clearly discussing the outcome of the hearing and had an aura of self-satisfaction about them. After a brief conversation the two men shook hands and separated. As his solicitor walked away Bird looked up and spotted Farmer. A slow, confident smile slowly crept its way across his face. For a moment Farmer didn't move, then a minute tremor ran through her as she realized that Bird's car was parked on double yellow lines. She turned to Adams, 'The bastard's on double yellows, go and book him.'

Adams looked at her despairingly. 'What's the point, ma'am?'

'The point is, he's breaking the law, Inspector, now do your duty.'

Adams sighed inwardly before setting off in Bird's direction.

CHAPTER FIVE

It had been almost a month since the last killing and he was ready for the next. He hadn't expected the court to come to the decision it had, but he was pleased. Although the time had gone quickly it hadn't been wasted. He pulled a green file from his cabinet and spread its contents on to the large oak table in front of him. Photographs, maps, information sheets; he'd left nothing to chance. He felt he probably knew more about the day-to-day movements of Frances Purvis than she did herself. In many ways murder was an intellectual challenge and one that he'd risen to. He'd selected alternative places to commit the killings, and to dump the bodies afterwards, in case the first locations proved unsuitable. He'd even walked around them, getting to know them intimately and assessing possible problems. He'd never felt more confident in his life. The James mission had proved how important planning was, and his death had gone like clockwork. It had been pleasant to discover how easy it had been to kill him. He'd felt no sense of remorse, no pangs of conscience; in fact, he'd enjoyed every moment, much as he imagined a general winning a well-planned battle might feel. Revenge, he decided, was a positive concept not a negative one and he fed off the emotion it generated eagerly. The elation he felt after the killing had lasted for days and was certainly better than any drug he'd tried. In fact the high was better than anything he'd ever felt before in his life and he was keen to repeat it.

He went through every detail of the plan one more time, making sure he'd memorized even the smallest detail. Testing himself, going over and over the plan in his mind. Once he was satisfied, he collected the contents of the file together and closed the folder, clipping the photograph of Frances to the front of it and after one last look at her face, dropped it into the section marked 'pending'. He was confident, but he didn't want to tempt fate. He leaned down by the side of his chair and picked up the small, black, leather bag. He pulled it sharply on to his desk and, unclipping the top, began to examine the contents. The black bag, he thought, added a rather macabre touch to proceedings. It reminded him of one of the three things which were the hallmarks of pictures of Jack the Ripper. His top hat, his cloak, and most of all, his small, black bag, inside which he kept his instruments of death. He pulled the dissecting knife from the dark interior and began to examine its edge. Despite having been used once, it was still sharp and well honed. He wondered idly how many times he would be able to use it before its cutting edge dulled and he would have to replace it with another. He flicked his thumb gently across the blade before slipping it back into its protective sheath and returning it to its rightful place inside the bag. He then examined his syringes and needles. They were fine, packed away inside their individual pockets. He couldn't use those twice but it didn't matter, he had plenty of them.

He considered the last two objects he pulled from his bag to be the most important. The small, bronze-coloured wind chime with its long cord stretching between the two holes at the bottom and top of the chime and the long garland of ivy which he had only recently cut. He ran it through his fingers admiring the leaves. He hadn't realized what a very attractive plant it was. It had grown around him for years, yet only now, when it had become such an important part of his scheme, had he begun to appreciate its beauty and subtlety. He dropped it back into his bag which he closed with a click before placing it back on the floor. He'd hesitated at the prospect of taking on two people at once but He seemed to be guiding him in that direction. He'd formulated a plan, of course, but two people presented particular problems, and had required a considerable amount of thought. He was going to enjoy this one for then it would be finished, and he could rest again.

Frances was sorting out her wardrobe when her father entered the bedroom. She'd already piled up her old clothes on the bed ready to hand in to the local Oxfam shop, whilst keeping back a few of her favourites, those with particular memories. She held one such article from of herself, turning to face her father, 'Remember this?'

Malcolm looked slightly bemused and clearly couldn't.

'It's the one I wore for Aunty Kitty's wedding. You

remember, when John got drunk and was sick down
the front of it. Look,' she pointed to a small section at
the front of the dress, 'that stain never did come out.
Worn once and ruined, and he never offered to pay for
another one.'

Malcolm nodded encouragingly but there was clearly
something else on his mind. Frances remembered his
moods and throwing the dress on the bed with the
others, she waited for him to speak.

'I can't come to the good parenting class tomorrow
night, sorry.'

Frances didn't disguise her disappointment. 'Why?
You know this is important.'

'It's the last time, I swear. An old case has gone wrong
and I've got to be in London to work on it.'

Frances folded her arms and looked away in disappointment.

'I'll stop off at Hamleys tomorrow and get you both
something nice.'

She looked back at her father, 'Promise it'll be the
last time?'

He held his hand up, 'Scout's honour.'

Frances scanned his face looking for the lie but it
wasn't there. 'In that case you can drop off at Armani
and get me something nice.' Malcolm threw his hands
up in mock horror.

'But God knows what the class is going to do without
its star turn.'

Malcolm laughed, 'I'm sure I'll more than make up
for it next week.'

'I'm sure you will,' Frances agreed.

*   *   *

He had been surprised to see him leave. The fact that a taxi collected him and he was carrying an overnight case indicated that he might be away for a while, but the exact length of time couldn't be determined. After all his protracted planning, it appeared that they would be separated at the moment of retribution after all. With her father away, what would Frances' actions be? They really were making life very difficult for him, and they'd suffer for it. He realized there was nothing to be done, and he would just have to wait and watch and hope that he would not be too inconvenienced. The following week was going to be very busy and he wanted this sorted out quickly or it might be weeks before he could try again.

Marcia Evans looked up from her microscope and squinted at the clock on the laboratory wall while her eyes adjusted to the change in focusing distance. Two-fifteen, only ten minutes had passed since the last time she'd looked at the clock. She rubbed her eyes gently, trying to relax them and prepare them for the next assault. Even at twenty-four she was beginning to find the strain of long hours over a microscope taking its toll on her eyes. She hated the idea of wearing glasses, subscribing to the Dorothy Parker adage that men never made passes at girls who wore glasses. Still, she consoled herself, she could always use contact lenses. Despite her concerns, she placed her eyes back on to the top of the binocular microscope, adjusted the focus again and lost herself in a world of fibres and stains.

*   *   *

Sam paced anxiously back and forth across her sitting-room floor stopping occasionally to look for inspiration into the roaring log fire which crackled and spat, forming unearthly shapes within its hot flickering interior. After a string of late-night call-outs she had felt justified in taking an afternoon off, and besides, she needed time to think. Farmer would not be interested in her seemingly wild theories, so she would have to find some evidence in support of her ideas before approaching her. The problem was that no matter how she tried to dismiss the case from her mind, she felt compelled to follow up her theories. The dilemma was troubling. It was a lonely vigil with only Bernard, her cat, to share her turmoil. He watched her languidly from the sofa at the far side of the room, his head turning from side to side, like a spectator watching a tennis match on the centre court at Wimbledon, stopping only occasionally to preen himself and stretch indulgently. Finally, Sam stopped and, looking out of her back window through the rain towards the woods at the top of the hill, came to a decision. Walking quickly into the hall, she picked up the phone and dialled.

Marcia was in the process of replacing one slide with another when the phone rang at the far side of the laboratory. Even this was a welcome break for her aching eyes. She jumped off her stool, walked across to the phone and lifted the receiver. 'Marcia Evans . . .' She recognized the voice instantly. 'As I live and breathe, it's Dr Ryan. Whatever can a poor girl like me do for you?'

Marcia knew at once by the tone of Sam's voice that she wasn't in one of her lighter moods. 'Marcia, I know this might sound odd, but were any garlands of ivy handed in with the evidence from the James case?'

Marcia was slightly confused by the request but accepted it at face value. She dropped her humorous tone to match Sam's and scanned the evidence through her mind. 'I don't think so, would you like me to check?'

She walked across to a small pile of neatly stacked papers close to her microscope and began to search through them, carefully looking at a couple twice to make sure she hadn't missed the obvious, but there was nothing. She returned to the phone. 'No, no ivy, garland or otherwise.'

Marcia heard Sam breathe out in a disappointed sigh. 'Was it important?'

'I'm not sure. Maybe, just a hunch really.'

'If any comes in, I'll give you a ring.'

Sam replied with a sort of distant hum which told Marcia that her mind was already far away, lost in some complex thought pattern in an effort to resolve whatever nagging problem was bothering her. Finally, the problem having been resolved in her mind, she spoke up, 'I was wondering whether you were interested in going to the medics' dinner tomorrow? I've got a spare ticket.'

Marcia was tempted but, given the amount of work she had, was concerned that she would either be too busy or too tired to merit the expense. 'I'd love to, but money's a bit short this month.'

'My treat, there'll be lots of young, handsome . . .'

Marcia began to weaken, her mind racing as she tried to plan a way of reorganizing her work commitments. She felt like Cinderella wanting to go to the ball but being thwarted at every turn. 'I've got nothing to wear.' Sam realized Marcia was almost persuaded and pressed home her advantage, 'Richard'll be there . . .'

That did it, Marcia realized she'd have to go. 'OK, I'm convinced. Where and when?'

Sam knew she'd have to be careful with the next part and made the comment quickly, hoping Marcia wouldn't notice. 'Four o'clock in St Mary's churchyard for drinks at six in the Master's Lodge. Dress is smart, black if you've got it.' She wasn't quite quick enough though.

'Hang on, hang on. I'm sorry if I didn't hear you right but did you say graveyard?'

'Yes, I was wondering if you'd do me a small favour first?'

'Wear my glad rags to a cemetery? No chance, no chance at all.'

Although it was still early in the evening people had already begun to arrive at Bird's club. The two detectives watching the club guessed that they were employees arriving early to open up the place. Bird had been amongst the first to arrive. He parked his Porsche on the street outside the club before making his way inside. DC Jock McFadyed's camera clicked, taking two photographs in rapid succession. The first caught Bird as he climbed out of his car and the second was a strange back shot as Bird entered the club. While McFadyed took his photographs, his partner, Peter Morant, jotted down the time of Bird's arrival at the club, the car he was driving and any other details which he thought might be of relevance. When he'd finished he put the clipboard back at his feet, folded his arms, and continued his desultory stare out of the front windscreen of the car. He hated observations more than anything else he could think of. They were long, boring, normally fruitless and played havoc with his social life. He should, he thought, all things being fair, which they weren't of course, be down at the Dog and Bear with his missis, downing a pint and swapping a few lies with George and Glenda. Instead of that, he was watching some prat who was probably well aware that he was under surveillance and was very unlikely to drop litter, never mind commit a murder. He glanced sideways at Jock.

'I spy with my little eye something beginning with W.'

Jock looked back at him feigning interest. 'Windscreen.'

'Right.'

It was Jock's turn. 'I spy with my little eye something beginning with . . .'

Morant intervened, 'W?' Jock nodded, Morant continued, 'Windscreen.'

Jock shook his head at him, 'You're bloody good at this game, aren't you?'

'Practice.'

Jock agreed with him, 'I'm a bit like that with sex.'

'Especially when you're on your own I've heard,' grinned Morant.

Jock scowled across at him and the two men began to laugh. As they did, Morant noticed an attractive young girl walking towards them. She was carrying a tray with two glasses on it. She walked across to the passenger side of the car and Jock wound down the window, a sinking feeling in his stomach. Smiling, she looked in.

'Mr Bird said he thought you looked a little fed up so he's asked me to bring a couple of drinks across.'

The two detectives looked at each other, both suspicious and a little astonished. The girl continued, 'He said he'd have brought them across himself but he's had to go out.'

The detectives groaned in unison. Jock took the drinks and passed one to his partner. 'She'll have our balls on a pole.'

Morant raised his glass to the girl who smiled at him, 'What the hell, they can't hang us twice.'

The two detectives emptied their glasses in one.

Sam and Marcia looked at each other for a moment before Sam finally plucked up the courage to knock on the shed door. Almost immediately the door swung open and the church sexton, shovel in hand, and looking annoyed, stood before them. Sam spoke up, 'Dr Ryan, I rang the vicar.'

The sexton wasn't impressed by her rank or her connections. 'You're late. Vicar told me you'd be here at four, it's half past. I've got better things to do than hang round here waiting for folks.'

Sam was apologetic, she could be little else. 'Sorry, got caught in the traffic, you know what it's like.'

He stared at her for a moment without speaking, then threw his shovel over his shoulder and stepped out of the shed. As he walked towards Marcia she found herself stepping backwards and for a instant actually contemplated running. The only thing that stopped her was the sexton's Jack Russell. The small dog came running up to her wiggling his body and wagging his tail as he tried to establish whether she was friend or foe. Marcia crouched down and stroked him and he rolled over on to his back. 'Nice dog.'

Without speaking the sexton moved off into the graveyard followed by Marcia and Sam. As they walked between the ancient gravestones and tombs Sam couldn't help but contemplate what a beautiful place it was. Here, surrounded by death, was life in all its abundance. She'd never seen so many varieties of wild flowers in one place before. Rare ivies crawled along and through the old tombs while trees and bushes sprang up from the centre of ancient graves like the fingers of the dead searching for the light. With autumn had come the changes and, unlike the human remains she normally dealt with, here death was beautiful. As if in dying the leaves and the plants wanted one last chance to show how wonderful they had been in life. It was a place she thought she would visit again.

They finally arrived at the tomb they had been looking for and the sexton turned to them. 'Lot of trouble for no good reason if you ask me. You'll find nothing here, the police turned the place upside-down. And they didn't put everything back after them.'

Sam looked at him. 'They didn't know what they were

looking for.' She walked across to the tomb. The lid had a large section missing in one corner and Sam considered that she could probably squeeze through. She turned to the sexton. 'It was you who found him, wasn't it?'

He put his hand up to his nose and squeezed. 'Smelt him more like, right stink.'

Sam nodded, 'Better have a look then.' She pulled a small torch from the inside of her bag and pushed it into a pocket before handing her bag to Marcia and beginning to squeeze through the hole. It was a tight fit but she was just about slim enough to make it and was soon crouching inside the dark interior. Sam pulled the torch from her pocket, clicked it on and began to shine it around the interior of the tomb. The air in the tomb was heavy and damp with a muggy oppression. Despite the police search, spiders had already begun to re-colonize the crevices and there seemed to be dozens of webs. The floor was not as clean as Sam had expected as much of the debris had merely been stirred around rather than removed. Old detritus was forming a thin, slimy carpet overlain by fresh, dry, crisp autumn leaves. She began to run her hands carefully through the leaves, occasionally picking one up to examine it more closely. She tried to be systematic but it was difficult. The space was small and cramped and offered little room for manoeuvre. Every now and then a disturbed insect would scamper from under her hand or across her body in a bid to escape the danger she posed to its sheltered life. As she was resigning herself to abandon the search her torch finally picked up the shrivelled, but nonetheless distinctive, shape of an ivy leaf. She brushed the leaves away from her prize to reveal it fully before carefully picking it up and squeezing herself back out of the hole and into the fresh, sharp, night air. She shivered slightly, not so much from the cold, but more from relief and pleasure at having her expectation fulfilled.

The sexton looked at her. 'You've found something then?'

Sam smiled at him and holding the garland of ivy aloft, watched it lift gently in the breeze.

As the red-robed appeal court judges finished reading their judgment the court erupted. The defendant leaped to his feet and, looking across the court towards the public gallery where his friends were standing and cheering, threw his arms above his head and punched the air with delight.

A firm hand was placed on Malcolm Purvis's shoulder. Turning, he found himself facing his client's solicitor, who stood smiling with his right hand outstretched in thanks. The two men shook hands warmly before Malcolm looked back across the court towards the dock. His client, a smartly dressed, plump man in his mid-thirties, was sitting back in his seat, his head in his hands, crying like a small child, the initial euphoria of the verdict having deserted him. Normally Malcolm would have waited and spoken to his client and the family, basking in the praise which occasions like this always brought. On this occasion, however, the trial had dragged on, it was getting late and he couldn't wait to leave. He made his way quickly but quietly out of the court and into the cloakroom, slipping out of his wig and gown and making his way to the main entrance. At the bottom of the court steps was an army of journalists and television reporters. As he appeared, they surged forward towards him and he froze. Fortunately it was not him they were interested in, but his client, who had just emerged from the court-house behind Malcolm with his family and solicitor. As they were engulfed in a sea of cameras, tape recorders and notebooks, Malcolm was able to slip through undetected. At least, he thought, they were convinced of his innocence, which was more than he was. He hurried along the street towards his chambers which were situated about quarter of a mile from the court. When he finally reached them he dashed up their wooden steps, two at a time, emerging at the top exhausted and having to grip the banister tightly to stop himself collapsing.

'You'll give yourself a heart attack if you're not careful, Mr Purvis.'

The voice was that of his clerk, Michael Scott, who was waiting for him outside his office holding an attractive large royal blue pram which he gently rocked up and down with both hands, humming a lullaby to an imaginary child concealed inside. He waited patiently for his boss to regain his breath. Finally, having recovered sufficiently to stand up, Malcolm looked across at his clerk. 'Well done, Michael, just right, great.'

'We aim to please. Bit old-fashioned for this generation though, don't you think, sir?'

Malcolm was indignant. 'Rubbish. It's exactly the same make we bought for Frances.'

'Twenty odd years ago. Times have changed, and so have young women.'

Malcolm looked down at the pram and then back at his clerk. 'She'll love it. It will be just perfect for my grandson.'

'She's had the baby then, has she?'

'No, not yet, what makes you think that?'

'Grandson?'

'Well, granddaughter then. It's all the same as long as it's fit and healthy.'

Michael smiled and nodded as his boss took the pram from him and began to imitate his action by looking into the pram and rocking it gently. He decided he could take no more and retreated along the corridor towards his rooms.

There's nothing worse than an expectant grandfather, he decided.

Frances took a final sip of coffee from the mug on the kitchen table before grabbing her coat from the stand in the hall and pulling on her large woolly hat. She felt the cold, always had, even when she was a child. Her father had spent hours rubbing her feet in an attempt to keep the chilblains away. It hadn't always worked, but she enjoyed the personal contact with her father. She took one last look around to make sure everything looked its best. She had spent the whole day cleaning the house from top to bottom and filling it with freshly cut flowers. She remembered her mother doing that and had planned it as a surprise for her father when he got home, a token of her gratitude for his support and acceptance.

She glanced at her watch, she was late. Racing out of the front door towards her car she pushed the key into the lock of the driver's door and turned it. The car was as old as the one Bird had given her. It used to belong to her mother and Frances was convinced it gave her father immense pleasure just to watch her driving it. As she opened the door she was distracted by the sound of rustling from a bush close to the front gate. Frances turned and strained her eyes to see what had caused the disturbance and, although the drive was illuminated by street lamps, it was still impossible to recognize the figure which rose to standing as she watched. It was his voice, not his appearance, which gave him away. A cold shiver travelled down her spine; it was Bird. He slowly walked from behind the bush and stood only a few paces away from her. Frances' breath caught in her throat and her stomach churned within its confined space above her baby. Her hand moved instinctively over her stomach.

As Bird took a step closer, Frances fumbled wildly with the alarm she had, at her father's insistence, taken to carrying concealed in her coat pocket. Her fingers, without any conscious direction, triggered the alarm. The noise it made was extraordinary. It was loud, she had expected that, but as the sound bounced off the walls and bushes it seemed to fill the whole drive with a long, wailing cry. Frances was taken by surprise. She dropped the alarm and held her hands tightly to her ears in an attempt to keep the worst of the noise out of her head. Bird was caught completely off guard and spun around defensively, prepared for imminent attack from an unknown enemy or the arrival of a fleet of police cars. Lights along the road began to flicker on and doors opened. Frances' neighbour looked across his fence towards her, trying to shout above the din.

'Are you OK? What's the problem?' He looked across at Bird who glanced at him before his nerve finally deserted him and he fled from the driveway, jumping into his sports car and roaring off along the street towards the city.

Frances was freed from her inertia and retrieved the alarm, flicking it off. The sudden silence was almost deafening. She stood for a moment longer bringing herself back under control. Her neighbour, who had remained on the opposite side of the fence, shouted across again, 'Is everything OK, who was he?'

Frances felt that every nerve in her body was quivering but she turned to reassure the agitated man. 'Everything's fine now, thank you, Mr Miles, just a bit of a dispute with an ex.'

'Well, if everything's OK?'

Frances nodded and he walked back towards his house. Despite her best efforts she began to shake uncontrollably. She opened the car door quickly and sat inside grabbing hold of the steering wheel to support herself and breathing heavily. She felt sick and faint and for a moment contemplated going back into the house and missing the class for once. Finally, she decided that Bird had already affected her life enough and she wasn't going to be afraid forever. She wound down the car window and took in several deep gulps of air, wiping the tears which had forced themselves out of her eyes from her cheeks with the arm of her jacket. Finally, as she began to feel calmer, she straightened up in the seat, turned the key in the ignition and reversed out of the drive.

The disembodied voices of the choir singing inside the minstrel gallery, high above the Old Hall, floated majestically across the candle-lit tables. People waited, some with their eyes closed, absorbing the sounds which had been heard in this place for hundreds of years. Others looked about them at the peculiar shadows which danced across the portraits of the college's former masters hanging around the hall, making the forms shimmer and move for an instant, giving them life once more. When the singing finished the diners' attention was drawn to the High Table at the front of the hall. Professor John Watkins, the Master, stood, a crystal glass of wine in his hand, 'Ladies and Gentleman, the Queen.'

As he raised his glass the rest of the diners stood and in unison echoed the toast, 'The Queen!'

After the loyal toast was drunk the assembled crowd sat back on to their long oak benches and the room immediately filled with the buzz from the chatter and laughter of dozens of people. Sam sat looking exquisitely elegant in front of a portrait of one of the more severe-looking masters. During the short trip between Mary's churchyard and the college, Sam had somehow managed to slip into a short, black dress, brush the cobwebs from her hair and touch up her make-up, so that in the subdued and soft candle-light she was as perfectly turned out as all the other guests.

Marcia had become separated from her as they'd filed into Hall from the Master's Lodge, and now sat opposite a rather handsome man of about twenty-seven. Their body language as they executed an animated conversation revealed that were clearly getting on well. Sam smiled to herself, feeling slightly jealous of their youth and promise. She remembered rather wistfully the brief liaisons she'd enjoyed during her university days. Relationships then were light and very fluid. It was difficult for anyone outside her immediate circle of friends to determine which of the group had formed particular attachments; all were demonstrably affectionate with each other. She couldn't pinpoint the precise time at which relationships had begun to be more demanding and an encumbrance in her life, which was increasingly focused upon her career and her ambitions.

'Make a handsome couple, don't they?'

The comment burst into her reverie like an echo from those carefree days. It had come from the woman sitting opposite her. Sam looked across at her. 'Yes, they do, don't they.'

'Oh, to be young.'

'Sometimes.'

The woman put out her hand. 'I'm Janet Owen, I think you know my husband, Richard?'

Sam nodded. 'The police surgeon?'

'Well, he tries to be, I think he's getting a bit old for it to be frank.'

Sam smiled reassuringly across the table at her, trying not to show her complete agreement. Janet, however, wasn't so easily fooled. 'I see you're in complete agreement with me.'

Sam's embarrassment was masked by a slight commotion at the far end of the table. Trevor Stuart was sitting further down the table next to a young and attractive blonde girl. His hands were all over her and she was giggling with delight. He was making it quite clear to the assembled green-eyed men that she belonged to him. Despite her general liking for Trevor, Sam felt herself more than a little disgusted by him.

Janet looked back at her. 'How does he do it? If they get any younger they'll be wearing nappies.'

Sam remained focused on the lewd actions of her colleague. '"Now, how do we see ourselves getting that first-class degree, my dear?" I should think it probably goes something like that.'

Janet looked back at Trevor who was now nibbling his girlfriend's neck. Finally, sickened by Trevor's openly lecherous behaviour, Sam returned her gaze to Janet. Although she was in her mid-forties she was still in wonderful shape with a beautiful face and athletic figure. Which was more, Sam thought, than could be said for her husband, Richard. She couldn't understand why so many of her friends continued to look so good while their partners went to seed.

'Where's Richard this evening, not on call surely?'

'No, he's around here somewhere, looking to expand and probably chatting about the latest murder he's dealt with.'

'The James case.'

Janet looked across and seemed to be surprised for

a moment that Sam knew which one it was. Then her face relaxed as she remembered, 'That's the one you're working on as well, isn't it? That's why he's so worried.'

'Worried?'

'After you made a fool of him in court the other day.'

Sam was taken aback. 'I didn't make him look a fool.'

'He thought you did, especially over the cadaveric spasm.'

'There was no reason a GP, even one of Richard's experience, should have recognized that.'

'You did.'

'I was lucky, that was all. I don't want to fall out with him over it.'

Janet smiled, 'You won't, just pricked his male pride, that's all.'

Sam smiled, appreciating but not convinced by Janet's reassurance. She changed the subject. 'Richard tells me you're retired?'

'Semi-retired, if you please, I'm still doing a bit of locum work.' She held up her right arm. Her hand looked swollen and bruised and a number of her fingers appeared bent and unnaturally twisted. Unfortunately, this prevents me from doing more. Nothing to be done, about it, though, arthritis just does that. Too many years of delving around in cold, unpleasant places. I've been offered a few good roles in Peter Pan though.'

Sam smiled at her bravery. 'How do you cope with work?'

'Not much I can do. The pills control the pain but another couple of years . . .' She shrugged. 'I'm considering turning to psychology.'

'Delving around in minds instead of bodies, eh?'

'Something like that.'

A commotion at the far side of the table attracted Sam's attention. Trevor Stuart had climbed on to one of the benches with his young friend. He was clearly drunk and enjoying the attention. Two bowler-hatted porters moved quickly towards him and pulled him down from the table. On the way down he slipped and fell sprawling to the floor dragging his young friend with him. Sam shook her head in disgust and decided to leave.

Frances was beginning to regret going to the parenting class. It wasn't just the effect Bird's visit had on her, or the lectures themselves, she enjoyed those, with or without her father. It was the weather. When she'd left home it had been as clear as bell but in only a few hours a thick fog had descended over the whole town restricting visibility to only a few yards. It hadn't been so bad in the city where the buildings broke up the fog a little and the street lights combined with those in shop windows to penetrate the gloom. But the mile or so of country lanes which led to Frances' home were very different. They were dark with no artificial illumination and nothing to break up the swirling banks of fog that drifted across the fields and blanketed the roads. She leant forward over her steering wheel, straining her eyes to pick out the road in front of her. Even her headlights failed to penetrate the dense shrouds, which reflected white light straight back at her. She kept her speed down to below twenty miles an hour. She knew this road well and must have walked and driven it hundreds of times, yet in the fog it looked completely different. She tried to estimate how far from home she was but could discern no landmarks by which to judge it.

It wasn't a severe impact, just a jolt really. Fortunately Frances was sitting back in her seat at the time and her seat-belt held her firmly. She looked up into her rear-view mirror trying to distinguish who had collided with the rear of her car. She couldn't see much, just the dark outline of a long wide car. Although it didn't look like a Porsche, it suddenly occurred to her that the car might be Bird's. For a moment, and despite all the promises to herself, she was afraid again. She watched in her rear-view mirror as the driver's door opened and a figure walked around the car to the passenger's side. The figure crouched down and smiled in at her. She smiled back, leaning over the passenger seat and unlocking the door. He pulled the door open and stepped into Frances' car.

Standing by his study window, he watched as the white smoke disappeared over the village roof-tops. It was burning well. He knew he'd have to return to the garden later and pick up all the bits that the fire had failed to consume. Buttons, metal brooches; he'd always been slightly surprised at how many bits were left behind. Once he'd collected them he would dump them at various locations around the country so they would never be found, and even if they were, they wouldn't be linked to any of the killings.

He'd been disappointed that they hadn't been together, that would have saved time. Still, he had been lucky. He'd lost her for a while in the fog and thought he'd have to start planning it all over again, but then he'd quite literally bumped into her. He'd thought it was just good luck at first, but then he felt His hand guiding him through the mist to his ultimate destination.

'Two files completed, eighteen to go,' he murmured to himself. He reached forwards and pulled one down at random. He'd started to mix them up regularly so he'd have no idea who his next victim would be. After he'd selected his first three victims he'd decided that God should really be dictating the fate of the rest. They were all going to die, of course, but he felt he didn't have the right to decide the order, only God could do that. He opened the file, spilling its contents on to the desk and examined them. Most of the files contained basic details of a person's background, name, address, age and sometimes details of their place of work and car. The most important detail was the photograph. He'd managed to get one of every person. He was quite proud of that. He pinned the photograph on to the cork board by the side of the desk so he could look at it constantly and be reminded of what each one did.

He remembered this one; she'd been on the jury. He recollected the expression on her face when she saw him looking at her after they had announced the verdict. He hoped she'd remember him when her time came.

*　　*　　*

It was midday by the time Sam reached the village of Little Dorking. Although she'd set off straight after her morning list, the fog that had come down unexpectedly the night before still lingered and made driving both slow and difficult. By the time she reached the small Fenland village, however, the worst of the mist had been burnt away and the sun had begun to shine through its thin diminishing veil. She parked her car outside one of the local pubs, The Black Dog. It was a beautiful place, long and white with a thatched roof and small leaded windows. For all its beauty, however, Sam thought that the sign which swung gently outside its front entrance seemed strangely out of place. It depicted a large, snarling, jet black dog with bared teeth and red penetrating eyes. Sam couldn't help thinking that a picture of a black Labrador with a pheasant in its mouth would have been more appropriate. As she stepped out of her car she noticed two women watching her from the opposite side of the road. Their stare made Sam feel uneasy. There was something unusually intrusive about it, almost hostile. She decided to try a friendly smile but the moment she did the two women turned away and continued with their conversation, except that Sam felt sure that they were not really talking to each other, only waiting for another opportunity to stare at her. She turned and hurried into the hotel.

The reception desk was empty so Sam rang the bell on the desk and awaited a reply. The inside of the hotel was almost as charming as the exterior. Modern, but with sufficient of the original detail left to give the place a sense of age and interest. Opposite the desk was a large, open fireplace whose black sooty interior was clearly used regularly. At the bottom of the fireplace Sam noticed a series of interconnecting white rings. They reminded her a little of the Olympic emblem, only crude and slightly more spaced out. The receptionist, a short, plump, middle-aged woman finally arrived at the desk and smiled expectantly at Sam.

'Can I help?'

It was a warm smile and Sam appreciated it. 'Yes, I was wondering if you could give me directions to the Reverend Shaw's house?'

Still smiling, the receptionist walked out on to the street and Sam followed. With her arm extended like a mobile sign she gave her directions, 'Follow the road to the centre of the village and cross by the old memorial. Carry on following the road until you reach the old blacksmith's shop, then turn left on to Swallow Road and you'll see the vicarage on your right, about a hundred yards further along.'

As the woman began to move back towards the hotel Sam's curiosity finally got the better of her. 'Why have those white rings been painted at the bottom of the fireplace?'

'To stop witches coming down the chimney.'

'Ah.' Sam wasn't sure whether she was expected to smile or acknowledge the comment sagely. Finally, the woman turned and disappeared back into the hotel and Sam set off to follow her directions through the village.

Like many of the Fenland villages it was an old and

quaint place. A mixture of the old and the modern thrown together in a planning catastrophe. Whitewashed cottages with their small windows and doors leaned uncomfortably across uneven pavements and looked oddly out of place next to the modern shops and houses with their PVC windows and large glass shop-fronts. When she reached the market place she crossed the tarmacked road on to the cobbled surface. At the centre of the square was a large stone obelisk with several steps leading up to it. At first Sam thought it was a rather bland war memorial like hundreds of others in the area, commemorating the dead from two world wars. But as she got closer her curiosity was piqued. Etched on to the front of one of the base panels on which the obelisk stood was a crudely cut inscription:

IN SACRED MEMORY OF MABEL STEER
PUT TO DEATH BY BURNING ON THIS SPOT
IN 1722
THE LAST WITCH TO BE BURNT IN ENGLAND

Sam looked at the stone for a moment and imagined the screams of the woman as the flames began to lick around her body and burn her flesh. She remembered the pictures she'd seen in Simon's room and hoped that her end had come before the flames had reached her. The poor woman's only sin had probably been to practise a primitive form of medicine, an early ancestor of her own profession. But clever women intimidated men, and still did, she thought. Worse still, they intimidated the church, that bastion of male supremacy.

After one final look at the long brown stone she moved off towards the far side of the village. The directions she had been given were impeccable and she soon found herself walking up the gravelled path of a large redbrick Victorian vicarage. She'd seen similar buildings before but they had almost exclusively been turned into old people's homes or office buildings. This one, although looking a little run down and neglected, was clearly still used for the purpose it was intended and had a charm all of its own as a result. It had been Sam's dream for many years to own a house like this, but she knew it wasn't practical for one person to live in such a large place. When, and if, she ever had children she could perhaps consider it. Though, given her terrible luck with men, she was becoming increasingly pessimistic about the likelihood of children. She walked up to the large white door and hammered loudly upon it. She heard her knock echo through the house but there was no response. The sound of soft padding on the gravel made her turn her head and look along the side of the house. Plodding towards her was an old brown Labrador bitch. Her head was down but her tail wagged gently from side to side in a friendly expression.

Sam crouched down and stroked her head and ears. 'Where's your master then, eh? Where is he?'

As if understanding her question, the dog turned and began to make her way towards the back of the house. Sam followed. As she rounded the corner she was confronted with a view of a striking garden. At first sight it had the appearance of wild disorganization but Sam could discern a plan and realized that a discriminating mind had been at work.

She watched the labrador as it plodded its way across the garden to a figure in a thick Aran jumper kneeling by the side of the vegetable patch and lay down beside him. Sam made her way towards the figure, admiring the skilful combination of wild and cultivated plants. As she approached, the figure spoke without turning, 'You must be Dr Ryan?'

Sam was taken aback, 'Yes, but . . .'

Continuing to pick snails off his vegetables, he answered her question, 'Don't be so surprised. Simon Clark told me you might visit, and as no one else ever visits me in the middle of the day it wasn't a very clever deduction.'

Sam chuckled, impressed. 'Oh, I see.'

'I understand you're interested in the murder of old Charlie Ironsmith?'

'Yes.'

'Let me just get these last couple of . . . there that's got them.' He dropped his last two victims into a large bucket of salt water. 'Only way to kill them really. Tried pesticides; they kill the slugs all right but just about every other useful creature in the garden as well.' He looked into the bucket. 'The evenings are the best time, of course, but I was away last night. Fortunately the day's damp enough to tempt them out at the moment. Got over a hundred one night, quite a record, eh?'

Sam looked into the bucket of dead molluscs. As she looked up she noticed the Reverend Shaw looking at her closely. 'Simon described you very well.'

Sam felt slightly embarrassed by the vicar's attention and could feel her face begin to colour. He wasn't what she'd expected. Although he looked younger, Sam estimated he must have been at least in his mid-forties, tall and slim with a handsome chiselled face and a crop of curly black hair. Although her mouth didn't actually fall open she felt that it should. She also felt a sense of guilt at being attracted to a vicar. He noticed her discomfort and smiled at her. 'It's been a few years since I brought a flush to a woman's face.'

'There's no Mrs Shaw then?'

'She died.'

Sam felt embarrassed. 'I'm sorry.'

'Thank you, it's been a while now. Car crash, drunken driver. Still miss her.'

For a moment his face became sad and tense. Then he smiled and his face calmed again. 'Fancy some tea?'

'That sounds nice.'

They walked off towards the kitchen at the back of the vicarage discussing the finer points of cottage gardening and closely followed by the faithful Peggy.

Tom Adams was driving his car along King Street when he first noticed the commotion. He'd been forced to stop behind a queue of traffic which had, in its turn, been stopped by a coach full of Japanese tourists taking endless photographs of King's College. Patience was a virtue in Cambridge; it was a small town with enough activities for a large city and student life seemed to dominate everything. At times he found himself resenting their presence, but would then remember

how important they were to the economic life of the
city. They provided work for thousands of people, they
used the local shops, restaurants and cafés, and the
tourists who came to see the colleges and experience
their ambience added millions to local coffers. For now,
however, his concentration was taken up by a group of
drunken youths who were staggering their way down
King Street towards him. He thought they were students
at first, but as they drew closer they didn't look quite
right; wrong clothes, wrong attitude, these were local
kids who'd had too big a sniff at the barmaid's apron.
Suddenly, one of the youths leaped on to the bonnet
of a nearby car and began to jump up and down on it,
crumpling the thin metalwork into the engine. Adams
jumped out of his car but before he had time to intervene,
two uniformed police officers, helmets in hand, came
running along King Street towards them. The group of
youths standing on the pavement cheering their friend
on spotted them in time and, sobering up quickly, turned
and ran. The youth on the car, however, was not quite so
lucky and in his haste to jump down from the car slipped
and fell. Before he had time to scramble to his feet, the
two police officers were upon him. They lay him face
down in the street and handcuffed him before picking
him up roughly and pinning him up against a wall whilst
they radioed for help. Adams hadn't had a clear look at
the youth until they picked him up, then as he struggled
and shouted abuse at the arresting officers he turned his
face towards him. It was Ricky, Sam's nephew.

As Sam walked through the house to the sitting-room

she was surprised at how bright and modern it was. Victorian fittings and fitments which were an integral part of the structure of the interior remained but everything else she saw, from the curtains to the prints on the walls, was boldly contemporary and strikingly colourful. Even the crucifixes and other religious *objets d'art* scattered around the house were modern and highly stylized. Only one object looked slightly out of place, a large photograph of Shaw in army uniform surrounded by some very tough-looking men, all of whom were leaning on an ancient Jaguar car.

'Tea.'

Sam turned from the picture to see the Reverend Shaw enter the room with a large wooden tray containing two china cups, an old brown teapot and plates full of scones and jam. He put the tray down on a small side table and Sam walked across to join him. 'It's only English Breakfast, I'm afraid. I'm a bit old-fashioned about tea.'

Sam sat in the large armchair opposite him. 'That's fine. I'm not a smelly tea fan either. Do I detect a female hand in the décor?'

The Reverend Shaw began to pour the tea using a silver strainer to catch the wet leaves. 'Indeed you do. My wife had a love of the contemporary and ran a thriving small business in interior design for like-minded individuals before she . . . Well, anyway, I'm happy to keep reminders of her around me.'

'I hadn't realized you'd been in the army?'

'Territorial, I was the padre for a local parachute battalion.'

'Bit of an odd profession for a man of God.'

'I was attached to the medical corps, first aid, that sort of thing.'

'You don't think you could kill anyone then?'

'I shouldn't think so, but who knows? Depends on the circumstances, I suppose.' He changed the subject, 'Now what do you want to know about poor old Charlie?' He finished pouring and handed a cup to Sam.

'As much as you can tell me,' she sipped at her tea, 'I'm probably barking up the wrong tree but there are certain similarities between the death of Charlie and a murder I'm dealing with in Cambridge.'

'The James murder?'

'Yes, as it happens.'

'I read about that, terrible business, awful, so young. Any closer to catching your killer?'

'No, not really, the police have a suspect, but I'm not sure.'

'Any evidence?'

'A few fibres, but that's about all.'

The Reverend Shaw sat back, still interested. 'What kind of fibres are they?'

'One's from a woollen garment of some sort, and the others are horsehair.'

'Horsehair, how peculiar.'

Sam began to feel a little uncomfortable with his questioning and feared she had revealed more than she ought. 'They've both been eliminated. You seem very interested in the case?'

'Bit of an Agatha Christie fan; I find crime fascinating. Don't get much chance to talk of such things in a backwater like this. The Ironsmith case was the only interesting thing to happen in the village for three hundred years.'

Sam brought the conversation back to the subject. 'Simon tells me you're a bit of an expert on the case.'

'I know something of it, much of it village gossip though. You know what places like this are like. Chief Inspector Romer was your man.'

'Where can I find him?'

'Graveyard next door, I'm afraid. You're a few years too late.'

Sam was intrigued, 'What happened?'

'Nothing sinister, cancer, poor man. I officiated at his funeral, first one I did after coming to the village. The murder became an obsession with him, even after his death. He insisted that he was buried in the local churchyard, sort of a permanent reminder to the killer that he was still around. Caused quite a stir at the time. Only case he failed to solve apparently.'

'What can you tell me about Charlie?'

'You know he was black? I think he and his brother must have been the first black people in the area. There are still not that many. Anyway a lot of people were afraid of him.'

Sam cut in, 'Because he was black?'

'Partly, I think, but they also thought he was a warlock. A male witch. There were a lot of strange things associated with old Charlie, a lot of stories too.'

Sam became increasingly interested. 'Like what?'

'Well, the strangest one is in here.' He picked a heavy leather-bound book off the table by the side of his chair,

Folklores, Customs and Superstitions of the Fenlands
by the Reverend Clive Moulton, a predecessor of mine.
He was the first person to write about the legend of the
black dog. Didn't Simon tell you about it?'

Sam shook her head and remembered to take another
sip of tea before it cooled.

'The hotel in the village is named after it.' Sam
remembered the sign outside the hotel where she parked.
Shaw continued, 'In 1910 a ploughboy came across a
large black dog while working in a local field. He saw
it at the same time, dusk, on eight successive occasions.
The boy, who had been on his own when he saw the giant
animal, told the other farm-workers of his experience
but, of course, they just laughed and teased him. The
following evening, however, the boy was visited again
but this time instead of disappearing the dog turned
into a headless woman. The apparition then proceeded
to glide hair-raisingly through the youth's body causing
him to faint. The same evening the boy's brother was
killed when he fell under the wheels of a cart. Ever
since that time the sighting of the dog has always been
synonymous with a violent death of some sort.'

Although it was lunch-time Marcia Evans had decided
to work on in the lab. It was the only time she could
guarantee the solitude she needed to work on the ivy
they'd found inside the tomb without the risk of being
asked awkward questions. She examined it through a
powerful magnifying glass. The main interest of her
examination was the knot at the centre of the garland.
As she looked at it she tried to draw its shape on a

small scrap of paper. Once satisfied with her drawing, she put down her magnifying glass and took the paper along the corridor to George Bishop's office.

Her luck was in. George was sitting by one of the lab's work surfaces engrossed in this month's copy of *Yachting Monthly*, while at the same time trying to pull a small piece of his corned beef sandwich from between his teeth with his fingers. Although George was one of the lab's firearms experts he was also a keen yachtsman who'd written numerous books on the subject, the most important of which, for Marcia, was the definitive book on knots.

She knocked and entered the lab. George looked up. He was always pleased to see Marcia. She had to be the most attractive girl in the lab, he thought, certainly had the greatest legs. He watched her as she crossed the lab trying to imagine what she'd look like lying on top of him in the cabin of his boat. He'd invited her out for a day's sailing a couple of times but she'd always resisted. Although he was forty-three, overweight and married with three children, he still thought he was in with a chance. He finally pulled the piece of annoying meat from the back of his teeth and after inspecting it closely, wiped it on to his sandwich bag.

'You've decided to come sailing with me at last?'

Marcia smiled thinly, she'd often seen him watching her and when they had a conversation his eyes seldom roamed from her breasts. It didn't make her feel uncomfortable, just amused her. She was more than capable of handling the George Bishops of this world, but by occasionally flirting and acting the naïve innocent, she knew she was more likely to get what she needed from him. 'Maybe, depends whether you can help me with this?'

The merest hint that Marcia might be changing her mind about the trip had George interested. He wiped his hands down his lab coat and took the piece of paper on which Marcia had drawn the knot and examined it quickly.

'Do you recognize that knot?'

Bishop nodded. 'Good drawing, obviously good with your hands.'

Marcia raised her eyebrows at him, flirtatiously.

'It's a surgeon's knot. Developed in 1918 during the First War by a surgeon called William Speakman.'

Marcia continued smiling at him, eager for more information.

'It starts with a right over left, then a left over right . . .'

Marcia cut in, 'Sounds like a reef knot.'

Bishop looked impressed.

'I was a brownie.'

'Still got the uniform?'

Marcia gave a false laugh of amusement.

'Well, um, it's almost a reef knot but it does have slight differences. It's left over right, right over left, but the right over left again.'

'Do surgeons still use it?'

'Some. There are others, but this one's still in use.'

Marcia took her drawing from him and glanced at it again.

'Why do you need to know? One of your jobs?'

'No, but if I'm coming sailing with you I thought it might be a good idea to learn about a few knots first.'

She held both wrists together in front of her. At the sight of this Bishop's eyes widened and, thinking she might have pushed him a bit too far, Marcia skipped out of the lab, quickly returning to her own desk to ring Sam.

Sam reached into her bag and pulled out a small glass bottle containing a section of the ivy which she had found inside the tomb. She passed it across to Shaw. 'I found this inside the tomb, where James' body was discovered.'

Shaw held it up in front of his face and examined it myopically.

'I'm told you're a bit of an expert on ivy as well.'

'Expert? I'm not sure about that, but I certainly dabble.'

'Can you tell me anything about this? It's not all there I'm afraid, the boffins have most of it.'

Shaw leaned back, lowering the sample. 'It's rather brown around the edges, but I think I can help. You say it was found in the graveyard?'

Sam nodded. 'Yes, I think it might have been tied around Mark James' wrist.'

'It would make sense if you think, and you clearly do, that there is some kind of ritualistic element to the James murder. Most of these rituals are carried out on consecrated land.'

'I thought Charlie was killed at the top of a hill?'

'Oh, he was, but Primrose Hill certainly comes under

that definition. It's been associated with witchcraft and devil worship for as long as anyone can remember. When was your man murdered?'

'We're not entirely sure, he went missing on 20 September.'

Shaw nodded sagely. 'The day after, the twenty-first, is the Autumn Equinox, one of the witches' eight great Sabbaths. They're periods well-known to occultists, a time of psychic stress and hauntings. It comes just before the end of the month of the vine and begins the month of the ivy.'

'When's the next one?'

'Thirty-first of October, Samhain, Hallowe'en to you and me. The beginning of the Celtic winter. The dark forces come out with a vengeance for that one.'

Sam suddenly straightened up. 'But that's today!'

'Has anything happened?'

'Not that I know of.'

'Looks like you've got away with it then.'

Sam looked at him, uncertain whether he was making fun of her.

Graham Dawes looked at the two young golden retrievers as they bounded about their compound in his back garden. Although they were only six months old they were already huge and almost impossible to control. He'd tried training classes but they'd been an abject failure; he wasn't sure if it had been his fault or the dogs'. He was too soft, but now he was left with only three options. To have them put down, to sell them, or give them away. He thought he'd try selling them first and if that didn't work, well . . . he shrugged to himself. The two adolescent dogs jumped up at the fence, their eyes bright and clear and their tails wagging furiously. He'd have to walk them soon. A swift pint down the local and then he'd give them the run of the park for half an hour; that should do the trick, he thought. He stuck his hand through the fence and let them lick his fingers for a few moments before walking off to fetch their leads.

It was a large greenhouse and very impressive. Inside were rare orchids of every description and the variations of shape and hue were wonderful. Shaw was clearly proud of his collection and boasted that he cultivated plants from the four corners of the world. Sam walked in to the greenhouse and was assailed by a heady aroma; she looked around her in delight and dismay and located the source of the aroma as a *stephanotis* plant nestling amongst the flamboyant orchids. Sam put her nose close to one of the trumpet-shaped blooms and breathed in deeply. The smell was overwhelming and delicious. It had to be because the formalin was beginning to take its toll on her nose just as it had on dozens of her friends' and colleagues'. When the effect became too pronounced her time as a pathologist would be over. For of all her senses, smell was, for her, the most important. Even if her sight failed her at some time in her life and she couldn't see her garden and plants she could at least smell them, and she wasn't sure that life would be worth living without that pleasure.

As Sam and Shaw made their way to the back of the greenhouse the look changed dramatically. Here was the most comprehensive collection of ivy plants Sam could have imagined. Every shape, size, and shade were represented. The Reverend Shaw emptied the small section of ivy on to the bench in front of him before turning to Sam. 'When did you lose your faith?'

Sam was totally taken aback by the question and her mind raced for an answer. Shaw answered for her, 'When someone who was close to you died.'

Sam could do nothing but nod.

'I thought so, it's normally the case.'

'How did you know?'

'I watched you examine some of my crucifixes. I'm a bit of a collector. There was interest but no passion. I even thought I detected a certain resentment. Sorry to embarrass you. I'm a great people watcher, comes with the territory.'

'My father, he was murdered when I was young, I saw it happen.' Sam couldn't understand why she was telling him this, she'd never told anyone else. He smiled at her as if he understood and then returned to the ivy, leaving Sam unsure and more than a little rattled. It was a feeling she didn't enjoy.

'There are ten species of ivy and you have managed to find one of the rarer ones.'

Sam stepped closer to him and looked down at the ivy on the bench. 'Really?'

'*Hedera Hibernica*. It's the wrong one, but it's rare. There's only one type of ivy associated with the occult and that's *Helix Poetica*, the poets' ivy. It was the

189

one found around Charlie's wrist when they discovered him.'

'Are you sure?'

'Absolutely, your witches don't seem very well-informed do they?'

Sam raised her eyebrows at him.

'Let me show you.'

He reached up to a shelf in front of him taking down a large tray of ivy and putting it down on the bench. 'This,' he indicated to the tray of ivy, 'is *Helix Poetica*. Now, if you compare that with the example you brought me, the *Hedera Hibernica*, you'll notice several things.' He reached into his pocket and retrieved a magnifying glass which he had brought with him. He handed it to Sam who began to examine the leaves. 'You'll see that the veins on the *Hibernica* are far more pronounced and white in colour. The leaves are slightly larger too. The biggest difference will come later in the year when the *Poetica* will be covered with rather attractive orange berries.'

Without looking up Sam asked, 'What about the *Hibernica*?'

'That's only found wild in one area of the country, down by the Helford River in Cornwall. Although I understand that Kew has some fine examples.'

'Can it be propagated?'

'Oh yes, quite easily. As you can see it's an attractive plant.'

Sam handed back his magnifying glass and nodded. Shaw continued, 'I had a young man here a few years ago who was fascinated by the Ironsmith story. Even took cuttings of the ivy. He was going to write a book. Now, what was his name? Named after an animal of some sort.'

'Sebastian Bird?'

'Yes, that was it, Bird.'

Malcolm Purvis had arrived home early in the morning, having hired an estate car and driven back from London rather than catch the train the previous night. He wasn't sure how he would have managed going by train even in first class and the reports of thick fog had deterred him from attempting the journey until the morning. He lifted the pram from the back of the car before dragging it step at a time up to the front door.

He had become increasingly concerned about Frances. He'd left plenty of messages on the answer phone but she hadn't returned one. He unlocked the door and pulled the pram inside. The curtains were still closed and although the house was in darkness and he couldn't see them, the smell of the freshly cut flowers hit him at once. Their odour was everywhere, he hadn't smelt anything like it since his wife had died. This was Frances' work, he thought, and he loved her all the more for it. He turned on the lights and walked around the house calling his daughter's name. He even went into the garden, but there was no reply. Stepping down into the garage he noticed her car was gone too. Walking into the sitting-room he switched on the answer phone. The only messages were the ones he'd left, Frances had clearly never heard them. As the final message ended a dark apprehension began to descend over him. He picked up the phone and pressed in the numbers 999.

He'd enjoyed his pint, well three actually. The dogs had waited in the car for over an hour and now he felt guilty, so he'd driven on a few miles to give them a run across the Abbey grounds. It was an impressive sight, normally illuminated in the darkness by a dozen spotlights which shone their powerful lights upwards across the ruined walls. But the Abbey had been closed for some weeks now for urgent repairs and he had been forced to find a way across the fields and through a hole in a nearby hedge. He lit a cigarette as he watched his dogs race across the park towards the ruins, bounding and chasing each other in large circles. The nights were drawing in quickly now and the scene was gloomy. As the dogs moved further away from him he shouted to them, 'Pip, Max, here. Come here.'

They ignored him and raced towards the Abbey, jumping over a low stone wall and disappearing into the ruins. 'Bastards,' he thought, realizing he'd have to cross the park to fetch them. Dawes was a large man used to long drinks and short walks. He'd bought the dogs to provide an incentive to improve his fitness but he'd soon tired of them and as his inherent laziness took over, the walks had become shorter. As he made his way towards the Abbey the dogs began to bark furiously, frightened and confused at what they didn't understand. Their barking didn't sound natural and had a sort of hollow ring. For a moment Dawes was frightened but his curiosity got the better of him and he began to search for his dogs. He finally arrived at a set of steps leading down below the Abbey. The sound of barking was definitely coming from the bottom of the stairs. He called to them but there was no response. For a moment he was undecided but, finally plucking up the courage, he pulled a small torch from his pocket and slowly descended. He shone his torch on to a large oak door which stood half open with its metal lock hanging loose, having been forcibly ripped from its mounting. He squeezed his rather portly body through the gap between the wall and the door and found himself inside a large chamber. From its design it was clearly some sort of private chapel although in a poor state of repair. His dogs were both standing back from the altar at the far side of the chamber barking furiously at something lying prostrate across the top of it. Graham Dawes pulled their leads from his coat pocket and walked towards them. His approach didn't, as he had expected, calm them and for the first time he looked across in the direction they were barking to see what was causing them so much agitation. What he saw made him stagger back.

'Oh my God, oh my God!'

He grabbed the dogs by the collar and secured their leads, his eyes never leaving the awful sight by the altar as he dragged them backwards, finally turning and stumbling in panic back up the stairs.

CHAPTER SIX

The web covered her entire face like a grotesque veil refusing to reveal the beauty beneath. However, it failed to hide her agony. She had died hard, howling against her fate, her mouth open and fixed in a silent scream. Adams watched as the web's occupant, a large brown and cream spider, suddenly crawled towards its struggling prey. The fly had been caught directly over the girl's mouth as it had gone to lay its eggs in the deepest recesses of her dead body, and was now engaged in a life and death battle which it was bound to lose. Soon the fly was still and the spider began to wrap his web tightly around the paralysed body. He knew he shouldn't, nothing at the scene of a murder should ever be touched, but it was too much for him. He leaned down and plucked the spider from its web. It didn't come away easily and pulled part of the web away with it. Part of it had been attached to a long engraved silver ear-ring and as the web released it from its hold it rocked gently. Adams didn't want to kill the spider, he'd seen enough death for one day. He placed the small insect gently on to a nearby wall and watched as it scuttled off into a dark recess before returning to the scene.

Detective Superintendent Farmer arrived at the scene later than usual, in a vile mood. She'd been on the other side of the county on an enquiry when the call had come in, and her fool of a driver had not had the intelligence to mention it to her until she'd returned to the car. She consoled herself with the thought that she'd make sure he was back plodding the cold streets of Cambridge before the month was out. She gave no quarter; she had certainly received none during her career.

Logging in with the PC on the gate, she began to follow the taped path to the scene. Half-way towards the ruins she noticed Adams walking towards her. Without stopping for breath she started her interrogation, 'Who found her?'

'A chap walking his dogs.'

'I'm going to start a "man walking his dog" section, they seem to turn up more crime than we do.' Who is she?'

'Frances Purvis.'

The name made her stop for a moment as she began to feel the anger well up inside her. 'Bird's girlfriend?'

Adams nodded.

'Bastard. What did I tell you? There's going to be a lot of very awkward questions asked about this one. I hope the press hangs them out to bloody dry. I want him in, I don't care what you have to do, or who you have to do it to but I want him in.'

'It's all in hand. With a bit of luck they'll have picked him up by now.'

Farmer walked on without responding further, Adams followed. She descended the stairs quickly and was soon inside the chapel. She'd attended many murder scenes and seen more bodies than she cared to remember but despite that, this one still shocked her. Perhaps, she thought, it was because they'd met, she'd known her, although only briefly. It made all the difference. Most deaths, no matter how horrible, could be viewed with a degree of detachment and the only real grief was that of the family and friends, but that was expected and most members of the force learned to deal with it in this way. But when you've seen the difference between a vibrant life and an horrific death, it was brought closer.

She remembered Frances coming to the police station with her father to give them the information about Bird and James. Everyone, even she, had been struck by her beauty and zest for life. She had clearly slipped off the rails for a while and fallen in with an undesirable crowd, but she was intelligent and gave a clear and articulate account of what had occurred on the night of James' death; she'd have made a good witness, Farmer thought. Now all that was left lay at her feet, twisted and bloated like some dead animal carcass left in a field to rot. She watched Owen, the police surgeon, making his notes.

'How long's she been dead?'

'Couple of days, I think. Strangled. You'll have to wait for the pathologist to be sure though. I don't want to get into trouble again.'

Farmer looked across at Adams. 'Where is she?'

'On her way.'

'She always is.'

Farmer was secretly pleased Sam was late. She took a

perverse delight in displaying self-righteous indignation at Sam's inability to arrive promptly at a scene and she rather feared that one day Sam would arrive first. Still, by current evidence there was little chance of that, she thought smugly to herself. Farmer's thoughts returned to the body.

'This is a public park, why has it taken so long to find her?'

'It's been closed for the last couple of weeks for urgent repairs, some of the walls are in a bit of a state. The bloke that found her shouldn't even have been here. His dogs ran off and he followed them.'

Owen made his last few scribblings before packing his bag away. 'I'll let you have my report in the morning.'

Farmer nodded as Owen disappeared back up the stairs.

Sam had got the call as she drove back from Little Dorking. She had sworn at one time that she would never use a mobile phone but had slowly accepted its usefulness and felt she would now be lost without it. For once she knew exactly where the murder scene was. She'd been there with her mother the previous summer for a picnic. It had been one of the last occasions she could remember her mother still being her mother and not the rather sad figure she had become since her mind and memories had begun to decay. She remembered leaving her mother sitting in the warm sun while she explored the ancient ruins. Although still a majestic sight, the Abbey's decaying grandeur saddened her. She remembered standing on one of the last remaining walls and shading her eyes from the sun to look out across the ruins towards her mother who sat dozing happily under a large oak tree, relieved for the moment from the knowledge of the creeping inertia in her mind. She seemed to fit in well with the surroundings. The once consequential, now slowly decaying to the steady beat of time. Shelley's words floated into her mind: 'My name is Ozymandias, king of kings: Look on my works, ye Mighty, and despair!'

She spotted Richard Owen as she made her way towards the Abbey. He was at least wearing protective overalls this time. She had already made the decision not to stop and chat, she was late enough and nothing he could tell her was going to make the slightest difference to her own findings. When Owen saw her he waved and stopped, preparing to summarize his findings. She swept by him, 'Sorry Richard, can't stop. I'm late. I'll read your report later.'

Giving him a half wave Sam disappeared into the grounds leaving Owen feeling slightly bemused.

The moment she entered the chamber Sam had realized she was dealing with the same mind that had killed James. This time the cross, which had been cut deep into the front of the girl's body, was clear and vivid. By the side of the cord which had bitten into the girl's neck, was the long brass wind chime just as before. She looked across at the girl's left arm which was spread out by her side. Around her wrist and almost concealed by the clear plastic bag that had been tied over her hand, was a garland of dark green ivy. Sam crouched down and, gently pulling it clear of the bag, examined it carefully. At that moment she realized that whatever the murders were about, they had nothing to do with witchcraft. She laid the girl's arm gently back on to the ground and, opening her medical bag, began her preliminary examination.

PC Carver couldn't help feeling resentful that his lack of experience excluded him from most of the exciting events. When the body had been discovered the station had almost emptied as everyone went to help or just gape. Murder in this part of the world was still an unusual event and one not to be missed. He'd managed to get as far as the station yard before he'd been called back and told to cover the area car while everyone was busy. Still, he reflected, this was better than nothing. It was the first time he had actually been let out on his own in the car! Perhaps this was his big chance. Perhaps while the rest of them were stuck up at the Abbey he could make the big discovery and solve the case. They'd have to be impressed by that. He drove slowly along the main road feeling self-important and musing that he was probably the only effective law enforcement for miles. All those people relying on him for protection and he wasn't yet twenty-one; it made him feel good.

Whilst lost in his thoughts, his eyes picked up the shadow that moved rapidly across the front of his Panda. The dull thud and scream that came from the front of the car let him know that he had hit something. He braked hard and stopped, peering through the windscreen to see if he could spot what it was. He opened the car door just in time to see the vixen run, limping and screaming, through a farm gate into a recently ploughed field. The blood from her injured leg covered the ground by the side of his car and left a trail into the field. She's not going to get far in that state he thought, he'd have to try and finish her. He pulled his truncheon from his side pocket and began to follow the trail, using his torch to guide him. The field was large and black and there wasn't a sound, he'd never find her. She'd probably crawl into some shallow hole or under shrubbery and die quietly, he thought. He clipped his truncheon back on to his belt and was about to leave when he saw the car. It was parked tightly behind a hedgerow. He walked across to it flashing his torch across its length. At first he thought it might be a courting couple, but he soon discovered the car was uninhabited. He returned to the back of the car and flashed his torch across the number plate. Taking hold of his radio he held it close to his mouth, '1623 to Control, over.'

'Control to 1623, go ahead over.'

'PNC. Check please, Control.'

The voice at the other end seemed none too pleased at his request, 'Given the situation is the check considered necessary at this time?'

He thought it was. 'Yes, over.'

The voice was still exasperated. 'Go ahead, over.'

'Blue Renault registration number L, lima, seven eight four, Fox-trot, Yankee, Oscar. Over.'

'Stand by.'

While he waited he decided to examine the car further. From the impact damage at the back of the car it appeared to have been involved in a recent accident.

It worried him. Probably just pushed it in here while they arranged for it to be towed away, he thought. More stick when he got back to the station. His radio crackled back into life. 'No trace lost or stolen. Registered owner a Malcolm Purvis from The Gables, Fereham.'

'Thank you, control.'

He decided that at least he would pay Mr Purvis a call and see what was going on. He got back into his car and started it before turning the heater up to full blast and feeling the warm air drift over his exposed face and hands. He was about to pull away when his radio crackled back into life. This time it was not the control room operator but his inspector, 'Control 1623, are you still with the car, over?'

He called back, 'Yes, over.'

'Stay with it. We're sending up some help. It may have been used in connection with the murder up at the Abbey.'

PC Carver could feel the excitement begin to surge through his body. The radio crackled back into life once again. It was his inspector, 'And well done.'

PC Carver could almost feel his chest swell. He straightened his cap, pulled on his black leather gloves and returned to the field to guard his exhibit.

The preliminary examination finished, Sam packed away her tape recorder and pulled off her gloves. She glanced at her watch. 'PM at nine if that suits everyone?'

Farmer nodded, and as she was the only one who counted, Sam took it as an acceptance and left, closely followed by Farmer, eager for information. 'What can you tell us?'

Sam continued walking back along the taped path. 'I can't be entirely sure yet. I'll know more once I've carried out the PM, but I'd say she was almost certainly murdered by the same person that killed Mark James.'

'I guessed that much myself,' snorted Farmer. 'We should have Bird back in tonight.'

'You're still convinced it was him then?'

'Oh yes, it was Bird all right and if you'd come up with the evidence when I asked, that poor little girl in there would still be alive. I hope you can live with that.'

Sam stopped and turned angrily on Farmer, 'If the evidence had been there I'd have found it. It wasn't and I'm not going out on a limb for you or anyone else!'

Farmer quickly fired back, 'Even if it means an innocent young girl dies?'

Sam was equal to it, 'Don't you blame me for your cock-ups. You arrested Bird on nothing and then expected me to sort it out for you. Well, I don't work that way. Just try getting it right for once then perhaps that "poor little girl" *would* still be alive!'

Sam began to walk back along the taped path but stopped after only a few steps and turned back to Farmer, 'And for what it's worth, Bird didn't do it, you are wrong.'

For a moment Farmer was stunned and contemplated going after the rapidly disappearing pathologist but thought better of it, deciding to talk to her later after the PM when things had cooled down a little. She turned and walked slowly back to the scene. She was confident of her suspicions over Bird but Sam seemed equally confident and a small germ of disquiet was waiting to grow given a moment's weakness. She would not allow it to do so.

It had only taken Sam forty minutes to get home. She looked at her watch and sighed. It would be dawn soon. It had been very quiet when she'd arrived, only a high-pitched beeping filling the emptiness of her cottage. She walked across to the machine and switched it on. It was Marcia.

'I've made rather an interesting discovery about the knot in the ivy. Give me a call when you can. Oh, and thanks for the other night. I had a great time, I think.'

It was the only call and the machine switched itself off. Sam instinctively reached for the phone but then remembering the time stopped herself, writing a mental note in her head to ring Marcia the following morning. She decided it was hardly worth going to bed. Besides, she knew she wouldn't sleep, her mind was too active, full of calculations and theories. She changed quickly, slipping on her gardening boots before making her way out to the garden shed. It seemed the ideal time to finish planting the bushes she'd purchased a few days before. Switching on the security light which illuminated the garden, she collected her shovel and began to dig a large hole in the border at the far side of the garden. It was only here in her garden that she felt completely relaxed. Here she felt at one with her thoughts, emptying her mind of the day's rubbish and concentrating on the relevant. Although it was hard, she worked vigorously whilst her mind went over the circumstances of the two murders. She knew she wasn't just angry at Farmer but was also questioning herself and her own ability. What if Bird was the killer; perhaps Farmer was right, although the evidence was pretty circumstantial and weak. She wasn't a policeman after all, only a pathologist. Maybe this time she'd overstepped the mark. Had she missed something? Perhaps she could have made more of the evidence. If she had, then the murderer, Bird or whoever, might have been identified and the girl might still be alive. She bashed her spade into the ground in frustration and anger, breaking up the soil before shovelling it out and throwing it to the side. She decided the hole was big enough and began to drag the bush towards it. Suddenly a voice broke through the cold night air.

'Need a hand?'

Sam turned sharply to be confronted by the smiling face of Tom Adams. She was tired and in a bad mood. She didn't want to see Tom or any other policeman right now. She tried to make her feelings felt.

'You and Farmer are a double act, are you? Well, I've met the funny one so you must be the stooge.'

Adams smiled at the insult, he'd certainly been called worse. He walked up to her and started to help her pull the bush towards the hole she had just prepared for it.

'Stop me if you've heard this one, but do you know the story of the superintendent who's having to deal with two murders in a month and whose main suspect is walking around as free as a . . . Bird?'

Sam wasn't impressed. 'That's her problem.'

They reached the hole and dropped the bush into it.

'Thought it might be yours as well.'

Sam began to water the bush with the garden hose. 'Why should it be?'

'She's the first woman detective superintendent this force has ever had, and there's plenty of people that would like to see her take a fall. Some are already seeing this as their chance to give her a bit of a push. She might seem tough but she's still frightened of failing.'

Sam turned off the hose and looked at him. 'Aren't we all.'

Sam was suddenly pleased he was there. She looked into his face and wondered if he was as supportive of her as he was of Farmer. She found herself becoming slightly jealous of his relationship with his boss. Suddenly, realizing she'd been staring at him rather longer than was natural, Sam quickly turned her back to hide her embarrassment, beginning to fill the hole with soil. Adams was slightly nonplussed. For a moment he thought he'd detected a certain warmth but he was clearly wrong and realized that he was being dismissed. She was certainly no pushover, he thought. He hesitated for a moment, not wanting to end another encounter on a sour note.

'Do you need any more help with the Triffid?'

'No thanks, I've about finished.' She sighed and relented a little. She could tell by the tone of his voice that she'd made him feel awkward. She didn't really want him to leave quite so quickly.

'If you really want to help you could make some tea.'

'For two?'

Sam nodded and Adams disappeared into the kitchen.

*   *   *

Malcolm Purvis had searched everywhere. All her old haunts, friends, Bird's club and house and, although there was no sign of Frances, there was no sign of Bird either. It wasn't that he distrusted the police but they didn't know her as he did and he felt he had more chance of finding her. He'd even managed to get in touch with the woman in charge of their 'good parenting' class. She'd confirmed that Frances had attended the class and had left in good spirits, promising to drag her father there the following week, come what may. He parked the car in the garage, locked it and made his way inside. He looked at the pram, rocking it for a moment as he began to feel the weight of emotion take him over. The ring on the doorbell came as a welcome relief. He ran to the door and swung it open hoping to see his daughter's contrite face and to listen to her lame excuses, but he knew he wouldn't mind where she'd been. She would be safe, and that was all that mattered.

Policemen have a way of telling you everything without ever opening their mouths. He learned a lot about their facial expressions in court and prided himself that no matter how bland or disinterested they tried to make themselves, he could still read what they were thinking. So he knew what they'd come to tell him before they spoke and had to resist the temptation to slam the door against them. If he wasn't told then it wasn't true.

'Mr Purvis?'

'Yes.'

'I wonder if we could come in for a moment, sir?'

He stood for a second, barring their way. 'She's dead, isn't she?'

The inspector and the young policewoman by his side looked uncomfortable. 'Can we just come in, sir?'

Malcolm Purvis threw his head back, staring blankly through his tears towards the dark sky. The scream seemed to come from his very soul, its entire energy concentrated through his open mouth. Its intensity frightened the young, inexperienced policewoman and made her step back. The inspector had seen it all before and, wrapping his arms around Malcolm, held him firmly, like a father holding an injured child.

Sam was sitting on the small, wooden garden bench which she had sited at the back of her garden where it captured the view over the open countryside during the daylight hours. By her side Tom Adams sipped at his steaming mug of tea. Sam held her mug up to him.

'Nice tea.'

'Years of practice; you learn a thing or two in the police you know.'

Sam smiled, she enjoyed his sense of humour. 'I'm glad to hear it.'

Tom smiled briefly before his mood changed. 'I need to talk to you about Ricky.'

'You're not going to arrest him for the cigarette machine are you?'

'No, we came to an agreement about that one, but he has been arrested.'

Sam was shocked. 'Whatever for?'

'Criminal damage. He'd one too many and decided

to turn the bonnet of some poor unfortunate's car into a trampoline.'

Sam was exasperated. 'Are they sure it was him?'

Adams fidgeted in embarrassment. 'I saw him do it, sorry.'

Sam gazed across the darkened fields. 'Why should you be sorry, he did it. Bloody idiot.'

'He's young and he was pretty drunk.'

'That's no excuse. God knows what Wyn's going to say when she finds out. She's got enough on her plate without this. He's not likely to go to prison or anything is he?'

'I don't think so. I've had a word with the arresting officer, he's an old mate, I think I can probably sort it out. Depends whether we can square off the car's owner or not. Paying for the damage should do it.'

'You'll be lucky. Ricky's out of work and Wyn's having trouble making ends meet as it is. How much is it?'

Reaching into his jacket pocket, Adams produced an estimate and handed it to her.

'How much! What was it, a Rolls Royce?' She read it again. 'He's not a bad boy, you know, just having a bad time. If I pay up will it keep the little idiot out of court?'

'I can't promise that . . . But I'll see what I can do.'

'Thanks, Tom, I appreciate it.'

Adams had put himself out on a limb for her and having someone else take some of the responsibility she felt for her family was a welcome relief. He smiled and for a moment their eyes met. This time Sam didn't look away. Adams began to move his face slowly towards hers, giving her time to look away or pull back if she wasn't interested. She didn't move. It wasn't to be Adams' night, however, for just before their lips touched his radio suddenly crackled into life between them.

'Control to DI Adams, over!'

Adams pulled back slowly, not taking his eyes off her for a moment and answered the call. 'DI Adams to Control, over.'

'Superintendent Farmer's compliments, sir, and would you join her on the B784 about three miles outside Fereham. They've found the dead girl's car.'

'Twenty minutes, over.'

He slipped his radio back into his pocket and looked across at Sam. 'I've got to go.'

Sam nodded understandingly but disappointed.

'Oh, by the way, are you sure about what you said before?'

Sam was confused.

'About Bird being innocent.'

'I was angry, I'm not sure, but there are a few things that don't add up.'

'Like what?'

'The ivy around Frances' wrist; it's the wrong type, nothing to do with the occult.'

'There was an ivy plant in Bird's office.'

'Could you get me some? Might answer a few questions.'

'If I do, it's between the two of us. I don't want to find myself back in a funny hat walking some miserable beat.'

The sun was finally beginning to peep over the distant horizon, lighting up the fields and woodland beyond the edge of Sam's garden. Adams looked across at it. 'It's going to be a great sunrise.'

'The sunsets are pretty good too,' said Sam mischievously.

They smiled at each other in mutual understanding.

My, thought Adams, the Ice Maiden melts.

Adams arrived at the scene earlier than he had anticipated, the empty roads having hastened his journey. The scene was already basking in the beam of half a dozen mobile lights and the humming of their accompanying generators. Parked by the side of the road was a large, low loading lorry with two police officers preparing to lift the car out of the field and on to its back. He spotted Farmer watching one of the SOCOs take paint scrapings from the back of car. She looked across at him as he arrived, 'Good of you to come.'

Adams remained silent, keeping any excuses to himself. Farmer looked back at the SOCO who was examining the small slivers of red paint he'd managed to scrape from the car into a plastic exhibit bag.

'Are we sure we've got the right car, Bert?'

He lifted his large round face up in Farmer's direction. 'The registered owner is a Malcolm Purvis, who I assume is the dead girl's father, poor sod. And we found this.' He held up a long, patterned, silver ear-ring, identical to the one Farmer had seen swaying gently in Frances' ear.

'Anything else?'

'A few paint scrapings. Not as many as I would have

thought though. Our killer's trying to be clever, cleaned up after himself.'

Adams interjected, 'There goes the paint evidence then.'

'Oh, I don't know about that,' said Bert with a self-satisfied grin. 'He wasn't as clever as he thought, forgot the scene of the original collision. Managed to get a few good samples from the side of the road and the verge; should be enough to get a match.'

Adams walked over to the car and had a good look around it. 'Any attempt to burn it out?'

Bert looked across at him. 'No, I wouldn't be here if they had. Why?'

'If it's the same killer then I wonder why he didn't burn the car? He's been very careful up to now. He burnt James' car out.'

Bert looked across at Frances' car, 'They get careless, that's how we catch them.'

Adams nodded and walked back towards his two colleagues. Farmer began to follow the SOCO out of the field. 'When can you let us have something?'

'Give us a ring tomorrow afternoon, should have something for you by then.'

Farmer was not satisfied, 'Why is everything tomorrow with you people?'

'Ask me tomorrow,' chuckled Bert, as he walked away.

Farmer glared around at her team defying any sign of amusement.

Sam had arrived at the mortuary early for once. She wanted to go through Mark James' file thoroughly before starting the PM on Frances. She was already convinced it was the same killer and that he was either playing some kind of game or he really was a religious nut; Sam wanted to be sure that she wouldn't miss anything.

She hung her coat on the back of the door and walked across the room. There was a small brown envelope sitting in the centre of her desk with her name written in blue ink across the front. She opened it and put her hand inside pulling out a small piece of notepaper and a small section of ivy. She read the note.

'I normally buy ladies flowers, but I found this in Bird's office when we arrested him and thought you might find it interesting, Tom.'

She smiled, he'd come through with the ivy. She hadn't been sure that he would, she thought she might have been pushing their relationship a bit far. But she was wrong and pleased. Sam laid the ivy across the top of her blotter and took a magnifying glass. *Poetica*, she was right. She was convinced now that Bird had got nothing to do with these murders. If Bird was the murderer and trying to forge a connection with the occult, he would have known which variety of ivy to use, he even had easy access to some. However, trying to convince Farmer of her theories would still be difficult, she needed more evidence.

Malcolm Purvis was led gently into the mortuary, the inspector walking closely by his side. His face had lost all its natural colour and he was lined and aged. Inside he hung on to the final hope that a dreadful mistake had been made and that the poor unfortunate girl he was about to see wasn't Frances. For the first time since he lost his wife he prayed. Prayed that it wasn't Frances, that it was another girl, he didn't care who. He was aware of the selfishness of his thoughts but didn't care. As he entered the mortuary he saw Fred standing solemnly by the stainless steel trolley. The trolley was covered with a large, white sheet under which was hidden a human form. He stood by the side of the trolley, a rush of heat passing over him as his insides churned. The inspector spoke, gently, 'Are you ready, sir?'

Fred didn't move, awaiting the inspector's nod. Malcolm remained unmoving, trying to deny the moment that would change the rest of his life. The inspector tried again, 'Are you ready?'

This time Malcolm nodded. The inspector looked up at Fred who pulled the sheet away from the top of the trolley, exposing Frances' face. He didn't look down. He stared ahead, his throat swelling as the tears began to fill his eyes. Finally, the inspector gave his arm a gentle, persuasive squeeze and he lowered his gaze.

What he saw was not Frances but a bloated and blackened caricature of his daughter. He looked through the twisted distortions of her face at his lovely daughter who lay beneath. The tears from his eyes spilled down on to his face and he rubbed them away. 'Not now God, please not now. Don't leave me on my own.'

The inspector made a hushed request, 'Is this your daughter, sir?'

Malcolm nodded, 'Yes. It's my daughter.'

The inspector looked across at Fred who began to cover her face. Before he had a chance though, Malcolm grabbed his arm to stop him. He looked at Fred, the anguish clearly etched on his face. 'You will be gentle with her, won't you? She's suffered enough.'

For once there wasn't an amusing quip or thought in Fred's head. 'We'll take care of her sir, don't worry.'

Malcolm nodded and after one last look at his daughter's face, allowed Fred to cover it. As he turned to walk away Sam entered the mortuary. She was already gowned and ready for the PM. Malcolm saw her and understood what she was about to do. The horror of it finally made his legs buckle. The inspector moved quickly, throwing an arm around his waist, saving him from collapsing onto the floor and leading him carefully out of the mortuary. For a moment he looked up at Sam and their eyes met. Her timing had been bad and she knew it. She had a job to do and she was proud of her chosen profession but for the first time in her professional life she felt a sense of shame and lowered her gaze, unable to match his stare.

Although Sam found it difficult to remove the sight of Malcolm Purvis' face from her mind she was determined to put the experience to one side and throw herself into the PM. She had to banish from her mind that this had once been a person with people who loved her and were loved by her. Now she had an important job to do. The body could yield up the vital clues needed to catch the killer before he had time to strike again and she had to find those clues and find them quickly.

The body had already been removed from the bag and now lay still on the white marble slab while a group of white-suited SOCOs finished collecting samples. Sam looked around the room. As well as the usual array of people Adams was standing in the viewing gallery watching proceedings closely. She knew Adams didn't like watching the PMs. He'd told her that it wasn't so much the sights, as the smell, that really affected him. Well, there wasn't much she could do about that, that's the way humans were, smelly. Richard Owen was also in the gallery deep in conversation with Farmer. It was unusual for the police surgeon to attended the PM and she felt it was probably more to do with her than the body on the table. For a moment she wished she could be a fly on the wall but then changed her mind, who wanted to hear ill of themselves anyway. The SOCOs finished and Sam looked across at Fred, 'Everything ready?'

He nodded. 'There is one thing you ought to know. I think the body's been cleaned.'

Sam was annoyed and almost couldn't believe what Fred was telling her. 'Who the bloody hell's done that?'

'Nobody here, boss. I think the killer's done it. Trying to get rid of any evidence.'

Why? Sam wondered. Did the killer have a specific knowledge of forensics? Had something gone wrong this time so that the killer knew that he had left incriminating evidence? What sort of mind were they dealing with in these cases? She walked across with Fred and began her commentary as her world closed in around her.

'Post Mortem, 9 a.m., 1 November 1995. The body is that of a well-developed, and well-nourished, white female. She is sixty-seven inches tall and weighs one hundred and thirteen pounds.' She picked up her chart and examined the information. 'The remains are those of a Frances Purvis, twenty-four years old. She has brown hair and blue eyes. The body was discovered at approximately 11.30 p.m. yesterday, 31 October at Ruilex Abbey. Life was pronounced extinct by Dr Richard Owen, the police surgeon, at 12.42 a.m.'

She lay the board back down on a small table and began the PM. She'd done hundreds before, but despite this she tried hard to keep each one fresh and interesting, complacency only led to mistakes. After ensuring that the SOCOs had got all the photographs they required she cut the cord that was still embedded tightly into Frances' throat, being careful not to damage any knots. She did the same with the ivy around her left wrist. Both items were then dropped into exhibit bags and sealed by the SOCOs. She then scraped the nails, took swabs from the mouth, nose and vagina; examined the conjunctivae, the membranes connecting the inner eyelids to the eyeballs for the tell-tale bloodspots caused by haemorrhaging in cases of strangulation and asphyxia. Fred moved to the opposite side of the table and rolled Frances on to her side so Sam could examine the back of her body.

'There are no obvious signs of injury to the rear of the body.' She ran her hands through Frances' hair. 'The head also appears clear of any injury . . . what's this?'

She stretched the skin gently over a small puncture wound she discovered at the back of Frances' neck. She was surprised and slightly annoyed at herself for not noticing it at the scene. 'There appears to be a small puncture wound at the back of the neck, possibly caused by a needle of some sort.'

She looked across at the photographer. 'Can I have plenty of shots of this, please?'

The SOCO nodded and took several photographs from various distances and angles before Fred laid the body back on to its back. Sam then began to cut into the body. A large V-shaped incision was made into the neck and continued along the full length of the body. The cut was made slightly off centre to avoid interfering with the previous cuts that formed the upside-down cross. The neck muscles were then dissected off in layers, exposing the larynx, which were removed for examination together with the other neck and chest structures. Moving down the body she discovered the child. 'There is a well developed and apparently healthy, eighteen-to-twenty-week foetus present inside the uterus.'

Sam gently removed the child from its mother and passed its remains to Fred. She was saddened and wondered if the Reverend Shaw would still be so certain of his faith after seeing what his God allowed to happen to the innocent and the pure. She took a deep breath and continued with the PM.

CHAPTER SEVEN

M arcia Evans walked across the oil-stained, concrete floor of the laboratory garage. In the centre of the garage Frances Purvis' blue Renault sat covered with a large, clear, polythene bag. Inside the bag a white-suited SOCO, his nose and mouth covered with a face mask and his head with a disposable hood, prepared to evacuate the grey mist which filled the inside of the car, clinging to every surface. As Marcia watched, Alex Wood, the head of the unit, entered the garage and walked across to where she was standing. He was a short, stocky man tending towards the tubby with receding hair and a full beard. He was genial and hard-working but lacked ambition and the confidence needed to take him to the top of his profession.

'What are you doing here? Thought you were spots, specks and sperm.'

Marcia looked up at him, 'I thought I'd come and see how the other half live. What are they up to?'

'Just waiting for the super glue to clear. With a bit of luck it should cling to the sweat from any undetected prints.'

As Marcia watched, the glue's vapour slowly drifted

out of the car, dispersing through the air ducts in the roof of the garage.

'Lights didn't pick any up then?'

'None that we couldn't eliminate. This is our last hope.'

'We'll have to hope he wasn't clever enough to wear gloves then.' Marcia smiled but Alex did not respond. Marcia was well respected as a thorough and competent professional in her field and she was very friendly with Dr Ryan. Her presence made him uncomfortable and he didn't want his professional competence challenged. He stood supervising the activities of his colleagues who were by now back inside the car searching the interior's more inaccessible places with a high-powered light. Marcia crouched down to peep inside the car. The interior had been robbed of all colour and been transformed to a brilliant white, as if covered by a blanket of hoar-frost. The SOCO concentrated his light and magnifying glass on a small area of the interior under the driving column.

Alex spotted his interest. 'Found something, Bert?'

'Bingo, a couple of good ones. Have a look.'

Alex moved forward and Bert handed him the magnifying glass. 'Very nice, very nice indeed, better get the photographer in here.' Alex stepped out of the car with a smug look on his face and handed the glass to Marcia. 'Looks like our killer wasn't "clever enough". Want to have a look?'

Marcia took the glass and examined the two prints. They were clearly visible, sitting side by side, their white swirling loops and whorls starkly emphasized. When she had finished, Marcia stood up and passed the glass back to Alex. 'I'm impressed. This should help the evidence *stick*.' The SOCO took himself far too seriously and wasn't amused by Marcia's quip. She wasn't deterred though and continued, 'They're in a very unusual place though, aren't they?'

Alex was defensive and his reply was curt, 'I've found them in stranger places than that. Sometimes you're lucky, sometimes you're not . . .'

Marcia interjected, 'And this time you were lucky?'

Marcia's persistent scepticism was heightening Alex' discomfort. 'Yes, indeed, unless they can be identified and eliminated.'

She nodded uncertainly and walked out of the garage, leaving Alex seething with professional indignation.

The PM over, Sam stripped off her green gown and threw her gloves into a nearby bin before making her way into the small office by the side of the mortuary, closely followed by Farmer, Adams and Owen. The moment they entered the office Farmer began her interrogation, her voice sharp and to the point, 'Are we dealing with the same killer?'

Sam was tired to her bones with a weariness which had its roots in mental turmoil more than physical activity. She leaned wearily against the desk top and sighed, 'Almost certainly . . .'

Farmer, impatient for information, cut in, 'Just tell us what you've got and keep it simple.'

Sam was irritated by her attitude, 'The Jackanory explanation, just for you then, Superintendent.'

Adams and Owen couldn't help smiling at the professional conflict between the two women until Farmer caught their expression and turned to glare at them.

Sam continued, 'As you know, the injuries to the abdomen of both Mark James and Frances Purvis are unusual and identical . . .' She picked up several photographs from the desk and handed them around, keeping one for herself and indicating the injuries, 'and form this upside-down cross.' She outlined the cross with her pen on the photograph. 'By the way, your killer is left-handed.'

Farmer cut in, 'So was Jack the Ripper.'

Sam wasn't put off. 'The police didn't do very well then either, did they?'

Farmer scowled and Adams interjected, sensing a rising level of animosity, 'Any chance that it's coincidental?'

Sam shook her head. 'With identical cuts like those, I doubt it, but there's a bit more. Both victims were also garrotted, which in itself is interesting.'

Farmer cut in again, 'So they were both strangled, so are hundreds of others, I don't see what that tells us?'

'The fact that our killer has taken the time and trouble to make a garrotte might tell us quite a bit. Let me show you what I mean.' She opened the desk drawer and pulled out a length of string attached to both ends of a pencil. 'Here's one I made earlier. Can I borrow your wrist for a moment, Superintendent?' Farmer reluctantly agreed to it. 'It won't hurt.'

'Don't tell me, just a little uncomfortable.'

Sam slipped the loop over the outstretched wrist and

began to twist the pencil, slowly tightening the string and squeezing Farmer's wrist. 'Once the loop is around the victim's neck it doesn't require much strength to tighten it, a child could do it. All you have to do is twist the stick and the loop tightens, until, finally . . .' She twisted the pencil sharply turning the skin under the loop white and extracting a wince from Farmer. Her demonstration finished, Sam released the pressure and slipped the loop off Farmer's wrist. 'It was the main form of execution in Spain for hundreds of years.'

Farmer looked up at Sam, still rubbing her wrist. 'Remind me to cancel my holiday in Benidorm.'

'Although I'll have to wait for the lab reports for this one, I also think it likely that they were both drugged.'

Owen was surprised by this revelation. 'I don't remember your report on James mentioning drugs?'

'It didn't because there was no trace of any, but I think we'll find some in Frances' system.'

Adams cut in, 'What makes you think our killer used drugs?'

'Considering what our victims must have gone through before they were killed, I would have expected to have found some sort of defence injuries; bruises, scratches, or evidence of some form of restraint, rope burns around their wrists perhaps, but there was nothing. Given the time it took to find James' body the chances are that any drugs in his system would have had time to disperse and any small puncture hole would have been obscured as the body decomposed. However, there was a small puncture wound at the back of Frances' neck where I think she was injected. It would also explain why our killer went to so much trouble to hide James' body. By the time it was discovered all traces of the drug would have disappeared.'

Farmer wasn't convinced. 'Then why didn't our killer make more effort to hide Frances' body?'

Adams spoke up. 'He tried. The Abbey was closed for repairs. He wouldn't have expected anyone to be nosing around the old chapel for at least a couple of weeks. We just got lucky with the dogs.'

Farmer looked across at Owen. 'Bird's diabetic, isn't he?'

Owen nodded and Farmer continued, 'So he'd have easy access to syringes and needles.'

'Yes, but so have thousands of others, it doesn't necessarily make him a killer.'

Sam glanced across at him, she appreciated the support. Sam continued, 'There's something else you ought to know as well.' Her hesitation was barely noticeable, 'I found out that when he was at college Bird made a study of a murder that occurred in the Fens in the mid sixties. He did quite extensive research and later wrote a paper on it. The circumstances were identical to those of both Mark and Frances. The victim, an old man by the name of Ironsmith, was garrotted on holy ground and an upside-down cross was carved on to his body.'

Farmer's face flushed with anger. 'How long have you known about this?'

'Not long. I wasn't really sure it was relevant until now.'

'I'm the best judge of what's relevant. Not you. Any other evidence you're withholding?'

'I'm disclosing evidence not withholding it, that's my job, Superintendent. I found a similar garland of ivy to that found wrapped around Frances' wrist inside the tomb where they found James. There does seem to be a connection with the Fenland murder.'

Sam expected Farmer to explode but she didn't, she just sat passively, almost content.

'So, you came up with the goods in the end. Looks like we've got Bird bang to rights on this one. Well done.'

'There is one more thing I think I ought to tell you.'

Farmer looked at her suspiciously.

'It's the same thing I told you when we were at the Abbey. I don't believe Bird did it.'

Farmer's contented looked slipped and was replaced by one of enormous anger. 'Really, and why not?'

'The ivy, it was the wrong species.'

'I see. You've just given me enough evidence to get Bird convicted of two murders and now you're telling me he's innocent because some *plant* happens to be the "wrong type".'

'Bird wouldn't have made that kind of mistake; he would have known which variety of ivy to use to make it look like an occult killing. Christ, he had a pot of it in his office!'

Farmer glared across at her. 'How the hell did you know?'

Sam glanced, embarrassed, at Adams, realizing she'd just dropped him in it. Farmer picked up her look and realized immediately what had happened. She relaxed back in her chair, looked across at Adams and then back at Sam.

'So, there's a conspiracy is there? What else has been going on behind my back? I'll have both of you if there's any more tampering with the investigation.' Farmer knew she was being unfair but she felt betrayed by a close member of her team and she was finding it difficult to control her anger. Sam's face flushed with indignation and she prepared to unleash a tirade upon Farmer but, before either of them had chance to speak, Fred Dale entered the office.

'Sorry to interrupt but there's an urgent message for the Superintendent.' Farmer looked up. 'Can you contact the murder incident room as soon as possible, apparently they've matched the fingerprints they found in Frances' car with Bird's.'

Farmer's face was a study in triumph. She swung round to face Sam, 'Looks like we've got to arrest a killer.' She stood up and pulled her jacket from the back of the chair. 'In future, Dr Ryan, can I suggest you confine your "inquisitive mind" to your mortuary and leave the rest of the investigation to the professionals. You cut them, I'll catch them.' Farmer turned and left quickly without looking at Adams. As he followed her out of the lab Sam tried to catch his eye but he avoided her gaze, feeling angry and betrayed at Sam's indiscretion. He couldn't be sure if he had been used and discarded or whether Sam had made a genuine mistake in the heat of the moment. He would need time to think about this one and besides, there was Farmer to pacify. Sam turned to

Owen who shrugged nonplussed by what had just occurred.

Sam hated walking through the underground car-park, even now in the middle of the day it still had that feeling of impending danger and was the most oppressive place she knew. The sound of her every footstep echoed off the nearby concrete walls before bouncing back towards her, giving the impression of dozens of unseen people hiding in every dark recess and following her every move. As Sam reached her car she began to search through the rubbish which littered the inside of her handbag for her car keys. As she did, a sudden tingle passed through her as she heard the distinct sound of footsteps. Although they weren't close, they were certainly coming her way. An irrational fear overcame her. She tried to control it with the logic of her mind: hers was not the only car in the car-park, lots of people worked flexible hours at the hospital. Indeed, she had often had pleasurable encounters with colleagues she rarely saw during working hours in this very car-park. However, logic held no sway over intuition and pictures of the bodies of both Mark James and Frances Purvis filled her mind. She walked to the back of the car and strained every sense as she scanned the corridor to pinpoint who was there. She assured herself that it would only be another hospital employee making their weary way home but as she strained her eyes to break through the dark shadows filling the car-park's long corridors, the footsteps stopped, the silence spread like a blanket around her and she could see nothing.

She waited for a moment, controlling her breathing so that the air passed in and out of her lungs without a sound, waiting, hoping, to hear the sound of a car door slamming or the roar of an engine as it burst into life. She heard neither of those things and as she moved back towards her car the footsteps began again, only this time quicker and closer. Sam's search for her car keys now became a frantic scrabble, she began to throw things from her bag in her panic. Finally, she discovered them, hiding under a pile of crumpled receipts in a side pocket. She pulled them out of her bag and cursing, fumbled to find the car key before ramming it into the lock on the driver's door and throwing herself inside. She slammed the door behind her and locked it. Turning the ignition key she turned her headlights full on, forced the gear stick into reverse and accelerated blindly out of her parking place, cringing mentally in readiness for a collision. None came and she rammed the gear into first and raced along the car-park's corridors towards the exit. She couldn't be sure, it was just a fleeting image, but just as she accelerated away she thought she noticed a figure standing behind one of the pillars. As she passed it she glanced into her rear-view mirror but darkness had replaced the momentary light from her headlamps and she could see nothing.

She began to feel safe when she finally drove out of the car-park and into the well-lit hospital grounds. Her breathing slowed and she began to feel a little foolish, berating herself for letting illogicality take over. However, she persuaded herself that the incidence served to highlight the potential danger which the isolated, poorly lit car-park posed for the hospital staff, especially the female staff, and she decided she would make a fuss about it. It might have been nothing but then again . . . She'd get Jean to type out a report on the incident the following morning and insist that, at the very least, new lights should be installed.

As she pulled out of the hospital grounds the glare from a car's lights behind made her glance up into her rear-view mirror. The car behind was not only too close for comfort but had his lights on full beam. Sam put her hand up to the mirror in a vain hope of asking him to dip his lights, nothing happened, so she flicked her mirror down dismissing the glare. As she drove through the Cambridge traffic on her way out of the city the car remained with her, maintaining the same distance behind and keeping its lights on full beam despite flashes of annoyance from oncoming traffic. The car continued to follow her as she began to navigate the twists and turns of the country lanes which eventually led to her cottage. Sam could feel her mouth begin to dry as the fear she had experienced in the car-park returned. She accelerated, watching the needle on her speedometer increase quickly to a speed she knew was unsafe to drive at. Finally, the car behind made its move and began to overtake. Sam knew that if she allowed it to do so she would be finished. She pressed her foot down hard on to the accelerator but it made little difference; slowly but surely the car behind began to pass her. She glanced quickly to her right in a hope of seeing the other driver but although she could distinguish his dark shape at the wheel, she could make out nothing further. She knew little about cars but at this speed, and in her panic, she couldn't see this one clearly to identify its make. She could see that it wasn't new, it was too long and heavy and its lines had an old-fashioned feel, like one of the classic cars she occasionally saw driving around the streets of Cambridge. As it finally pulled ahead of her and began to brake, Sam saw her escape route, a small lane to her left. She braked sharply and threw the car around the corner before accelerating along the lane. As she reached a junction she stopped for a moment and looked back. The other car had reversed and was now racing along the lane towards her at high speed. With a sob of panic she pulled out of the junction and followed the signs back towards Cambridge. She looked down at her hands which, although gripping the steering wheel firmly, were shaking. In fact she felt as if her whole body had gone into spasm and had become uncontrollable. It was a relief when she finally reached the urban outskirts of Cambridge. She turned off the main road and travelled the side streets for a few minutes before heading back towards the centre of Cambridge. She knew she couldn't return to the cottage and decided to exercise her right to stay overnight at her old college, if there was a room available. She pulled up at a set of lights and was relieved when, looking into her rear-view mirror, the road behind her was clear. She put her head down on the steering wheel for a moment, trying to regain her composure.

The bang on the window made her jump and as she pulled her head off the steering wheel she screamed out. The windscreen washer who had, uninvited, begun to wipe down her front windscreen, jumped back in surprise. He'd had various reactions to his job but he could never remember making a woman scream before. He watched her for moment as she stared at him. He wasn't sure if she was mad or just scared. As the lights change from red to green she pulled away rapidly, sending the cloth he had abandoned on the windscreen, flying from the car and on to the road. As he ran to retrieve it, another car stopped at the lights. He turned and gestured to the driver with his cloth, but there was no interest. Pity, he thought, he liked doing the old classic cars; their owners were normally far more generous than most.

Sam was pleased she'd found Marcia on her own. Although she was still very shaken up by the incident she decided to keep it to herself for the moment as she knew Marcia would be horrified and worried by it.

Marcia was so lost in her work that she didn't even know Sam was there until she was standing by her shoulder.

'How did you get on with six-foot-two eyes of blue at the medics' ball the other night?'

Marcia jumped, and then smiled up at Sam. 'OK. Lured him back to my room with promises of seeing my collection of rare man-made fibres. He was sick all over my new carpet and passed out on the sofa. I haven't seen him since.'

Sam tried to hold back a laugh. 'Ah well, win some lose some.'

Marcia scowled at her, 'I'd just like to win *one*.

'Mind you, I haven't seen you with many, "to die for" men recently if it comes to that.'

'Wait, watch and see. I got a postcard only the other day from an old flame, Liam.'

Marcia was sceptical. She never had seen Sam with a man, which, given that she was an intelligent and attractive woman, was somewhat surprising. 'We'll see, we'll see.'

Sam smiled, 'I'm sure you will, soon. Thanks for the information about the knots.'

'You have no idea what I might have to sacrifice for that information.'

Sam felt it expedient not to probe too deeply into that remark for the moment. 'I thought we were on to something there for a while.'

'I take it you've heard about the prints then?'

Sam nodded. 'Farmer's like a dog with two tails. I was so sure.'

'These things happen.'

'But why use a surgeon's knot, why not a reef knot or granny knot or something.'

Marcia shrugged and crossed the lab picking up a report from a shelf on the opposite side of the room. 'I wouldn't give up hope just yet. I might have some good news for you.'

'She was drugged.'

'Who's a clever girl then?'

'Tubarine chloride, I found a concentration of it in her liver.'

'Tubarine, I thought that went out with Agatha Christie?'

'Apparently not. It's alive and well and living in

Cambridge. I had the toxicologists have another look at the samples from James, and do you know what? They found traces of the drug in some of the decomposed tissue.'

Sam was pleased with the result but they posed more questions than they answered. 'But why use Tubarine, why use any drug? They were both strangled not poisoned.' Sam quickly answered her own question, 'Tubarine doesn't have to kill, does it? Can't it cause paralysis if administered in the correct dosage?'

'Can do, but you'd have to know what you were doing. There's a fine line between paralysing someone and killing them.'

'So, a victim could still be alive when they were strangled, just unable to move. The ultimate nightmare. Where would our killer get it from do you suppose?'

'It's a curare alkaloid, comes from a South American plant, but most hospitals keep it. Couldn't be that difficult to get your hands on.'

Sam's thoughts returned to Reverend Shaw's greenhouse. 'Would it grow in an artificial environment, like a greenhouse?

'Perhaps, why, know someone who's got some?'

'I am not sure, maybe.'

Farmer and Adams looked across the interview table at a dishevelled and unkempt Bird. His arrogance had gone, he seemed somehow smaller. By his side, impeccably dressed as usual, was his solicitor, Colin Lane. Farmer began the interrogation.

'When was the last time you saw Frances Purvis?'

Bird remained silent for a moment. He wasn't being awkward, just confused. He'd spent the few hours before they'd come to arrest him just looking at a photograph of Frances. He hadn't really been aware of it before, but he loved her. He only knew that he had always been afraid of losing her, that fear had driven her away and now he'd lost her for ever. He finally replied, 'I can't remember.'

'Yesterday evening, wasn't it?'

'No, I don't think so.' Surely, he thought, it had been longer that.

'You were seen by several of the neighbours arguing with Frances.'

Bird realized he'd told a stupid lie and, although regretting it, continued, 'Maybe it was then, I don't remember.'

'In breach of your bail conditions.'

Bird shrugged, 'I wanted to talk to her, tell her it wasn't me, that I had nothing to do with killing Mark. She wouldn't listen, got upset. I didn't mean to do that, so I left. I wouldn't hurt her, I loved her.'

'You hurt her before, when you hit her, the night Mark went missing.'

'The one and only time, and I've got to live with that for the rest of my life. Love isn't easy, sometimes you do stupid things.'

'Did you know which was her car?'

'There was only one on the drive, a small blue Renault, I think. That must have been it.'

Adams asked the next question, 'Did you ever go inside Frances' car, the Renault I mean?'

'No, never, the first time I knew she was using it was when I saw it that evening.'

'So you've never accepted a lift or travelled in it?'

'No, never.'

Farmer jumped in, 'Then why were your fingerprints found underneath the dashboard?'

For a moment Bird was surprised, confused. 'They couldn't have been, I was never in the car.'

'Well, they were there and they're definitely yours. How do you explain that?'

'I can't, they must have been planted. You lot are good at that,' he accused.

'What, we took you to the scene at night and rubbed your fingerprints all over the car before we tucked you back up in bed? Come on, I think you'll find that not even Cambridge magistrates are going to believe that one.'

Bird just stared at her and didn't reply. Farmer continued, 'Where did you go after you left her?'

'Drove around for a while then went back to the club.'

Adams joined in the interview, 'What time did you get back to the club?'

'I don't remember, one, half past, look I was upset. Ask the doorman, Gerry, he might have a better idea than me.'

'We will. Were you alone during this time?'

'Yea, I needed some space to think things through, that was all.'

'Is that why you gave my men the slip outside the club?'

'Partly. Look they were never going to let me within a mile of Frances. I just wanted her to understand it wasn't me.'

Farmer interjected, 'Isn't it more likely that you went to see her to try and stop her giving evidence against you?'

'No, I just wanted her to know the truth.'

'But with her out of the way the main witness against you has gone and you're in the clear.'

'I'd rather do life than kill her, I loved her.'

'I thought you told us in the last interview that she was a free agent.'

'She is . . . was . . . but that doesn't mean I wanted to lose her, wasn't willing to fight for her . . .'

'Kill her?'

'No, no never! I'd never do that!'

'In your last interview you said that the wind chimes outside your club were there to ward off evil spirits.'

Bird shrugged.

'I understand you're a bit of an expert on the occult, written papers on it.'

'I know a bit, not exactly an expert though.'

'Come, come, I think you're being a bit modest; didn't you write a paper on some occult murders in the Fens? What was it, *The Fenland Murder and Enigma*.'

'That was a long time ago, I was nineteen. I wanted to make a name for myself.'

'Interesting though. Ironsmith was killed on consecrated ground, so were Frances and Mark. Ironsmith was murdered during one of the so-called witches'

Sabbaths, so were Frances and Mark. Ironsmith was garrotted and had an upside-down cross carved into his body. Surprise, surprise, so were Frances and Mark. Call me Ms Suspicious if you like but that's one hell of a coincidence, don't you think?'

'It's a well-known story, anyone could have found out.'

'It's not that well known. I'd never heard about it, you're the expert.'

Bird didn't speak. Adams continued, 'As the original murder was committed while we were all still kids, the chances are that the murderer of poor old Charlie Ironsmith is no longer with us, which leaves us with just one person who had the knowledge and motivation to commit the two murders.'

'Why would I murder them like that then, wouldn't it just draw attention to me?'

'Not if you thought we wouldn't find out.'

'You underestimate yourself, Superintendent.'

For a moment Farmer was caught off balance and she struck out, 'Did you kill her because you thought she was carrying someone else's baby?'

Now Bird was caught off balance. 'What baby?'

'Frances was pregnant when she was murdered. Your idea of an abortion, was it?'

Bird's solicitor, seeing the shock of his client, cut in, 'I must object to this line of questioning. It really is intolerable.'

Bird, tears beginning to run down his face, tried to defend himself, 'I didn't . . . she never told me. Was it mine?'

'She told her father it was yours, and she wanted you to have nothing to do with it.'

Bird became very still, staring straight ahead, not at anyone or, anything, 'I didn't know, I just didn't know.'

'Wouldn't you have cut her up if you had?'

Farmer was now on her feet leaning over Bird, feeling she was close to the confession she was desperate for. Bird remained silent. Bird's solicitor interjected again.

'My client is in no fit state to continue with this interview and I request it be terminated immediately so we can consult.'

'Interview terminated at 4.22 p.m.' Farmer moved her hand towards the tape recorder and clicked the machine off. She looked back at Bird. 'There'll be no bail this time. This time no one's going to want to know you.'

Bird looked through his tears into her face and slowly shook his head.

Sam and Marcia had moved to the opposite side of the lab where Sam's eyes were glued to a binocular microscope.

'What exactly am I looking at?'

'Paint flakes, the ones they found on Frances Purvis' car.'

'Any joy?'

'They're from a Jaguar saloon, Mark II, probably a three point eight 1963 to 66 vintage.'

'All that from a few flakes of paint? I am impressed, tell me more, Sherlock.'

'You see but you don't observe. It's all in the way the paint is layered. This one's metallic opalescent maroon.'

'Might be Inspector Morse then.'

'Wrong university, that's the other lot.' She changed the slide on the microscope and Sam took another look. 'If you observe the way the paint is layered you'll see that the first layer is dark brown, this is followed by red, pale cream and then green after which they spray the main colour, in this case, maroon, over the top. The combination was only used for metallic cars and then only between 1963 and 1966. They reverted to three undercoats after that. Except on the original "Knicker Ripper" itself, the old E-type, then they used it until 1968.'

Sam looked up. 'So why couldn't it be an E-type?'

'Elementary, my dear Ryan, because they didn't do E-types in opalescent maroon.'

'Brilliant! How rare are they?'

'There's still a few about, enthusiasts mostly. The police are trying to check on the owners but it's going to be a long job.'

Sam nodded. 'I've got to go. I've got an afternoon list.'

She rubbed Marcia's back affectionately for a moment before making for the door. As she opened it Marcia called across to her, 'By the way what's this I hear about you getting Owen a bollocking for not wearing his protective suit at the James scene?'

Sam smiled across at her. 'You should know better than to listen to rumours, Marcia.'

'He deserved it. You could have saved your breath. I don't know how the crime scene manager puts up with him.'

'No, I don't either.'

Marcia returned to her microscope and Sam closed the door quietly behind her.

Farmer and Adams sat opposite each other inside Farmer's office. It was a bleak place. The desk behind which she sat was old and had suffered years of misuse; they'd tried to change it several times but she'd always insisted on keeping it, calling it her lucky desk, whatever that meant. Grimy cream walls with the occasional black and white photograph of Farmer at some point in her career did nothing to lift the atmosphere. But the most bizarre object in the office was the large drawing of a tall, distinguished-looking chief superintendent in full uniform sitting behind Farmer's back, peering down menacingly into the room. It was new. Adams hadn't seen it before and kept glancing up at it.

'My father.'

Adams looked back at Farmer.

'The drawing you were looking at, it's my father. Didn't think I had one, did you?' Adams found himself feeling slightly embarrassed. 'They gave him that when he retired. He died a few years ago, it's been in my garage for ages. It started to go mouldy so I thought I'd stick it in here, brighten the place up a bit.'

'Hardly,' Adams thought.

Farmer continued, 'He was never the same after he retired. Lived for the job, it was more important to him than anything, even his family.' She knocked her fist on top of the desk. 'This used to be his desk, his office too. I think my mum was glad to see the back of him when he went. Heart attack on holiday in Yarmouth. They're all coppers my family; uncles, cousins. He didn't want me to join, though, said it was no place for a woman, he never forgave me for not getting married and giving him grandchildren. He was even more annoyed when I made inspector, not proud, you understand, just annoyed.' She turned and looked back at the drawing. 'I wonder what he'd think now, eh?'

For the first time since he'd known her, Adams felt a certain sympathy for her. Maybe it was something in his countenance which alerted Farmer that she had, perhaps, become too relaxed, but she quickly returned to the point.

'As soon as the paperwork's finished we'll charge him.'

'He did seem genuinely upset about the baby.'

'Maybe he was. Maybe he really didn't know, but maybe it was all an act for the tape recorder and jury. Even if he had known he'd still have killed her, no point being a dad and doing life. There'd be other women, other kids.'

'I suppose so but for a man with no previous to commit a murder like that . . .' Adams shook his head in disbelief.

'He'd got plenty of previous, it just wasn't on paper, we never caught him that's all. Do I detect a certain amount of doubt?'

'A bit.'

'Fancy it, don't you, Tom?'

Adams attempted to look innocent but knew exactly who she was talking about. 'Who?'

'Don't try and con a conner, Tom; the pathologist Sam Ryan.'

'Bit out of my class, ma'am.'

'You never know, she might fancy a bit of rough.'

Adams breathed out despairingly. 'Thanks a lot.'

'Look, you're a copper, if you want to get your leg over with the pathologist, fine, I hope you enjoy yourself, but you're letting it cloud your judgement.'

'I don't think so, I think I would have felt the same with or without her opinion.'

'Bollocks! Listen, don't let your prick rule your head, it's been the downfall of better coppers than you. The evidence we've got against Bird is overwhelming, we're all going to get a pat on the back because of it, so sit back, take the applause and don't spoil it by talking about bloody plants.' Adams realized she hadn't quite finished with him and remained cautiously silent. 'And just one more thing. If you do ever pull a stroke like the one with the ivy again, I'll not only have you off the case, I'll have you off the bloody force!'

'Yes, ma'am.'

'She's a service industry. She supplies us with information which makes it easier for us to catch the bastards that do these things, nothing else. If she and you remember that we'll all get along fine, if not, well, don't ever say I didn't warn you.'

Before Adams had time to defend himself or even explain his reasons for handing the ivy over to Sam, there was a knock on the door and a uniformed constable entered the office.

'Station sergeant's ready when you are, ma'am.'

Farmer nodded and the PC left the room. Farmer stood up and made for the door. 'Come on, let's get it done.'

Adams followed her along the corridor and down the steps that led from the CID offices to the station sergeant's office. Inside the office Bird stood with his solicitor. Adams couldn't help feeling what a pathetic figure he made. His eyes were red and swollen and his clothes crumpled and dishevelled. A feeling of loss and depression seemed to have pervaded him. The station sergeant passed Farmer the charge-sheet. Looking straight at Bird she began to read out the charge.

'Sebastian Bird, you are charged that between 20 September 1995 and 5 October 1995 in Cambridge you did murder Mark James contrary to common law.'

As Farmer read out the caution Bird just stared ahead at the wall behind her head. She continued with the second charge.

'Sebastian Bird, you are further charged that between 30 October 1995 and 1 November 1995, you murdered Frances Purvis contrary to common law.'

She repeated the caution. As she did Bird began to visibly shake and the focus of his attention moved from the wall to meet Farmer's stare. Suddenly with a half scream he came to life, leaping forward and grabbing Farmer by the jacket and screaming into her face, 'You've got the wrong man, you've got the wrong man!'

Adams and the station sergeant reacted and jumped between them sending Farmer crashing to ground and forcing Bird across a table with his arms held firmly behind his back. Adams knew Bird was a strong man who could handle himself, his reputation went before him, but as he held him across the table and handcuffs were wrapped around his wrists, Adams could detect no outward sense of aggression, just an inner rage, as if he was fighting against himself, trying to change what he was and put right what had happened.

Sam was only half-way through her list when Trevor Stuart entered the mortuary where bodies lay around in various stages of preparation.

'Got a minute?'

Sam looked up and waved her scalpel in acknowledgement of his request. She looked across at Fred. 'Put everything back and stitch up will you, Fred?'

Fred, who was just stitching together the remains of the last PM, waved his response and Sam made her way to the door.

'I hope this isn't going to take long, Trevor, I've got another ten to get through yet.'

They walked across to the small mortuary office and sat down.

'Farmer's on the warpath and threatening to go to the chief executive. Something about you withholding information.'

'Information that she wasn't bright enough to discover for herself. Who told you?'

'I have my contacts. Anyway, whatever the reason, I think you should be careful for a while.'

'What can she do?'

'She could certainly make life a bit awkward, depends how far she's willing to take it.'

'I could be in trouble then?'

'Not serious. She's not going to want to broadcast the fact that you found the information that led to Bird's arrest. But it might be worth watching your back for flying scalpels for a while.'

Although not happy, Sam appreciated Trevor's concern and judged it to be genuine. 'Thanks, Trevor.'

He smiled at her. 'All part of the service.'

As Sam prepared to return to the mortuary Jean Carr entered the office. 'Just a quick word, Dr Ryan, you haven't forgotten you're in court tomorrow with the Nash case.'

Sam had but she didn't want to admit it. 'Yes, yes, I'll be there.'

Jean could see by the expression on Sam's face that she had forgotten and was now finding it a serious inconvenience. 'You were warned.'

'I know, I know. Sorry, Jean, I've got a lot on my mind right now.'

Fred, still dressed in his mortuary gown and holding a stained needle in front of him with a section of twine hanging from it, stood by the door. 'Bad batch of gut. The bodies just burst open again.'

Sam watched as the colour drained from her secretary's face. She put her arm around her and squeezed her arm sympathetically.

* * *

Malcolm Purvis sat cross-legged in front of his television set, the hand control for the video recorder held tightly in his hand. He was watching a video of Frances with her mother. The film had been taken many years before at a local park and he had only just had it converted to video tape. As he watched, Frances hugged her mother tightly. The camera zoomed up to a close-up of their faces. Encouraged by her mother, Frances' small face looked right into the camera lens and, smiling, she spoke to her father, 'I love you, Daddy.' She put the flat of her hand against her lips and blew her father a kiss. He played the moment over and over, sometimes freeze-framing the picture, staring at his daughter's face.

Adams arrived at the house alone. He'd decided that perhaps Farmer's professionalism was not required in a situation like this. He knocked hard on the large oak door and waited. A few moments later Malcolm Purvis came to the door. Adams was careful and gentle, 'I'm sorry to bother you, sir, especially right now, but I need to take a statement.'

Malcolm Purvis stared at him blankly for a moment then stood to one side of the door and ushered him in. Adams followed him into the sitting-room where the video was still running. Adams sat on the sofa opposite the television and watched it. The picture had changed from the one Malcolm had been watching earlier. Frances, was playing on the Cambridge backs with her mother and a young boy. It was summer and they were rolling about in the grass, executing handstands and enjoying their young lives to the full.

'Is that Frances?' Adams indicated the television set.

'Yes, that's her. Took that eleven or twelve years ago now.'

'She was very pretty, even then.'

Malcolm sat by Adams' side and watched the screen with him. 'Yes, she was, took after her mother, thank God.'

'Is that her mother with her?'

'Yes, Anne. She died of cancer about a year later.'

Adams looked at Malcolm's face. He seemed to have aged since he'd seen him last. The lines on his face seemed more numerous and deeper and his grey hair had lost any distinction it may have given him. 'I'm sorry.'

'Frances took it very hard. And I was too busy and too depressed to cope. I let her down when she needed me, that's why it's my fault, you see.'

'I doubt it, life has a way of levelling things out anyway. She was home and she loved you, so you couldn't have got it that wrong.'

Malcolm looked across and gave Adams a half smile of thanks. Adams' attention was drawn back to the screen, 'Who's the boy?

'Mark James, would you believe. They'd been friends since they were young. Got him off a supplying drugs charge a few years ago. I normally wouldn't have taken the case but she was always able to get around me, and he seemed grateful enough.'

'Rather a tragic film, isn't it?'

'Yes, it is. I don't know why we've been singled out but there's been too much death connected with this family over the last few years.'

'We've charged Bird with both Mark's and Frances' murder. I just thought you ought to know.'

'Thank you, inspector, but it's all a bit late now, isn't it.'

Malcolm's face returned to the television screen and his daughter's laughing voice.

There was the usual scene of chaos surrounding Sam's kitchen, she was late as usual. As she scrambled to eat a slice of burnt toast while slurping down a mug of hot coffee and keeping one eye on the clock, she realized her car keys were not where they were supposed to be, on a small hook marked 'car keys' by the side of the kitchen door. Not that they ever were, but they were supposed to be. Giving up on the toast, she dropped it into the bin which was already overflowing with rubbish. It landed on the top, slid off an old can of beans and fell on to the floor. Sam was too busy looking for her keys to notice. Papers were lifted, pillows moved, even cat baskets emptied, but there was no sign of them. In her panic she decided to use the spare. Running to the drawer and opening it, she remembered that she was, in fact, already using the spare key. She slammed the drawer shut and was trying to create a mind picture of her movements since she last used the car when the doorbell rang.

Ricky stood in the doorway, a contrite look on his face. For once he was smartly dressed in jacket and tie and his hair was combed neatly; it was very out of character.

'Sorry, Aunty Sam.'

Sam stared at him for a moment, wondering what he was apologizing for. Then she remembered the dented car and the very large bill. 'I should think you are.'

'It won't happen again.'

'I'm glad to hear it. What was the outcome?'

'That friend of yours, Inspector . . .'

'Adams?'

'Yea, him. He got me a caution, that's why I've got me best Marks and Spencers on. Said there'd be nothing he could do if it happened again though.'

'You're lucky.'

'Yea, I know. He's a good bloke. I'll pay you back as soon as I've got a job.'

Sam smiled fondly at him and gave him a hug. 'Well, I've been thinking about the money . . .'

'You mustn't let me off, I will pay it back.'

'I wasn't going to let you off.'

It wasn't the reply Ricky expected.

'Come with me.'

She led her curious nephew through the kitchen and out into the back garden. She opened the shed door and emerged with a set of overalls, a pair of wellingtons and a spade, before continuing her journey to the top of the garden and a weed-covered wilderness of about half an acre that had once clearly been a much-prized vegetable garden.

'Well, here we are. Weeds go over there, you'll find the bags of compost in the shed but don't dig it in until you've cleared the ground and then make sure it's evenly distributed.'

Ricky's mouth almost fell open with the magnitude

of the job. He hated gardening at the best of times and had to be dragged screaming out of the house just to cut the lawn. This was in a completely different league.

'Nobody mentioned anything about slave labour.'

'Does your mum know about the caution?'

'No.'

'Do you want her to?'

'No.'

'Then get on with it, I'll be home about six. I'll run you back to your mum's then.'

She started to walk away from him. 'Sorry, I've got to rush. I'd have liked to watch you for a while, but I've got to call a taxi because someone's hidden my car keys. Should only take you a few days, then the debt's paid. It's a bargain if you ask me.'

Defeated, Ricky sat on the garden seat and began to undo his shoes. As he pulled up his foot, he noticed a set of keys lying next to him on the bench. He picked them up and called to his Aunt, 'Are these what you're looking for?'

Sam turned and, feeling slightly embarrassed, made her way back up the garden towards her nephew.

'The burglar must have dropped them as he fled across the garden, eh?'

Sam snatched them off him with an embarrassed 'Thanks.'

Tom Adams walked across the packed bar to the small brown table where Sam was waiting. He put her tomato juice down in front of her and, after taking a sip from his pint, sat in the chair beside her.

Sam raised her glass, 'Cheers.'

Adams responded before downing another mouthful of the clear brown liquid. Sam still felt annoyed with herself and embarrassed by dropping Adams in it over the ivy and was determined not to miss this opportunity to try and put things right,

'I wasn't sure you'd come.'

Adams sipped at his pint again, 'Nor was I. I must be going soft.'

'Then why did you?'

'Probably because I still think you're our best bet for finding the killer.'

'You don't agree with Farmer then?'

'She's the boss so I've got to support her decisions. But I've seen a few guilty men in my life, and I'm not convinced he's one of them.'

Sam sipped slowly at her drink giving herself a few seconds to summon the courage to make the apology. He certainly deserved it, but the words were difficult to say, 'I'm sorry, it just slipped out. I was angry and it was really stupid of me to let you down like that.'

As much as Adams liked and respected Sam, he wasn't yet in the mood to forgive, 'Yes, it was. Don't ask again.'

Sam had hoped it would be easy. It clearly wasn't going to be, 'It really wasn't deliberate.'

Adams thumped his pint down on the table, slopping some of its contents along the outside of the glass and onto the beer mat beneath, 'In this game, *Doctor* Ryan, trust is everything. Without it, you're buggered. Not only did you let me down, but you got me a bollocking from Farmer which I could well have done without. My entire career was under threat because I did you a favour.'

Sam had never seen Adams angry before and she didn't like it. Especially as she was the justifiable focus of that anger. 'Would it help if I talked to her?'

'No thanks. With your track record I'd probably end up inside.'

Sam was struggling, 'What did Farmer say?'

'Basically, that if I wanted to get you into bed then I should do it on my own time and at my own expense, not hers. She was right.'

Sam looked down and took another drink, nervous of asking the next question. 'Is that why you did it?'

Adams had no such reservations, and looked directly at her. 'Partially.'

Sam found herself in the peculiar situation of feeling both angry and flattered at the same time. Angry at his ulterior motive for helping and flattered because of his obvious and welcome interest in her.

Adams continued, 'It wasn't the main reason, though.'

Sam detected a softening in his voice, as if he felt that perhaps he had gone too far and was now trying to make amends. She looked up at him.

'You're a maverick, a one-off. You're the first and, I hope, last pathologist I have ever met who is willing to take their work outside the mortuary, and with the bottle to see it through. To be honest, if you weren't effective you wouldn't be tolerated.'

'Farmer doesn't think that?'

'Yes she does. But because of that, she also sees you

as a threat. When it comes to the credit for cracking this one, she wants it all.'

'I see.'

Adams turned towards her looking earnestly into her face, 'Sam . . .'

She was pleased that they were at least back on first name terms.

'Don't get involved any further, it could get dangerous and you're stepping on too many egos. If you push Farmer too far she'll react, and then we'll both be in the shit.'

Sam nodded, 'Ok.'

Adams smiled at her, pleased that at least she'd seen sense. 'Fancy another drink?'

Sam glanced at her watch. If she didn't go now it would be dark by the time she reached Little Dorking,

'Sorry, Tom, I've got to get back to the hospital, I've got a full list this afternoon.'

Adams was disappointed. Sam could see the disappointment in his eyes. He really was a very appealing man. She walked up to him and kissed him gently on the lips, whispering, 'You don't have to do me favours you know; you only have to ask.' She turned, picked up her bag from the table, and pushed her way back through the bar towards the door, leaving Adams flustered and frustrated.

CHAPTER EIGHT

He raged through the house. It had quite clearly been a big mistake, not in the original plan, not sanctified. These things took time. He appreciated that and had never skimped. The attempt to murder Dr Ryan had been rushed and had failed because of it. Now she was aware of possible danger, alerted and so on her guard. That would complicate the situation and could put at risk all the previous hard work; he would have to be patient. Frustration coursed through his veins like fire and it took a supreme act of self-will to remain rational. He gripped the edge of his desk and forced himself to be calm. Although Samantha would have to be killed, it would have to wait, he would have to return to the original plan.

With Bird out of the way his plans would have to change a little. The simulation of ritualistic killings had been a useful subterfuge and had served his purpose well. Two were dead and one would be lucky to see the outside of a prison cell until he was a very old and institutionalized man. Bird's release had been unexpected but had presented the opportunity to bring retribution in the same fashion a second time. Bird had even helped, behaving in a manner which perfectly complemented his purpose and assuring his eventual destruction. It was all quite wonderfully simple. Luck had been on his side, if that was a suitable description for His divine intervention.

New methods would have to be found to punish the remaining victims. A decision had been made at an early stage not to use the same method twice; with Mark and Frances it had been expedient and had worked well but now it was time to change. He lifted Malcolm Purvis' file and opened it, examining the scribbled note which he had written to himself outlining the type and method of Malcolm's nemesis. It was a good plan and should leave no clues as to the identity of those involved.

It was a very difficult thing for him to do but there was no longer any point in keeping these things. This time she hadn't gone away for a while, wasn't travelling the world or staying with her friends. She was dead and she wouldn't be coming home. He had his memories and his tapes and he treasured those, but they were all he had left. He'd spent the evening boxing up her clothes, her old toys and bric-à-brac. She would have wanted him to do that. He packed it all into the back of his car ready for his journey to the cancer research shop in town. The minutiae of a young, vibrant life was contained in only five cardboard boxes and two carrier bags. He had kept a couple of things, foolish sentimental items which she had loved and he couldn't part with. Her bear, Barney, which was the very first present he had bought her after she was born, and the black dress she'd worn to her mother's funeral when they'd offered and received love and support from each other. He shook his head in despair and grief. He'd had so many visitors since her death. People he'd forgotten existed. Friends from her past, old school friends, former boyfriends he hadn't seen for years, even people from the good parenting class they were attending. He'd welcomed them all and they helped him to retain her memory and remind him what a gentle loving child she had been. Many had said crass and foolish things, referring to life and death as if it was some game to be played by winners and losers. Others talked of His divine intervention and His will and plan for us all. They talked the platitudes of death, of peace and a better place. Malcolm listened patiently, understanding their difficulty and their fumbling attempts to comfort him, but he'd never believed; even now when it could have given him the greatest comfort, he still couldn't bring himself to compromise. For him heaven was here on earth in the pleasure he had derived from his love for his wife and daughter and now all that had been taken away from him. As he closed the boot of the car he looked up at the FOR SALE board outside the house. There was nothing left for him here. He'd decided to move into his London flat to see his remaining years out. Life could have little more of consequence to throw at him.

The FOR SALE board outside the house had brought proceedings forward. The original plan had to be scrapped and a new one would have to be made quickly. He'd watched as Malcolm loaded the back of his car with her clothes. He'd taken a perverse delight in having his own memories re-kindled. Bitter memories of undertaking the same tasks, of spending the entire night in her room packing away all her precious belongings and crying over every item until he felt himself teetering between sanity and madness. He hoped that *his* grief, *his* hurt, would be no less than his own. It was an ironic coincidence, he thought, but Frances would probably end up in the same graveyard as his daughter, 'united in death' he chuckled wryly to himself.

As soon as Malcolm's car pulled out of the drive and headed towards Cambridge, he made his way over to the house. Pulling a small notebook from his pocket he began to scribble intently. How many doors, where they were situated. The distance between the back door and the front drive, whether the drive was overlooked or not. How long the back garden was and where it led. He always liked to find at least two escape routes in case something went wrong. He worked very hard to avoid problems but God helps those who help themselves and so he prepared thoroughly. When he had finished and was satisfied that every eventuality had been covered, he made his way back to his car. The next stage was to drive around the area to familiarize himself with the layout of the roads, where they led, which were the dead ends, the short cuts. After half an hour, and assured that he had been thorough, he made his way home. As he drove into the Cambridge traffic he smiled to himself and thought, 'soon, very soon'.

They had been very grateful to receive the boxes and

had begun to unpack them at once. There was apparently a good market for the small-sized teenage clothes, especially in Cambridge. The elderly lady who took the clothes thanked him politely and asked him to send her appreciation on to his daughter. She had no idea who he was or what he was going through and he promised that he would. Once outside the shop he looked back into its busy interior. The clothes had already been supplied with wire coat hangers and were being hung on the long rails that stretched the length of both sides of the shop walls. As he watched, two girls walked up to the rack and took down one of Frances' dresses. He remembered it, she had bought it one summer on a trip to London. It hadn't been cheap but she'd looked so good in it that he had agreed to foot the bill. As he watched, one of the girls held it up against herself. It didn't look as good on her as it had on Frances, he thought. The girl noticed him looking and told her friend. She turned and they both stared at him as if he was a dirty old voyeur, lusting after their young bodies. Their stares penetrated his dulled senses making him feel uncomfortable so, turning away from the window, he returned to his empty car.

It was late afternoon by the time Sam finally managed to get to the village of Little Dorking and the Reverend Shaw's house. She was not entirely sure what approach she was going to adopt, it would be a case of playing the situation by ear. She parked her car on the drive, crossed the gravelled path to the front door and knocked. Although the sound echoed through the old house, there was no reply. Sam looked around the front garden half expecting to see Peggy's liver-coloured body marching up to her side to guide her once more to her master. This time, however, there was no sign of the affable dog and Sam made her own way to the back garden. She peered through several of the windows, looking for signs of life but there were none. She was quietly relieved, hoping that she could complete her task and go before the Reverend Shaw even realized she'd been there. She walked across to the garage and squinted into the gloomy interior through a gap in the old wooden doors. There were fresh pools of oil glistening on the concrete floor, indicating that a car was certainly still being parked there but the garage was empty and there was no sign of the car she had seen in the photograph on his sitting-room wall. The next source of her interest was the greenhouse at the far end of the garden. She cut across the garden and made her way along the damp, mossy path towards her objective. Even now, in the middle of her clandestine task, she couldn't resist pausing to stoop to catch the fragrance of the plants and flowers along the way. She had already decided that she was a smell junky and was convinced that one day it would probably get her into a great deal of trouble.

She slid the greenhouse door to the side and stepped in, carefully closing the door behind her. She wasn't entirely sure what she was looking for, a plant labelled *curare* would be helpful, she thought, or equipment of some description necessary for the distillation of illicit drugs, but unfortunately there were none of those things to be seen. Simply a large greenhouse with an abundance of plants and flowers of every description. She had at least taken the trouble to look at photographs of the plant she was looking for, not that it was much help in here. There was nothing particularly remarkable about it and it could thus be easily lost in this jungle of flora, something of a needle in a haystack. As she moved from plant to plant examining each in turn she began to fear that she would have to be there for at least a week to be able to cover all of the plants, then a voice shouted her name, 'Dr Ryan, Dr Ryan!'

It was the Reverend Shaw. Her immediate reaction was to jump guiltily and cast around for a hiding place but there was clearly little point as her car was parked on his drive and he was already calling her name. Her mind raced for a ready excuse as she slowly left the greenhouse. Outside, the Reverend Shaw was walking up the path towards her with Peggy, tailing wagging at the sight of her, leading the way. He gave her a cheery wave. 'Afternoon, and to what do I owe this pleasure?'

She waved back and then crouched down to stoke and fuss Peggy. A feeling of apprehension grew within her and she mentally berated herself for allowing herself to get into these situations in the first place. It was as if two sides of her personality were in conflict with each other for control of her spirit. One half that said, go to work, come home, lock the door and remain safe, and the other half needed to feel the adrenalin rush through her body to confirm her hold upon life. Despite her logic and her natural instinct for self-preservation, it was her more reckless half which frequently prevailed over the cautious side.

'I wanted another look at some of your ivies. I, er, thought it might tell me something I didn't know. I did knock but you weren't in, so I . . .'

'And did it?' His voice was fresh and energetic as if her interest in his subject had excited him.

'No, not really,'

He looked disappointed so, encouraged, she embellished her lie, 'It was very interesting though.'

He appeared to brighten at this and the two of them walked back down the path together towards the house companionably discussing his garden. Sam had already made a note of many of the garden's more interesting and unusual aspects and had decided to incorporate them into the plans for her own garden. It was well planned and well stocked with the kind of variety only a large garden such as this could support. As usual, talk of gardens had a relaxing, almost soporific effect upon her jangled nerves. As they reached the drive, Sam looked across at the car parked next to hers. It was an ageing Ford Escort which looked as if it had seen better days. Shaw remarked her interest, 'Bit of a wreck, isn't it, but it gets me from A to B and repairs are cheap.'

'A two-tone car.'

Shaw looked baffled as he stared at his car's dark blue paint.

'Blue and rust.'

He appreciated the joke and laughed heartily.

'Bit of an odd car for a man like you though, isn't it? I rather had the impression that you were more of the classic car type.'

'I used to be, but it had to go, cost far too much to keep.'

'Was that the one I saw you standing next to in the photograph?'

'The one in the photograph? Yes, that was it.'

Sam pressed him further, 'I'm afraid I don't know too much about cars. What kind was it? It was a beautiful colour.'

'Jaguar Mark II, in opalescent maroon.'

Sam felt her mouth suddenly grow dry as the adrenalin began to run. This time it wasn't fear, it was excitement.

'I bought it from a local farmer – the bodywork was in good shape but the engine was a wreck. I spent over a year renovating it. Ah, but it was worth it in the end.' Pride and affection were evident in his voice. Sam tried to control her excitement. After all, she considered, it didn't have to be the same car, there must have been hundreds produced in that colour but it was an exceptional coincidence.

'Who did you sell it to?'

'Some local man, about six months ago now. I miss the car but not what it was costing me.'

Sam was struggling to remain casual, 'Can you remember his name?'

'Well, no, not off the top of my head, sorry. Middle-aged chap, grey hair, knew a lot about the car. I felt sure she would have a good home.'

'Do you remember where he lived?'

'Cambridge, somewhere . . . hang on, if you're interested I still have the receipt, I'm a bit sentimental like that.'

He walked back into the house closely followed by Sam and Peggy. When he reached the sitting-room he began to rummage through an old sideboard drawer. After a few moments he emerged triumphant with a small scrap of white paper in his hand. 'Here it is. I knew it was around here somewhere. Old Simon Clarke put him on to me so I didn't have to advertise.'

Sam was almost beside herself with excitement. Her voice changed in tone with the stress. 'Who was it?' she squeaked.

He unfolded the paper slowly, if Sam hadn't known better she'd have sworn he was doing it on purpose to try and heighten her excitement. 'Yes, here it is, Dr Richard Owen, Owl Coats Farm, Swanham, Cambridge.'

There was an urgency in Brian Watton's voice when he called that had made Marcia drop what she was doing and react immediately. She wasn't quite sure why he'd called her, she'd certainly never had anything to do with fingerprints. She finally decided that he must have heard of her interest in the case and decided to pass any new information he'd discovered straight on to her. She hurried along the corridors until she reached Brian's lab and entered. Brian was a real ale drinking bear of a man. He stood well over six feet in height and was built like the proverbial brick privy with a thick, black beard and heavy glasses. However, Marcia liked him a lot. He belonged to the dying breed of happily married men and she felt genuinely comfortable with him. Despite having been around fingerprints for most of his working life he was still an enthusiast.

He ushered her to a chair before turning on the small slide projector situated on a stand at the back of the room. The image of four fingerprints close together were thrown up on to the wall.

'I wasn't sure at first, but the more I looked at

the prints the more convinced I was that they were wrong.'

Marcia looked intently at the prints but was unable to detect any obvious flaws. 'They look OK to me.'

Brian got up from his seat and, using the tip of his finger, pointed out the problems, 'Flatten your hand. The length of your fingers are uneven. Your index finger is smaller than your middle finger, your ring finger is larger than the index finger, but is smaller than your middle finger and so on. Now,' he said with a theatrical air, 'if you take a look at the prints found in the car, the tips of the fingers are in line.'

'So?'

'This only happens when a person is picking up a cylindrical object of some sort, like a glass for instance. Not when they've just placed their hand on to a flat surface.' Marcia pulled her chair up closer to the screen. 'The ridges are too heavy and spread as well. You only get this kind of pattern when pressure is applied to enable an object to be lifted.'

'So, are they Bird's prints?'

Brian nodded his head, 'They're Bird's prints all right, but I don't think he put them there. I think they might have been planted.'

Marcia was unconvinced. 'But how? I thought that sort of thing came within the realms of detective fiction.'

'Good fiction maybe; let me show you.'

He went across to the sink at the far side of the lab and filled a glass beaker with water before returning and handing it to Marcia. 'Now, just hold that for a few moments.'

After a few seconds he took the glass from her, took it over to one of the tables and, using a Zephyr brush, dusted it with aluminium powder. When he'd finished he showed Marcia her own prints, which the powder had revealed from the surface of the jar.

'Now, if we cut a strip of this tape,' he cut the tape from a roll on the desk before returning to the jar and rubbing the tape firmly over Marcia's prints, 'and press it against your prints making sure . . . there . . . are . . . no . . . bubbles . . . then I should be able to lift your print from the surface of the glass.' He peeled the tape back carefully, removing Marcia's prints. 'There you are, your prints neatly lifted off the glass.' He showed the print to Marcia who could clearly see the loops and whorls of her own fingers. 'Now, if I take this beaker,' he lifted another glass beaker off the work surface, 'and press your prints down hard on to its surface I should . . . be . . . able . . . to, yes, there you are.' He peeled the tape off the glass with a flourish and handed it to Marcia. 'One set of prints moved from glass A to glass B. Proving it was *you that did it*.'

Marcia looked at her prints on the jar, both impressed and concerned at the same time.

'Now, if you look carefully, you'll notice that the tips of your fingers are all even, just like Bird's. And to make absolutely sure there is no comeback, I just blow off any aluminium residue with my little brush.'

'Are you sure about this? I mean, you're an expert, is your average killer likely to know about this sort of thing?'

Brian shrugged, 'Depends whether we are dealing with

your average killer. I don't think we are. Perhaps Mr Bird's made some very clever enemies.'

As Farmer and Adams walked along the corridor of the police station one of the many blue-suited detectives called out to her, 'Excuse me, ma'am, but there's a serious problem, you're wanted on the phone in the control room straight away.'

Farmer looked at Adams who shrugged. Farmer turned and followed her subordinate officer back along the corridor. He opened the door for her and she entered. The room was pitch black and she strained her eyes to be able to see inside. Suddenly the lights were switched on and a dozen murder squad detectives began to sing, 'For she's a jolly good fellow'. They were all wearing party hats and most had either cans of lager or wine in their hands. Draped across the top of the room was a large banner bearing the words, WELL DONE BOSS. She glanced at Tom with a quizzical look and he smiled back, clearly having been aware of what was going on. She turned to face the body of police officers with a frown, 'Have you lot got nothing better to do than hold parties when you should be out there nicking villains?'

Their voices came back as one, 'No!'

Farmer smiled, 'You bunch of lazy bastards, someone had better give me a drink quick before I turn nasty.'

There were roars of approval, a can of larger was pushed into her hand and someone turned on the music. Adams looked at her and raised his can; she raised her can in salute. They both took deep and long drinks.

*　　*　　*

Sam arrived home earlier than she had anticipated. She was caught on the horns of dilemma which she was having difficulty resolving. If she went to Farmer now she'd have to accuse Owen of being the killer and explain to Farmer why she was still involved in the case when she'd been warned to restrict her work to the lab. There had to be another way of establishing the truth. Her thoughts were disturbed by the sight of four youths, all in their late teens, walking along the lane towards the main road and all looking both dirty and exhausted. She concluded that they must be casual workers making their way home from the farm a further quarter of a mile along the track from her home. She pulled the car on to the drive and walked around to the back of the house to see how Ricky was getting on with the job she'd given him. She stared up the garden and, although she could see his spade leaning up against the garden shed, there was no sign of her errant nephew. She walked to the top of the garden to make sure he hadn't sneaked away for a quick cigarette in the small wild copse at the bottom end of the garden. As she reached the vegetable patch she was amazed to find that not only had it all been dug over and the weeds cleared but the compost had been forked in as well. She had to admit that she was exceedingly impressed.

Ricky's voice suddenly called across the garden to her, 'Tea's ready when you are!'

She looked back towards the house to see her smiling nephew waving at her. She waved back. Picking up the spade she scraped it clean and walked back to the shed, hanging it with the rest of the tools across one of the shed walls. As she did, she noticed that the smell in the shed was different, as if someone had been smoking in there. The obvious culprit was Ricky and although she objected to his smoking she was prepared to overlook it under the circumstances. She picked up a plant pot which was sitting on top of one of the shelves. It was full of cigarette stubs, thirty or forty of them. Unless Ricky had become a chain smoker of mammoth proportions he had not spent the day alone. She suddenly understood where the four youths she had passed on the lane had come from and she smiled to herself. Taking the pot down to the bin by the side of the house she emptied its contents before kicking off her shoes and walking into the kitchen.

The smell of curry hit Sam as she opened the kitchen door. It wasn't one of her favourite dishes but as Ricky had made it she decided it would be churlish to make a fuss. She walked across to the stove where Ricky was standing, stirring his evil brew with a large wooden spoon. Sam kissed him on the cheek and sniffed in deeply. 'Curry, one of my favourites. I'm surprised you've got the energy after all that gardening.'

'If you get stuck in and give it your best it's surprising how much you can get done.'

Sam nodded in mock agreement. 'I see you're still smoking?'

Ricky looked awkward. 'Just the odd one now and again.'

'I think you're being modest, there were at least thirty in the pot.'

Ricky was silent.

'So how did you get them all to help?'

Ricky decided to act the innocent. 'Who?'

'Those four friends of yours I saw walking down the path when I arrived.'

'Oh them, they just popped around to see if I was OK.'

'That was lucky, wasn't it?'

Ricky gave a short, false laugh, 'Yes, it was.'

'So they did it out of friendship?'

Ricky couldn't see the point of lying any further, 'All right. They owed me. They were with me when the car got damaged and I didn't grass them up. This was just their way of saying thanks. Sorry.'

Sam didn't want to detract too much from his efforts, especially as they had all been made on her behalf. 'Very enterprising, I'm impressed. You're obviously going to go far, my boy.' She rubbed his back gently. 'Well done.'

Ricky smiled at her, began to stir the pot with renewed vigour.

To Sam's surprise the meal wasn't that bad and she actually found herself enjoying it and the company of her nephew, who talked almost non-stop as he served up the curry. Sam opened a bottle of red wine and sat listening to Ricky discuss his plans for the future. He still wasn't sure what he wanted to do. Sam suggested being a chef and, although he wasn't entirely against the idea, had to admit that with the exception of curries and having worked in a fast-food restaurant for a while, his culinary abilities were limited. At the end of the evening Sam phoned to order a taxi for him and he left. She suddenly felt very lonely. She'd never experienced it before, preferring her own company and thoughts but now, without Ricky's exuberance, the cottage felt cold and empty. As she began to pack the dinner plates into the dishwasher the phone rang. She hesitated for a moment, letting the answer machine take it so that she could see who it was before committing herself to talking to them. She recognized the voice at once and ran to the phone.

'Sorry, Marcia, I was in the bathroom.'

Marcia's voice was excited and Sam realized something had happened. 'The prints they found in the Purvis car, they were planted.'

'What! are you sure . . . does Farmer know . . . are they releasing Bird?'

'They're double- and triple-checking before they tell the police but they seem pretty convinced.'

Sam's mind was still racing as Richard Owen's connection with the murder came to the front of her mind again. 'That fibre, the one we think came from Owen's jacket, have you still got access to it?'

'Which one, the one from the James murder or the one from the Purvis murder?'

Sam was confused, 'Which one from the Purvis murder?'

'I found some more fibres on the cord around her neck, the same as the ones we found at the James scene.'

Sam felt herself getting annoyed with her friend. 'Why didn't you tell me?'

'I did when you came to the lab the other day. I asked you how the crime scene manager coped with him.'

Sam remembered the flippant remark and its importance suddenly became apparent. 'Did you manage to match them with Owen's jacket?'

'It was the same type of fibre we found at the James

scene.' so I just assumed it was his. Obviously didn't bother wearing his protective suit *again*.'

'But he did he was wearing his protective suit at the Purvis murder!'

Sam arrived at Owen's house early, hoping to catch him in. There was something wrong, a nagging doubt at the back of her mind. She needed samples from his jacket, if only to allay her worst suspicions. Neither Richard's nor Janet's cars were anywhere to be seen but still, she knocked loudly on the front door to be sure. She waited for a few moments but there wasn't a sound.

She walked to the rear of the house and peered through the back windows, there was no sign of life. Although she might not be able to get samples from Owen's jacket, it seemed stupid to miss an opportunity to have a good look around. She knew if she got caught she'd be in trouble, but she decided it was a risk worth taking. She crossed the neatly trimmed lawn to the greenhouse. The garden was one of the most boring and predictable she had ever seen. It was mainly laid to a rectangular lawn with a selection of plants and shrubs in narrow borders around the edge. It was a garden designed to give its owner a minimum amount of work and a minimum amount of pleasure. The greenhouse, like the garden, was small and uninspiring, mainly full of tomato plants in grow bags and very little else. She crossed the garden again, this time towards the garage and peered in through one of the small windows at the side of the building. It was only a small garage, but crammed inside, swathed in a dark-coloured tarpaulin, was a car.

Sam began to feel her heart beat a little faster. She had been surprisingly calm up to that point, only half believing her suspicions. Sam walked to the front of the garage and grasped both doors, giving them a violent shake. But they were securely locked and offered no prospect of entry without considerable effort and inevitable damage. The two small windows at the side of the garage were also firmly closed and so she walked round to the other side where there was a single door. Without much hope she pulled at the handle and, despite her expectations, the door was unlocked. After catching momentarily where dampness had caused the wood to swell, it gave way and the door flew open throwing her off balance. With one last glance along Owen's drive she took a deep breath and entered the garage. Whatever the make of the car, hidden under its heavy covering, it was certainly long. She moved slowly to the front of the garage and, crouching down, lifted the front of the tarpaulin to reveal the front end of a maroon Jaguar. She stared at it for a moment as if it were a living thing, wondering what stories it would reveal when the SOCOs began to work on it. A coldness crept over her as she pictured the fear and pain of Mark James and Frances Purvis and tried in vain to connect the bumbling, affable Owen with the cold, cruel persona of their killer. Pushing her thoughts to one side, she began to examine the front of the car. The middle half of the nearside wing was crumpled and bore a number of deep scratches which had ripped the paint from the bodywork across its front. Sam could also see that the front bumper was missing. It looked as if one half had been ripped from its mounting while the other had been carefully removed.

She ran her hand along the smooth, dark paint checking for an area from which a scraping would not be noticed. She decided that one more scratch by the side of the already damaged area would be hardly noticeable and so, taking a penknife and a small plastic bag from her handbag, she began to scratch away at the paint until she was sure she had enough for a comparison. Then, dropping her penknife and the paint back into her bag, she replaced the cover over the front of the car. There was new little doubt in Sam's mind, Owen was the killer.

Sam pushed the garage door firmly closed behind her and she had just got back to the side of the house when she heard him call.

'Samantha!'

She whirled round. Owen's voice sent a shiver down her spine and for a moment she found herself unable to move. Willpower and an inbred survival instinct finally made her turn and, smiling, she gave him a cheery wave. Owen made his way up the garden towards her. She noticed that he had on the same smart blazer he'd been wearing the night James' body had been discovered. Now, in the bright sunlight it seemed far more vivid than she remembered and there could be no doubt, it was unquestionably blue.

'What a pleasant surprise! What are you doing here?' She could feel her body tense and a slight tremor begin. She knew she had to relax, it was important for her to appear normal if she was to bluff her way out of this situation. Drawing on all her mental reserves she affected a matter-of-fact air, 'I tried the front door, but there was no reply. I thought I might find you pottering around the back.'

'Well, you've found me. I had to pop down to the shops; my car's in the garage so I had to walk. Still, I'm sure it did me good. Coffee?'

All she wanted to do at that precise moment was run screaming into the road calling for help and pointing out to the world that friendly old Dr Owen was in fact a homicidal maniac and should be locked up for ever. Instead she found herself dumbly nodding her acceptance, 'That sounds lovely.'

She followed Owen into the house through the front door. She had never felt so alert in her life. Her eyes darted from place to place, continually looking for the quickest escape route, or some object which she could use as a weapon. By now her heart was pounding so hard that she felt sure Owen would notice it, even through her clothes. She tried desperately to remain calm.

'I only half expected you to be in, thought you might be at your surgery.'

'I get Thursdays off. Janet covers for me, she likes to keep her hand in. Now, let's see about that coffee.'

He made his way into the kitchen taking off his jacket and dropping it carelessly over a chair. Sam saw her opportunity and began to make her way carefully towards it. She had only gone a few steps when a shout from the kitchen stopped her.

'Black, no suggar, is it?'

Sam called back, 'Yes, that's right, thanks.'

Taking in a deep breath she plucked at the jacket with

her fingers, pulling away whisps of fibres and dropping them quickly into a white paper tissue she pulled from her bag. As she began to close the tissue Owen returned from the kitchen with the two steaming cups of coffee. Sam quickly brought the tissue up to her nose and pretended to sniff.

'Got a bit of a cold coming by the sound of it, like me to give you something for it?'

Sam shook her head. 'No, I'll be fine. Thank you.'

Owen put his coffee down on a small table and walked across to one of the window blinds. 'You'll have to forgive my back for a moment but I've got to get this thing restrung, the last cord broke.

While his back was still to her Sam slipped the tissue into her handbag. Now, as I take it this isn't entirely a social call, perhaps you'll tell me what I can do for you?'

Sam swallowed hard.

'I've come up against a bit of a brick wall over those last two murders. I thought you might have some ideas on the subject?'

'I thought they'd got that man Bird in for it?'

'They have, but I'm not convinced.'

'Really, might one ask why?'

Owen turned. He had a long white cord in his hand which he continually wiped across his palms. The movement seemed to have a hypnotic effect on Sam and she found herself becoming transfixed by the movement like a snake's prey waiting for the deadly strike.

'Too many holes.'

'Like what?'

The movement of his hands seemed to increase as he clearly became more agitated.

'The fingerprints, they were planted.'

'Planted? How can you tell?'

'The technician at the lab discovered some inconsistencies.'

'First I've heard, when did all this happen?'

'Yesterday evening.'

'Will they be letting him go then?'

Sam's breathing began to imitate the rhythmic movement of the cord through Owen's hands. She sipped at her coffee, affecting normality, trying to calm herself. 'I've no idea.'

'Well, let's hope they at least shut down that club of his.'

Sam nodded her false approval. Owen stopped pulling the cord through his hands for a moment and excused himself, 'It's too long, I'm going to have to cut it down a little. Back in a second.' He disappeared into the kitchen. Sam considered bolting for the door, she wasn't sure she could take much more. She realized, however, that if she did it would alert him and he might slip away before the police could stop him, he might be lost for ever. He returned to the sitting-room after only a few moments but this time instead of walking across to the blind he stood behind her. Sam glanced back. He had the cord wrapped tightly around one hand while he cut the other end with a scalpel. He looked at her, 'Sharpest thing I've got in the house, cuts through almost anything in a moment.'

Sam gave him a nervous smile and forced herself to turn

away in a parody of casual interchange, whilst expecting at any moment to feel the cord being looped around her neck or the sharp cut of the scalpel as it forced its way through her neck.

She continued with the conversation estimating that at least the sound of his voice would tell her where he was. 'I didn't know you had an interest in Bird's club?'

The reply came back sharply and with a hint of anger, 'I don't, but one hears stories. Bad influence on the young, deserves to be closed.'

Sam noticed a photograph of a young girl on the top of the fireplace and seized upon it as an excuse to stand up and cross the room, moving away from Owen. 'She's pretty, who is she?

'My daughter, she was eighteen when that was taken; she'd just got into Trinity Hall to read law. Her whole life was before her.'

'Where is she now?'

'Dead, she was killed a few years ago.'

Sam felt embarrassed and surprised. She suddenly realized how little she really knew about Owen. She'd always liked him as a friend and a colleague but they had never been close and she'd certainly never pried into his personal life. She doubted that anyone else had either. He was very adept at simulating intimacy without revealing anything of himself. Owen suddenly turned towards her and from the look in his eyes Sam could tell he was about to make his move, about to finish a job he had started days before when he tried to force her off the road.

Farmer was in the interview room when the call came

in. The place was winding down, computers were being removed, staff were clearing their drawers as they prepared to return to section. The DC who answered the phone did so in a very disinterested manner, 'DC Parker, murder incident room.' He listened for a moment, then called across to Farmer who was sorting through a stream of witness statements with Adams, 'It's for you, boss, forensic lab, I'll put it through.'

As soon as the white light began to flash on the phone Farmer picked it up. 'Detective Superintendent Farmer, can I help you?'

The voice on the other end of the phone was unmistakably that of Brian Watton. She knew it well, and she knew how good Brian was; he'd been the inspiration behind the resolution of more than one case in his time. What he told her this time, however, she didn't want to hear. Adams looked up as the room went quiet.

'Are you bloody sure? . . . Do you realize what you're doing? . . . Yes, I'm sure.' Farmer slammed the phone down hard on to its cradle. 'Shit, shit, shit, shit, shit, shit!'

Adams and the rest of those in the room remained silent, waiting. Farmer finally stood up and looked across at the remaining detectives. With a deep sigh she addressed them.

'Well, there's good news and bad news. We're back to square one. The prints on the Purvis car were planted and we've all been made to look a bunch of tossers.'

One of the DCs spoke up, 'And the good news?'

She snarled across at him, 'That was the good news,

the bad news is, all leave and time off is cancelled until we catch this bastard.'

She looked up at her WELL DONE banner which was still draped across the ceiling, 'And get that down before I strangle – sorry, garrotte – someone with it.'

Sam felt convinced that Janet Owen's timely arrival had been her salvation. She had apparently finished her surgery early and come straight home. Her arrival had broken the spell of the moment and taken the glaze out of Owen's eyes. She couldn't remember being more relieved to see someone before in her life. She hadn't wasted any time and despite the look of surprise and bemused incomprehension, Sam had made feeble and hurried excuses for leaving and fled the house. She tried desperately to control her rising panic but her hand was shaking so much that she had serious difficulty in getting the key into the lock. She pulled her coat around the side of her hand trying to hide her panic. Finally, the door opened. She jumped inside and pulled the car out of the drive, accelerating quickly along the road, leaving Janet waving earnestly from the front door. She hadn't travelled far before the tears which were filling her eyes and blurring her vision forced her to pull into the side of the road and stop. She pulled her mobile from her bag and dialled, desperately trying to see the numbers through her tears. Finally she managed to get through.

'Marcia Evans, please.' Sam tried to control her voice which threatened to fail her as the ache in her throat reached a crescendo and paralysed her vocal cords,

'Could you find her please, this is Doctor Ryan at the Park, it's very urgent.'

Marcia's concentration was almost tangible as she looked hard down her microscope. She changed the slides several times before finally looking up. Sam was sitting on a bench at the far side of the lab. Although several hours had passed since her encounter with Richard Owen, she still hadn't managed to regain her composure completely. She looked back at Marcia expectantly.

'The paint layers and colours are identical. I'm ninety per cent sure it's the same car. Where did you find it?

'It was parked in Richard Owen's garage.'

'The police surgeon?' Sam nodded. 'So I was right all along!'

Sam gave a forced half smile. 'What about the fibres from his jacket?'

Marcia walked across to a plump young girl working on the bench next to hers. 'Any joy, Jenny?'

The girl looked up. 'Well, I'll need a bit more time to be sure, but I'm almost certain they're *not* the same.'

Sam felt she should have been surprised but she wasn't. 'How are they different?'

The girl placed the fibres Sam had collected from Owen's jacket under an ultraviolet light. 'If you look hard, you'll notice that under the light it shows up bluey-green.'

Marcia and Sam examined the fibre closely as Jenny changed the sample.

'The samples we retrieved from the scenes are a much

more intense, flat blue. These are definitely not from the same garment.'

Marcia looked up at Sam. 'Are you sure it was the same jacket?'

'Yes. Well, it looked the same. It was certainly blue.'

'It was dark last time you saw it, you might have made a mistake. He's bound to have more than one jacket, and they're all bound to be dark. Can't see Owen buying a red one.'

Sam had been so sure. 'No, I suppose . . .'

'He's hardly likely to give us evidence that's going to incriminate him, is he?'

'No, I'm sure you're right.'

'We've got enough with the paint samples anyway.'

'I hope so, I'd hate to lose him now.' Sam looked back at Jenny, 'I didn't manage to pick anything else off the jacket that might help, did I?'

'Not much, a few plant hairs, that's all.'

Sam suddenly found herself becoming interested again, her optimism returning. 'What kind of plant hairs?'

Jenny shook her head. 'I'm not sure. Have a look.' Sam walked across to the microscope and peered in. She examined the hairs for a few moments then straightened up, a look of triumph on her face. 'I know what they are, *Hedera Hibernica*. They come off in the hundreds when you come into contact with it. They're difficult to get off as well.'

Marcia walked across to Sam and put her arm around her, 'Time to call Farmer, I think. This thing's getting a bit too dangerous for country girls like us.'

CHAPTER NINE

It was almost over. He knew the moment he walked up the drive and saw her coming out of his garage. The involuntary tightening of her grip on her handbag as she saw him was so revealing. She had worked it out, she had come looking for evidence and had found the car. He was sure paint scrapings would be inside her handbag. Scrapings which would match samples collected from the damage caused when he had collided with Frances' car. She had wrestled hard to act calmly, but it hadn't been entirely successful. He knew her well enough to be aware of her agitation. He could see it in her eyes, in her body language and the taut lines of her face. He'd even watched her from the kitchen as she had taken samples from his jacket and concealed them in a tissue and her feeble pretence of a cold. Even after she had fled from the house he had seen her hands shaking so much that she couldn't get the key in the lock of her car. He'd almost pitied her, so locked inside her fear, and contemplated offering to help her. Perhaps he should have killed her when he had the chance. If Janet had not come home he probably would have but what would have been gained from that? She'd probably already told someone where she was going and the game would have been up anyway. Besides, killing her now was not what He had ordained. And departing from His clear intentions would have made him a common murderer, and he had never been that. He wasn't convinced he had the stomach for it. Despite his anger and frustration at the way she'd thwarted his plan, he still liked Sam. She was honest and diligent and would undoubtedly do more good in this world than he, once his mission was complete.

He didn't know why but God had quite clearly decided that his mission was nearly over and that he had done enough. Mercy was, of course, within God's gift but not his. He had one more score to settle before he could feel any sense of justice. What was important now was to buy time and cover his tracks as much as possible so the mission could continue. He felt remarkably calm for a man who knew he must spend at least the next ten years in prison. They called it life; he supposed for man of his age they were probably right.

He walked outside and to the top of the garden where he pulled a large box of matches from his pocket and began a fire. He watched as it took hold of the dried wood and leaves and the grey whisps of smoke drifted into the damp, windless atmosphere over the adjoining gardens. He waited until the flames had taken a firm hold before piling more wood and leaves on to the top. When he was convinced that the fire was established he collected a spade from the shed, walked to the line of bushes at the back of the garden and dug the ivy bush out of the ground. The plant had blended in well with the evergreen bushes, and was difficult to spot unless you knew it was there.

He had to wrest its long tendrils from their anchorage points on the fence before throwing it on to the fire. It didn't burn well, but it did burn. Then he returned to collect the fallen leaves and any remaining branches and roots before filling the hole and levelling the ground and returning to the house.

Malcolm Purvis watched as the removal men carried item after item of furniture out of the house and into the back of the removal van parked in his drive. He planned to put most of it into storage, sell those items which he no longer needed and give the rest away to local charities. The flat in London was fully furnished so he had no immediate need for most of his furniture, but much of it held memories and each piece had been chosen with care, much discussion and good-natured banter with his beloved wife. He waited for them to bring out the large piano and watched them struggle down the steps with it before he went back into the house and up the stairs to Frances' room. It looked so forlorn now with her bed stripped and all her toys gone. He stood for a moment while memories engulfed him, glimpses of past Christmases, birthdays, tears and joy, grief and illness. He wondered if those memories and his grief would be etched into the very fabric of the house to reappear as unwelcome ghosts to future generations of owners. He tried to empty his mind for a moment to see if he could sense her presence but she wasn't there, even her smell had gone. The fragment of comforting words she had once spoken to him drifted into his mind, 'Wherever you are Daddy, so am I.' He was comforted. He decided that this would be the last time he entered this room. It was only an empty shell with no life. Finally, he walked across to the window, drew the curtains and left the room, closing the door quietly behind him.

The liquid was measured precisely into the syringe. When the vial was almost empty the plunger was gently depressed sending liquid squirting into the air to fall on to the carpet. The calculated amount of drug was sealed inside the clear plastic tube and it was dropped back inside the black bag which was closed and locked. The phone rang twice before it was answered. After a short conversation the bag was pushed under the desk and the room vacated.

The fire was burning well when Owen returned to it, his arms full of files, photographs and notes. Even the ivy seemed to be burning well now. He spilled the contents of his arms on to the fire and began to poke at the ashes with a long stick, trying to stoke it up. There was something about fire which he really enjoyed. It was created of strange pictures and images. He found the crackling and spitting comforting too, but most importantly it was a purifier. They'd known that almost since time began. It destroyed only to renew. Now it would destroy most of the evidence against him and renew his chance of finishing his work. He picked up one of the files which had slipped out of the reach of the flames and examined its contents. He remembered this one, Michael Kemp, 64 Denning Lane, Cambridge, a 43-year-old self-employed builder. Lived with his wife and one son. The other son was at college in Nottingham. He had two vehicles, an old, blue Ford van, registration number LLD 453E and a series three BMW, black, registration number M256 PDR. He looked at it one more time before throwing it on to the fire. It caught light almost at once. The edges of the file turned black and curled inwards before bursting into flames. He really didn't need the files any more but they had become like old friends, comforting and familiar. He'd spent so much time researching them, reading and re-reading every detail that the information was almost a part of his very being. He would miss them but he didn't need them.

After giving herself a final cursory once-over in the mirror, she pulled down the jacket of her suit, flicked the last strands of hair away from the side of her face, marched quickly out of the ladies' lavatory and headed towards the chief superintendent's office. Although she always endeavoured to look smart, she wasn't normally so precise about her appearance, but on this occasion she knew that not only was her position as head of the enquiry in doubt but her future career with the Cambridgeshire Constabulary.

The large, black plaque bearing the inscription, DETEC-TIVE CHIEF SUPERINTENDENT. MARK WORDS QPM, covered the entire top third of the door and confirmed her arrival at her destination. She wondered, facetiously, whether the plaque was there in case he forgot who he was. She took a steadying deep breath and knocked. A loud but firm voice echoed imperiously into the corridor from inside the office, 'Wait!'

He was on his own, of course, and the only person he was expecting was her but they had to play these little power games and she was in no position to prevent them. It had been like this during her whole time with the force. If they weren't trying to touch her up or persuade her that an episode between the sheets with them would increase her promotion chances, then they were putting her down, making light of her success, and blowing up out of all proportion her failures. She'd seen so many women join full of ambition only to have it knocked out of them by the system. And if one did beat the system and exhibit some success, then of course they had to be a dike. She knew that was the common denunciation of herself, and her lifestyle afforded ample affirmation of the presumption. Late thirties, unmarried, living alone; what else could she possibly be? Well, she wasn't, and she was damned if she was going to indulge in a pointless defence of her sexuality with any of them.

'Enter!' The voice boomed into the corridor once more. She breathed in again, pushed down the handle on the door and entered the office. It was typical of the style of office preferred by senior officers and could be summed up in one word, plush. Thick carpet on the floor, an oak desk, drinks' cabinet, television and video, a couple of large comfortable chairs for cosy, chummy meetings and the shelves and walls covered in mementoes and trophies from police forces around the world. He eyed her carefully, making his annoyance felt, and setting the tone of the meeting immediately, before directing her to one of the not so comfortable chairs in front of his desk. They were strategically placed. Not close enough to be too intimate, but not so far away that he would have to raise his voice above a reasonable whisper to be heard. They took a pride in sounding reasonable, she thought, they never were, but they liked to sound it.

'Well, we're in a right bloody mess, aren't we?'

Farmer watched him, resenting everything about him, but she remained silent.

'You've managed to make this force look complete bloody fools and you've done it all by yourself. We'll just have to hope he doesn't sue us for every penny we've got. God knows what your father would have said if he'd been alive. He wasn't the soft touch I am . . .' She waited for it. 'He was my detective inspector when I first joined the CID.' She mouthed the next bit in her mind, she'd heard it so many times before. 'He was the best boss I ever had, hard you understand, but fair, you knew where you were with him.' She knew for a fact that her father thought Mark Words to be the biggest prat who had ever been allowed into uniform. She'd tell him one day, hopefully at his retirement party when she'd got his job and he could kiss her arse. For now she settled for sounding reassuring.

'We've still got him for breaching his bail conditions.'

'Clutching at straws a bit, aren't we?' Farmer knew she was but couldn't think of anything else to say. 'That is, if you haven't managed to cock up that one as well?'

For a moment she fantasized about leaning over the desk and punching him in the face. He stood up from his desk and began to pace around the room, his hands behind his back with his 'let's have the cards on the table' conversation look on his face.

'I took a chance when I appointed you, Harriet. It was a sort of thank-you to the memory of your father really, to pay him back for all he did for me . . .'

Would that be when he tried to get you thrown off the job? she thought.

'I really believed that you, above all people, especially given your background, could handle the job.' He stopped for a moment and looked at her. 'I was wrong.'

Farmer couldn't remember hating someone so much in her entire life. She'd often heard it said that anyone was capable of committing murder, but until that moment she hadn't really believed them. After that, everything else the sanctimonious old bastard said just sounded like a distant echo.

'You've let me down, Harriet, you've let the force down and more importantly, you've let yourself down. I really do not have any other . . .'

The loud knock on the door stopped him mid-flow and he told the unknown intruder to wait but it was too late, Adams was already in the office.

'Excuse me, sir, but there's been a bit of a development.' He looked across at Farmer. 'Those paint scrapings you managed to find, ma'am, well, they've come up trumps, you were right all along, it was Richard Owen.'

Farmer was as surprised as Words but tried not to show it. This time it was Words who began to look uncomfortable.

'Do you mean the Police Surgeon?'

Adams glanced across at him. 'Yes, sir.'

'Good God, I had dinner with him and his wife on Saturday! Are you quite sure?'

'Yes, sir, very sure.'

Words returned to his desk and sat down. 'Looks like you might have the opportunity to redeem yourself. Better go and sort it out and make sure you keep me informed. I'll wait here and have a heart attack.'

Farmer nodded and made her way to the door which was being held open for her by Adams. She looked up at him as she passed. Normally she wasn't very good at thank-yous but this was the exception. 'You're a prince, do you know that? a bloody prince.'

'All part of the service.'

They exchanged wry smiles briefly before disappearing down the steps to the car-park.

Sam and Marcia were waiting outside when Farmer and Adams arrived supported by at least a dozen other uniformed and CID officers. They'd heard the sound of the police sirens as they raced through the rush-hour traffic for almost five minutes and so, presumably, had Owen. The white smoke which the two women had seen drifting over his house had lent an intensity and urgency at the sound. All Sam wanted to do was to rush into the house and prevent him from destroying any more evidence. She had experienced one frightening episode with Owen and she wasn't keen to experience another. Next time she might not be quite so lucky. The police cars came to a screaming halt outside Owen's house and dozens of police officers piled out. They moved into action like a flock of birds, responding instinctively to information and directions undetected by mere onlookers. Two sealed off the driveway to the house, several ran into the gardens of the adjoining properties, while others rushed up to the front door and smashed it in with a hydraulic ram. As Adams and Farmer dashed from their car, Sam and Marcia followed. They ran up to the back gate which led out into the garden and pulled on the handle, but it had been securely locked. Two hefty kicks from Adams' boot, however, sent the door crashing off its hinges and the small party spilled through.

As Adams ran towards Owen, he desperately threw the last few files on to the centre of the fire. Adams launched himself at Owen and, pulling him to the ground, forced his arms behind his back, handcuffing his wrists together.

Owen laughed and screamed hysterically as he was restrained, 'You're too late, you're much too late!'

Adams shouted to the uniformed officers who had followed him into the garden, 'Get some water – get this bloody fire out!'

The two officers rushed towards the kitchen as Sam and Marcia, shielding their faces against the heat, attempted to rescue as many of the smouldering files from the edge of the bonfire as possible, stamping on them to smother the creeping ribbons of fire which threatened to engulf them.

Finally, one of the police officers returned with a hose-pipe and began to douse the flames. Adams pulled Owen to his feet and, deferring the privilege, pushed him in front of Farmer who had now entered the garden from the back of the house.

Farmer stared coldly into his eyes. 'Dr Richard Owen, I'm arresting you on suspicion of the murder of Mark James and Frances Purvis. You are not obliged —'

Owen suddenly lunged forward to within a few inches of Farmer's face, 'Prove it!'

Farmer, unflinching and with contempt, continued to stare into his eyes and finished the caution before getting two of the uniformed officers to drag him out to her car.

The fire was extinguished and teams of SOCOs were already arriving to search and clear the house. Sam and Marcia carefully sifted through the charred remains around the fire trying to rescue anything that might help build up the case against the former police surgeon. Marcia found several ivy leaves and showed them to Sam who confirmed its species before Marcia dropped them into a small brown envelope. Sam found several metal buttons which looked as if they might have come from a girl's jacket, as well as a small piece of black cloth. Of the files they had managed to pull off the fire, only two were of any use. Adams and Sam flicked through them: flakes of black, shrivelled paper breaking off and swirling into the air.

'Look at this, they must have been his next victims.'

Sam stared incredulously at the files.

'Places of work, where they drank, the routes they took,' said Adams. 'Look, even where they shopped. Talk about "Who Dares", it's like an SAS operation.'

Sam took the file off him and looked at the photographs. 'I wonder how many we missed?'

'Doesn't really matter, they're safe now, they'll never let him out.'

'But why? Why would someone like Richard Owen turn into a homicidal maniac?'

'He'd obviously been thinking about it for a while. These must be the best laid plans for murder I've ever seen.'

Farmer approached them, taking the file off Sam and handing it back to Adams. 'Well done, Tom.'

'It wasn't me. It's Dr Ryan you've got to thank, she found the paint samples, not me.'

Farmer looked at Sam then back to Adams. 'Give us a minute, will you, Tom?'

Adams walked away and joined Marcia who was still hunting through the remains of the fire in the hope of finding something extra. As soon as they were alone and Adams out of earshot Farmer began, 'What did I tell you about getting involved in this enquiry?'

'I didn't have any deliberate intention to interfere, circumstances just dictated it. I handed over all the information as soon as I had it. I don't see what else I could have done. If you want to make an official complaint, then that's up to you.'

'Oh no. Not even I am that stupid. Have the world know that it was you who cracked this case and not me? I'd be a laughing stock. He'll be locked away, in a nice secure hospital where he belongs, and this will be our little secret. A perfect ending for all concerned.'

'Fine.'

'Look, I'm not very good at this sort of thing, and part of me still feels that you were in the bloody wrong, but well done – and thanks.'

Sam knew how difficult such a statement must have been for Farmer and appreciated it all the more.

Farmer continued, 'To be quite honest, if you hadn't stuck your nose in where it wasn't wanted not only might I have been off the case, I might have been off the job.'

Sam was conciliatory, 'Thank you. I *am* a bit of a nosy cow; it comes with the job.'

'Well, I think we can both be grateful for that.'

'What will happen to Bird?'

'We've still got him for the breaking the terms of his bail. I expect we'll drop that if he decides not to sue us. It normally works something like that.'

For the first time since Sam had known Farmer there was a hint of mutual understanding.

Shouts and screams from the front of the house sent them scurrying to the front gate. Standing at the bottom of the drive and struggling with two police officers was Janet Owen. She was angry, confused and crying bitterly as she watched her house being searched by a team of white-suited SOCOs and armfuls of her clothes and belongings being unceremoniously removed.

'My clothes. Where are they going with my clothes?'

Sam looked across at Farmer. 'I'll tell her. I've met her before.'

'She'll have to come in for questioning.'

'I understand, but if it wasn't for her I might be dead now, so give me a chance to calm her down first and I'll drive her in to see you after that.'

Farmer nodded, 'OK, I've got her old man to interview first anyway.'

Sam made her way back down the drive and through

the cordon. Janet recognized her at once. 'What the hell is going on, Sam?'

'It's Richard, I'm afraid. They've arrested him.'

'For what?'

'Let's go to my car and I'll explain.'

'No. If you know something, tell me now.'

'I'm sorry, Janet, but they've arrested him for murder. He's responsible for the deaths of Mark James and the Purvis girl.'

The effect of Sam's words on Janet was total. The colour drained from her face and her eyes glazed over. As she fell forward in a dead faint, Sam caught her and with the help of one of the nearby police officers laid her gently on the pavement, slipping off her jacket and using it as a cushion under her head. She shouted at the young PC by her side, 'Get an ambulance!'

She picked up Janet's left hand and began to stroke it rhythmically while she waited for help.

Adams watched Owen closely as he signed all the appropriate forms and disclaimers in the station sergeant's office. After he had finished he was escorted to an interview room in the company of his solicitor. The two video cameras had already been turned on. One showed a general view of the room revealing Farmer and Adams sitting opposite Owen and his solicitor. The second camera stood back from the table but showed a close-up of Owen's head and face. In the murder incident room a closed-circuit television showed the interview to the rest of the squad. Farmer began.

'We are making enquiries into the murder of Mark

James and Frances Purvis. I believe you can help us with those enquiries.'

Owen remained silent for a moment, scanning the two officers' faces. 'If you mean did I kill them and then cut them up, yes I did.' He smiled into the camera close to the table. 'And, what's more, I don't regret a thing.'

Mr Robertson, his solicitor, leaned across and spoke quietly to him, 'Do you realize the full implication of what you are saying?'

Owen looked back at him. 'Oh yes, I do, it's time for the truth I think, don't you?'

Sam had been joined by Trevor Stuart as she waited outside the busy casualty department at the Park Hospital where Janet had been taken for treatment. She was glad to see him and was surprised to find herself throwing her arms around him and hugging him closely. They sat down together and Sam outlined the situation. For the first time since she'd known him, Trevor had lost his humour and listened intensely to every word she said. When she'd finished he took her hand.

'I think I might understand his motivation at least.'

Sam was surprised. 'Why didn't you say something before?'

'It didn't seem relevant, not until now anyway.'

Sam waited expectantly.

'I think it has something to do with his daughter, Claire.'

'I thought she died in an accident?'

'Well, it was an accident of sorts. A drugs overdose at a party.'

'How long ago did all this happen?'

'Three years ago. Claire wasn't the angel Owen liked to portray her as. She was a bit of a bad lot actually. Ran around with the wrong crowd, got involved in drugs and started stealing to feed her habit, even from her parents. How they put up with it I'll never know. I think Janet was aware of what was going on but Richard wouldn't hear a word against her. Claire's death hit him hard. Janet did what she could, she's the strong one in the relationship, but it was still over a year before he went back to work. I don't think he's ever fully recovered. He found God as well and became a *bore*-again Christian.'

'Any other children?'

'No. She was all they had.'

'Where did the party take place?'

'I seem to remember it was in a local club.'

'Bird's Nest?'

'Yes, that was it, Bird's Nest.'

Marcia's laboratory was filling rapidly with the clothes and other paraphernalia from Owen's house. Each item had already been carefully bagged and labelled and now awaited the attention of one of the white-coated technicians. While some lifted fibres off the clothes with taped hands, others organized the fibres on to slides and began to examine them. Everyone knew it was going to be a long job but it didn't blunt their enthusiasm to ensure that nothing was missed.

Trevor had left by the time Janet emerged from the cubicle where she was being treated. The doctor had wanted her to stay in for the night, concerned about her condition, but she persuaded them that her husband's needs were greater than hers and assured them that if she experienced another bout of fainting she would return. Finally, she signed the release form and rejoined her friend.

Sam had parked her car directly outside the department in a slot which indicated 'Casualty staff only'. She helped Janet into the passenger seat and they began the short drive to the incident room. Sam was at a loss to know what words might comfort her. An awkward silence descended over them, broken finally by Janet.

'I knew he was ill, had been for a while. He never got over the death of our daughter from a drugs overdose a few years ago, you see. But I never thought he could . . . kill anyone. I still can't believe he'd do such a thing; he's such a gentle man. You know him, Sam, you know he couldn't do a thing like this.'

'I think the evidence against him is pretty strong. You never noticed anything?'

'No, he had his den and I was banned from that, called it his little bit of liberty, wouldn't even let me dust in there.'

'Is there anything you can think of that might help his case, explain his state of mind at the time of the killings?'

'He kept a diary. Would that be of any help?'

'It might be, where is it?'

'He kept it in his safe at the surgery.'

'Will it still be there?'

'Unless the police have already searched the place.'

'Would you mind if we went and had a look?'

'Not at all if it helps. He's ill you know, not bad. If those people hadn't supplied Claire with those evil substances she'd still be alive and I would probably be a grandmother by now.'

Sam tried to be sympathetic but she remembered how Frances' body looked when she'd first seen it, and the hurt in the eyes of her father when she'd seen him at the mortuary. She found it hard to feel any real understanding for Owen's actions.

'There's just one thing, my dear, can I go in alone? I know where it is. I won't be a moment but I'd like to be the one who breaks the news to the staff. They're going to be upset enough when the police start taking the place apart. It'll be better coming from me.'

Sam nodded in agreement. A few moments later they were outside Owen's surgery and Janet was disappearing through the swing doors.

Farmer persevered with the interview. Around the monitor in the incident room there was standing room only and, in a normally bustling and noisy office, the silence had a tangible quality. Farmer leaned back in her chair; she hadn't expected the confession to come quite so easily and hoped the rest of the interview would go as smoothly.

'Why did you kill them?'

Owen was totally calm and in control of himself. 'It wasn't murder, more like an execution, devine retribution, they killed my daughter.'

'How?'

'Drugs. They gave her drugs. She overdosed, died in Bird's club. He knew how ill she was but he just left her to die.'

'So what was Mark and Frances' involvement?'

'They took her there, gave her the drugs, as many as she wanted; you see, she had the money, that's all they were interested in. She was a wonderful daughter until they got their evil hands on her.'

'Frances Purvis wasn't evil.'

'Oh yes, she was, she was the worst of the lot. Claire had no idea about the kind of people they were. Pimps, prostitutes, pushers. They introduced her to all that. Do you know where they found her? In the cubicle of a public toilet.'

Adams cut in, 'I thought you said she died in Bird's club?'

'She did, but that's where they dumped her.'

A PC knocked and entered the interview room, passing Adams a sheet of paper.

'According to the information we have, your daughter died of an overdose. The conclusion of the inquest was that it was accidental. Nobody murdered her.'

'They might not have stabbed her in the heart or shot her but they murdered her just the same. You didn't know her, did you? She was the sweetest thing you ever met.'

'This report here states that your daughter had convictions for theft, robbery, violence and prostitution. James never supplied your daughter with drugs. Bird and Frances had tried to get help for your daughter, they knew she was ill but, by the time the ambulance got there she'd climbed out of a window and disappeared. They tried to find her, they wished they had. They were as upset as you were.'

Owen wasn't listening, 'Lies all lies. You're just part of it.'

'Part of what?'

'The cover-up. Do you know what the coroner said when he gave his verdict, "A tragic loss of a young life." Tragic, tragic. I'll show you what's tragic.' He rolled his sleeve up exposing his arm. The bottom half of which was covered in the tell-tale puncture marks of a drug addict. 'I'm an addict just like she was. It's the only way I can cope, you see – to stop the memories pulling me down and tearing me apart. That's what the tragic death of a young life does to a family, it destroys them. I think I could have coped if someone had been punished, but no one was. James walked free from court. Frances wasn't even charged. It was one big cover-up because certain people didn't want their precious reputations damaged.'

'Who was that, Dr Owen?'

'That's for you to find out. You lot couldn't catch a cold, never mind a murderer. Something had to be done, so I decided to do it.'

'What about the people who loved Mark and Frances? Did they deserve to suffer?'

Owen looked indignant. 'Yes, of course they did. That was all part of it, they were responsible for the kind of people their children became. I hope they rot in hell.'

'What about your wife, Janet? Who's she going to turn to now you're locked up?'

'What difference will that make? We both died on the

same day as Claire; you can't do any more to either of us. You were lucky it was only three, I wanted to kill a lot more.'

Adams looked across the table at him. 'We only know of two bodies. Where's the third?'

'That's for you to discover.'

Adams could feel himself becoming agitated. 'Is there a third body, or hasn't it happened yet? What the fuck are you up to?'

Owen smiled confidently. 'Later, I'll tell you later.'

Jenny was staring intensely down her microscope. She looked up and shouted to Marcia. 'I've matched the fibres with the ones from the jacket.'

Marcia walked across the lab to her friend who was sitting next to a dark herringbone tweed jacket.

'I thought you said the threads *didn't* match Owen's jacket?'

'Richard Owen's jacket didn't match, but this isn't Richard Owen's.'

Marcia was feeling slightly confused and agitated. 'Whose is it then?'

'It's a small woman's. The label inside says Janet Owen, so I guess it must be hers. I've found traces of ivy hairs as well.'

Without waiting for any further explanation Marcia ran to the phone and began to dial.

Farmer and Adams walked away from the cell block where they had just incarcerated Owen. Despite Farmer's optimism, Adams was not feeling complacent. Farmer noticed. 'Look, if there *is* another body we'll find it sooner or later. We can't do the poor sod any good now. Besides, there probably isn't one, he's just playing games with us. You know what these bloody psychos are like.'

'I don't think there *is* another body. Not yet, anyway. But there's going to be. There's something very wrong.'

'Not while he's locked up there isn't, and that's going to be for ever.'

They walked into the custody sergeant's office and he handed the forms to Farmer. She filled in the sheets, making an accurate note of the time the interview with Owen had taken place. Adams leaned over the desk and watched her. Suddenly he burst into action and, grabbing the form and the pen from Farmer, scribbled three or four incomprehensible words across the front of the sheet before drawing a line through all four and shouting to the station sergeant to follow him. He made his way quickly back to the cell block and Owen's cell. The station sergeant opened it. Owen was lying prostrate on the bed, his eyes closed, looking perfectly relaxed. Adams spoke up.

'Excuse me, sir, I've made a slight error with the paperwork. I wonder if you would be good enough to have a look at it and sign to say you've seen the error and accept it.'

Owen pulled himself to his feet slowly and examined the detention sheet. Farmer reached the door of the cell and watched with interest as Adams passed him the pen. Owen signed the mistake slowly and handed the pen back to Adams before returning to his bed and lying down.

'You're right-handed then, sir?'

Without opening his eyes Owen replied, 'Most people are, inspector, it's a well-known fact.'

'Maybe so, but our killer isn't; the cuts on the body were made by a left-handed person. You've an accomplice, haven't you? Who is it? Who the fuck is it?'

Owen opened his eyes lazily for a moment, waved a dismissive hand, and then closed them again. As Adams pondered what to do he heard the sound of running feet coming down the corridor. Chalky White, one of the team's two detective sargeants, handed Farmer a note. She read it in a glance and looked across at Owen. 'It's your wife, isn't it? Your partner in these killings is Janet.'

Owen sprang up and looked at the policemen who filled his cell and applauded. 'Well done, gentlemen, well done.'

Farmer looked at Adams. 'Where is she?'

A horrible realization suddenly gripped him. 'She's with Dr Ryan.'

Owen smiled. 'Now you know who the third body belongs to.'

He was lying, but he guessed it would keep them away from Purvis long enough for Janet to finish the final part of their mission.

Adams spun around and grabbed the front of Owen's shirt, pulling him to his feet and slamming him against the cell wall.

'Where is she, you bastard? Where the fuck is she?'

'You're too late! You're *far* too late. It'll be over by now.'

Adams brought his fist back and punched Owen as

hard as he could in the stomach, sending him crashing to the floor before pulling his head back up by his hair.

'I'll ask you one more time, where is she?'

The station sergeant moved forward to pull Adams away but Farmer stopped him just in time to see Owen vomit all over Adams' shoes and trousers.

Sam was still waiting outside in the car. She looked at her watch, Janet had been gone for almost half an hour and she was becoming increasingly bored with listening to a Radio Four play about life in the slow lane. She'd tried to phone Marcia to see how things were going, but she'd forgotten to charge the battery on her mobile phone, and it was hopeless. She climbed out of her car and walked into the surgery. A pleasant-looking middle-aged woman was on the reception desk.

'Excuse me, I'm looking for Dr Owen.'

The receptionist smiled at her. 'I'm afraid you missed her, she left about twenty minutes ago.'

Sam couldn't conceal her surprise. 'But I've been parked outside for the past half hour. I'd have seen her.'

'She took the back stairs, said she had to get to some emergency.'

'Which is her office?'

The receptionist pointed to a blue door at the far side of the surgery. 'It's in there, but I don't . . .'

Before she had a chance to finish her sentence Sam was inside Janet's office. Lying on the table were several small jars of Tubarine, two of which were empty. Although the computer was on, the screen saver obscured the open file. Sam moved the mouse and brought up the information.

At the top of the screen was the name, Malcolm Purvis, followed by his address and everything a would-be killer would need to know. There was even a photograph. She recognized him from the mortuary. Undoubtedly the rest of their intended victims would be on the same file. Sam ran from the office into the reception. The woman she had seen earlier was on the phone. Sam glared at her.

'Who are you phoning?'

The receptionist looked frightened and replied nervously, 'The police.'

Sam grabbed the phone from her hand making her jump back with a scream. She shouted into the phone, 'Write this down. My name is Dr Samantha Ryan. I'm the forensic pathologist at the Park Hospital. Ring Detective Superintendent Harriet Farmer and tell her that Janet Owen is also involved in the murders and she has gone after Malcolm Purvis . . . Yes, she knows where he lives. For God's sake be quick, tell her I'll meet her at the house.' She slammed the phone down, apologized to the receptionist, who had retreated to a safe distance at the far side of the office, and fled from the surgery.

It had taken Janet longer than she had anticipated to reach the Purvis house. Road works and the late arrival of her taxi had slowed things down considerably. She paid the driver and walked across the road to the house, holding her small black medical bag tightly in her hand. She didn't bother with the front door but walked directly to the back. She climbed the few steps leading to the kitchen door and knocked; there was no reply. She tried the handle. To her delight the door opened and she stepped inside. Making her way slowly along the corridor she listened intensely for any sign of her prey. When she came to the phone in the hall she pulled the wire from its socket before crouching down and removing a syringe and a long white cord from her bag. It wasn't what she normally liked to use, it was from the blind in her front room, but it was handy and strong and she was sure it would do the job well. The house was barren, almost empty of furniture. She walked slowly into the sitting-room. She was impressed by its size and décor and admired the taste. Strange squeaking sounds, a little like a distressed mouse, filtered to her. She followed the noise to an old, white sofa. She couldn't help feeling that it looked totally out of place in such fine surroundings. Hanging over the edge of the furniture was a pair stockinged feet. She moved slowly and quietly around to the other side of the sofa before moving in. Lying in front of her was Malcolm Purvis. Pressed in his ears were two small headphones which led to a personal stereo finely balanced on his chest. He appeared to be asleep which was a great advantage to her. Raising her arm she plunged the needle of the syringe into Malcolm's neck.

Richard Owen was slumped on his bed crying, his face in his hands, while Adams watched him from the hallway outside. Their frantic efforts to locate Sam and Janet had come to nothing, though every policeman in the county had been alerted.

Farmer walked into the cell and sat by his side.

'One more killing isn't going to bring her back, it's not going to make the slightest difference to anything.'

Owen kept his face hidden in his hands. 'It will to us. It balances things up, puts our lives back together.'

'You might think it will, but it won't take the pain away or bring back Claire. There's no more purpose to it.'

Finally he lifted his head from his hands. 'Our *purpose* ended when Claire died. Revenge isn't a negative quality, it's a positive one. It's the only thing that keeps us both going. It's a powerful force. It has allowed us to achieve things we never thought possible.'

'Like murder?'

'Yes, just like murder.'

'Whose idea was it?'

'Janet's. She was always the strong one. She couldn't do it alone because of her hands, so we did it together, but she always liked to be there at the kill.'

'Who thought up the ritualistic stuff?'

'She did, it was so sweet. We found out that Bird had an interest in it and it went from there really.'

'Who did the actual killing?'

'We both did, a shared experience you might say.'

'Is that why you used the garrotte?'

'Yes, it was the only way she could do it, and it fitted in nicely with the witchcraft theme.'

'Is that why you used the drugs as well?'

'It made things so much easier. But they knew what was happening to them. They were conscious all the time. So we made sure they understood why before we finished it.'

The phone rang in the lobby and the station sergeant picked it up. He listened for a moment before slamming it down and running into the cell. 'Message from Dr Ryan, sir. She says that Janet Owen is going after Malcolm Purvis. She'll meet you at his house.'

Adams was half-way down the hall before the sergeant had finished speaking.

Owen screamed from the cell, 'You're too late, you're much too late!'

Sam arrived quickly at Malcolm's house, having driven like a maniac from the surgery. She hoped that the police, when they received the numerous complaints from the public, would be generous. She tried knocking at the front door but when there was no reply she ran around the back.

Climbing the steps to the kitchen door she found it was open. She called inside, 'Hello! Hello? Is anyone there?'

She stepped inside the kitchen, straining her ears for any sign of movement. As she walked along the hall she continued to call, not that she thought anyone was going to hear her any more, but it was somehow comforting. As she approached the sitting-room door she noticed the telephone lead lying on the hall carpet where it had been pulled from its socket. All her instincts told her to run, and she would have if she hadn't seen Malcolm's body lying across the sitting-room floor close to an old sofa. She ran across to him, her own safety dismissed from her mind for a moment. She rolled him over on to his side and felt his pulse, it was weak, but still there.

As she began to pull the shirt away from his throat a loop was passed quickly over her head and secured around her throat. She was pulled sharply backwards, the rope twisting at the back of her neck. She grabbed the cord and tried to pull it away from her throat but it bit so tightly that she was unable to get her fingers underneath. She threw her arms blindly behind her, grabbing at anything which came within reach, but it was futile. She could feel her strength ebbing away. Her lungs were screaming for air, her ears ringing and her eyes and face suffusing with blood. She pulled ineffectually at the cord a few more times but as her swollen tongue was forced from her mouth the darkness began to close around her.

The sight that greeted Adams as he burst into the sitting-room stunned him for a moment. Janet Owen was sitting behind Sam, her long grey hair dishevelled and thrown over her face as she pulled wildly at a white cord which was wrapped around Sam's throat. Sam lay in front of her, her body jerking unnaturally as spasms passed through her. He raced across the room. Judging the situation too desperate for reasonable force, he kicked Janet Owen hard in the face, sending her reeling backwards before collapsing unconscious on the floor, her jaw broken and blood pouring from her mouth. He knelt down by Sam and picked up her lifeless body. As the room filled with police officers he screamed at them, 'Get an ambulance! For God's sake, get an ambulance!'

Farmer knelt down by his side and put her arm around his shoulder.

Adams, his composure returned, looked down at Malcolm Purvis' unconscious body on the stretcher.

'Will he be OK?'

The paramedic nodded. 'I'm no doctor but I think so; he'll have one hell of a headache though.'

Adams turned to Sam who was sitting on the garden wall with a blanket around her. 'I thought I'd lost you.'

She could hardly speak, and whispered her hoarse reply, 'I thought you'd lost me, too. What about Janet?'

'She's gone. For ever I hope.'

'What will they do with them?'

'Lock them up and throw away the key with luck. But they'll probably get lots of care and consideration as well.' He said it with a sarcastic tone to his voice.

'Why did they go after Malcolm?'

'He defended Mark James, got him off. They never forgave him, or his daughter.'

A paramedic pulled up a mobile chair in front of her and helped Sam into it. She waved limply at Adams as they wheeled her into the back of the ambulance. He waved back. Farmer walked across to him.

'What are you doing here?'

Adams shrugged. 'Thought you might need some help.'

'Yes, I do. Go and get a witness statement off our intrepid pathologist. You might as well travel in the ambulance with her.'

Adams hesitated for a moment.

'Well, off you go then.'

Farmer turned and walked back towards the house.